For a thoroughly
enjoyable meeting
that was meant
a meet

♡ M8 † Keyes

Molly's Daughter

Other Books by Margaret Frings Keyes

Inward Journey: Art as Therapy
Open Court Publishing Co., LaSalle and London; 1983 (rev.)
The Reality of the Psyche Series

Staying Married
Les Femmes Publications; Millbrae, CA 1975

Out of the Shadows:
Uses of Depression, Anxiety and Anger in the Enneagram
Molysdatur Publications; Muir Beach, CA 1988

Emotions and The Enneagram:
Working Through Your Shadow Life Script
Molysdatur Publications, Muir Beach, CA 1992 (rev.)

The Enneagram Cats of Muir Beach
(with drawings by Fran Moyer)
Molysdatur Publications; Muir Beach, CA 1990

The Enneagram Relationship Workbook:
A Self and Partnership Assessment Guide
(with drawings by MK Brown)
Molysdatur Publications; Muir Beach, CA 1991

Margaret Frings Keyes

Molly's Daughter

A Three Generation
Story Exploring:
**What Do Women
Really Want?**

Arseya Publishing • New Jersey

Library of Congress Control Number: 2008932967

ISBN-13   978-0-9745185-8-9

Cover/text design by Curtis Tow Graphics, New York, NY

Printed in the United States by The Wall Street Group, Inc.

Published by Arseya Publishing
New Vernon, New Jersey
www.arseya.com

FIRST EDITION

For us all

To celebrate the moments
when one frame slips into another
and everything is seen freshly
— and understood differently.

Acknowledgements

This book represents nine years of off and on research in the archives of the public library of Butte, Montana, the archives of the ILWU (the International Longshore and Warehouse Union) and conversations with friends in the Fort Point Gang Thursday Morning Walkers (a collection of Union Leaders, Abraham Lincoln Brigade Volunteers in the Spanish Civil War, and supporters of past and present leftist movements).

The components that make this book into a novelized family memoir are family and personal stories. Giving Gram and myself, plus some others, alternative names served my need for fictional freedom to write true stories. The more specifically detailed our stories, the more we discover we share in common. Old family maps are useful to know our current choices and the direction of our shared life journey.

Many writer friends have read the book, in its several versions, and I have benefited from their suggestions. Certainly, Rosemary McGee, Monica Moore and Jack Ragsdale, seaman and historian, have been most valuable in the final shape-up. Penelope Bevan, writer, and Steve Bankston, computer system designer, were also helpful. The writings of Bill Bailey, ALB fighter and waterfront activist were immensely useful to me, as well as the comments of other students, clients, friends at the Fromm Institute, and particularly my adopted grandsons and god-daughters.

Contents

PART III LIZBY

PART IV THE UNFOLDING

Part I

Butte, Montana

Prologue
(Dave Gillmore JFK doctoral research on Social Intelligence)
Interview transcript — Lisby Keyes, February 10, 2006

DAVE: Research shows most men sense danger and immediately take
  steps to deal with it — some form of fight or flight. Women are
  wired differently — feeling non-verbal signals as thoughts and
  emotions, before action. Talk comes first, usually with other women
  — then sometimes, a different view of what's happening,.

LIZBY: Well, I guess it depends on the urgency and time you've got, but
  that's the way it was for me with my grandmother — 'Sit down.
  I'll put the kettle on,' she'd say. 'We'll have a cup of tea, and talk.'
  Humm, You know, it fascinates me that our brains are wired to
  connect. We understand so much more than ever gets said in
  words.

DAVE: You experienced that with your grandmother?

LIZBY: (laughs) Actually, I watched her with other people. She'd read the
  cards, tell their fortunes. I didn't get what she was doing until I was
  older, of course, but she was giving them little hunches, other ways
  to think about what was bothering them. Not too different from
  what I do.

DAVE: Where did you grow up?

LISBY: Here in San Francisco, with Montana summers during childhood.

DAVE: This is kind of a Mecca of activism.

LIZBY: Lots of anti-war and social activism, The San Francisco Mime
  Troupe, and before that the "Beat Poets," but during the 30's, labor
  was where the action was.

DAVE: Uh, was your family religious or spiritual in any way?

LIZBY: Yeah, I grew up in the Sunset district; everyone I knew was
    Roman-Catholic — mostly Irish, German, the Italians were in North
    Beach — but 1st and 2nd generation and definitely working class.
DAVE: Oh, OK, so does Catholicism still influence you? Has that evolved
    or changed related to your upbringing?
LIZBY: Well, I got out of the Sunset by winning a scholarship to Notre
    Dame des Victoires, which was *downtown*!
        French Catholicism was different culturally. Those nuns had
    a lot of concern about social justice and what was going on after
    World War I. Germany was bankrupt when my father left. He
    sailed the world in three masted ships before he dropped ship in
    California. My mother was born in England but her father was killed
    in the mines of Montana. My grandfather, incidentally, was part of
    the union labor organizing movement when Butte was the world's
    hottest trouble spot in mining.
DAVE: Did you sympathize with socialist or communist movements of
    that time?
LIZBY: Oh lord! When I graduated from high school my mother was
    scared to death. I wanted to go to UC Berkeley. (laughing) She
    knew my inclinations, my concern and caring and she was
    convinced I'd turn communist as soon as I walked through Sather
    Gate! So she bribed me to go to Lone Mountain by allowing me
    to go first to art school for a summer — even paid my tuition —
    unheard of previously.
        I had worked from the time I was in eighth grade . . . What
    was the question? I dropped it.
DAVE: Sorry, um, just in terms of, have you felt a connection to socialist
    and communist movements?
LIZBY: Yes, particularly the need for socialized medicine.
DAVE: Socialized medicine, huh. That's cool.
LIZBY: I was ambitious . . . but my root interest was, and is, in the
    connections we have with one another . . . . I know I'm wearing a
    different body, but if Gram were around, she could get behind my
    eyes, and understand what we're exploring — Yeah, we talked
    when times got bad . . .

Chapter One

Lizzie

September 1918

At three o'clock a cold wind blew steadily from the Flats below Butte. Dark clouds building in the sky promised snow before dark. Eleven-year-old Frank Dyer was folding his newspapers on the corner of Wyoming and Main Street when his sister Molly joined him. They could see the huge gallows frame of the Con Mine below them where the metal cages dropped almost a mile into the ground. Both of them were bundled into heavy sweaters.

"Frankie, your elbow's poking through the sleeve. Let me take a look." Frank held his arm up and Molly pushed her finger through the hole. "Give it to me tonight to darn. I can't knit a new one until Johnny's sweater is finished."

"I've still got my jacket to wear," Frank said. The steam of his breath clotted in the air.

Butte was stark bare of trees. It did not have lakes like Vancouver, or rows of little brick houses like Newcastle-upon-Tyne where they had lived with their grandfather a few years back. Butte was just a big hill mining-camp with gray slag heaps, iron head-frames over elevator shafts, smoke stacks, and dirt roads. Not a blade of grass anywhere. Saloons and gambling houses, rooming houses, churches, and schools all mixed together between the mineshafts.

Frank shoved the last folded newspaper into his bag, stood, and brushed the dirt from his knickers. He was two years younger than Molly, but just as tall. His rusty hair was not a true red, but he had a quick enough temper to control a choice corner to sell his papers.

"Hitch up my bag and I'm ready to go," he said.

"Wait a bit. I need to stretch the cramp in my leg." Molly stamped her feet before she helped fit the bag over his shoulders. "D'you know if Pa's got a union meeting tonight?"

Frank started to answer, when a noise shook the air. A crack like a packing case had fallen and split, but much louder.

"What the..." Men were running in the Con mine yard. "Something's wrong with the hoisting engine," Frank said. "Jesus, look at it!"

Another crack, a couple of chunks from the roof of the shaft house buckled over. They could see the hoisting wheels on top of the gallows frame. The spokes had stopped.

"The shift's down. It's not time for the men to come up," Molly said, "but whatever was in that cage dropped like a rock."

She looked at her brother. His face was white. The engine house. The cables. She felt like she was going to vomit. She reached to help Frank struggle out of his bag. He dropped it, and they started to run.

"Maybe it was just timber for bracing the tunnels," he said.

✖   ✖   ✖

Men huddled around the shaft house. Once in a while someone would peel off and run into a building. The children had to wait at the fence. The only person who stopped to say anything to them was an ore car loader. He said he didn't know what happened, but he'd heard some guys were in the cage when the cable broke.

"What could make it go like that?" Molly asked.

"A busted clutch or somethin'. The cable rope's almost an inch thick wrapped in steel wire. They keep it lubricated with tar and that one was done less than a week ago but, Christ, did you see the roof go up?"

They went to the gate and waited. Time had never before seemed so empty. The whistle blew. Men started coming out and Frank demanded, "What happened?"

"Some guys got it when the chippy cable broke at 2300 feet," one of the men said. "The main cable's still working, but that shaft's deep."

Molly grabbed hold of the fellow's arm, "Who got killed?"

"I don't know. They're trying to get the bodies out of the sump now." He pulled back, but looked at her with sympathy. "Your Pa's working down there, ain't he?"

"Yeah, Packy Dyer," Frank said. "He's an engineer."

"Jesus," the man said.

Molly whispered, "Maybe he's topside somewhere. Engineers don't always work below. Run and have a look."

Frank ran everywhere he could think of. No sign of his father nor anyone who'd seen him.

✖ ✖ ✖

It was three hours before they got the bodies up, two of them. When they put a sheet over the first stretcher, the children could see it was a little runt of a guy, not Pa.

When the second stretcher came up, Molly knew. She could see Pa's sweater, the match of her own. "Is he dead?" she cried.

Someone tried to hold her back.

"You try to stop us," Frank yelled, "I'll knock your block off." He reached and lifted the sheet. Molly clutched Pa's body in her arms. He was soaked with sump water, eyes half open but not seeing. No cuts — but his body was twisted the wrong way.

Someone was screaming. Molly didn't recognize her own voice. After a bit, she felt herself being held, tears other than her own splashing down her face. Walt, Jack, men who'd worked to get him out. Pa's friends.

Jack's voice, "Christ, how're we going to tell Lizzie?"

✖ ✖ ✖

The day had not yet turned dark when Flanagan stopped by Lizzie Dyer 's kitchen with a bag of scones for their afternoon tea. Lizzie bit the tip of her tongue as she stared at the tea leaves clinging to the bottom of the cup. One tightly folded leaf had refused to yield to the scalding water. It lay like a door between the blob of shapeless leaves and a sprinkle of broken bits near the rim. What could a closed door mean between a shapeless something on one side and a shattered something on the other? Lizzie used the fingers of both hands to hold and turn the porcelain cup, a treasure carried from England to Ireland to Canada and now to this wild place in Montana. No matter the angle, no picture poked through the leaves.

"Drat!" She frowned. "It's black as a piece of coal. My pictures are stuck in the leaves today and won't let themselves be seen."

"You did fine with my tea." Flanagan reached her hand across the kitchen table to look at the cup. "Why don't you pour another cup for yourself?"

Lizzie shook her head. Her toddler, Pat, played underfoot on the braided rag rug, banging sticks of firewood together. A locomotive now, Pat chugged his stick with its resiny smell of pine under her chair and advanced into the tunnel of her skirt. She pushed him away without a glance and returned her cup to its saucer on the flowered oilcloth.

The room, warmed by a huge coal stove, was brightly lit by an electric lamp hanging from the ceiling. A small window above the sink and another in the door to the alley showed the afternoon had turned dark. Large snowflakes drifted through the air outside.

"The leaves don't work that way. I don't know why, but the pictures have their own ways," she said. "Your cup was clear as day. A tall man is going to enter your life any time now and bring you good fortune." They both laughed. Flanagan worked as a hostess at the Gold Dust Casino, and men were inclined to share their good fortune with her when they won.

Lizzie liked the contrast between them. At thirty-two, Lizzie wore her straight black hair pulled into a twist held on top of her head with a multitude of hairpins. She had fair English skin and flirtatious eyes. Despite her ample bosom after six breast-fed children, she was light on her feet, with a dancer's erect carriage that set her apart from most women.

Red-haired Flanagan, big-boned with a lazy swing to her walk, always gussied herself up in fancy clothes. She changed her first name to suit her mood. When they had met two years before at the Young Old Timers Dancing Club, she said she had only one name, Flanagan. Lizzie later heard some men call her Fanny while others called her Edna, but to Lizzie she was Flanagan.

They were close as sisters.

Packy, Lizzie's husband couldn't understand what she saw in Flanagan, a woman he found disreputable, "that floozy in the Park Street gambling joint." Still, he would not gainsay the friendship. For years, Lizzie had followed him about to mining camps where conditions were rough and there were few women companions. In Vancouver, when Johnny was born, the first white child on the island, only an Indian woman had been there to help.

Today, Flanagan's day off, the women shared a cup of tea and a bit of gossip as usual. A hungry cry that Lizzie did not want to hear came from the bedroom. "James has to be fed. D'you mind?" she asked.

Flanagan looked out the kitchen door window and checked the light. "Lord, I didn't realize it's almost dark," Flanagan said. "I have to be going. Will I see you Saturday night?"

"It's payday, but probably not. Packy put some Christmas presents on lay-away at Hennessy's, so there won't be much left over for Keno this week. Come to dinner on Sunday, though. The men always like it when you're around to hear their tall stories, and so do I."

Lizzie picked up the baby from his crib. He quieted to a gurgle, his little fish mouth opening, searching. She returned to the kitchen, a shawl tossed over her shoulder. Flanagan pulled her hat fashionably low over her curls, shrugged into her sealskin coat with its matching muff, and then blew a kiss from her gloved fingers. She left the warm kitchen for the alley, where the storm had thickened into a heavy snowfall.

Lizzie, holding the baby at her shoulder, pulled the rocker closer to the stove. James nuzzled her breast under the shawl and her milk flowed, a pulse of pleasure. Her husband and the men wouldn't be in until after dark, but where was Molly? She should be home peeling potatoes to start the stew.

Johnny, her six-year-old, joined Pat playing under the table. Lizzie took little heed of them. They were building a tower from pots found in the cupboard. Lizzie liked to imagine what her life would be like with servants to pick up after the children, scrub the floors, wash and hang the clothes to dry, and do the ironing, *endless ironing*. How nice it'd be! Her mother's grandfather, Sir Wilfred Lawson, had servants. Lizzie needn't have been a wife and mother. Things could have been different! Instead of having all these children, she could have been a dancer. But no, nothing would do; she had to marry Packy — Francis

Patrick Dyer. What if he hadn't swept into Newcastle, with his laughing eyes and his stories and songs?

Even so, she might have resisted him, but she caught Kate making eyes at him. That did it. Her sister was such a sneak. Kate once got Papa to give her a gold bracelet he had bought specially for Lizzie. Well, Kate was not going to get Packy! Lizzie said yes to him that very same night. And lived to regret it sometimes, but what choice did she have?

She turned James to the other breast, put her feet on the base of the stove, and slowly started to rock. Packy could always make her laugh, but he was so hotheaded. The drink. Every year, he took the pledge not to drink. It never lasted. His fiery temper got him into trouble. This awful union he was in. No, she just wouldn't think about it.

She closed her eyes and settled more deeply into the rocker. She would put her mind on nicer things. A famous dancer, Mr. McFarland, manager of the Newcastle-upon-Tyne Theater, had assured Papa that she had a great future. Lizzie drifted on the edge of sleep, traveling around England in a special rail car with trunks of beaded, sparkling dresses, furs, and jewelry. Locals vied with each other to be part of her troupe. The darkened theater, the music tuning up, brass horns, fiddles and piano, the lights, blue, red, then bright yellow as the heavy velvet curtain rose, and herself twirling, gliding, and utterly splendid.

The baby finished nursing and lay asleep in her arms. She looked at him, momentarily puzzled, then held him up to burp with his warm flesh nuzzled into her neck—a dear little cuddler, but . . . . She sighed.

✖ ✖ ✖

Boots thumped loudly on the narrow outer porch that ran on two sides of the house. The men were home earlier than usual. Something must have happened. Lord, she hoped it wasn't the start of another strike. The union activities in Vancouver had almost ruined them.

The alley door opened abruptly. Why did no one use the front door? Her thought trailed off. Where was Packy? She had a sick feeling. The shattered leaves! She got to her feet as men crowded into the kitchen, five, six of them. They pulled off their hats and stood, awkwardly silent. That terrible expression on Jack's face! So many men! Molly and Frank there with them, shocked white faces and terrified eyes.

Jack sobbed and reached to gather her into his arms. "Lizzie, Lizzie! Somethin' terrible's happened."

"Dear God, Packy's hurt," she screamed. "Dear God, tell me he's not dead! Please."

Walt's voice broke, "Wha kinna tell you . . . The chippy cable busted."

She only caught fragments. A chippy cable. The auxiliary line that brought rock ore to the surface. What would Packy, an engineer, be doing on it?

"Packy and Bill Moran, the shift boss . . . nothing . . . no one could stop the cage then . . . plunging down the shaft . . . deepest in the world. We worked for hours and only just managed to get them up."

More voices joined in. She could not separate the sounds. She could not breathe. Jack sat her down. Molly took the baby. Someone brought her water. Johnny had buried his head in Molly's shoulder. Pat, whimpering, clutched her leg. Death in the mines was common enough. Every week three to four men died from accidents, but not Packy — not her husband. Her arms were weak as water. Her body shook.

The first couple of days, Lizzie took to her bed and did nothing but cry. Molly did everything she could to distract her, kept the boys out of her way, brought her tea and rubbed her back the way she used to like. Lizzie would not nurse James, but he was ready for real food anyway, so Molly could feed him. A neighbor, Mrs. McCaughy, took care of him during the day. Mrs. McCaughy had a soft spot for his blue eyes and smiling ways. Black Irish, she called him, just like the baby she had lost. Lizzie did not talk much about Packy, just about how terrible life was and how she did not have anyone or anything. Molly couldn't take that kind of talk for very long.

"What are we, for God's sake?" she burst out. "Pa wouldn't want you carrying on like this."

Lizzie seemed to come to her senses a bit after that. She listened to what the neighbors were saying and even asked about the Widow's Pension.

The wake, the funeral mass, the long drive to Holy Cross Cemetery following her husband's coffin, passed in a blur. Lizzie watched the men lower the coffin into the grave. She would never again feel Packy's arms pull her close; hear his teasing whisper when they danced. Everything slowed except her thoughts. The priest's words were empty sounds.

Her eyes wandered to the headstones in the graveyard. Families kept their graves up when they visited the dead. Soil on the Flats was different from the arid ground of Butte itself. For some reason, lilacs thrived on chemicals from the smelter that destroyed other vegetation. Their scent mingled with smells from the dumps, the butcher-town slaughterhouses and, worse, the arsenic in the air that Marcus Daly said gave Butte women their beautiful white complexions.

How could she ever stand to visit the grave?

Copper metal. The Great War in Europe took more and more of it and the mines worked day and night. Butte drew men like Packy from all parts of the world. They crowded into the mining camps and worked for wages and the war effort instead of wild frontier dreams. But Butte's six graveyards now held more men than worked in the mines. If collapsing mineshafts, fire, deadly gas or violence did not kill the miner, silicosis would. But what did so much death have to do with *her,* now that the worst had happened. What did anything matter?

After the dirt was shoveled on top of the casket, Lizzie let herself be led home. Jack, Packy's mining partner and closest friend, headed to a nearby saloon with the rest of the men to conclude the traditional Butte funeral. Eileen McCaughy and other women of the parish brought food not only for the day of the funeral but also for the week.

"Don't worry about cooking," Eileen said. "I'm baking beef steak pasties tomorrow. I'll bring some round for you and the children. There'll be enough for the men's lunch pails, as well." Lizzie tried to thank her, but Eileen brushed it aside. "It's no trouble at all. You'd do the same."

The weeks passed. Lizzie wept less. Flanagan came with carrots, onion, and beef bones to make soup. Walt Davis, who rented a room, and Jack McKenna, who owned half the house with Packy, shifted for themselves for the first few weeks and then gave Eileen money to make their pasties.

Just as well. Lizzie hated cooking.

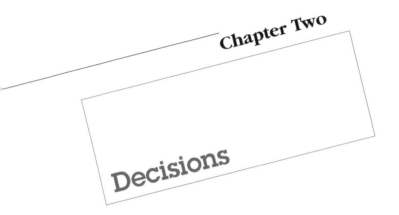

Chapter Two

Decisions

November 1918

F rom the window of an opulent office in the Anaconda Copper Mining Company, Lizzie could see the snow of winter piled high and the Rocky Mountains white against dark gray skies.

The insurance man said, "You can use the two-thousand-dollar death benefit to pay off the mortgage as well as Jack McKenna's share of the house, but are you sure you want to do that?"

"Yes," said Lizzie.

"You won't be returning to England?"

To take care of her father's house? She shook her head. No question. She had not owned property of her own before, couldn't. It made little sense to stay in Butte, but she felt freer here than she had in England. This place, the people, had more life than any other place she'd been. Lizzie looked at the bluff-faced man. He meant well, but she could not imagine sharing her real worries with him.

"I plan to stay in Butte," she said.

"With your six children, you're eligible for the widow's pension. You can apply at the courthouse and it will pay you between eighteen and twenty four dollars a month."

"I won't take charity, thank you." And even if she did, how could she manage to feed and clothe the children and take care of herself on so little?

He smiled. "Well, there are always men looking for good home cooking. You'd do better to turn that place into a boarding house and get your kids to help."

What did this man know of her children? Nothing. Her older sons had learned to survive, but they did not always mind her. Only Packy had kept them in line. A feeling of panic rose in her throat. How would she manage them alone?

She stood. "I'll take my leave now. Thank you for your help."

✖   ✖   ✖

Lizzie unlocked the front door and stepped across the threshold into the small entryway of her home. She pulled off her hat and gloves and looked about. A hump-topped trunk brought from England held the family linen. It sat beside the staircase under a wooden-framed mirror flanked by clothes hooks on each side. The narrow staircase beside the front door climbed a few steps, and then forked left to the top floor, where Walt and Jack stayed in wintry dormer bedrooms and an upper parlor heated by a Franklin stove.

Her house. Lizzie glanced into the long narrow parlor where the children slept, then pulled the door shut. The unfinished apartment below kept the floor of the children's room cold. She did not want the chill to get into the rest of the house. *The children!* She had not given the little ones a thought since she left them with Eileen this morning, but what she needed first was a quiet cup of tea. She carried her coat through the kitchen to the carved wooden closet in her bedroom, and then returned to fill the kettle with water.

In the two months that had passed since Packy was put to rest, Lizzie had heard sullen talk that the accident was no accident, but what good did that do? When men were killed who happened to be union leaders, no one thought it an accident. The Anaconda Copper Mining Company did not want unions, particularly the IWW, interfering with their profits. Only money mattered. She couldn't see the boundaries of the town, but Packy said they had been drawn with as many fancy loops and holes as a Swiss cheese to exclude the mines from taxes. Butte's wealth flowed east to absentee owners without a nick.

She stirred up the coal in the stove, tossed in kindling, and then put the kettle on top. So maybe Packy was killed, but maybe the cable just broke.

Maybe machinery grew tired working 24 hours a day to keep the war in France going. The coroner said Packy's death was "due to shock from injuries." The Company disclaimed any responsibility — as if they had nothing to do with the equipment that failed.

Knowing what happened would not bring her husband back. She had told him not to make trouble, but he always treated her ideas as if they were a child's. A year ago last August, masked vigilantes dragged Frank Little, the IWW union organizer, from his boarding house bed through the streets and hanged him from a trestle. Everyone knew they were ACM hired thugs, even the probable killer Ed Morrissey.

Packy wasn't an anarchist Wobbly. He was on the Union Council that called a strike after a terrible fire killed a hundred and sixty-three men. The National Guard sent by the governor put down the strike, and Packy and the others were marked as troublemakers.

"Why do you want to fight them?" she had asked. "Even if they give you a dollar or more a day, you'll never make up the money you lose when you go on strike."

"Men have only the hours of their lives to sell for food and shelter, nothing else," Packy replied. "If we wake in the dark, go to work and come home in the dark and never see the sun, how are we anything but slaves?"

She had heard this Irish rhetoric before. "You see the sun on your day off," she snapped.

Packy laid one hand heavily on the table and scowled at her. "The bosses stole this mining land, they don't pay taxes, and they've taken over two billion dollars from Butte — *two billion*. Lizzie, Can you even imagine it? What gives them the right to squeeze the last nickel from our work? Four dollars and two-bits we get for a day's work, cramped in tunnels, prying and carving hard ore from walls that can collapse at any time, while we're breathing the poisons that we cough out with our lungs!"

"No one forced you to leave England," Lizzie said. "The mines in Butte pay more money than anywhere, you said."

Packy continued as if she hadn't spoken. "Don't we deserve enough time each day free from work to see our children? To eat a meal with our families? Shouldn't we be able to look around the country and see what's here?"

"What have you been doing all these years, but looking around, seeing the

Chapter Two • Decisions 1 7

world?" she asked. "Papa wanted you to take his business —"

"Four years building rows of brick houses for your father was enough," he said.

"So you had us traipse after you to Sligo while you farmed your family land, then off to Canada you went, leaving the land to your thieving grandfather, and me with Molly, Tom and the baby Frank just born. . ."

"You insisted on staying!" Packy protested.

Lizzie ignored his comment. "I don't know why in the four years you were away you didn't decide you had enough of the mines, too, if they're as bad as you say."

"Lizzie, don't you think this is better than the old country?" he asked.

She softened. "Yes, I do. It's just . . ." She paused, trying to think. "It's just that I think you like to fight more than anything."

Packy laughed.

"It doesn't matter what about," she said. "You enjoy the fight itself."

"Not with you, Lizzie."

After that, he just laughed and would not talk to her about any of it. And look where it got him.

✖   ✖   ✖

Lizzie measured black tea into the caddy and poured boiling water over it to steep in the pot. She sat at the table and rested her chin in her hands as she gazed at the letter propped against the sugar bowl. Now, she had her own decisions to make. Her father wrote that she should come back to England to stay with him. He would send her sister Bess, the only one still at home, to help. Lizzie shook her head. No, she had said her good-byes to the old country.

She realized, with a start, that she was no longer grieving for Packy. She was supposed to be sad for a whole year. Was she that cold-hearted? Her sister Kate thought so, and selfish to boot, when their mother died and Lizzie refused to take on the care of their younger brother and sister, but Lizzie knew what you gave up, you couldn't get back.

Well, now she had other things to concern her. How was she going to manage without Packy's wages and without accepting charity? She could take in more boarders. Her sons, Tom and Frank, could sell more newspapers.

She clenched her hands together. It wouldn't do at all. She did not *want* to stay home, day in and day out with children and cooking for boarders. What did she want? Something she could choose for herself — *not* have to accept what other people wanted her to want.

It just wasn't clear yet.

She poured her tea and lifted the fragrant cup to her lips. Jack would marry her in a minute if she would let him, and weren't all the women in the parish expecting it? Eileen commenting what a handsome man he was, and Mary Kelly hinting that no one would be surprised if she took the step when the year of mourning was up. But Lizzie knew something about herself she had not known as a girl. She did not want to birth any more babies. They came along so easily. It used to seem that all Packy had to do was look at her and she was pregnant again. If he hadn't gone to Canada without the family, she'd probably have three more children to care for!

Flanagan had taught her last year how to use the French cap, but James was living proof that *that* didn't work. No, remarriage was not what she want-ed, and to be a dancer in show business was a daydream. Lizzie wrinkled her nose and shook her head. With her belly dropped from childbearing, she didn't have the stomach muscles anymore.

She only seemed to know what she didn't want. She'd be daft to choose the life wives and widows lived. She looked around the kitchen. It was just too — ordinary!

Flanagan had said she would be better off turning the children she had over to the Paul Clark Orphanage.

Lizzie was horrified, at first. "What kind of woman would give up her own children?"

"Most of the children in the home have two living parents," Flanagan had said, "but they're going through hard times. The orphanage is temporary for them."

Lizzie sipped her tea. She had to think about money to support them.

✖   ✖   ✖

Saturday night was bath night. After supper, Lizzie helped Molly heat the water and bathe the little ones, but Tom and Frank still were not home. The boys used to do dishes with their father and sing old favorites like *Coming Through the Rye* and *Danny Boy.* Tom had a singing voice like his father's. He kept trying to deepen it, but he would always be an Irish tenor. Frank had his father's tougher side. Packy had taught him how to box.

What could they be up to, staying out so late?

Then Molly and Lizzie took baths and Molly went to bed.

Jack sat in the parlor upstairs reading his paper, waiting for his cup of tea before bedtime. How Lizzie longed for a life with lots of other men and women around, a life in which she could laugh and talk and dress up. She could not imagine herself spending the rest of her days like this.

Jack brought his paper downstairs into the kitchen. "Lizzie, I think you should reconsider." He was going to make his argument again that she needed him to take care of her. She definitely did not want to marry *anyone*, but never in a hundred *years* would she consider marrying Jack. She could not tell him she thought him dull-witted, with not a spark of fun in him. He would keep the boys in line, but — no, he was impossible! She breathed in sharply through her nose. She had to look interested as he rambled on. He was impossible to deflect with a light-hearted story. He always said what he had to say, thinking if you didn't agree with him it was not clear to you and he needed to repeat it.

She needed a job, Lizzie thought suddenly. Maybe it would not be so bad to send the children to the orphanage for a year or so, like sending them to boarding school. Lots of children in England went to boarding schools. She could bring them home again when the little ones didn't need someone with them. Maybe she would talk to Flanagan again about this.

Jack droned on.

She'd talk to Flanagan tomorrow.

Chapter Three

Changing Places

January 1919

izzie waited for Flanagan to join her in the lobby of the Thornton Hotel. She shifted her seat to be able to watch both the front and the side doors. There was an opening for a chambermaid on the third floor, and in ten minutes Flanagan would introduce her to Mrs. Bonner, the head housekeeper. Lizzie hadn't told Molly where she was going. "Take care of the little ones, and I'll be back in a couple of hours," she had said.

The only question now was whether Mrs. Bonner would take a chance on someone who had never had a job. "Nora Bonner isn't known for her soft heart," Flanagan had said, "but she owes me a favor."

Almost a quarter hour. Where was Flanagan? Lizzie fairly itched with anticipation. She could not bear it if she didn't get this job. She had not worked for money before, even as a girl on the stage. Having her name listed among the dancers was enough, that and the fun of banter with the actors.

Lizzie looked around the huge lobby. The Thornton was a grand hotel, the most impressive place in Butte. Five stories high with a hundred rooms, a saloon, a barbershop, and a bowling alley;

its warm, orange brick exterior was carved with Tudor arches and stone balconies. A cast iron and glass canopy ran the length of the building, and famous people came through its beveled glass doors all the time. When Teddy Roosevelt visited in 1906, the manager had pulled aside the drapes so his hundreds of admirers could watch him eat a breakfast of steak and eggs.

She could imagine herself living here as a guest. The Christmas decorations were down already, but the room itself was a celebration. Its elegant red-and-gold patterned rug had been woven in Belgium. Like the high crystal chandeliers from Austria, the rug complemented the carved plaster ceilings. The lobby was filled with overstuffed horsehair sofas, dark walnut tables, lamps, and ferns the likes of which Lizzie had not seen since she left Newcastle. The copper kings knew how to treat their friends when they brought them in from the East Coast.

This was the place where mine bosses and politicians met, but also where entertainers stayed — the vaudeville actors, dancers, musicians, and comics who traveled from Broadway to Butte, Seattle, San Francisco, and Virginia City.

Finally, Flanagan appeared with the bell captain. She was out of breath and puffing a bit. "This is Jocko," she said. "He'll bring you up to Mrs. Bonner."

With pockmarked skin, a narrow fox-like face, and a mouth full of little crooked teeth, Jocko was only an inch or two taller than Lizzie, maybe five foot five, but skin-and-bones thin. A cocky one, with curly brown hair and eyebrows stuck out in tufts, he winked at her. "Don't worry, Angel. Herself's in a great mood today. You'll be working here in no time."

Flanagan squeezed her hand and gave her a raffish smile. "He's right. You've got the luck you need. I'll wait."

Mrs. Bonner, heavily corseted, must have weighed two hundred pounds under her stiffly starched apron. She had the flushed face and wheezing breath of one who suffered from a heart ailment. Her office was narrow, no larger than a double closet. Steam-heated, it had a tightly closed single window covered with chicken-wired opaque glass. The skin between Lizzie's breasts and a trail down her backbone began to run with sweat. She feared she would faint. From behind a desk heaped with account books, Mrs. Bonner explained the terms of her employment.

"You can start at the first of the month, with Thursdays off. You'll be on probation, but if you can handle the work, you'll get the job."

Lizzie let herself breathe again.

"Each maid has her own floor with twenty-five rooms. You can expect to work about nine hours a day and a half hour for lunch."

Twenty-five rooms!

"Do you have any questions?"

"How much will I be paid?" Lizzie stammered.

"Six dollars a week." The amount was small, barely above the widow's pension. "We have a fine class of guests, so your tips will probably add a couple more dollars." Mrs. Bonner rose from her desk and led Lizzie to the laundry where she would be expected to pick up fresh linen each morning, then to the windowless maid's room on the third floor with more supplies and a maid's cart that Lizzie would push down the hall from room to room. "The guests leave all sorts of newspapers and magazines, including the *Police Gazette*," Mrs. Bonner said. "You can take your pick."

Lizzie listened to the instructions with only half her mind. Mrs. Bonner's tone was brisk and impersonal, her pictures of hotel work hard. She sounded like Packy. But in one more month, Lizzie would have the job and be earning her own money! Her whole body was humming with excitement by the time she turned to take the elevator to the lobby. Her own house, her own job, her own money — her own life!

The elevator door closed. Now — the children. Maybe, somehow, she could work it out — if she let Mrs. McCaughy have the baby, and let Molly take care of the house and other children . . .

✖ ✖ ✖

Molly swept snow from the porch. She watched rivulets of water forming under the snow rimming the alley. Water seeped down cracks in the rocky soil. Like her mother's moods, the snowdrifts had crystal crusts in the morning, yet melted a little during the middle of the day, before they froze again in the night. It had been a bitter winter and it was not getting better.

Ma was tight as a fiddle. That morning she hardly even looked at the mirror when Molly laced up the boned brocade corset for her. She put on a petticoat, and then her wool serge dress trimmed with ruffles, before she spoke a word. Finally, she pointed to a slip of paper on her dresser. "Look at that."

The paper, an official county court report, said 12-year-old Tom and 11-year-old Frank Dyer had been caught breaking into Dillon's Grocery Store. It was the third time Tom had been picked up for truancy.

"The court worker gave it to me yesterday," Lizzie said, "I told him the boys are more than I can manage. He said they're headed for the Industrial School on the Flats, if this keeps up."

"Oh, Ma!" Molly clasped her mother's arm.

"He said I should think about using the Paul Clark School for all the children until I get on my feet."

"Ma, you can't let them be taken away."

Lizzie stiffened her spine and tightened her lips. "It's a *very* nice school that one of the copper kings set up when his son died. Most of the children have one or both of their parents, so they're only in for a year or two until the parents can take them home again."

"It's an ORPHANAGE!"

"It's better than the Industrial School," Lizzie snapped, "and that's where the boys will go —." She sobbed then and bent over, brushing her hair to hide her face. She would not look at Molly.

The Industrial School was a two-story building with a ten-foot fence around it. Molly knew Judge Mike Donlin handled troublemakers by giving one- to three-year sentences for almost anything. But Tom and Frank weren't hooligans.

"The court worker said this is a hooky-school known for curbing Butte kids' exuberance."

Exuberance? "What's that?" Molly asked.

"Trouble-making," her mother said. "The court worker told me boys at the school tend gardens, take care of livestock, and learn useful trades, instead of making trouble. I am taking the boys to talk to the judge this morning, but I have already decided. If the judge says they should go, I'll agree. They need this for their own good. I can't manage them anymore. They pay me no mind." She pulled on her cotton lisle stockings and leather pumps.

Molly clamped her lips together.

"Wipe that look off your face," Lizzie said. "I've already talked to the boys. It is not me who's sending them away. It's the court."

Molly followed her mother into the kitchen and cried when she called the boys. Frank stood wooden-faced and wouldn't give Lizzie a glance. Tom looked crestfallen, as if he just couldn't believe it. Molly couldn't see how her mother could bear it. Wasn't Tom her favorite son? Johnny and Pat were frightened and didn't understand, but Lizzie just seemed to get harder.

The day was sunny but growing colder from the wind. The air was heavy with bitter, yellow sulfur fog. It was not much of a walk to the center of town. The courthouse was on the corner of Montana and Quartz Streets, not far from the post office with the big statue of Marcus Daly he'd put up of himself for finding copper in his mine after the silver ran out. Molly bundled up James and Pat in snowsuits and would have followed Lizzie to the courthouse but Lizzie saw her intention. "You're not to leave the house," she said.

Tom and Frank, spanking clean in their brown wool jackets, knickers, and knee socks, went with their mother. Molly ached for them. When they left, she tried to distract herself with a book, but she gave up after reading the same page in *The Scarlet Pimpernel* three times. She just sat and worried about what would happen.

Two hours later, Frank returned by himself. Lizzie had gone on with Tom to do some marketing. Frank said he had not spoken a word to Lizzie going, coming, or during the hearing.

"But what happened," Molly asked. "What did the judge say? What did he decide?"

"Ma had old Donlin thinking butter wouldn't melt in her mouth. She was the helpless widow needing time to get on her feet while being overwhelmed by responsibility for all of us. Judge Donlin actually asked her how she thought he could help her!"

"What did she say?"

Frank made his eyes big and sad, and mimicked Lizzie: "Oh, Judge, do you think the children would be better off in an orphanage for a year or two?"

"She didn't," Molly said, but she knew it was true.

Frank resumed his normal voice. "I think Donlin was surprised, maybe even didn't like the idea, because he asked her if she'd ever been to an orphanage and what she knew about them. In the end, he went along with her, because that's what she seemed to want. He told her if she changed her mind, she could have us back. Just to call him."

"How could she? What does she think she's doing?"

"She doesn't think. And there is worse. There is not room at the Paul Clark Orphanage. We are going to the state orphanage in Twin Bridges," Frank said. "And *you* have to stay with Ma."

✖   ✖   ✖

The house was warm and dinner in the oven when Lizzie arrived home, but she dreaded what was coming. She could not look at Molly or say a word when she took off her good clothes and changed to her gingham housedress. She filled the kettle and put it on the stove. Molly stood by the kitchen table, watching. Lizzie knew her daughter was ready to pounce, but she would not give her an opening. She would stay calm and reasonable and Molly would have to understand.

"There's no choice, Molly," Lizzie said. "The court won't let you take care of the boys." Molly said nothing, just held onto the back of the wooden chair. Lizzie could not tell if her eyes were glittering with tears of fury or pain or both. "The boys have to go to the orphanage for a while. Walt and Jack will stay until the boys come home again, and I will rent out the parlor rooms. We will put a cot in my bedroom for you, and you can take care of the house. I can't work and manage everything."

Lizzie knew she was saying it all badly, and her words sounded cold and harsh to her own ear. But how could she help it, with Molly staring at her that way, with such a black look? Her eyes grew twice their size when she was angry.

Molly's voice rasped as she shouted, "You've decided everything, talked to everyone, haven't you? But not to me, not to Frank, Tom, Johnny. Pa wouldn't have let you do this!" She stood trembling.

Lizzie looked at her feeling her own eyes of ice.

"We'll see about that, Miss!" she said. "How can you refuse to see that what's happening is for the boys' own good? You can stop your noise, Molly," Lizzie spat at her. "You always got your way with your Pa, but no more. Frank and Tom have been committed by the court, and the younger boys will go with them so they can be together."

Lizzie lowered her voice, tried to regain the conviction she intended. "It's just like a boys' boarding school. This is hard enough for me without you making a fuss."

"You've got to let us be together." Molly's tears broke and she wailed, "The boys need me!"

Lizzie pulled herself up straight and spoke in a calmer voice. "You couldn't go, even if you wanted, because the girls are kept someplace else entirely. You would never see your brothers. This way, we can go by train and visit. Besides, I'll bring them home, as soon as I can."

Molly flung her broom down, kicked the coal bucket over, and hollered at Lizzie. "You're no mother! What kind of mother tosses her children away as if we're nothing to you?"

Lizzie shouted, "Mind your tongue. Just who do you think you're talking to?" Molly knew her Pa would have slapped her for saying such a thing to her mother.

"I'm sorry," she mumbled.

Lizzie gave her a cold-eyed look. "If you don't want to take care of the boarders, you can go into service and support yourself. Families of mine officials on the West End are always looking for someone to care for their brats and do their housework," she said. "They don't pay much more than food and a bed, but if that's what you want, I won't stand in your way."

Molly walked to her alcove in the front bedroom, lay on her bed, and sobbed.

The next day, Molly and Frank bundled up Johnny for a walk. No crying, no words spoken, just silence and stillness. They trooped past the slagheap of the Anselmo Mine behind the house and on to Big Butte Hill. There was not much snow left after the warm spell. They climbed almost to the top, but their exertion made it harder to breathe the thin cold air. They stopped and sat on the rocks of the big M painted white on the side of the hill. In the distance were the graveyards and smelter on the Flats, then the great white-capped mountains of the Rockies with masses of dark clouds accumulating. It looked like another storm coming, but they still had a few hours.

Molly took out the egg sandwiches she had packed in the lunch bucket, gave one to Frank, and split the other with Johnny. They could see the city spread out below them, like a little village under a Christmas tree. A milkman with his horse and cart was struggling over the rutted road.

"Do you remember Pa's buckboard when we came from England?" she asked.

"Yeah," Frank said, "I remember the tub-bucket contraption in the middle filled with coal and hot stones."

"It was snowing when he met us at the boat in Vancouver. He tucked us all snug into that cart with Indian blankets around us, and we rode for miles. The snow stopped and the stars came out. When we got to our tent, I could hardly believe it. It was a wooden floor with the sides and top part canvas and part wood. Not much house, but that wide lake with all the trees was the most beautiful place I could imagine," she said. "So still, not a sound, just the crunch of the wagon wheels on the snow."

"Until the wolves started howling." Frank said.

"Yeah. Then Pa told us about *Call of the Wild* and promised to read it to us. He took us out and hugged us, and cried, he was that happy to see us."

"Then I was born," Johnny said.

"Well, we had to wait a year for you."

Molly pulled Johnny to her lap and cuddled him. "You'll be too big for me to lift soon," she told him. "You were only ten days old when we had to skedaddle from Canada, after the strike started. And when those Pinkerton gunmen tried to kill Pa."

Frank looked at her out of the corner of his eye. "Pa wasn't a saint, you know. D'you remember his temper the day he came home and found Ma scrubbing the floor on her knees but no dinner on the table? He kicked the bucket of water across the floor, saying that was work that should have been done during the day, and not when a man came home hungry for his supper."

"That was the drink in him talking."

Frank gave a short laugh. Molly stayed silent then. Frank wanted to stay mad. He did not want to talk about anything that might make him cry.

Molly knew her father had loved them all, but her especially. He named her Molly, Gaelic for 'giving-praise'. He talked to her about everything, the miners and the bosses and what you needed to know when you went on strike, and stories of what happened in Ireland from before she could remember. She really missed Pa, especially on New Year's when they should have sat around telling each other all the old stories. Ma forgot to do it this New Year's, or maybe she didn't want to because she'd feel too sad.

Frank was right about Pa's temper, though. But he never hit Ma. Molly

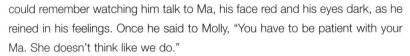

could remember watching him talk to Ma, his face red and his eyes dark, as he reined in his feelings. Once he said to Molly, "You have to be patient with your Ma. She doesn't think like we do."

Huh, nobody thought like her — except maybe Flanagan. Her mother was plenty smart, though, in figuring things out to get her own way.

Molly got to her feet, tagged Frank, and sped away. "Can't catch me!"

"Can too!" He chased her, his sullen mood forgotten.

"Wait," Johnny hollered and started scrambling down the hill. "You forgot the lunch pail. And *me*!"

�֍   �֍   ✖

Molly could hardly sleep. The full moon filled the night with light, but her feet were cold. The hot water bottle she had brought to bed with her had long since cooled, so she hugged her knees, trying to make a warmer ball under the blankets. She wondered if Ma was sleeping. Taking the children to the orphanage was wrong, yet Ma did not seem to have any sense of it. She could not stop her, but Molly had to do something.

She got up from her bed and felt her way across the carpet to the cabinet that separated her alcove from the parlor. She eased open the drawer that held the moneybox with all the money the miners had given to the children at her father's funeral. A weight of silver dollars filled her hands as she returned to bed, tucked the money under her pillow and fell sound asleep.

The next day, she went down to Hennessy's and bought a book for each of her brothers, *Peter Rabbit* for Pat, and *Treasure Island* for Johnny. Johnny was only five, but it tore Molly's heart out that he so badly wanted to read and now she could not teach him. She picked out an extra book for him about myths, full of beautiful pictures of Greek gods and strange animals. Then two books about the Hardy brothers for Frank and Tom. And she wrote, "I love you. I love you. I love you," in each book, so her mother couldn't return them even if she wanted to. Molly spent every cent from the box.

That afternoon, Molly and Flanagan joined Lizzie and Jack who were taking the boys on the train. Molly said good-bye to the boys in the Great Northern Railroad Station, against the background noises of the great steam engine preparing to depart. Even Frank let her hug and kiss him, and her brothers all hugged her back, hard. The books were a surprise and these unexpected gifts did make them feel better. She told Johnny he should look at each picture and make up a story to tell her.

Lizzie did not make any fuss about the books, at least not then. She just gathered the boys up and went with Jack on the train. Molly thought maybe Lizzie felt a little heartsick at what she was doing. She looked peaked around the mouth. She had packed a big picnic basket and made her special raisin pie that the boys liked, but she couldn't seem to find any words to say. Jack looked uncomfortable with his chin tucked down into his stiff collar, but Molly knew he would go along with anything Lizzie wanted.

Flanagan took Molly for tea and saffron cake in the Hotel dining room after the train pulled out. Neither of them felt like eating.

✖   ✖   ✖

Lizzie had known she couldn't let her guard down with Molly. The slightest show of weakness, and Molly would have broken her down and had her saddled with the boys again. She had to stay firm and resolute if she was going to start a new life.

She was hardly able to stand it on the train, though, with Frank and Molly so angry and the half-day train trip with the little ones so miserable. They usually loved her raisin pie, but Frank refused to touch it and little Johnny was so upset, he threw up. Johnny and Pat were distracted by the excitement of the railroad trip and the new sights for a while, but mostly they were subdued and silent. James, the baby, slept and did not seem to realize she was leaving until the end. He stared at her when she handed him to the matron, then started howling and reaching for her. He kept screaming as she walked out the gate. Her own tears fell then, and all during the trip home. She begged Jack to reassure her that the children would be all right and that she was doing the right thing. He tried, but what could he say being as fond of the children as he was? It was so hard to feel disapproved of. She had never experienced it before. She could tell that Eileen and most of the other women in the parish did not like what she was doing. Except Flanagan.

She would bring the boys home as soon as she could. It shouldn't take too much money to finish the apartment downstairs. The men would help. With that rented, she would not need boarders. She could bring the children home and continue working to support them. The only alternative she could think of, to spread them out among friends to be cared for, would not be better. This way they had each other. She had to do this. She kept saying the words inside, repeatedly.

When Lizzie got home, she tried to say something to Molly about her theft of money for the books. She told Molly the books were absurdly expensive. "You've no sense about the money it takes to buy things."

Molly looked her in the eye. "The boys need more than books. They need me. Books are all I can give them."

Lizzie glared at her and Molly glared right back.

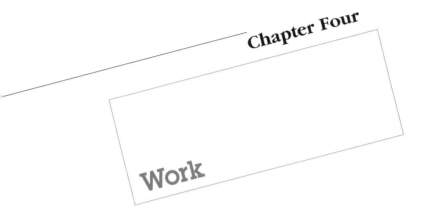

Chapter Four

Work

February 1919

izzie had not worked so hard in her life. She was too tired even to think about missing the children. By the third day, every muscle in her body protested the drudgery of lifting mattresses and tucking in sheets. Scrubbing tubs produced a backache that sent her to bed unable to move and this raised her first doubts. Did she so much want the independence of a job that this was better than cooking for a few boarders and caring for her children?

She managed to hobble to her station the next day. As she stood in the laundry room, the idea of lifting fifty sheets to her cart filled her eyes with tears. If Jocko had not observed her at that very moment, she thought later, she would not have survived the first week of work.

"Need a bit of help, Lizzie?" he asked, lifting the first pile onto her cart.

"Umph," she murmured, unable to talk.

"You've never used those muscles before, at least not for so many hours at a time — right? Tell you what, I'll ask Mrs. Bonner if Annie can give you a hand this afternoon, and in an hour I'll be up to see you. I'm a great one with a carpet sweeper."

Lizzie bit her lips together tight to keep from bawling and sniffed her gratitude, still unable to speak. Large tears rolled down her cheeks. She was terrified to let Mrs. Bonner know she couldn't handle the job, but she had no choice.

Lizzie managed to complete a few rooms before Mrs. Bonner appeared. Her small eyes twinkled in her ruddy face. "Well, well," she said, "you've made it through half a week. I had my doubts, but you're going to be a female Samson." Mrs. Bonner plunked herself onto the vanity bench. "Do you still want the job?"

"Oh, yes,"

"Tomorrow, then, I'll put you on the top floor with Annie. She can show you a few shortcuts and the easiest way to bend and brace yourself when you scour the tubs."

Why didn't you show me? Lizzie wondered as she looked at the fat little woman, who seemed so amused by her pain.

Jocko appeared a few minutes after Mrs. Bonner left. He held a bag in his hand and with him was a round, freckle-faced woman with a smile that showed missing side teeth. She was perhaps ten years older than Lizzie.

"This is Annie," he said.

Annie smiled and picked Lizzie's bottle of chlorine and the container of Bon Ami cleanser from the cart. "We don't have to wait 'til tomorrow."

Jocko smiled his fox-like grin and handed Lizzie the bag he carried. "I've brought you a bag of Epsom Salts, a bottle of Sloan's Liniment, and a jar of Vicks VapoRub," he said. "Go home and soak in a hot bath with the Epsom Salts. Nothing works as well."

"If it didn't hurt so much, I'd hug you. You're both so kind."

"I'll collect later," Jocko said.

"This'll get easier, you'll see," Annie said. "Later on, I'll talk to you about joining the WPU, the Women's Protective Union for waitresses and chambermaids."

Lizzie went back to work. The talk alone seemed to have taken away most of her soreness. But she was not going to get mixed up in any union. This job was too important to risk losing.

✖   ✖   ✖

The house was completely silent. Molly sat by the stove and thought about how to start a strike. She had to get the boys back. Pa would say the important thing was to make her demand clear, then not give in. Ma had refused to talk to Judge Donlin about when the boys would come home. Molly had to make her see what would happen to the house when Molly wasn't around to keep things in order, make the dinner, and lace up her corsets.

Molly would up the stakes as high as she could.

But first, she had to find a job, and there were almost no jobs. A couple of months after Pa died, the war ended, and now copper wasn't needed the way it had been, so the ACM was laying off thousands of miners. When the miners went on strike or were laid off, their wives scrambled around to find any kind of work.

Well, strikers had to know what they wanted and to be prepared for a long fight, Pa had said. Ma did not know anything about strike strategy, or Joe Hill or anything else important. Ma never listened.

"Pa, help me!" Molly prayed silently.

Chapter Five

Molly

April 1919

M olly pushed the storm window open a crack to catch the scent of wet leaves. Fresh cold air swept into the stuffy, overheated parlor. What a wild stormy day it was, filled with wind, sleet, and rain. She wanted to get out into it, to walk pushing into the wind, feeling it try to push her back. Both she and the wind were stubborn. She had hours to wait, though. The children were kept indoors when it might rain.

Two months ago, Flanagan had told her the McPherson family needed a live-in girl to take care of their children. Molly applied and the McPhersons hired her because of her experience caring for her younger brothers. Lizzie still refused to bring the boys back, so Molly left home as soon as she got the job. She carried on her strike part-time. On Sundays, her day off from work, she went to Mass and had dinner ready when her mother came home from the Thornton. But *every* Sunday first thing, Molly asked her mother, "When are you going to bring the boys home?"

Lizzie always answered, "As soon as I have enough money." But as time went on, she got angry and impatient with Molly. Molly did not let it stop her. Lizzie didn't want to see Molly each Sunday and have this same conversation, but Molly was her own strike committee. Her mother having guests didn't stop her questions either, because she would ask Lizzie right in front of them, and she didn't smile or say anything else during the meal. It was what miners call a *lockout*.

✖   ✖   ✖

Molly pulled the window shut and looked about her. The McPherson house was probably four times bigger than Lizzie's, with a porch and pillars supporting a balcony up above. There were fifteen rooms and three stories, if you counted the attic where she and Cook had their rooms. Molly could look out her dormer window and see the iron head frame of the Anselmo Mine on the lower slope.

A housekeeper, Mattie, came in during the day to clean the parlors filled with chairs and sofas and a grand piano; potted plants and ferns everywhere, and carved wooden cabinets teeming with cut glass and painted porcelain. Then Mattie still had to clean the upstairs family bedrooms. Molly tried to imagine herself, Ma, and the boys living in these big rooms, but it was hard to picture.

Cook, whose long name was never used, shopped for food and prepared and served the meals. She got along easily with Molly, and they told each other stories. Cook's were all sad. She and her husband came from Sweden and all of her children died before the age of six. Finally, her husband died and she had just herself to care for. Sweden was even colder than Montana in the wintertime.

Molly told Cook about her great-great-grandmother who was a lady-in-waiting to the queen. Cook gaped at the idea of anyone talking to a queen, so Molly told her that the queen and her great-great-grandmother were the same age as little girls, and they used to bounce on the mattresses in the royal bed-chamber. When she bounced the little ones on their bed later, Molly told them the story too, and made up other tales about how the queen loved to play hide-and-seek in the garden.

Molly took care of the children during the day and washed up the dishes and kitchen after supper. Mrs. McPherson didn't spend much time with the children. Most afternoons she went to her social and charity meetings, or her dressmaker. She wore a different fancy dress almost every day and her picture was in the society pages of the *Montana Standard* once a month at least.

Susan and Bobby, ten and eleven years old, were as close as twins, and Billy and Mary, eight and seven, were easy enough to care for. Molly missed her brothers when she was with the children. They were like the boys, the way they loved stories of any kind and going on adventures that Molly made up while they tramped for miles among the little hills and gulches.

This day, because of the storm, they stayed home on the back garden porch. Molly told them a story from *The Tales Of King Arthur's Round Table*.

"The Green Knight had knocked King Arthur down and as a penalty the king had to solve the riddle: 'What do women really want?' He had a year to do it or he'd have to marry Lady Ragnell, the sister of the Green Knight, a horrible hag with a wart at the end of her nose." The girls wriggled and screamed when Molly told them how ugly Ragnell was. "Every time Lady Ragnell spoke, pieces of coal and spit fell out of her mouth. Anyway, King Arthur couldn't answer the question, but his best friend Sir Gawain offered to take his place."

"To marry Lady Ragnell?" Mary made an ugly face.

"Yes," Molly said, "and the people at the court felt the same way you do when Sir Gawain and Lady Ragnell got married and went to their bedroom. But then something happened. When Sir Gawain got ready for bed, he found the frightful Lady Ragnell had turned into a radiant, enchanting woman. 'You kept your word to marry me and this is your reward,' she said. 'You may have me as you see me now, by day when other people are around, or by night to be seen by you alone.'

'Madam,' he bowed to her, 'you are the one who must live your life. The choice is yours.'

Lady Ragnell smiled and laid her hand on his. 'You have destroyed the spell,' she said. 'I can now choose to be as you see me all the time.'"

"I don't get it," Bobby said. "Was she an ugly witch or not?"

"Both," Molly said. "Lady Ragnell was a good witch and really beautiful, but she was under a spell and couldn't use her power until someone told her she could choose to be what she wanted."

"Was she still able to turn back into a hag when she wanted?" Susan asked.

"Why would she want to do that?"

"For fun," Susan said. "Anyone try to bully her around, she could scare the heck out of them."

"Shush, Susan. Nice little girls don't use such language."

Susan grinned. "It's witch language."

"Yeah, let's be witches for our adventure," said Mary.

"Naw, I'd rather be King Arthur battling the Green Knight," said Bob.

So, their adventure became a melodrama with Mary — as the fair-maiden-to-be-rescued — tearing around the porch and into the kitchen crying, "Save me! Save me!" Followed by the wicked Green Knight yelling, "I've got you in my power!"

Susan, as Lady Ragnell, put on her most fearsome face to wither Billy, the Green Knight, at a glance. Bob claimed that it was not fair to wither the Green Knight before he got a chance to fight him. So, he became an ally of the Green Knight. He and Billy consulted in whispers, disappeared into the house, and returned with a blanket. They ran at Susan and dropped it over her head. "You are invisible and totally in our power," Bob declared.

"That's what you think," Susan shouted as she fought free. Mary, forgetting she was the fair-maiden-to-be-saved, joined her sister. They raced into the house to find pillows and the battle was on.

Until Mrs. McPherson came home from her tea party and demanded to know just what was going on.

"Oh Mummy, it's the greatest game!" Billy said.

Mrs. McPherson fixed Molly with an icy stare. "This is not acceptable. I expect you to keep the children in order. If you want to keep this job, such behavior will not be tolerated in this house. Is that understood?"

Molly nodded. "Yes, ma'am."

Mrs. McPherson said, "Now clean up this mess."

Billy's eyes welled up with tears as his mother left, and Susan whispered, "I'm sorry I got you in trouble."

Molly thought of Mrs. McPherson as some kind of witch herself, but of course, she could not say that to Susan! Witches have a lot of power when they are mad. She winked at Susan, "Out of sight in the gulch is a better place for witches to play."

Later, she walked by herself when the children were at their music lessons. Then the utter desolation of the ground, without a weed, without even a grass blade, drew her into long, long thoughts. So many things were not right. She'd like to change that. But how did women ever get power?

November 1919

Lizzie seemed happy with her job. Molly heard her tell Flanagan the maids and bell boys knew everything that was going on in Butte. She said, "It's better than reading novels." Molly suspected that her mother never went to Mass now that she was working. Church had been more important to Pa. Molly missed school, but at least she had books and the *Daily Miner* to read. Miss Nichols, the librarian, picked out five or six books for her to read each week when she went to the library.

She wanted to check on what she heard at the McPherson dining table. Molly helped with serving when the family entertained, although mostly they went to other people's parties. Their guests were always ACM people. Molly kept her ears open and enjoyed listening to their talk. They certainly had different views from Pa. Butte had been under martial law since the beginning of the War, and the soldiers were still around. They expected violence when the Mill and Mine Workers Union finally went out on strike to protest the layoffs. Congresswoman Jeanette Rankin offered to mediate, but the ACM people hated her for having cast the only vote against the war. They said they definitely were not going to let *her* have a say. Molly did not know who the Congresswoman was, or why she was a pacifist, but Molly thought she was brave to say what she thought.

When the strike ended, it had not done anybody any good. A lot of families left Butte.

✖   ✖   ✖

It was Molly's fifteenth birthday, the ninth month of her own strike. Once a month, Lizzie switched her day off so she and Molly could take the train to Twin Bridges State Orphanage, seventy miles each way, to visit the boys. But Lizzie still had not asked that the boys be sent home.

The McPhersons would have given Molly her birthday off, but Lizzie would have none of it. "Nonsense, I'll come by with your cake and a present I've made for you." Molly knew her mother. Lizzie wanted to take a gander at how the McPhersons lived. "Mind, I don't want you saying anything about the boys," Lizzie had said. "Dropping dirty linen in front of the McPhersons would just give them something to talk about."

"Huh?" Molly thought. At least Ma knew that putting your kids in an orphanage was dirty laundry.

Molly would not have said anything to the McPhersons about it anyway. The McPhersons were a bloodless lot. Nobody laughed or joked. Nobody sang or told stories. Molly wasn't sure if it was because they were Protestants or because they were mine owners, but all they talked about was money.

Mrs. McPherson invited Lizzie into the front parlor, and Lizzie gave her the cake. "Would you like a cup of tea?" Mrs. McPherson asked.

When she brought the flowered teapot in its cozy, Mr. McPherson came in, and put the water kettle on a trivet. Lizzie showed off Molly's present, wrapped in tissue paper and laughed and talked to Mr. McPherson.

"Four embroidered handkerchiefs I stitched myself and a sachet of lavender for Molly's hope chest," she said.

"Butte must have the prettiest girls in the world," he said.

Mrs. McPherson wasn't as amused as her husband when Lizzie went on to talk about how she was married at sixteen and how she was such a great dancer that Packy couldn't keep his eyes off her. Molly felt her cheeks begin to burn and a sick feeling in her stomach.

"The tea's ready," Mrs. McPherson said in a frosty voice.

Lizzie took the cup with a satisfied smile and trotted out more of her stories. Her husband was a champion heel-and-toe walker. He was a musician. He played the fiddle and the brass horn. He acted sometimes, and was a stagehand for a group of performers that toured Great Britain. Ma told them how the traveling groups hired local girls to fill out the chorus, and that she was always hired, because she could do the splits and kick higher than anyone.

Mr. McPherson wanted to know what the "splits" were. Molly tried to cough to give her mother some kind of signal. But no, Lizzie had to show him. Right there in the front parlor. One leg in front, the other behind, down to the floor she went, her back straight as a board, both arms lifted and a mischievous smile on her face to show it was no trouble at all. Her ankle length skirt hid all but a little lace on her slip, but bunched up sufficiently to show her trim legs and small French heeled shoes.

Mr. McPherson laughed until Molly thought he would collapse. "And will you show me how high you can kick?" he asked.

Lizzie knew he was teasing and dimpled up in that way she had. Mrs.

McPherson kept a stiff smile on her face. She did not like what was going on, but she didn't know what to do anymore than Molly did.

Molly could just hear what Mrs. McPherson would say to her the next day about "you people" as if they were some strange animals a refined lady couldn't imagine. Molly could have strangled her mother, but it also tickled her to see Mrs. McPherson's thin little mouth tighten even smaller.

Lizzie liked to be teased, and men liked to tease her. Packy did, and her son Tom as well. Only Frank would not give her a bit of it.

Molly shook her head. Lizzie did not touch a drop of drink other than tea, because she fancied her complexion so much, but sometimes she acted like she did not have good sense.

✖   ✖   ✖

Her shenanigans were probably what gave Mr. McPherson the idea that he could tease Molly the following day. Except he did not understand that teasing was public talk, you did in front of other people. Next day he wanted to say things to Molly when they were alone in the dining room. There was something thick about him, like he did not have all his wits. Molly did not want to embarrass him, so she found something to say and slipped away. She knew from Pa that mine officials used words different from the way miners did; you couldn't trust them.

A couple of days later, when she was washing up after supper, first thing she knew he had her cornered. Liquor was on his breath and he was trying to put his mouth all over hers. Fortunately, or so she thought at the time, Mrs. McPherson heard Molly struggling to get away, and she ran downstairs to the kitchen. Mr. McPherson, looking sheepish, left the room.

Mrs. McPherson hissed at Molly: "I know what you're trying to do, Miss, but you don't know who you're dealing with. You're going to be sorrier than you've ever imagined possible."

It was little more than a week after the "Day of the Splits," that police officer William Beebe arrived at the front door to take Molly to a court hearing. Mrs. McPherson had told the police she had stolen a ruby ring, and that she had a habit of lying from the beginning of her service in the house.

"I put up with it at first," Mrs. McPherson said. "Now, I know no one can believe a word Molly says. I hoped to help her, but the girl is obviously impossible and ungrateful." She said this with such hatred it took Molly's breath away. Her mouth was open. She could not believe this was happening. Mrs. McPherson hadn't said a word to her beforehand. She could not have looked Molly in the face and told such a lie.

Molly's temper exploded, "I've never said *anything* untrue!"

"Maybe the royal family will vouch for you, then," Mrs. McPherson sneered.

Cook — the children — they must have told her about the family stories. Molly shut her mouth tightly. She would not explain, wouldn't put her stories to Mrs. McPherson's ridicule. This woman was a liar.

Molly knew why she would not tell the truth. So did Mr. McPherson. He had come to the door, but did not say anything. He tried to slip Molly a silver dollar, half a week's wage, when she took her satchel from the house, but she stared him in the eye and let it fall to the ground. He covered it with his foot so Mrs. McPherson wouldn't notice.

Molly felt the police officer believed her when she said, "I don't have the ring because I didn't take her ring." But what would her word be in front of a judge? The McPhersons were important people. She was not.

"I think you'll be better off out of there," the policeman said in a soft voice.

✖ ✖ ✖

Lizzie came to Molly's hearing. Molly told her the whole story and she knew it was the truth. When Judge Donlin said Molly had to spend six months in the Convent of the Good Shepherd, Lizzie cried. She promised Molly that she would bring the boys home. They would work things out. It was the closest she ever came to admitting that she was wrong for what she did — letting the children be scattered.

She pulled something wrapped in a handkerchief from her purse. It was the steel pocket watch Pa used at work. It was in his pants with his pocketknife when he died. The tears were still in her eyes as she pressed it into Molly's hands. She did not have to say anything. When she hugged Molly and Molly hugged her, Molly knew her mother loved her and she loved her mother in return.

Lizzie said she could not manage the boys without Molly, but as soon as she came out, they would go to the orphanage and collect them. Like Pa said, a strike can take a long time, but it is the only strength you have got at the bargaining table. Ma had finally given in.

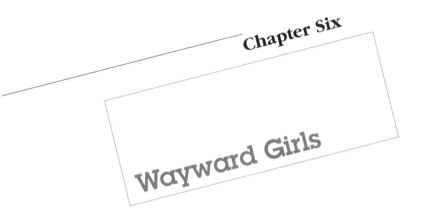

Chapter Six

Wayward Girls

Molly picked up the pamphlet the Judge had given her. It said the Convent of the Good Shepherd was "a haven and a place of learning for troubled and wayward girls." It probably was not as bad as it sounded, though, because the nuns taught things like bookkeeping. Molly thought she would like to be in school again. Maybe she could become a famous bookkeeper. She wondered what bookkeepers did.

✖ ✖ ✖

The court worker brought Molly to the Convent Gate. Sister Mary Magdalene, a nun with the slight hint of an Irish brogue, answered his ring. "Follow me, dear," she said after the court officer left. "I'll take you to the dormitory." She moved quietly in her white woolen habit, unstarched wimple, and black veil. She had a way of brushing her veil back, as a girl might do with unbraided hair, but when they reached the stairs Sister grasped the banister tightly and had difficulty climbing.

The four dormitories were exactly alike, six iron cots on each side of the room with a closet beside each bed. The whole place smelled of disinfectant and, at first, Molly could hardly breathe. Sister unlocked a large closet at the end of the room and gave her two sets of underwear and bloomers, long brown stockings and garters, a dark blue woolen dress, and two white cotton pinafores. "Not very pretty, but you'll find they are practical." She smiled at Molly, "I hope you won't mind them too much."

Molly nodded, but her neck felt stiff.

Sister took her to the washroom. It had tubs in separate stalls with wooden doors, and a deep sink with a single faucet under the window. She showed Molly where her basin and towel were kept under a long wooden shelf with small mirrors over it. Molly would fill her basin at the sink when she wanted to wash up.

"You'll work in the kitchen this month," Sister said, "when you aren't in class. Later, you might be assigned to the laundry, the garden, or general house cleaning chores."

Molly could see the locks on the doors and windows. She went to one of the windows. The garden was large but surrounded by a high wall. "The girls have a recreation hour in the late afternoon. You can spend it in the garden or the library, but you can't go outside into the street."

Molly pricked up her ears when Sister mentioned the library. What she loved to do most in the world was read, but when Sister said that about being locked in, Molly could not stop the chill that passed through her. Sister must have seen how heartsick she was because she suddenly stopped, put her arm around Molly's shoulders, and gave her a quick hug. She took her hand and led her to sit on a bed. She plumped herself down on another to face Molly.

"I don't know all that's happened to you, dear," Sister Mary Magdalene said, "but I see from the way your eyes tightened, looking into the garden, that you've suffered and been hurt. This probably seems like a prison to you, but I hope you will soon feel it's a safe place. Then you can catch your breath for a while and find what you need to live."

Her voice was so kind Molly felt tears well up in her eyes, but she could not say anything.

Sister asked, "Do you know the story of the Good Shepherd?"

Molly nodded. The shepherd who leaves his flock while he hunts for one lost lamb was sometimes a gospel reading at Mass.

"Well, our order was founded to show that aspect of God's love. We get to be His eyes and arms. He loves each of us — you, the same as me. If you get lost or into difficulty, He wants to find you and bring you back safely into His care."

Molly did cry then. She just bawled. She cried and cried. All the tears in the world were in her. She could not stop. Tears for Pa, tears for herself, tears for her brothers who had been sent away. She did not notice that Sister moved and was holding her until she saw Sister's white wimple under her mouth all damp and limp.

Sister gave her handkerchief. "Blow your nose, Molly." Molly was surprised to see tears in Sister's eyes. "The other girls won't be back in the room until late afternoon. You might like to take a bit of a nap. I'll be back. We can have a cup of tea, and then I'll bring you to the afternoon class."

Molly did take a nap. She felt safe — and she loved this shepherd lady, Sister Mary Magdalene.

✖   ✖   ✖

Molly had not spent much time with girls, so she couldn't imagine what it would be like living with them. For one thing, most of them did not like Sister Mary Magdalene. They mocked her brogue and what Trina called her 'pie-in-the-sky-by-and-by' talk when she taught religion.

The only time for talk without the nuns around was in the dorm for an hour before lights out but, sometimes in the dark, the girls talked late into the night. The first evening they had been friendly enough. They asked Molly's name and where she lived. They were impressed when Molly said she had five brothers and assumed they were all older than she was. Molly did not tell them different.

Then Trina Olsen asked what she was in for. Trina was huge, almost six feet tall, and probably weighed 180 pounds. "Yeah, Miss Innocent, where did you stash it?" she asked.

"What?" Molly asked.

"The ring you stole," Trina taunted her. "And what else did you get away with, Miss Big Eyes?"

The others watched to see how Molly would take this attack. Her stomach felt tight and her heart raced. She felt gritty and cold as a piece of copper ore.

"I took nothing." Molly looked Trina directly in the eye, " Anyone who says

I did is a liar."

"Hoity-toity," Trina said. Looking at the others, she mocked Molly's accent, "she too-ook nawthin."

Molly refused to say another word.

They ignored her then, and gossiped about a girl who had once lived in the dorm.

Gertrude Krueger, a pal of Trina, only smaller with masses of blond hair that she was winding up with rag curlers, asked "Do any of you remember Helen, the crybaby who was here a year or so ago?"

"Yeah," another girl said. "She was the squealer, a tattle-tale, who always ran to the nuns with how mean everyone was to her."

They laughed.

Trina did not look at her, but Molly knew something bad was going to happen.

Molly narrowed her eyes and watched everything that went on. She remembered when the family first came from England. Frank and Tom wore dark green wool suits and their school caps. The local boys made fun of their clothes, pushed them around, then stole their caps and ran off. Tom tried to laugh it off, but Frank was tough. He knew he had to fight. He ran after the biggest bully and they slugged it out. Frank's nose got broken and he was so bruised he could barely get out of bed the next morning. But he never had to fight another fight.

Next morning, Molly knew something was wrong. The others were getting dressed and chatting. She looked around and no one paid any attention to her. She checked her satchel. Sure enough, Pa's watch was gone. She marched over to Trina and said, "You've taken my watch and I want it back."

"O-oh," Trina said, mocking her. "Miss Innocent is missing a watch." She looked around, checking her audience. "I too-ook nawthin." She widened her eyes and stared at Molly. "Anyone who says I did is a liar."

"That watch must be put back." Molly kept her voice as even as possible. Then she turned on her heel and walked downstairs to the kitchen. She had to prepare oatmeal for breakfast while the other girls were at Mass. She put the water pot on the stove to boil, then clutched at her waist. "Oh, the elastic on my bloomers! It's broken. I have to change."

"Be quick about it," Sister Imelda said. "You still have to set the places."

Molly raced up the back stairs to the dorm. Nothing in Trina's closet or bed. She pulled Gertrude's apart next. Nothing . . . Where would she put it? . . . Molly thought carefully . . . Yes, there Pa's watch was — tucked into a toe of an old pair of shoes, under Trina's bed. Molly thrust it into her pocket under the pinafore and raced down the stairs. She flew around the dining room, setting each place in order. When the girls filed in after Mass, she helped Sister Imelda distribute bowls of hot porridge to each person.

When Molly was helping clear the tables after breakfast, Sister remarked with annoyance, "Will you look at this. Two of them did not touch their porridge. Why they don't refuse food instead of wasting it, I'll never know!"

True, and one more meal should do it.

When lunchtime came, Molly dipped up soup into the bowls, two of which again held three extra tablespoons of salt.

She did not doctor the dinner. When she returned to the dorm after cleaning the dishes and dining room, Gertrude was sitting on her bed, laughing. "OK, you win! How did you know where to look — and when did you find time to do it?"

Molly smiled but didn't say anything until Gertrude told the others she was in cahoots with Trina and what Molly did was funnier than anything they had ever thought of doing. They were glad Molly was in their dorm.

Trina added, "I didn't think it was funny until I got a dinner I could eat."

The convent had a huge laundry on the first level. The girls' work in the laundry paid for their keep. The chapel took up half of the first floor above the laundry. Sister Magdalene's brother Father Emmett Healy, who taught at Carroll College as well as the Convent, said Mass there most mornings. The parlors were used for classrooms except for the one Sister Superior used as her office, and one other for visitors. Sister Magdalene's brother visited her every Wednesday afternoon. Molly could hear them laughing in the parlor or see them walking in the garden on sunny days. One day, Fr. Healy passed Molly going out the front door. "You must be the union agitator," he said and grinned. How'd he know that? For once, Molly had nothing to say.

The kitchen where she worked was behind the dining hall. Then there was a library on the third floor and the dorms. The nuns lived in the cloister, a fourth floor with separate small cells and a larger common room.

December 1919

Each letter Molly wrote that Christmas to Ma and to the boys began the same way: "I haven't time to write much, so many things are going on. Today we are preparing for Christmas, but, of course, we won't put up the tree and crib until Christmas Eve. I baked cookies all morning and now have free time without class." She didn't write that she cried with each letter, she missed them so much.

February 1920

Molly didn't mind Lent with meatless meals, mostly bread and soup. There was plenty of both and sometimes they had fried potato sandwiches. She was work-ing in the kitchen again and liked baking bread, especially pounding the dough.

Learning shorthand was magic. She could type 32 words a minute and knew a little bit about bookkeeping now. She'd learned more than business courses, though. Most of the girls at the Convent had hard lives compared to hers. Gertrude, who was fifteen, almost sixteen, came to the Convent when the police shut down her mother's business. Gertrude did most of the after-lights-out talk and she'd told them a lot of things Molly didn't know.

"What do you mean by 'down the line'," Molly asked one night. The lights had just been turned off and they were scrunched down in their beds as usual.

"You don't know anything, do you?" Gertrude said. Sometimes she was still a know-it-all pain-in-the-neck.

"First came the miners to work in the mine.
Then came the ladies who lived down the line," she sang to Molly.
The other girls laughed.

Molly was embarrassed and said nothing. She should have known Gertrude was talking about whores.

Gertrude laughed, too, but then she explained. "All mining camps have lines," she said. "A dozen or more shacks and tents get set up as soon as miners start working. Butte's line was on Galena Street. When more miners came, the saloons, gambling and music halls were everywhere — like weeds. Every one of them had runners to the line.

"One place, the Casino, is still on Galena Street. It used to have a saloon, a dance hall, a prizefight ring, a theater, and its own cathouse! More than a hundred girls worked there. The doors never closed. There were a lot of guns and fights. On the south side of the street, the girls lived in tiny little rooms called cribs. When times were flush, a girl could make up to sixty dollars a night. Each crib had its owner's name on the door. 'French Erma,' 'Fat-Ass Annie,' 'German Jess,' and lots of others."

Molly listened to Gertrude in stunned silence, glad that she couldn't see her burning cheeks.

"I'll tell you about one of them," Gertrude continued. "German Jess was also a pick pocket and smart as a whip when she was junked up. One night, she was picked up for the usual charge. The man who accused her of rolling him, though, could not prove it, so the judge let her go.

"She threw her arms around the judge in gratitude. He was embarrassed, but he got her off and tried to rearrange his robes. A few moments later, his honor discovered his watch, his wallet, and his tiepin were missing. He sent a police officer to re-arrest Jess, but not a trace of the missing articles could be found. The judge had to let her go again.

"About a week later a package was delivered to the judge's chambers. Everything was in it. There was no explanation."

The girls hooted. Gertrude really could tell a story.

"That's the 'red-light' district," Molly said, pulling up a distant memory of something Flanagan had said to Ma.

"Yeah, except it changed when parlors like the Dumas House were built. They catered to the sons of the copper kings, and the copper barons." Gertrude told them about the silk draperies, upholstery, art treasures, and ornate furniture that went to furnish the parlors, each run by a *Madam*.

As they listened in their beds to Gertrude's voice, it was like watching a fairy tale. They could see the neatly dressed colored maids and Chinese servants greeting the guests at the doors. The Madam, covered with diamond rings and necklaces, stood among the girls and offered champagne in sparkling cut-glass goblets.

"Over the years, different women ran the houses," Gertrude said. "One of them was Pansy Krueger, my mom. For a long time, she did all right for herself and for us — my sister and me. Most of the money, after the entertainment costs, went to Ned her business partner who did the bookkeeping. The parlors were closed two years ago, but the reform didn't last."

Molly never could think of a thing to say after Gertrude talked. She seemed to know everything, and Molly didn't even know the words she used. She told sad and funny stories, but she never talked about herself. Molly wondered how could she stand not having a family who cared about her.

One day, while she and Molly were assigned to wash down the walls and windows of the dining room, Molly asked, "How come you're here?"

She didn't answer for a while. Molly thought she was probably making up a lie to tell her. Gertrude wrung out her cloth made from a flour sack and hung it to dry on the stepladder. Molly refilled their basin with water and vinegar. They had to keep busy to finish by afternoon classes, but they were alone for now.

"After the war started, things changed for Mom. When the line — the entire district — was closed two years ago, hundreds of girls were turned out, most of them homeless and penniless."

"But you weren't one of them," Molly said.

"No, but I didn't know Mom was a hophead. She had to have her drugs everyday or she went crazy. She and my sister opened a boarding house and kept some of their own customers, but not like at the parlors. I saw a lot of things that scared me. When the police closed the boarding house, they sent me here for my safety, or so they said."

Again, Molly couldn't think of anything to say. She took Gertrude's hand.

"Ned, Mom's partner, beat her and I know he made her do things she didn't want to because I heard her crying. I tried to make her leave him, but she screamed and wouldn't listen to me. Nellie, my sister, wasn't any help. She doesn't have all her wits."

Molly reached over and hugged Gertrude. She sobbed. Molly let her cry and held her, like Sister Mary Magdalene had done with her.

✖   ✖   ✖

That afternoon in religion class, Molly asked Sister Magdalene, "Why do some people have bad things happen to them?"

Sister looked at Molly for several moments, eyes squinched, puzzling out what to say. "God wants us to make choices," she said. "Sometimes it's just to endure something we can't change." She took off her glasses and rubbed her eyes with one hand. "Life gives us different problems," she said. "When bad times come, we have to find what choices we can make with them." She paused again. "Our choices make us who we are."

"You mean it's like a problem-to-be-solved with a solution?" Molly asked.

"It's not so logical when the heart's involved. What's worrying you, Molly?" she asked.

"Well, when someone's Ma is a drunk, or beats her up all the time, or something like that," Molly said.

Sister's eyes flicked then softened. "That's hard, isn't it?" She said, "A parent who beats a child does a terrible thing." Sister Magdalene looked at the crucifix hanging in the back of the room for a few moments. "Have you ever thought about the 'miracle' that Jesus did most often?"

"Healing the sick?" 'Trina guessed.

"No, casting out spirits," Sister Magdalene said. "Think about that word. What do we mean when we say 'So-and-so is mean-spirited, or has a selfish spirit or a violent spirit, or even . . . that someone is drinking alcoholic spirits?' Doesn't it mean something that moves in and, sometimes, can take over a person's will, take away choice?"

Some girls nodded. "At first it's invited in and sometimes it's good," Sister Magdalene said, "like having a creative spirit, it enlarges us, but a bad spirit narrows the choices we see. The spirit that wants drink or drugs, that spirit doesn't let the person think anything else is as important as what it wants. That's the kind of spirit that Jesus cast out. He did it only when the person wanted to be free to make choices again."

"What about today?" Gertrude asked. "Can a bad spirit get cast out?"

"We have to pray," Sister Magdalene said, "first, that we won't catch it, because it's contagious like scarlet fever. When someone hurts us, we want to hurt back."

Molly gulped. She knew she had wanted to hurt Ma like that. Sister Magdalene seemed to read her mind.

"We all do things we know are wrong, but we can ask forgiveness," Sister said. "Jesus preferred the company of sinners like thieves and prostitutes, people who know the truth about the dark will in us, to hypocrites, who are people who pretend to be better than they are, richer, smarter, holier or whatever — as if they never made bad choices."

Sister said some other things, but Molly didn't hear her. She was preoc-
cupied with her own thoughts. She woke up again when she heard Gertrude's
voice.

Gertrude had hung on to their question. "What can you do with your
mother, though, if she takes drugs and does other things that hurt you?"
Gertrude asked.

Sister fingered the long wooden rosary beads that hung from her leather
belt. She spoke to Gertrude then. "What Jesus did was call it what it was —
name it. You have to do that. When your mother's craving for drugs is quiet, it
doesn't mean it's gone away." She moved her chair closer to Gertrude. "When
you talk to your mother, you don't agree that everything is going to be better, no
matter what she says. You get someone to help you."

"Why does it happen, though?" Gertrude looked miserable.

Sister took both of Gertrude's hands in her own, "Sometimes, when you
feel utterly devastated, another door opens and you see your pain is just a
human experience, a very ordinary event in ordinary lives, yet through it you're
connected with everyone who suffers anywhere, and separate from all those
who don't know and don't care if they inflict the pain." She spread her hands in
her lap, palms up. "It's difficult to say how, but . . . in that instant you understand
something important about God."

"But God could change the mother," Gertrude said. "Why doesn't he?"

"It's puzzling, isn't it — for everyone to have choice seems to cause so
much pain."

This seemed dumb to Molly. Wasn't a child's care more important? Like
with Ma and the boys?

Sister shook her veil back. "It's something like seeing everything at once,"
she said, "and how everything, good and bad, fits with everything else."

"I don't get it," Gertrude whispered to Molly.

Molly did not answer. Sister still had not answered her questions, but
maybe, there were no answers.

April 1920

It was spring and beautiful dogwood blossoms were bursting out everywhere.

Sister Mary Magdalene and Molly were pals, or as close to it as you can get with an old nun. Molly helped her dig and plant even after their work period, and they talked about everything. Sister gave Molly copies of the *Daily Miner* when she finished reading them. They were really from Father Emmett who taught English literature, Journalism, and a course called the Encyclicals on Social Justice, at Carroll College. The Encyclicals were letters the Pope wrote about the common good and the rights of labor to just wages and fair working conditions. Sister Magdalene and Molly talked a lot about these letters and what Emmett thought.

"It was a close call whether Emmett would be a union organizer or a priest," Sister Magdalene said. "Paddy, our oldest brother, was studying to become a Jesuit. He was the funniest, smartest, most loving man in the world." Sister turned and watched the birds for a moment. She was blinking away tears.

"The summer Emmett turned sixteen, Paddy was killed in the mines." Sister pressed her lips together. "It was a stupid accident. Paddy shouldn't have been there, but he wanted to know what men like your father experience deep in the earth. So he took his last seminary leave to spend two months as a miner. An ore carrier failed, and he was crushed to death." Sister took a handkerchief from her pocket and brushed her eyes.

"Emmett and I were both mad with grief." She glanced at Molly as she folded and put the handkerchief away. "Emmett has the same hunger for community and justice you have. Nothing would do but he had to go down into the mines and work to see what was going on. He came back angry at the bosses who were so careless with men's lives and furious at the men them-selves who tolerated such conditions. He decided to become a priest that summer."

"Can a priest be a union organizer?" Molly asked.

Sister smiled. "No," she said, "but they sent him to Rome to study and that's how we got interested in the Encyclicals — through his letters."

✖   ✖   ✖

There was another strike going on in Butte. A week before the strike was announced, a ten-foot high cyclone fence had appeared overnight around the entrances to the mines. Molly followed the strike day by day, even though her news was a week later than things happened. *The Daily Miner* reported that the very day the strike was to be called, the owners hit the miners with a lockout.

Shacks appeared behind the fences, again overnight, and the scabs had already been trucked in. *The Daily Miner* ridiculed the *Montana Standard*'s claim that the unions had been taken over by irresponsible radicals who were making wild Communist demands.

Pa had told Molly that the *Montana Standard* was a paper puppet voice for the ACM, so she knew the *Daily Miner* was telling the truth.

She mulled it all over. The next day in class Molly asked Sister, "Can an evil spirit invade a whole group of people — like the ACM?"

Sister frowned a bit before answering. Sometimes she told Molly she gave her a headache with all those questions. Then Sister Magdalene said, "I think some groups have a mean spirit, a spirit that lacks generosity, and again we have to be careful not to let it contaminate us. But Pope Leo XIII says we have to stick up for our rights and help each other like the miners do when they go on strike."

Molly grinned. When Sister quoted from the Encyclicals, she sounded just like Pa. "What about when the owners put up cyclone fences, like they did last week, then lock out the miners and bring in scabs?" Molly asked.

"We have a right to fight, but we can use only force that's necessary. The miners can't kill the scabs," Sister said.

"Well, who's going to help all the miners the goons kill?"

Sister Mary Magdalene threw up her hand. "Enough, Molly. You are not going to trap me into another hour of talk. We're not going to discuss strike strategy nor call names." She laughed, "You're so hungry to know everything!" Then she put her hand on Molly's shoulder. "In every part of your life, every day, even facing the ACM," she said, "you're going to know *love* differently, and you'll find things you never suspected."

May 31, 1920

The birds were singing in the garden when Molly woke. She never had thought she'd be sad to leave, but she was, a little. As she changed the bed linen, she thought, this is the last time. She went to Mass and thought, this is the last time. She did her chores in the laundry and thought she wouldn't miss this at all. Same with breakfast and lunch, except this was the last time.

As she ate her oatmeal, Gertrude leaned over and whispered, "Remember when you put in the salt?" They giggled.

Except for Sister Magdalene and Gertrude, Molly would not miss the Convent of the Good Shepherd. They both walked with her out the front door and down to the gate. Sister gave her a little book, *Poems* by Gerard Manley Hopkins. "Some poetry you might enjoy someday," she said. Molly looked at her. Sister was making a tie with her like Molly did when she gave the books to her brothers. Molly blinked hard, but could not hold her tears back. The nun gave Molly her handkerchief with a half-smile. "Don't fight your tears, they're heart teachers."

Molly gulped and nodded.

"Write to me if you want to, Molly. I may only answer with a few lines, but I'll take whatever you write into my prayers."

She gave Molly a hug.

Gertrude held her satchel and books on her lap.

"Mom and my sister are still working 'down the line' no matter what the police think," she said, "but I'll make a different life. Studying with you has been fun. I'll look up that business school Sister Magdalene told us about when I get out next year."

"I'll see you there," Molly promised. Gertrude was selfish, sometimes Molly didn't trust her, but with all that, she still liked her.

"You shouldn't wait," Molly told them. "Ma is always late."

"I'm not waiting for your mother." Sister Magdalene tucked her handkerchief into Molly's pocket. "I'm with you."

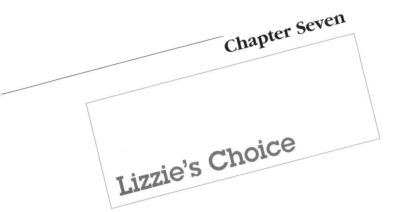

Chapter Seven

Lizzie's Choice

Lizzie stepped from the streetcar with a light heart. Helena, unlike Butte, was a garden city. Heavily leafed maples screened the sidewalk path from the sun. The grove of trees in front of the Convent, still a block away, hid most of the building from view.

Lizzie saw Molly waiting at the gate with another girl and one of the nuns. Molly had grown taller. Even with her long braids, she no longer seemed a child. Lizzie stumbled slightly on the uneven path. She was not certain she'd know how to handle her daughter now that she was almost grown. It had been hard enough before. As she looked at Molly's face, she almost could be looking at her sister Kate, they were so much alike — their gray eyes and straight-ahead look. She reached out her arms; Molly ran to her. The moment of strangeness passed. They hugged and smiled into each other's eyes. Lizzie pushed a strand of hair from her daughter's cheek.

Molly introduced her to Sister Magdalene and Gertrude, then hugged them good-bye while Lizzie gathered up her satchel and books. They were on their way home.

It was six months since she last saw Molly. She'd kept her

word and visited the boys on the one Sunday a month she could trade off with Annie. Why did these institutions all limit visiting to Sundays? Judge Donlin was not at all surprised when she called him to say she was ready to take the boys home.

In a gruff tone he said, "Puzzled me how you could let them be gone almost two years. When do you want 'em?"

"Thursday is my day off. I'll pick them up then."

"See that you do. I'll send the order up today."

Where had his kind sympathy gone? Lizzie felt a little spurt of indignation. Hadn't she put every cent she could get her hands on into the house? Walt and Jack helped to finish the apartment below. She had the rent from that now, and the boys would have the upstairs rooms. Walt was moving with the McCaughys to Virginia City to try his luck at silver mining and Jack decided to follow them when he finally understood Lizzie would not marry him. Maybe Judge Donlin was stiff mannered because he did not understand the business with Mrs. McPherson's ring. His sending Molly for six months to the Good Shepherd School was outrageous for that trumped-up charge.

It had been a long time for her without the children. She felt sad and uneasy whenever she visited them. They all wanted so much to come home. She was lucky a couple of the maids offered to do her rooms at the hotel. Today she picked up Molly, then on Thursday, the boys. She'd take an extra day off to get them settled and into the routines she needed to run the house.

✖   ✖   ✖

Lizzie looked about her. Early morning sunlight streamed into the kitchen from the open door to the alley. The distant clang of ore dropping into a rail car at the Anselmo Mine was the only sound in the balmy air. No sulfur fumes. The thunderstorm last night must have cleared the sky. The room was bright with the light and warmth of summer.

Three nights of cleaning and polishing after the roomers left and the house was ready for the boys. When Bill Henderson arrived, they would go straight to the Orphanage. Lizzie had not admitted it to Molly, but the house did feel cheerless without the children. Now it sparkled. She had even washed the parlor's lace curtains and stretched them to dry on the pins of a wooden frame. Molly helped her put them up again.

Lizzie's heart raced with excitement. She checked the clock above the kitchen table. Bill should be here in half an hour. He had offered to take her and Molly up to Twin Bridges in his Packard touring car. The boys' clothes and books would be sent back by train, but Bill had room to bring everybody home in his car.

She went to her bedroom to try on the new hat once more. It had a scarf to keep out the wind. She tied it and checked her left profile in the mirror. Perfect. Hat off and on the bed again. She took the stopper from a vial of cologne and touched a drop to her wrists, ear lobes, and the base of her throat. She looked at the clock in the kitchen once more and put on the kettle for a cup of tea.

✖   ✖   ✖

Bill. Six weeks ago, she found him in a hotel room. His face lathered up, he was stropping his straight edge razor. His long bushy eyebrows lifted as he managed a whistle. "I knew the Thornton was the classiest hotel in town, but I didn't know they'd started hiring beauties as chamber maids."

Lizzie blushed and backed out of the door. "I'll come back later. I thought this was a check out," she said.

He rushed after her. "No, don't go. I like to see a pretty woman at work."

Lizzie smiled at him but moved her cart firmly to the next room on her list. A sporting type. He would have a woman in that bed before nightfall. The next two days the room was occupied but looked as if it had not been slept in. The third day she found him dressed, shaved, and ensconced in a chair when she opened the door after knocking.

"Don't go away," he commanded. "I've saved you the trouble of making my bed for three days, and you owe me that time."

Lizzie blinked her eyes and tried to look skeptical. "Sit down," he said, "I haven't met a woman who speaks English for six months." He smiled. "You can give me fifteen minutes, can't you? And Nora Bonner doesn't have to know."

Lizzie laughed. Now she could see he was older than she had thought from the morning glimpse of muscled arms and hairy chest. He was a lanky man with white hair, blue eyes, and the wrinkled leathery skin of one who lives outdoors. It was difficult to tell his age, but she imagined him to be 15 or 20 years older than she was. He was definitely a flirt.

"How do you know our housekeeper?"

"I stay at the Thornton every time I'm in Butte," he said, "spring and half of summer, for the past five years. I give Nora a hard time because I either demand lots of service or I throw fits and will not let the bellboy or maid in to disturb my litter. I use the room as my office. I roared at her when I was here five years ago and threatened to string her up by her starched apron if I ever caught anyone lifting a paper out of the excellent disorder I create." He smiled at Lizzie. "This time, I'm going to change my routines. The maid is not to disturb my litter but is to come in and talk to me for fifteen minutes while I have my morning coffee." His lips twitched. "And I promise to treat her with the highest respect and not to make her uncomfortable. Does that sound like something you might consider?" He was so charming, Lizzie laughed out loud.

"What do you want to talk about?"

"You," he said.

He seemed to relish her coffee-time stories, and he continued to make his own bed. "Just bring me fresh sheets and towels," he said.

She dramatized tales guests had told her and her own view of the foibles of hotel life. Before long, however, the focus shifted to his own adventures. Lizzie knew how to listen to men. Attentively, with small questions to help them put their stories in the funny, or heroic, light they wanted. She learned he was a mining engineer who taught at the Montana School of Mines part of each year. The rest of the time he took care of business for the Anaconda Copper Mining Company, surveyed mines they might want to acquire, and did, "other things I'm good at."

One morning he told her he had bought a ranch from a discouraged homesteader. "Poor old sod went land crazy in the wheat boom of the war years and lost his shirt. I picked up the thousand acre spread for next to nothing." Bill planned to stay the summer while he taught and into the fall, "to put my little farm in shape before I leave for Chile and the Oppenheim Mine again."

He continued to flirt, said he liked to dance and wanted to get married again. He had been widowed for two years and thought that was long enough to live without a woman. Still, he didn't offer to take Lizzie dancing or to dinner during their morning talks. She wasn't surprised. He had the look of one who went his own way.

He was a favorite topic of gossip among the bellboys and maids. From Jocko, Lizzie learned he spent most evenings at the Vaudeville Theater shows, or gambling at the Silver Bow Club, but she also knew he went to dinner parties on the West End. One night he escorted Mrs. Watters, a wealthy widow, to an ACM banquet at the Thornton.

"How did you like the banquet?" Lizzie asked him the next morning.

"Politics is another name for high roller gambling, so it was an entertaining evening."

"Is Mrs. Watters a politician?"

"Oh, you noticed," he grinned. "I'd like to think you were jealous, but you've already told me that bellboys and maids know *everything* that goes on in the hotel and probably in Butte, even as it happens."

Lizzie blushed. "Maybe not everything."

Finally, he had said, "Lizzie, I don't know why I waste my time with some of these pretentious dinner parties when you're so much more fun. How about a trip to the Columbia Gardens, then a steak dinner at Meaderville on your day off?"

Lizzie said it would have been lovely, but she was picking up her children who had been away at school. His eyebrows rose in query, but she added nothing. She'd told him she was a widow but hadn't mentioned the children before. He suggested that he would be pleased to go with her and pick them up.

✖   ✖   ✖

Two minutes more, if he was as punctual as he was at the hotel. Yes, there was the sound of his car. She called to Molly, still upstairs arranging surprise gifts for the boys. She grabbed her wrap, pinned the hat to her hair, lifted her chin and, with a swift, satisfied glance at her profile, she went to the door.

The road consisted of endless hairpin turns. Molly was pale and her forehead damp as she looked bleakly out from the back seat. Bill gazed at her sympathetically. "I used to get car sick myself until I learned to drive. Why don't you curl up on the seat and try to sleep. There's a pillow back there."

Molly closed her eyes and slid out of sight.

Lizzie answered Bill's look of inquiry with a smile. "I have a seafarer's stomach. Nothing upsets me."

"I've noticed that," he laughed. "How did you happen to put your children in an orphanage?" Bill's directness never failed to astonish her. No way to evade a question that he intended to have answered. She looked at the mountain landscape, ridges upon ridges, uncompromising. A momentary image of herself, a prisoner in the dock. Judge Donlin, Bill Henderson, her husband Packy, and Molly all looked at her demanding an answer.

Why did her thought of doing this for the boys' own good seem not such a good idea now, particularly for little Johnny, Pat, and baby James?

"I don't know," she answered. "It seemed like the only way I could manage." She brushed her eyes with her fingertips. "When Packy was gone, it was the first time in my life I didn't have a man to tell me what to do. A couple of men would have married me in a minute . . . I didn't want them. I couldn't think of marriage." Her voice faltered. Bill continued silent. "But I didn't have enough strength to deal with my oldest sons. I thought a boarding school would be better for them." She straightened her back against the leather seat. "The orphanage has been that for them. Now, though, I know my own strength and I can do whatever's needed."

She considered her words for a moment. Her fluent account surprised and touched her. It was the truth, of course, except it left out that she did not care much for the company of children. She loved them, of course, but she did not like to feel bound by them. She preferred to be with men and women who could talk of what was going on in the world. She intended, come what may, not to marry a bore. Yes, above all, she wanted a life that entertained her.

"Maybe you won't have to," he said.

She peeked at him. She had forgotten what he was responding to. He frowned as he drove with absent-minded skill, slowing and banking into the curves of the road.

"You needed a man to take care of you, but those louts around you weren't up to it, and you were smart enough to know it."

Oh lord, his words and tone . . . he sounded like Jack. He was going to offer her advice. She'd scotch that and give him a little taste of his own question medicine. "How is it that you didn't have children?"

He looked at her with a flash of impatience. "We're talking about you."

"Why?"

He paused, and then laughed. "Right. The current topic is my lack of chil-

dren." His face sobered. "My wife and I both wanted them, but after five mis-
carriages we gave up hope. At least my wife did." His silence lasted a couple of
minutes this time. Lizzie felt uneasy but knew he did not want her to speak.

He finally drew in his breath and continued, "Her disappointment and my
long absences in Brazil, Chile, and Australia were too much for her after a while.
She took to the consolations of the bottle. It got worse. I had to have a full time
attendant with her for the last five years of her life. I was glad when it was over."

Another silence, then he turned to her. He sighed and smiled. "Enough of
that — except I'm glad you're a teetotaler, beautiful, and have lots of kids." She
smiled back at him and placed her hand on his, but she was uncomfortable feeling sorry for him — wary — like it wasn't the right feeling.

The rest of the trip was easy. Lizzie glanced into the back seat. Molly's
color was better, her mouth slightly open with the slow paced breath of sleep.
Bill talked about the geology of the Rockies and entertained her with stories of
old prospectors.

The boys were waiting on the front porch of the orphanage. James and
Pat had been placed in different cottages according to age group and seldom
saw one another, but they had not seen Molly for six months. Now, they only
had eyes for her. Pat gave her a shy grin. James, at three, was no longer a baby,
but he demanded to be held in Molly's lap. Johnny, now a tall seven year old,
held his mythology book under one arm and clutched her with the other, looking into her face.

"I can read everything," he whispered.

Frank grinned at Molly, but said nothing. At thirteen and fourteen, he and
Tom looked broad-shouldered and almost full-grown. Only Tom hugged his
mother without reserve and teased her about her straw hat with its flowers.
"You're going to out-gussey Flanagan," he said.

Bill Henderson took in the scene without comment. When the hubbub
calmed down, he said, "Maybe you boys would like to look over my car and help
me crank up the engine." Even James was willing to desert Molly for this feat.
Bill continued to hold their attention by showing them how to work the gears
while they drove to the orchard next to the orphanage. They sat in impressed
silence.

"Could I try that?" Frank asked.

"Why, sure," Bill said, "I expect I could even show you how to work a trac-
tor, if Lizzie brings you out to visit my little farm."

Frank glanced at his mother. "Can we?" he asked. Frank had not asked
his mother for anything from the time Pa died, and seldom before that.

Lizzie smiled at Bill. "You do take the cake. What can I say?"

Bill raised his shaggy brows at her without cracking a smile. "Whatever do
you mean, ma'am? I told you I was an independent coot, 'cept with kids."

During the long drive back, he filled the boys with stories of his ranch and
the trout stream that ran through it. Lizzie looked at him with fascination. He
was fatherly and gentle. He promised to take the boys fishing on a Sunday as
soon as they were settled back in school. By the end of the journey, which
included a rainbow trout dinner at Meaderville, Bill's place in the family was a
taken-for-granted reality. Only Molly seemed to have any reservations. She was
quiet when he spoke and asked no questions.

The next morning, Lizzie told the children to sit at the table after breakfast
chores. She gripped her teacup with both hands. "I'm glad to have you home
again," she said, "but things have to be different." She took a deep breath and
began to speak her mind. She scowled to let them know she was determined.

Lizzie spelt out the work each of them had to do. "Tom's in charge of
heating the house — putting up the screens in summer, the storm windows in
winter, keeping the house supplied with kindling and coal. He also will shop for
food.

"Pat and James will help Johnny with the kitchen chores." Five-year-old
Pat, examining a spider web in the corner of the ceiling, turned his head when
she demanded his attention, but his eyes slid back to the spider.

"Everyone will make his own bed, change the sheets on Saturday and
hang his clothes properly. Frank will help Molly with the wash and cooking.
Frank, I'll hold you accountable to see everyone does every speck of the work
by the time I come home at night." Frank would not look at her when she gave
these orders, but it did not bother her. He would come round.

She looked around the table. "There'll be no getting into trouble with the
law either. Otherwise, no outings, fishing trips, or anything else. If you don't keep
the rules, you go back to the orphanage."

Johnny and James, open-mouthed and quiet, seemed terrified by the scowl on her face. That was just fine; being a mother to growing boys required strength. They had to know who was boss. Pat seemed to be in a daydream and not listening. She'd have to watch him but she was satisfied with the others' responses. Her temper flickered out.

Now, the gifts. Lizzie loved to give gifts almost as much as she liked receiving them, big dramatic ones, if possible. She brought out dozens of packages. Each child had new clothing — sweaters, shirts, shoes, everything. When the room was filled with packages and paper, she sent Johnny to fetch a box left with Mrs. McCaughy.

Johnny pushed the alleyway door open. He held a squirming mongrel pup who was trying to lick his face. Frank dragged in the wooden box that would serve as his doghouse.

"His name is Spot," Lizzie said before the hubbub began.

It was wonderful to have money. Packy had made big money, but he spent it. Lizzie found it amazing to have money of her own. Her tips were far more than Nora Bonner had led her to expect and almost doubled her wages. More and more regular guests — theater folk, politicians, engineers, salesmen — asked to be on her floor when they returned. She enjoyed listening to their unbuttoned talk, admired them, and made them laugh. Their tips paid for the gifts she bought for the boys and, tucked into her apron pocket, the certificate for lifetime tuition at Butte Business School for Molly. Molly could take as many courses as she wanted, whenever she wanted, no matter how long it took.

Now no one could accuse her of not loving her children.

✖   ✖   ✖

Saturday morning, shortly after 9 o'clock, Lizzie tapped on the door of the corner suite. "Maid service," she called. Bill opened the door and pulled her inside.

"Lizzie, your family is a prize — handsome, smart, and every one of them a talker." He lowered his voice. "Any man would be proud of them. Let me take them up to the ranch for a week."

"I'm sure they'd love to go."

"I haven't been able to get them out of my mind. I didn't realize I was so bored. I want to know each of them, show them how to ride . . ."

"James's a bit young for that, don't you think?"

"A boy's never too young to be trained to sit easy in his saddle and hold the reins. It's part of learning to take charge of a situation, part of a man's task to hold the right . . . ." He hesitated and chose his word, "attitude. Just a matter of finding a good horse — and instructor. Rafferty, one of my cowhands will be perfect with them. God, I'd forgotten how much fun boys can be — and how much I wanted sons."

"I warn you. They're a handful," Lizzie said.

He removed the towels from her hand, slipped his right arm around her waist, and pulled her close. "Now, I need to find out if you're half the dancer you *think* you are," he said.

July 4, 1920

It was the 4th of July. Molly sat on the sofa and looked at the thunderclouds building up. She hugged her legs, her knees pulled up under her chin, a Jack London novel lying discarded by her side. The air had that odd smell before a storm. Soon there would be flashes of lightening and fat warm drops of summer rain streaking down the glass.

She hoped the weather would clear up before the big parade downtown. The boys had gone, but Molly was not in the mood for oomph-pah-pah band music. She could not think what to do with herself. Why was she so uneasy?

Spot pawed at the door with little pleading squeals. When Molly let him in, he shook himself, jumped on the couch and put his head on his paws. She returned to her seat and he snuggled his head onto her lap. She rubbed his ears, absent-mindedly.

Ma had done what she promised in bringing the boys home. She was different though. She didn't read tealeaves or tell fortunes with the cards anymore. All those rules she set out — and the expression on her face — the boys were scared of her. She was all honey with people on the outside — Street Angel; House Devil. Could Ma have one of those bad spirits inside that Sister Magdalene talked about?

Spot thumped his tail and raised his chin so she could scratch under it. Molly laughed, but her thoughts jumped back into the troubles. Frank as the straw boss worried her. He was hard on himself and going to be just the same with the others. The boys were still little; they needed to play more. Frank had put Johnny in the corner for two hours because he did not clean the stove right. That was what Sister Magdalene would call "misusing power over another." She had told Frank so, but he was cranky and short-tempered even with her.

Johnny said he and Pat had cried themselves to sleep each night in the orphanage, but Frank didn't cry. He did farm work, and he wouldn't take any guff from anyone, even the animals. A horse crowded him against the corral one day and he hit it across its head with a board. The horse had no spirit after that.

Molly hugged Spot and he licked her hand. Then he settled down to sleep by her side.

Frank had so much to do, and his newspapers to boot. He and Tom paid three cents for each paper whether it sold or not, and could only charge four cents. Further trouble — the mayor of the Newsboys' Union decided they needed to strike for better rates and Boy Scouts were acting as scabs. The Boy Scouts lived in the West End and did not need the money. Why were they doing this? Did the rich always take advantage of other people, just because they could?

Pat was a worry, too. He did not cry, but he did not talk to her like he used to. Ma said Molly worried too much when Molly tried to talk to her about Pat's . . . what was it? Lack of gumption? Something about him just seemed wrong to her.

On the other hand, getting the business school tuition was great. She had sputtered and almost choked when her mother told her. Pa gave great gifts, but she had no idea Ma would do such a thing for her. That certificate must have cost every cent Ma made for two, maybe three months.

She had raced over to Burkart's Department Store, where the school had the top two floors, and signed up for a course in double-entry bookkeeping. She could hardly believe her luck when she also found a bulletin board that listed a job vacancy at Gamers Restaurant and Bakery.

She had to lie to get the job, told them she knew how to operate a cash register. But she would figure it out.

Then Ma wanted to take her to her friend Millie's studio for dance lessons. "It's time you learned to use those long legs," she had said. "Millie might use you in the chorus line for the vaudeville act she's putting together."

Molly didn't want to follow her mother's ideas, but she would find time for the lessons. She liked to watch the dances Millie's group put on at the Greens, a park outside of Butte filled with trees and grass.

The Greens real name was the Columbia Gardens and it was owned by the Anaconda Copper Mining Company, just like they owned most everything else in Butte, even the street cars. The boys went by themselves on Thursday mornings during summer when miners' children could ride the streetcars and get into the Greens free. The boys did not bother with the dance pavilion or carousel. They preferred the Ferris wheel and a roller coaster with open cars that could scare a person to death. Sometimes they brought pansies home, the flowers kids were allowed to pick.

They preferred to go with Bill, though. He was a regular part of the family now. Every Sunday, if he didn't take them fishing, he took them to the Greens. He was ace-high with them. Ma spent her day off with Bill and didn't return until after supper. Saturday night he took her dancing. All of the boys wanted their mother to marry him. They thought living on a ranch would be great. Molly did not know what she thought. Maybe there was something wrong with her. Everyone liked Bill, but she didn't. He was smart and had a lot of money, but wasn't he part of the ACM, like the McPhersons? How could Ma have picked up with him? She acted like she did not even remember Pa. And Bill was so old. Ma said fifty-six was not that old, but it was old enough to be Molly's grandfather — and Ma's father.

A u g u s t   1 9 2 0

Bill brought the family to his ranch. It took three hours to get there, even in his fast car. The last part of the trip over a rocky, rutted road brought them into a broad grassy meadow with the ranch house on one side and the bunkhouse, feed barn, and stable on the other. A chicken coop and what had once been a vegetable garden were behind the main house.

Rafferty, the ranch manager, was in a corral with a wild mustang filly when they arrived. She was blindfolded with a lariat around her neck, tied close to a center post about six feet high. The air was filled with dust. A couple of men dressed in leather chaps with spurs on their boots and flannel shirts tucked into their jeans were hanging on the seven-foot-high fence. They looked exhausted.

"They're breaking her," Frank hollered. When Bill stopped the car, Frank flung the door open and ran to the breaking pen. The boys tumbled out and followed him. The corral rails of peeled lodge pole were close together and easy to climb. "Can we watch?" Frank asked Bill.

Bill looked at him with a slow grin. "You want to see a mustang broken fast?"

"Sure."

Bill turned to Lizzie. "Let's have a bite to eat first. You and Molly probably won't want to see this." He went over to the corral to talk to Rafferty.

Molly decided nothing would drag her from Frank's side, but she got out the picnic basket for Ma with the baked chicken and potato salad. Bill brought Rafferty back with him to wash up before lunch. Bill set up a table on the porch and brought out glasses and a pitcher of water from the cooler.

"You can watch from the fence," Bill said. "Rafferty will tell you what's going on and answer your questions when I'm breaking the filly." While they ate, he explained that young horses, foals, were either fillies — females, or colts — males. Most of the colts would be 'cut,' gelded, and only the best allowed to grow into a stallion who'd be used to breed other horses. Bill said, "Rafferty breaks mules to use in the mines, but I'm breaking my own horses for the ranch."

Molly wanted to ask about the mine mules, how they got down in those little cages. Pa had said they were all blind after a few months. She decided she had better not ask too many questions if she wanted to find out what happened when a horse was broken. What was it that broke?

When they finished eating, Bill put on his chaps, boots, and spurs. Molly clambered up the side of the corral with Frank and Tom. The younger boys looked through the rails and Lizzie stayed in the house.

"That pole in the center is the snubbing post," Rafferty explained. "It's about a foot in diameter and when you get close you'll see it's been gouged, kicked, and gnawed. No one man can hang on to a wild mustang. Using the post gives us a space to control the horse."

"How'd you get her penned up?" Frank asked.

Rafferty snorted. "It took more than me. Look at that little filly." The horse's sides were heaving, and she looked tired and sweaty. "She may have sore feet from all that kicking, but she's still rank and willful. It's us who are exhausted from dragging her."

Molly had gasped as she watched the filly attack the post, but only asked,

"What does 'rank' mean?"

"Uncontrollable," Bill said, "but that won't last long. She's hurting now and we're letting her think about it."

He explained he had bought the filly that morning from some Indians who hunted wild horses in the mountains. "Just before you got here, we led her to the post without a blind fold, so she'd learn about tying. You notice her tail and back legs are a nice slimy mess. Horses pee when they're nervous. D'you see how scarred the post is? They kick forward with their front legs, bite, rear, and just plain old attack the snubbing post. Her front legs are bloody from striking out at the pole before we blindfolded her. The blindfold prevents her from fighting, not knowing where the enemy will come from next."

The cowboys threw the saddle blanket over the blindfolded horse, and Bill heaved the saddle onto her back. Then he cinched up the girth so tight it took the wind from her. She fell to the ground and had to struggle to regain her balance. A cowboy bridled her, put the bit in her mouth and strapped the halter on her head.

Rafferty told them, "Now he's going to let her go and get the hell out of the way, because the horse is going to explode." A rope attached the halter to the snubbing post. It was long enough for her to reach almost to the rim of the corral and she bolted as soon as her head was released. She reared and threw her head back trying to get rid of the bridle and bit. She tangled herself up in the reins and fell. Molly was frantic thinking she must be slicing her gums and tongue to pieces, but Frank said the bit was placed across the part of her jaw in back of her teeth. It would not hurt her.

That was not how it looked to Molly. The bit and the rope terrified the filly and she was furious to boot. Bill was standing to one side, letting her fight herself until she gave up. They pulled her into the pole again, and Bill drew her head back until her nose almost touched the saddle. He tied the rein to the horn. She could only walk in circles now trying to get away.

Rafferty muttered to himself. He did not seem to like that she was tied so tightly. He squinted his eyes and did not say anything. When Bill felt she had learned this lesson of giving her head, he again snubbed her to the post and climbed into the saddle. This time she did not have the blindfold. He let her fight. She was helpless, so it just exhausted her.

She kicked and went through every maneuver she could think of to get him off, while he kept forcing her to walk in tight circles to the left. After about five minutes, he brought her head to his right knee on the other side and repeated the process, making her walk in tight circles to his right. Her front legs, her back legs, her whole body was covered with lather. When he released her head, she flung her neck back and green slobber flew from her mouth. Molly laughed when a glob of it hit Bill's shirt. He signaled the men to confine her head again to the post while he took a break to smoke a cigarette.

Then it started again. The filly must have been sore, hurting, and exhausted. She had no strength left to resist. There was too much she could not do anything about. She was confined to the corral, she had this man on her back, and she was forced to move to the direction of the reins. She gave up. She just stood with her legs spread, shaking and dripping sweat. He kicked her and the boys yelled and whooped to get her to move. Then there was a long process of Bill moving the reins over and under her, slapping and kicking one side then the other, forcing her to move at his will.

He had broken her. That meant she could not do what she wanted, only what he wanted, or she would be hurt again. He turned her over to the cowboys to brush the sweat from her.

Everyone except Molly was excited when it was over. The cowboys all said the filly put up a great fight. Molly had a metal taste under her tongue and her throat ached as if she had been screaming.

They were all going to learn to ride horses now, even Ma.

The rest of their visit was tame compared to that. They looked over the ranch house, and Bill took them to see the trout stream in the hills to the west. The ranch house needed another floor to be added and would be finished when Bill came back from Chile the next spring. He'd live there instead of at the Thornton.

✖ ✖ ✖

The next week, Ma had on ruby earrings in a gold Tiffany setting and was proud as a peacock.

"Bill says I bring him luck," she said. "This is my cut from his four-day winning streak at the Silver Bow Club."

"Do you think you'll marry him?" Molly asked.

Ma tried to evade the question, but Molly asked her again.

"I don't want to be married." Ma laughed, but her eyes gleamed in a way that said there was more to this than she allowed.

Afterwards, Molly overheard the two of them talking in the parlor. They thought she was napping, but she woke and opened her eyes a crack to see what they were up to. They were talking about Lizzie's dancing club and little theater group. Apparently, it went without saying that Ma would quit her job if she married Bill, but she hadn't realized he wanted her to give up her little theater group.

"Do you mean I'm not enough for you, Lizzie?" Bill asked. "Do you have to have an audience to tell you what a beauty you are?"

"Pooh to my beauty. That isn't it, at all." Ma sounded exasperated.

"We'll go to every first night in Butte, when I'm in town. You just won't be center-stage."

"I've never been center-stage. It's not attention I want so much as the troupe. We are all in it together — the music, the lights, our satin and silk costumes with crystal beads, and the excitement. On opening night, the curtain rises, and all our hearts beat faster. We can hardly breathe. Oh, it's impossible to explain. It is magical, and we make it happen. You either know it or you don't." She turned to him abruptly, "You play the piano; it must be like that. You have the piano and I act."

"I don't want to share you, Lizzie."

"Oh Bill, you don't even want to let me dance with other men."

"Not in the clubs, but you'll have plenty of opportunities to dance with much more interesting people . . . and it won't be just in Butte either."

Ma shrugged helplessly. "You don't understand, and I can't explain."

"Some things I do understand, though." He bent over and kissed her lightly on the lips. She turned her head into his shoulder and clung to him.

Molly shut her eyes again. Did Ma think she had everything she wanted? What did she do with *her* uneasy feelings?

O c t o b e r   1 9 2 0

Bill wanted Lizzie to quit her job and marry him right away, but she would not consider it. He finally left for Chile, and Lizzie had a ring with enough diamonds in it to almost reach her knuckle. They planned to have the family spend a week at the Ranch when he came back and then they would decide when and where they would be married.

March 1921

Flanagan placed her thermos of tea on the hotel room table with a bag of rock cookies she had picked up at the pastry shop. "I must be getting into the change-of-life," she said. "Hot-flashes and hot feelings." She sat in an armchair and wiped her brow with a man's large handkerchief. Flanagan had a habit of stopping by in mid-afternoon to help Lizzie finish her late checkouts. Then they would pick a suite with a sitting room and talk. From the third floor, they could look north to the tall iron gallows frame of the Original Mine and watch its shadow grow longer.

Lizzie yawned as she sat down. Bill had been gone five months, and she was in no hurry to finish the day. "You're not that old," Lizzie said.

"Forty," Flanagan said. "My mum went through it even earlier."

"What's bothering you?"

"Oh, something's out of whack. I get angry or sad for no reason at all. This morning I was crying my eyes out about you."

Lizzie was startled. "About me?" She tried to imagine Flanagan sitting on the edge of bed in her chenille bathrobe, her eyes streaming with tears. She could not picture it.

"It doesn't matter — probably just the vapors." Flanagan pulled her purse open and took out a pack of cards. "I've brought the cards and Lent's over, so how about reading our fortunes?"

Lizzie flushed. "I don't think I have the gift anymore. I did not give it up. I just lost it."

"G'wan, some priest frightened you."

"No, what do priests know? But Bill hates . . ."

Flanagan frowned. "Lizzie, in some ways you're not yourself with that man."

"Because I don't read the cards?" Lizzie lifted her chin and stiffened her back. She did not like criticism, even from friends.

"Not just that," Flanagan said. "Don't get me wrong. I — I don't know about this marriage business."

Flanagan poured a cup of tea from the thermos. She wiped her forehead again with the crumpled handkerchief. "I shouldn't say this. It's still the vapors talking, but I don't think you want it — the marriage, I mean." Flanagan shook her head with a puzzled frown. "You go along with what Bill wants, but your feelings aren't with him. And you don't speak your mind either."

"What d'you mean? I always . . . "

Flanagan interrupted again. Her face looked splotchy. "I keep thinking about how things should be — and should have been."

Lizzie said nothing. This was a whole new side of Flanagan. The change must have affected her. Lizzie sat forward in her chair, forearms on her knees. She wondered if Flanagan had wanted to tell her this before, if she had sat in her kitchen, head in her hands, hurting, but unwilling to say anything.

"How do you mean?"

"I've known lots of men in a lot of different ways," Flanagan said. "Most of 'em carry grief inside, you can hardly believe. They think they want our bodies. I think they want our ears, someone to listen to their stories."

"What does this have to do with me not quarreling with Bill?" Lizzie snapped. She did not want it, but she felt her impatience rising.

"Lizzie, I've gotten your back up and I didn't mean to, but . . . well, it's like you don't want to question Bill. I think if you risked getting angry with him, like you used to with Packy, you might learn something."

Lizzie glared at Flanagan. How did she dare? She was jealous. She didn't want Lizzie to have this wonderful man. She was . . . just like Lizzie's sister, Kate. Lizzie's gaze shifted, aware of her friend's wan face and tired body. No, Flanagan didn't understand. Flanagan felt wretched, but she would never want Lizzie to be hurt.

"I . . . I'll have to think about this," Lizzie said. Then, to her surprise she burst into tears. "Oh Flanagan, I *have* been laying out the cards. I didn't tell you the whole of it. I keep getting the jack of diamonds in the wheel of fortune, the trickster with no heart. Nothing comes when I try to see the future."

"I don't know the cards like you do," Flanagan said. "But maybe you can't see something. I don't know if you see Bill the way he is. Why did his first wife drink herself to death? Why doesn't he have friends?"

"Bill's got all sorts of invitations. He is busy all the time. His wife couldn't have children and she was lonely." Lizzie's words were terse. "What's that have to do . . .?"

"Business and political friends."

"What else do men have?"

Flanagan looked down at her teacup. She shrugged and gave Lizzie a weak grin. "Maybe I'm just upset with myself." She unbuttoned the top of her blouse. "Topsy-turvy. I didn't know the change was like this. Sometimes it's like standing at the seashore with wave after wave of feelings and memories washing up and swirling around me."

"D'you ache?"

"My body does, at night, but it's the thoughts that come as I wait for sleep."

"What's upset you?"

"I don't know that it's just one thing. You know I have a son, Joe, somewhere." She paused to smile. "I could be a grandmother!" She shook her head. "I haven't said much about him — as if he didn't matter. I left him and Ned, his father, when Joe was a year old and ran off with another man. I was seventeen. Ned never forgave me and his bitterness kept us from getting together, although I tried . . . . I haven't heard anything about Joe for five and a half years. I'm afraid he may be dead.

"Friday, I learned Ned was out at Gaylen TB sanitarium. I tried to visit, but he refused to see me." Flanagan's eyes brimmed with tears. "This past week, I've thought about the hurt I did to them and how I still feel for them."

Lizzie stayed silent. Flanagan had such strong, passionate feelings. Her own upsets were trivial in comparison. Still, she did not know that she'd like to look so deeply into her own heart, or anyone else's for that matter.

"I've wasted too much time," Flanagan said. "I looked to love and be loved like some kind of a fire storm. Those loves never lasted." She turned her haggard eyes to Lizzie again. "My kind of love is too wild for you, I guess, like it was for Ned, but that got me to thinking about you. And how I wished you felt more —" Flanagan bit her thumb nail as she searched for the word, "More overwhelmed, somehow, and that you'd give yourself to it, if you're going to marry Bill."

Lizzie moved to her friend's chair, sat on the arm, and rubbed Flanagan's back and neck. She bit back her words to explain and defend herself. That Bill was a good catch; the boys loved him; they wanted a father and Lizzie liked being with a strong, attractive man. Her friend's pain was more important.

She could not remember what she'd felt for Packy; but it wasn't what Flanagan described. She said nothing for several minutes as Flanagan regained control and wiped the tears that continued to seep from her eyes.

"Look," Lizzie said, "I'm going to get my electric ring and brew us a proper pot of tea." She left the room and returned with her teapot, her heater, a canister of black tea and two china cups.

When the ritual was complete, she filled her cup and looked at Flanagan again. "I think next Thursday I should go out with you to see Ned. I think he will see you if you keep going. It's just hard for you to do it alone, and if he doesn't see you, you still won't have to come back alone. And we can do it again the next week."

"You'd do that?"

Lizzie nodded. "If we're going to get back to having gossip and good times together, we've got to get you in from the waves." She bent over and hugged Flanagan. "What would I do without you?" She pulled a fresh handkerchief from her pocket and stroked her friend's cheek. "I don't want to be out there with you, but I'll stand on the shore with a long rope tied to your waist."

Lizzie went to the bathroom to get a damp washcloth that she offered Flanagan.

"You make me think, though. I envy your passion, but I don't want it for me." Lizzie moved to the hotel room vanity and sat down to look at her face in the mirror. "I've delayed and delayed, but I still don't know what to do." She pulled the hairpins from her hair, shook it out, and then slowly bound it back into place again.

"Now that I have the children home again, my little theater group, our dancing clubs, and my work, I'm happy. The work isn't hard and I make lots of tips. I've got everything, friends I want, guests I like to talk with. I can't imagine life on a ranch as even one tenth as interesting. You can think I'm silly, but when Marshall Foch of the Allied Armies stood on the hotel balcony the other day and spoke in French to the press, and all the nabobs could hardly get enough of him, I was thrilled to my fingertips.

"I sound frivolous, but this is what I love most, my independence and the delicious, even the sad things that happen each day, including our gossip and stories.

"Bill doesn't matter more than all these other parts of my life. I don't want to lose him, but I don't want to give up any part of myself."

April 1921

Easter week arrived and so did the anticipated visit to Bill's ranch. Lizzie surveyed the water pump beside the sink. It was a device Bill was proud of constructing. No more frozen pipes, he explained. The water came straight up from a hot spring deep in the earth, like Old Faithful at Yellowstone. It was almost May and unseasonably warm for Montana, so he kept cold water in a jar in the icebox and a large pitcher in a cooler that opened off the porch. The hot water, however, was an engineering feat. The ranch and bunk houses each had two bathrooms with all the hot water you could possibly use. All very fine for taking baths — but what about the tea? What a peculiar aftertaste it left.

Bill, back from Chile for a month, had only yesterday brought her to the ranch. His letters had not mentioned business during the half year he was away, but whatever he did must have been wildly successful. He had been closeted in meetings at the ACM headquarters on top of the Hennessy Building every day and most nights for three weeks running. His elation was evident in his springy step and easy laugh. It was like his four-day winning streak last year at the gambling club, his fatigue showing up only in his edgy temper. Shortly after he arrived, he fired the ranch cook, when she questioned one of his orders.

None of this was apparent to the boys, however. Bill had missed Christmas with them and had not sent presents. "No time to shop in Santiago," he explained, and herded all the boys to Hennessy's to buy fishing poles and high rubber boots. "You'll need them for the mountain streams when you come to the ranch." Then he disappeared again into his business meetings.

She was surprised to find he had settled into the ranch as well as he had. Where had he found time? He must not have slept at all. He insisted that Lizzie and the children have the Ranch House with its four bedrooms and spacious attic. He said he'd bunk with the hired hands.

The huge kitchen was filled with boxes of supplies. "This is grub for the week," he announced, when they arrived. "You and Molly can figure out where you want it to be stashed. I won't have time to find another cook, but Mrs.

Rafferty, who cleans house, will lend you a hand. If you think of anything else we need, let me know. I'll have to go into town every other day for meetings. First thing tomorrow though," he grinned at the boys, "we're going hunting. We're going to get us some quail." The boys wanted to know if they would have guns. "Why, of course you will," he said. "We'll go in my office right now to look at them."

Lizzie saw that the office held every bit of the creative litter he had forbidden the hotel staff to touch. Loose papers covered his desk mixed in with open notebooks; scratch pads filled with figures, and roughly sketched diagrams. In addition, large ledgers sat on the bookshelves with boxes of records. Several hunting trophies, a Big Horn sheep, a grizzly bear, a moose and an elk's head were mounted on the wall over the stone fireplace. A gun rack held an impressive collection of guns behind its glass doors.

"It looks like I'll have game for mincemeat pie."

Bill was too busy with the boys to do more than acknowledge her comment with a brief smile.

Next morning, he left with the boys before breakfast. He dropped them off two hours later with ten fat quail. He had already dressed the birds so they were ready to bake. Lizzie made him stay for a breakfast of bacon slab strips, eggs, hash-browned potatoes, and plenty of ketchup. The ranch hands had already eaten.

"You can fix the quail for supper. There's sage and other spices in the cupboards," he said. "I should be home by sundown."

The boys described Bill's skills in detail at breakfast and how he had taught them to load and unload the guns. They were still excited after they finished the dishes and went off to find horses and explore the ranch.

Lizzie sat on the porch steps for a while to finish her tea and watch the migrating birds. She had not had free time for more years than she could remember. She needed to put on a hat to guard her skin against the sun, but for the moment, she felt wonderfully heavy and lazy. Finally, she rose, stretched, and returned to the kitchen to set up burlap for the rug she was working on. Molly had gone back into Bill's office to look at his bookkeeping records.

Lizzie tacked a 48' by 60' double piece of burlap to a wooden frame in front of her. She pulled several large flour sacks filled with strips of woolen cloth from worn out pants, coats and jackets to her side. Over the years, she and

Molly had cut the cloth into pieces one half inch by three inches and sorted them according to color. The strips lay ready to be twisted, hooked through the burlap, and secured on the other side. So many clothes were black, though. Wouldn't it be wonderful if people wore yellow, soft rose, and sea blue winter woolens? Nonetheless, the rug would be a victory worth celebrating. She had managed to carry off some of the Thornton drapes when they were replaced, so this rug would have ivory and mossy-green heavy satin strips in its center. Later, she would mix rust-colored wool with strips from a golden-brown hound's-tooth overcoat for a thin, inch-wide border, then perhaps straight black for four inches to the edge, depending on how it looked.

Four o'clock. Lizzie looked up from the rag rug she was hooking. She pulled a final green strip through the burlap to finish the center, and then stretched her back. "Time for tea," she called out to Molly and rose to put the kettle on. She put out the cups, the cream and sugar, and a tin of cookies. Where was that girl? She went to the office. Surely, she was not still in there.

Molly was at the desk, now heaped with ledgers. "Oh, Molly," Lizzie said. "You've got to put that away. I know you want to learn everything about book-keeping, but you should never touch Bill's records. He's ever so particular that not the least thing should be touched."

Molly glanced up at her mother. "Ma, do you remember when the miners went on strike last time and a week before the strike was announced, a ten-foot high cyclone fence appeared overnight around the entrances to the mines?"

Lizzie nodded.

"I was at the Good Shepherd and followed the strike day by day in the newspapers."

Lizzie bit her lower lip. "Molly, I don't want to know this."

"Too late, Ma. I've seen the order signed by William Henderson and payment for ten-foot high cyclone fencing to be delivered by truck prior to the lockout of the miners. There is also payment for trucks to meet the train at Missoula and transport Pinkerton gunmen to Butte. The dates match when the scabs were trucked in at night to work and live under guard behind the cyclone fences at the mine." Molly closed the ledger and moved it back to the shelf. "Bill's the person the ACM uses to break strikes."

"Molly, I can't think about this now. You must promise me to say nothing to Bill until I can think about it. Come and have some tea with me."

Molly regarded her mother without expression.

"Not another word," Lizzie said.

"I'll put the books away and I won't talk about this, I promise you," Molly said, "but I do want to ask him some questions about the ACM."

Lizzie frowned. "Molly, I mean it. Not a word out of you about this. Now, come and have your tea," she said.

Lizzie did not like to cook, but occasionally she put herself out and produced a great meal. There was no bickering among the boys. They were still excited from the day but tired enough not to protest an early bedtime. Bill had been affable at dinner. He answered Molly's questions readily. Anaconda had bought the Chile Copper Company from the Guggenheim family for 70 million dollars. It had been secret until the financial details were concluded last week, but they expected to extract as much as a billion dollars worth of copper from Chuquicamata, a huge mine in the northern Chilean desert.

"What will happen to Butte?" Molly asked.

"Oh, there's still plenty of copper in Butte."

"But could the mines be shut down if the ACM made more money in Chile?"

"I suppose the corporation could make that decision, but it's not likely. They have a lot invested in Butte." Bill looked at Molly with a half smile. "I didn't know you were that interested in mining."

"There's a lot I don't know," Molly answered, "like what's a corporation?"

"A corporation is a legal entity for business purposes. It's treated like a person, a peculiar immortal kind of person that has only one function, to make money for the stock holders. The one sin a corporation can commit is to *not* make money."

"Sounds like a person with no heart," Molly said, "like a Frankenstein."

Bill's eyebrows drew to the center of his forehead.

"Molly, that's enough," Lizzie said. "It's time to clear the table."

✖   ✖   ✖

"Lizzie, you strike me as a woman doing her damnedest to avoid dealing with a rattle snake in the barn. Am I imagining things, or have you stopped talking to me?" Bill asked.

It was Saturday. They had finished a late breakfast and sat in the kitchen. The heat of the sun and the after-smell of fried bacon surrounded them. Molly and the boys had left at dawn on horses with one of the cowboys who would fix them a breakfast cook out. Lizzie adjusted the hairpins into the bun at the base of her neck. She smiled at Bill, and then puckered her lips briefly. "I *have* been worried about your plans," she said. "I don't know that I want to be married so soon as June."

"Our plans, Lizzie," Bill corrected her. "You put me off last year, and June is still a month away. What's bothering you?" He leaned back in his chair, thumbs tucked into his belt.

Lizzie flashed a look at him, then dropped her eyes. "I'm not sure I . . . well, maybe I'm not cut out to live as a rancher's wife."

Bill regarded her silently. She stretched her neck and shoulders; then looked at him uncomfortably. She did not share her daughter's mistrust of Bill. He probably had reasons that justified what he did as part of the ACM. She didn't want to think about it, but she supposed . . . No, she didn't know about any of the mine business. The miners were as unreasonable as the mine owners. It was not her concern. What upset her was the prospect of giving up her life and the friends she had made for herself.

"We're not kids, Lizzie. We could live in town, but I don't think you'd enjoy rubbing elbows with the dinner party crowd."

He looked at her, his blue eyes seemed hard as granite to Lizzie. "I think enough of you to want to make you my wife, and your boys are like the sons I've always wanted, but I want you to want me as your husband, and I thought you did."

His face was impassive, his voice even, and he looked at her without blinking. Lizzie felt nervous. She had gotten herself into something she was not sure she could get out of.

"Let me put on a pot of tea," she said.

"Stop fidgeting." He said. "Tell me what's on your mind."

Lizzie dampened her lips. He was angry, like he'd been with the cook he fired. She found it hard to choose what to say from the concerns bunching up inside her. She had said them to him before — but separately, and he didn't take her seriously. He had shushed her with a kiss.

She moved to the kitchen rocker and sat, her palms open in her lap. "You don't want me to work, but I'm going to miss my work friends, and so much that's going on at the hotel. It's a whole world. I can't imagine any place more exciting to be." Lizzie wrung her hands. "I don't know what I'll do with my time out here in the country. Cooking, making rugs, crocheting, church socials — they will not be enough for me. I like to dance and play keno, and act in the theater group at the Empress. I had an audition at the Fox Theater last month, and they have a bit part for me in Romberg's *Student Prince* next fall. I — I love my life in Butte. I love you, too, and of course the boys do, but I'm completely torn."

Bill pushed the front of his chair back to the floor. His voice grated. "Who the hell do you think you are? You act like you're some sort of lady-in-waiting in a fairy tale castle. Every day is a new pageant presented for your amusement. People come from far and wide to bring you stories, gifts that you don't have to pay for. You are nothing, Lizzie. You're nothing but a cinder girl who cleans out the slops." He rose to his feet.

"Wait a minute," Lizzie protested. She was stunned with a mixture of shame and anger.

"Not even a cinder girl. Take a look in the mirror. You're a middle-aged woman who lives in illusions. You have them coming out of your ears. You don't have a clue what your sons need and could be. You see only yourself, stage front and center and fifteen years younger than you are."

Lizzie put her hands to her ears. This was unbelievable. What had happened to him? She hadn't willingly hurt him. She only wanted something of her own life. His wealthy friends, his world of power and money . . . better than hers? For him maybe, but not for her!

"God knows what role you cast me in, the prince probably, who rescues Cinderella. Well, let me tell you lady, I'm not. I have never claimed to be a good guy. I've never rescued anyone. Like you, I will not be bored. But unlike you, I play for high stakes and let the devil take the hindmost."

Bluebeard, a fleeting figure in Lizzie's mind's eye.

"You don't grasp high stakes any more than your friends do. Friends? You offend me — hotel servants and keno cronies — trash for God's sake, don't you see the difference? If cream rises to the top, what remains on the bottom? Those who don't have what it takes. If you don't realize what being my wife could mean to you, the things you would have, the life you could lead with important people, with *important* stories, and what I could do for your children, I'm fortunate indeed to get living proof of your trivial mind and concerns."

He then slammed out the door, leaving silence echoing in the emptiness of her mind. What had happened? Nothing he said made sense. She was too shocked to cry. Strange she wasn't more offended, her usual response to criticism. Was she as he described — selfish, caring nothing for her children, only for her own amusement — in fact . . . like him as Flanagan saw him? Living her life to avoid boredom, seeing people only as part of her play? She felt such shame. Maybe . . . no, this was outrageous . . . Yet she didn't want to lose him . . . Why was everything that mattered like death, all or nothing? The hours stretched vacant. She did not know what to do.

It was over. She knew it was over. She hadn't foreseen how it would feel. So empty, silent, blank. She had told him the truth she knew of herself, that deep instinctive truth that she wanted everything she had and not to give up any of it. To give up her friends would be to give up herself. Had she made such a mistake and lost the one opportunity of her life for remarriage? Surely there would never be a man again with so much charm, so much of everything any woman would want.

Afterwards, she told Flanagan she could not remember what exactly he said, only that she felt her very skin had been flayed from her back. She shuddered.

"He didn't come back until after nightfall. It was fierce," she said. "I didn't sleep a wink. The next day, he was smooth as glass when he brought us home. The boys didn't know anything was going on. I know they miss him, but . . . I've only seen him once since. He seemed completely himself, again. I tried to give him his ring back, but he insisted I keep it. 'You're the most magnificently frivolous woman I've ever met,' he said. 'Keep it as a tribute.'"

"I'm glad you didn't insist too hard about the ring," Flanagan said with a small wink. "Think of it as a trophy for a filly that wouldn't be broken. And Lizzie, believe me, he doesn't know all he thinks he knows about high rollers either."

"You mean he didn't recognize one of them?"

"No, not you," Flanagan laughed. "High-rollers don't see much except the dice."

Chapter Eight

Passage Point

July 22, 1923

M olly sat behind the cash register at Gamers Bakery and Restaurant; chin in hand, looking at large flakes of snow drifting through the air outside. Several inches had fallen since morning. Such freaky weather — mid-summer snow! No place on earth had weather like Butte.

At eleven in the morning, only a handful of patrons were scattered along the coffee bar at the rear. No one occupied the ground floor tables nor those on the open balcony that circled the restaurant. The wrought iron railings of the balcony and the cheerful green interior mocked the threat of the day. Kitchen warmth, the rich smell of cinnamon rolls, saffron bread, and Cornish pasties wafted from the slatted doors behind her.

When she took this job, Molly had not expected to be working at it three years later. But bookkeeping jobs had dried up when the banks collapsed. She was lucky to be working at all when the trouble hit; lucky to be kept on to work part time. Molly drummed her fingertips on the glass counter. It would not do, though. This was not enough of a life.

The door jingled and turned her attention again to the weather, as another customer pushed through the double glass entry doors and stamped snow from her shoes. Molly's bobbed hair and short dress were fashionable, but she wished she had pulled out her winter woolens this morning.

The bleached blonde approaching the register was a real flapper. She wore a skirt even shorter than Molly's with a hip hugging silk over-blouse and a black curly lambskin jacket over her shoulders. Her long pearl necklace was ultra chic as were her eyes, heavy with eye shadow and mascara, but now fluttering at Molly.

"Remember me?" she asked, in a throaty voice.

"Gertrude!" Molly gasped. "How did you find me?"

"When I got into town yesterday, I looked up the business school — remember our dream? I asked where you were. Simple."

"What happened? Did you go to school?"

"After you left, I got your letter but there was too much going on to write. It's just taken a couple of years longer to get here.   I stayed with an aunt in Helena at first."

"Do you need a job?"

"I can type, but that's it," Gertrude said, "and I don't need a job right away, because what I came to ask you is whether you'd like to move on to Seattle, or down to San Francisco with me?"

"God, I'd love to, but I don't know."

"I hear there are a lot of jobs on the West Coast."

Molly gave Gertrude a Clara Bow demi-smile and smoothed the back of her bob with one hand. "Well, it'd be hard to leave my other job — I dance in the chorus line at the Astonia Theater." She laughed. "Of course, they haven't paid us for the last three months, but neither has any talent scout invited me to leave for the big city lights."

"Come with me to the Barbary Coast, my dear," enticed Gertrude.

Molly giggled, then rang up a customer's check. "Look, come back at 3 o'clock. I have two hours free then. Ma wants me to drop off a cake for her friend Annie's retirement party. She's at the Finlen Hotel, it just opened, have you seen it?"

"The Thornton isn't the center of the world anymore?"

Molly laughed. "You haven't seen the Finlen — nine stories high crystal chandeliers hanging from a thirty foot ceiling in the lobby and the Gold State Banquet Room. It's got a restaurant, coffee shop, night club, and all kinds of businesses on the mezzanine."

Molly nodded to an entering customer and turned again to Gertrude. "Ma rules over the fifth floor. The Thornton housekeeper took Ma with her when she moved over. You'll get a kick out of seeing it, but we don't have to stay. I can bring you home with me. Do you want a bed tonight?"

"No, I'm staying with my boyfriend, Fred Winfield. He's the one who's grub-staking me to go to California, but I'll be back to see you at three on the dot."

It was like a delicious piece of candy under her tongue. California, sunny California where they did not have freak snow storms in the middle of summer. Where she would be unknown and could be anything, anyone. Where she need not serve coffee and cakes, and where she could try out being a flapper like Gertrude. She shivered at the possibilities.

She did not have to be Pa's substitute anymore, either. Despite the financial troubles of Montana, everything was going well for the family. Tom had a job as a salesman for Best Foods. No danger he'd go down in the mines. Johnny had a job after school running numbers from the Silver Bow Club. Pat, to everyone's surprise, had been elected president of his grammar school class. His black Irish looks must have counted for something, because he was still shy. And James was clowning his way through school taking nothing seriously.

Frank, on the other hand, had gained all kinds of attention playing left end for the Butte High Bulldogs, but he still had not forgiven Ma for *not* marrying Bill Henderson. "And what's she excited about now?" he'd ask. "President Warren G. Harding — he *talked* to her in the Finlen and is so handsome — that scum who betrayed Montana. The Teapot Dome scandal. She won't hear a word of it. Well, what can you expect from a royalist — in Butte!"

Molly had laughed. Even when she didn't agree with him, Frank was funny when he mimicked Ma. Molly had tried to tell Frank her own reservations about Bill and learned that Frank knew more than she did about him, without going through his records. Bill was from West Virginia where he had played a major role in preventing unions from getting a foothold in the coal mines at the turn of the century. Apparently, he was doing the same thing now in Chile.

Still Frank had not seen anything that much wrong with him. "It's a game, Molly, like football. Winning is what counts." Molly had been flabbergasted. How could a son of Pa think that way? Frank still did not understand that people suffered when things were stacked against them. She realized that they fought about most ideas. She shrugged. Today she was tired of family matters.

California. It wasn't possible. She didn't have near enough money. The minutes dragged their way around the clock and finally it was three. Gertrude pushed her way through the glass doors.

When they reached the Finlen, they went to the elevators, just as if they were guests. Molly waved at Jocko, who joined them, briefly.

"They're on the top floor, Angel, in the south-end suite," he said. "And be careful, they're trapping bear today. Completely full of themselves."

The girls heard laughter as they approached the room. Annie was wiping her eyes when they entered. The coffee table was heaped with tissue paper, small gifts and teacups. The maids from all floors of the Finlen sat about on the chairs and sofas of the Presidential Suite. Even the housekeeper was there. Nora Bonner appeared to be choking with laughter. "Oh Molly," she panted, "Your Ma . . . she's in great form . . .   the stories she tells!" Nora took a deep breath, straightened her face for an instant, and then collapsed in laughter again.

"Lizzie," said Annie, "Tell the one about the priest's donkey. That's my favorite."

Lizzie demurred with a shake of her head. "It's someone else's turn." She feigned embarrassment, one hand to her cheek. "You've listened to me long enough."

"No, don't say that." Nora Bonner belched her dissent.
Molly watched her mother glance with her bright, mischievous eyes around the room. Flushing the crowd, Molly thought, for the proper pitch of anticipation. Lizzie wriggled back into her chair and launched into her story.

"There was this priest," she said, "who wanted to raise money for his church. Someone told him there was a fortune in horse racing, so he decided to buy a horse and enter him in the races. However, at the local auction, the going price for horses was so steep, that he ended up buying a donkey instead."

Lizzie raised her eyebrows high in sympathy with the priest's predicament. "Since he had the donkey," she said, "he figured he might as well go ahead and enter it in the races, and to his surprise, it came in third. The next morning the papers read: *Priest's Ass Shows*. The priest was so pleased with the donkey he entered the race again. The next day the papers read: *Priest's Ass Out Front*."

Smothered giggles. Molly watched her mother focus her large gray eyes on Annie.

"The bishop was naturally upset with this kind of publicity," Lizzie said. "He ordered the priest not to enter the donkey in another race. The headline the next day was: *Bishop Scratches Priest's Ass*. This was too much for the Bishop. He ordered the priest to get rid of the animal."

Annie was holding her hand over her mouth, barely able to contain her-self. Molly noted Lizzie's pause before the double punch.

"So the priest decided to give it to a nun in a nearby convent. Headline the next day was: *Nun Has Best Ass In Town*. The bishop fainted, and then informed the nun she would have to dispose of the donkey. She finally found a farmer who was willing to buy the donkey for $10. The next day the paper stat-ed: *Nun Peddles Ass For Ten Bucks*. They buried the bishop the next day."

As laughter ricocheted around the room, Gertrude, also laughing, pointed to the teacups. "Is that just tea?"

Molly nodded and looked at her mother with affection. Lizzie had taken the world she found and made it the world she wanted. She could be mean, petty, and trivial, as Frank insisted, but she was also . . . magnificent was too grand a word . . . it was simpler. She was also solidly, unashamedly, herself. Abruptly, as if she had just finished an inner argument, Molly turned to Gertrude and hugged her. "We'll do it," she said. "I'm coming with you to California."

September 1923

The two girls, each with an arm wrapped around the other's waist, leaned against the window of their Pullman car, waving good-bye. Molly knew the boys would be all right without her. The edge of excitement — or was it fear she felt rising in her chest — was about going off without a job, without a plan. Fred Winfield, the gauche but good-natured son of a minor copper baron, had staked not only Gertrude but also Molly for their California journey.

"Don't give it a thought. He's rolling in money," Gertrude said. "He could lose this much at the gaming tables in a single night."

Gertrude was plain giddy, but Molly's mind was still in a whirl. She looked down the platform at her brothers until the Empire Builder bent round on itself and cut them from view. Lizzie was at work, but had encouraged Molly to try out California for a couple of months. "Call me if you want to come home and I'll wire you the money." Molly's eyes dampened with tears.

"This is what I want to do, but I've never before this left them willingly," she said.

Gertrude ignored the tears. She reached into the diminutive petit-point bag that hung from her wrist and pulled out an ivory cigarette holder and a packet of cigarettes that she laid on the seat beside her. She then extracted a small silver flask. She uncorked and raised it. "Prohibition hooch," she laughed. "Here's to us and to adventure!"

Part II

San Francisco

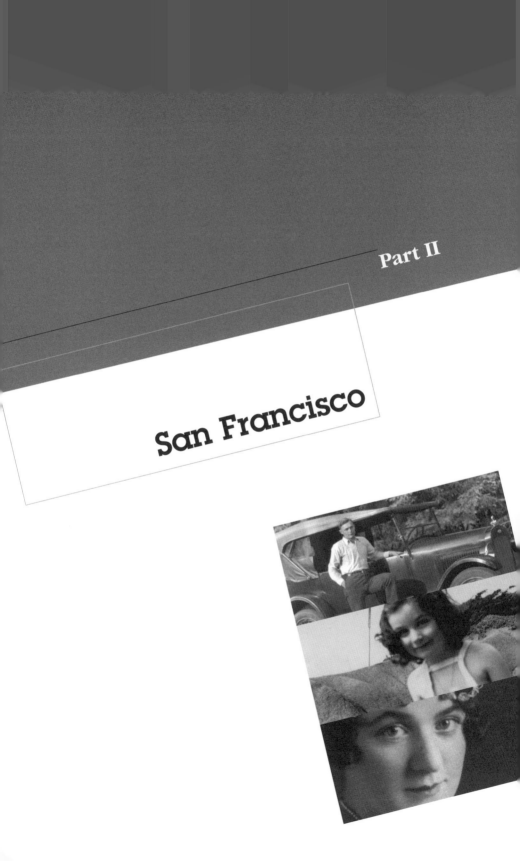

Chapter Nine

Molly

October 1923

The smell of strong coffee filled the room. Molly edged the last segment from her grapefruit shell, then pushed her breakfast dishes away. The radio crackled with static but no one was listening. She glanced at Gertrude lounging in a cream crepe dressing gown on the living room couch. The apartment, at the rear of a building on Russian Hill, had a bank of curved bay windows in the corner and Gertrude looked the picture of a fashionable flapper at home — without a care in the world. That was the problem. Gertrude did not take anything seriously.

Fred's grubstake was an example. Gertrude didn't intend to repay it. Molly should have known that, but she had not let herself question Gertrude enough. She wanted to be out of Butte. The stake paid their rail fare, the rent for rooms at the Y, and all their expenses while they located work. The same week they arrived Molly found work as a bookkeeper at Barton's, a fancy grocery store, and Gertrude took a job as a receptionist for a shipping company. Gertrude, however, refused to accept the part of her paycheck Molly offered toward paying off the loan.

"Are you goofy, Molly? You don't owe Fred or me anything. Surely you knew that was money for my loving companionship services rendered. Fred doesn't need the money, and he doesn't expect it back."

"You both called it a grubstake."

"A joke. His daddy is a hard rock miner who made it big. You know that."

"But aren't you going back to marry him?"

"You're kidding! I never said anything like that."

Molly felt baffled, the way she had felt sometimes with Gertrude at school — that Gertrude was laughing at her for not knowing something obvious. Molly, who was used to knowing what was so — and saying it, felt foolish. She hated feeling foolish.

Gertrude lived by two rules, "Nothing's worth doing unless it's fun," and another that she said her mother had given her, "Presentation is everything." Molly did not know what *that* meant either, until Gertrude showed her. Gertrude not only spent all of her first paycheck on clothes and make-up, but also insisted they move to a flat on Russian Hill with a view of the bay.

"It's our setting," she said, "it tells people who we are. The rest of Fred's grubstake can pay three months of our rent. After that, we'll split it."

Molly accepted the situation but it sounded as if she was a jackass for not understanding. She would get a place of her own when she could afford it. People could judge her by who she was, not by where she lived.

"I don't know why you think we should live together," she blurted without thinking further. Gertrude looked up from the fashion magazine she was leafing through.

"I like you," Gertrude said. "We have a good time together." She put the magazine down and straightened up, hands on her knees. She considered Molly a moment and then laughed. "I like the way you walk and move, as if you don't even notice the attention you get, with your dark hair caught back by combs into waves and curls. And you're smarter than I am, not always chattering away, so when you say something, people pay attention. Makes me jealous, but it's okay."

The stiff feeling in Molly's face relaxed; her temper flickered out. Gertrude always knew what to say; she said what people probably wanted to hear, unless she was needling. Gertrude crinkled her eyes at Molly, "I like you, and you like me so it's simple." She returned to her magazine. Molly reached for the crossword puzzle of the newspaper and once again decided to mind her tongue about things with Gertrude that bothered her.

The first months in San Francisco slipped by quickly. Molly loved the city from the moment she stepped off the train in Oakland and saw it from the ferry that brought them across the bay. The waves of the ocean and the waters of the bay fascinated her. On foggy nights, ship bells and the sounds of foghorns reached through the thick, gray blanket straight into her heart. Sometimes she could see blue-green and white lights from anchored ships that dotted the harbor. It was melancholy and wonderful at the same time. On other nights, the towns round the bay glittered with a million lights. Better yet, when the moon was full, the water itself became a sea of silver.

Russian Hill, where she and Gertrude lived, was a mixture of apartments for the young and mansions for the wealthy. Gertrude was sociable and their apartment soon became a place where people dropped by, knowing they'd be welcome. Most were immigrants from Butte and many of them were Irish. They all knew each other and liked San Francisco's combination of fog, hills, and sea. "Butte's a great place to be *from*," they told one another, "but San Francisco's the place to *live*." As Gertrude discovered the German enclaves, more Germans appeared at the apartment, but Molly thought her fascination with these foreigners would not last. Gertrude was a big-city girl. Molly could not imagine her staying interested in the mountain hikes all these back-to-nature Germans seemed to love. Mt. Tamalpias was nice to look at, but Molly could leave it at that. Even in the mountain chalet of the Nature Friends, it was beer and muscular polkas to accordion music — period. Gertrude wasn't sentimental about her German family roots. It must be something else, Molly decided, but it baffled her.

April 1925

Molly walked down from their apartment into North Beach. Telegraph Hill lay just ahead. Most of the city's artists and writers lived on that hill past the Italian bakeries, cheese makers, and greengrocers' shops. Only a few coffee houses were open, and she was grateful for the quiet. She had not thought much about noise while living in Butte, but living with Gertrude was another matter. So many people in the apartment, so much talk. Sunday morning Mass in St. Peter and Paul's church was Molly's time to drink in the silence and vastness and collect her thoughts. Then she walked across Washington Park to the Bay City Grill to join Gertrude for breakfast.

Gertrude, elegantly draped, sat in a wood-paneled booth sipping a Ramos' gin fizz from a coffee cup. She shifted her bright eyes to Molly when she entered, and the first words out of her mouth were a challenge. "How come you still go to church?" she said. "I don't."

"Not so fast," Molly said, "let me order." She glanced at the menu and smiled at the waiter. "Black coffee and panettone toast." She turned back to her friend. "I just do, and I don't get it that you don't."

Molly was not used to the amount of talk Gertrude insisted on — most of it about politics, sex, or religion — everything people were not supposed to talk about.

"Well," Gertrude said, barely pausing, "When my mom moved West, she left religion behind with the uncle who raised her. She didn't tell us anything Jewish except jokes with great Yiddish words." Gertrude took another sip from her cup. "But the priests and nuns at Convent of the Good Shepherd told us all sorts of things that don't work." She caught the waiter's eye and signaled that she too was ready for coffee and toast. "Turn the other cheek and all that *stuff*."

Molly grimaced. "It's hard to practice if people think you're a fool, but that's what the drill is, yeah." Gertrude half dropped one eyelid and raised her eyebrow.

"My brother Frank is different from me. He never gives an inch in any kind of fight," Molly said. "He says the other guy will take over. But I choose what I want to fight about and how, like when I wanted Pa's watch back from you and Trina."

"You used salt!"

"Salt or words, I use what I've got."

"So that's why you still go to church, to plot revenge."

Molly laughed and punched Gertrude's arm. "No, it's for a better class of conversation."

"I guess we have different temperaments." Gertrude shrugged. "You're certain about everything, and I'm a doubter. We see things differently."

The toast arrived. Molly dipped a piece of the hard rusk into her coffee and bit it. "I don't know, Gertrude. I think we see different things."

Prickly arguments with Gertrude were routine, but Molly liked exploring the city with her. With twice as many men as women living there, both girls had more invitations than they had time to consider. Gertrude worked in the sumptuous offices of the Matson Shipping Company near the Chamber of Commerce. More often than not, she would call Molly in the middle of the day at Barton's. "Are you free for dinner tonight? I met these guys who want to take us out to Tadich's Fish House." Or Jack's, or Ernie's, or the Cliff House, or any other restaurant Gertrude fancied at the moment.

When the Financial District closed down for the night, flower stalls folded their slats, and the street hawkers went home, they enjoyed a less visible part of the District. The best restaurants and clubs for dancing opened. If Gertrude and Molly stayed up late enough with their dates, they could watch the produce markets between the Financial District and the waterfront begin to come to life again at 3 AM. Half the fun for Molly was being with Gertrude, who enjoyed crazy things — taking the ferry at midnight to dance on the deck, or buying out all the remaining flowers from a flower stall before it closed for the weekend.

They both liked to shop, although Molly seldom bought anything. Gertrude's love for glitzy clothes brought them into the downtown shopping district north of Market with its nearby live theaters and palatial hotels. One day Molly saw a small sign taped to the glass door of a building opposite the Geary Theater. It noted a change in the rehearsal room for a tap dance session.

"Wait," she grabbed Gertrude's arm. "I'll meet you at Hale Brothers in the shoe department. I'm going to find out about chorus line auditions for shows at the Geary." She ran the three flights of stairs before she stopped to breathe and find the studio number. Each floor had two large studios with high ceilings and hardwood floors, a mirrored wall, and exercise bar. Actors rehearsing and the sounds of musicians and dancers were everywhere. Molly slipped into a room where an older woman was supervising warm-up dance exercises. The woman turned her head, raising her eyebrows in inquiry.

"I-I'm Molly Dyer, a dancer," Molly said. "Could you tell me where the pre-show auditions are held?" The woman looked at her. "Perhaps, you are a dancer," she said with a slight smile. "You, nonetheless, must know the professional drills. Look at the bulletin board and call me if you'd like me to evaluate your skill, beforehand." She turned her attention back to the troupe.

Molly looked at the bulletin board beside the door. Most auditions for upcoming shows conflicted with her work schedule. Then she flushed with embarrassment. She had stumbled into the studio of Helena Walinska, the world famous choreographer. She could not possibly afford her fees. She took a card and left. She would have to think about this, though. Maybe dance lessons were not a bad idea. It was much easier to get jobs if you knew someone.

February 1926

"Betty took me to lunch yesterday," Gertrude said one morning, "and have I got an earful to tell you!"

Men from Butte ran a score of prohibition saloons hidden in the Mission District. Inevitably, Gertrude had discovered another "aunt," this Betty, running a house of prostitution as part of the business. Gertrude loved gossip. Her third rule for living might be, 'Get to know everybody and who's doing what to whom.' She also enjoyed telling Molly how things worked.

"This town isn't like Butte," she said. "Gambling and prostitution are illegal, so everyone either pays or accepts graft. There are over a hundred houses, most of them run by or connected to the McDonough brothers, a couple of bail bond brokers. Have you heard of them?"

Molly shook her head.

"Betty told me she had to pay them six hundred and fifty dollars to open her house, and that was just the start. She has to give them a monthly payoff, as well."

"Payoff for what?"

"Well, the McDonough brothers have got city officials on their payroll to take care of *any* contingency — building inspectors, permits — you name it. If you don't pay, nothing gets done. The main payoff is divided among the police captain, the Special Detail, and the McDonoughs, who jointly control the rackets."

"Sounds like free enterprise taxes," Molly said.

"Betty also has to take care of Larry McDermott and Vin Gallegher, the patrolmen on the beat. Betty says even the streetwalkers have to make payoffs so the police don't beat them, or worse."

Molly knew Gertrude was needling her. The police, of course, were most of them Irish Catholics. Molly said nothing.

"Those hypocrites do okay for themselves down here," Gertrude said. "They get payoffs from the bookies, the bars, the lotteries, the abortionists, just about everybody. There is a thousand dollar vagrancy law that allows them to pick up anyone, so it is great for a shakedown. 'Pay up or else.'"

Gertrude glanced at Molly out of the corner of her eye with a small smile.

"Betty says the police even take graft from legitimate businesses for protection. At election time, the police help the politicians by getting campaign contributions and turning out the vote. No one can touch them."

Molly didn't needle or respond to needling. She preferred an all-out fight when her own sense of justice was outraged. Butte police under Jere Sullivan had been known for their tough integrity and kindness. Even her brothers had no complaints. There was no talk of rackets and payoffs; the police simply turned a blind eye on folks who took care of a human need. She was not going to quarrel with Gertrude about crooked Irish police in San Francisco.

May 1926

In the library, Molly found novels by Upton Sinclair that pointed to causes of corruption beyond the city. Unemployment, hunger, and police brutality seemed to be growing. A lawyer Molly had met at a band concert in the Park sponsored her membership into the Mechanics' Library, one of the city's oldest institutions. She loved wandering through the stacks with their beautiful curling wrought iron staircases and finding the treasures of books they held. The library was on Post Street near Montgomery, the narrow canyon where banks, insurance agencies, stock companies, and brokerage houses crowded into tall buildings. On her day off, Molly walked to the library past the Stock Exchange. She looked through the ground floor windows at the shirt-sleeved clerks erasing intricate stock quotations and scribbling others on large green blackboards.

Pa used to talk about the mine owners and their stock. How the ACM would do anything to keep the little stock market numbers climbing, no matter what it cost working men who created their profits. Making a strong union was the miners' only protection. Molly sighed. She did not think she could work as a union organizer — bookkeepers weren't blue collar workers — but it troubled her. Wasn't Barton, her boss, telling her to put her money into stocks to increase her savings? Could she do this without becoming part of the exploitation? Why weren't workers paid stock as part of their wages, so they could share some of the profits they made possible?

She did not want to think about it, but the question kept poking in. Was greed like an infection? A greedy spirit? She didn't understand it. If she kept giving away her extra money, maybe it would not be a problem.

Gertrude and Molly looked into the steaming crab pots at Alioto's. It was Saturday afternoon and a fresh supply of Dungeness had arrived. Gertrude smiled at the fisherman and held her hands up. "I want one this big, and will you crack and clean it for me?"

"Such a pretty lady," the boatman bantered with her. "What's your name?"

"Trudy," she said. "Trudy Krueger."

He wrapped the crab and threw in extra crab legs. "You come back, soon, and meet Mario, my son."

As they walked away from the fish market, Molly looked at Gertrude with widened eyes. "Trudy! Since when?"

"I just decided this minute. But lots of people call me that." She giggled. "Well, Fred did and Dante does."

Dante Podesto was a diver who owned his own salvage company. He was a handsome, hairy man with a flashing grin, and very married. The men who interested Gertrude often were older and wealthy, but not, to Molly's knowledge, married. "Is Dante, uh . . . Are you . . . "

"Nah, we have lunch together. Nothing to it."

Molly doubted that. "What about his wife?"

"I'm not taking her husband away. In a year, I'd be bored out of my mind."

Molly said nothing further. She still didn't know how to talk to Gertrude about anything when they differed about shoulds and oughts.

February 1928

A chorus line audition call! Molly could hardly believe it.

"Yes, six o'clock tonight. The side door in the building across from the Geary Theater — I'll be there." She put the telephone down softly, a smile spreading across her face. She hugged herself and shouted, "Trudy, they liked me! I made it through the tryouts! They want me to come in for the final audition!"

Gertrude hugged her, too. "Want me to come with you and cheer?"

"No, let's celebrate later."

Molly changed into her tap shoes and rehearsal skirt behind the stage. One shoe was missing a nail. She pushed, and the tap held tight. It would do.

The drill called for three steps up a staircase and down. Halfway through the session, Molly twisted her foot on the back step and fell to the floor. The dance director rushed to pick her up. "Can you stand?" he asked. She took a wobbly step and winced.

"I think I've sprained my ankle."

A dancer next to her felt the swelling ankle with her fingers. "Nothing seems broken, but you should get it taped. Do you want me to go with you?"

"The Harbor Emergency Room is only a few blocks away. We'll call a cab for you," the director said.

Molly felt embarrassed, more chagrined than hurt. She insisted on going to the emergency room alone. It was not fair to let another dancer lose her chance. They helped her into a cab and now she ached, but that was not the real hurt. She knew she would not get another chance. Why hadn't she checked her shoes earlier?

She had talent as a dancer, but she was not a star waiting-to-be-discovered. She simply wanted to be part of something bigger. The sense of being someone special that she had from childhood required more of her mind and heart than being on stage, but nothing seemed to call it out. If only she had let Trudy come with her, she wouldn't be alone. They could laugh at the end of another great career — and it would not hurt so much.

It was after seven. No one was in the tiled waiting room of Harbor Emergency except a nurse reading a magazine. The nurse helped her onto the examining table in a curtained alcove, and left to call the surgical resident.

Doctor Chelsea Eaton, rumpled, tired, about five foot ten with dark brown hair, looked like he had been sleeping and still was not quite awake. He touched the swollen ankle lightly. "How'd you do this?"

"The tap on my shoe caught on a stair."

"Hmm." He didn't comment further while he probed the ankle. Molly flinched.

"There's nothing wrong." He sounded annoyed.

Molly snapped, "Then stop bending it. It hurts like blazes."

He looked at her, startled. "Sorry, I meant you have no broken bones. I'll bandage it for support." He pushed his stool back toward the medical cabinet and reached for gauze, scissors and tape. "If you take some aspirin to stop the inflammation and keep off it for a couple of days, you could be dancing again in a week."

Molly noticed then that his eyes were awake, green-gray, like her own, with darker flecks in the iris. He had a long thin nose with a slight hump near the bridge. His manner, no longer self-effacing, was quite focused — on her.

He looked at her steadily while he taped her ankle. Molly felt her testiness drop away and her frown relaxed as this young physician asked about the audition and casting drills. He said he was a surgeon in his last year of training at the University of California Medical School.

"Not much time for theater, for me. How'd you get started dancing?"

The conversation itself was like a dance. He led with a flow of skilled words, questions, and small stories. Molly felt she had no say at all, in where it was going. She followed, and liked his interest.

Finally, he said, "I'm off in twenty minutes. If you want to wait in the green Chevy out front, I'll give you a lift home."

She agreed, an unfamiliar sparkle running through her body.

✖   ✖   ✖

They discovered they shared one thing in common, English ancestry. Molly had been born in Newcastle-upon-Tyne and his father in London. That justified their trying out a recently opened steak and kidney pie diner on Polk Street.

The place smelled of fried onions. A waiter with a red vest and Cockney accent suggested they start with a pitcher of Watney's Ale. In the end, they agreed the steak and kidney pie was dismal, but the home brew in the back room was great. Laughter filled the evening as they competed in telling stories of how bad English cooking could be until it became a hilarious rivalry. Molly confessed she had claims to bad cooking on her English mother's side, but she really considered herself Irish. Chel's humor ran to puns, most of which Molly didn't get, but she read his face and laughed or groaned in what seemed the appropriate places.

No matter what they talked about, it seemed to Molly that Chel knew everything about everything. She loved the quick cartoons he drew on napkins or any other paper at hand, and she was awed when he said *Colliers Magazine* had once published a short story of his.

"This was a great evening for me," he told Molly when he brought her home. "Do you know the Avalon Ballroom on Divisadero? I'll take you there next weekend."

He did not ask. She did not agree. It was understood.

The Avalon Ballroom was up a wide flight of carpeted stairs with carved metal torchlights along the sides. Molly felt peculiar, coming in and having her hand stamped while Chel paid for them. Was this just a dance hall? It was not like the dance clubs in Butte, where everyone knew everyone. Why hadn't Chel brought her to one of the hotel ballrooms, the Palace Hotel, or the Mark? Only the orchestra dais was fully lit. The rest of the huge hardwood floor was warmed by a soft glow from wall lamps on floor-to-ceiling pillars. Mirrored walls allowed the dancers to watch their performance. There were men standing around who hadn't come with partners and extra women sat beside the bar. Who were they?

When the music started and Chel took her arm, her pleasure returned. Charleston, fox trot, black bottom — Chelsea knew every step of every dance, every variation, and endless improvisations of his own.

"Confess," Molly said, "you're really a dancer masquerading as a surgeon."

He gave her a half-grin and shrugged away his skill. "Belle, my mother, insisted on Mrs. Parks' dancing classes after school — white gloves, polished shoes, the whole gamut. It was better than the piano lesson alternative."

"The girls must have lined up to dance with you."

"I've never had a partner like you, Molly. You follow like my own breath."

She could hear the strong beat of his heart as he held her head against his chest in a slow fox trot. This was wonderful, but crazy. What was she doing here? Doctors did not date miners' daughters.

Nevertheless, he wanted to be with her. His hours were irregular. When he called her in the daytime, he wanted to walk and to sketch. He liked to explore the city in the same way she did, soaking up the atmosphere of one district at a time. He had a book with tales of the city that he used as a sketchbook. Using orange ink over the black and white text, he made line drawings that illustrated the area without obscuring the printed words.

The way streets cutting into Market Street were named made no sense, but the tangle of districts they searched was clear enough. The waterfront, called "The Embarcadero" from Spanish days, crossed the foot of Market in front of the Ferry Building. Huge docks lined its curving shore. It was fascinating, but not a good place to walk with the constant dock activity of loading and unloading trucks and rail cars in the street. Chel took Molly up the steep wooden stairs that climbed Telegraph Hill, so he could sketch the full sweep of the waterfront.

An easier area was Chinatown. The Chinese lived as if they were in Peking, with their own schools, society, and newspapers. Even their own telephone exchange. Molly wished she had Chel's talent to draw the small temple-like structure where a handful of operators worked, women who knew by heart thousands of subscribers' names and all their telephone numbers. "You have to come down and see this to believe it," she wrote on postcards to her family in Montana. But she didn't mention Chel.

Molly showed some of his cartoons to Trudy. "He's drawn me as this exotic cat, with the arm bangles I wear and dark glasses, and here's himself — an amorous mouse with a beret — endlessly thinking up things to interest the cat."

Trudy examined the drawings. "You're right. He could make money as a cartoonist."

"He's irresistible!" Molly said. "Every week I learn something more that fascinates me. He knows all these things about writers and writing and has been telling me stories that are like what these people write, only the stories are his own. I don't know where he finds the time to write so much, but he says it's an obsession. Last night he told me about a murder in San Francisco that could have been written by Dashiel Hammett." Molly giggled, "He also told me one that sounded like your *Fanny Hill* stories."

"I've watched him when he's here in the apartment," Trudy said. "He doesn't sparkle for other people. In fact, he seldom has anything to say."

"He values privacy as much as I do," Molly answered. "That's one thing that draws me to him."

"You know the line men use to get women to go to bed with them?"

"Sure. My brothers used to show off their knowledge — and lack of experience: 'Tell her she's beautiful, tell her you love her, then tell her you need and want her more than anyone.'"

Trudy laughed, "Except this guy tells you how smart *he* is, then how bright and special you are because you can tell how wonderful he is. And pretty soon you're going to go to bed with him."

"You're too cynical."

"Oh yeah? Have you ever talked to him about your interest in the unions?"

"Well, no."

"You try it. Bet you a dollar to a doughnut in five minutes, he's talking again and you're listening."

Molly laughed, but with a small cringe inside. She had already crossed that boundary.

Chapter Ten

Winter 1928

M olly stretched her arms overhead, then in front of her as she arched her back. Her thoughts scattered like thistledown in the wind. She kept trying to gather and order them in precise small tasks. Must not think of Chel, must not drift. She counted the day's cash from Barton's Gourmet Foods and entered the figures on a deposit slip.

Her office, with glass from ceiling to desk level, was situated on a balcony and overlooked the street level of the store. She could see clerks still cleaning and restocking shelves, but the cashiers were long gone. Molly tied the money into a small canvas bag for deposit, then checked the time on her wristwatch. Her heart beat faster, but she would not let herself leave for another ten minutes. She didn't want Chel to find her waiting on the street. How in the world could she get into the playful mood he expected?

At twenty-four, after four years in the city, Molly looked, dressed, and felt like a San Franciscan. A long rope of pearls, her only jewelry, gleamed against the shaded blue crepe blouse that deepened the color of her eyes. Her skirt, a deeper blue, flared soft-ly to mid calf over silk stockings. It was a Saturday outfit, appropri-ate for office work, but ready to be dressed up for evening. She added costume bangle bracelets to her arm before she slipped on a hip-length jacket that matched her skirt. She took her purse and gloves from the topside drawer of her desk and ran a comb through short, waved, dark hair clipped close in back. She checked her face in a small silver compact, moistened the Maybelline brush with her tongue, widened her eyes, and then brushed up her lashes. It had been a long week at Barton's, but it was over at last. She slipped on her high heels from under the desk and her cloche hat from the rack before she walked to the back office wall safe. The money would stay there until Monday.

There wasn't much cash. Most customers in Pacific Heights had charge accounts; telephoning their orders into the store in the morning, and having them delivered in the afternoon. Molly had spent the day posting charges, sending bills, and crediting payments. She saw that Jay Barton himself was closing up his ledgers. He usually was not here this late.

Barton, a tall man in his fifties with a ruddy face and slightly stooped frame, was not a typical greengrocer. His double-breasted dark wool sack suit had been recently pressed. His fedora and overcoat hung on the clothes rack. The beige kid gloves on his desk matched his spats. Barton had inherited the business and came to it as a connoisseur of good living. The goods he chose made Barton's the Mecca of opulent foods in a city that prided itself on its appetites. A widower and popular figure in the social scene frequented by his customers, he had the reputation of a playboy, but Molly found him a gentle, somewhat wistful man. He gave her stock market tips each week and advised her to invest as much of her salary as she could.

When she reached his desk, he yawned, then smiled at her. "How're we doing?" he asked.

"You probably should look the bills over. Maybe you could write a note on some of them," she said. There hadn't been many payments during the past month. She made good money, twenty-four dollars a week — what Pa used to earn, but some of the accounts owed more money than she earned in a year.

"Oh, they're good for it. Don't be such a worry-wart, Molly. Go out and have a good time this weekend." He gave her outfit an appreciative glance. "That fellow you introduced me to last weekend at Coffee Dan's, is he waiting?"

She nodded. She did not like to talk about Chel. He was like a precious book, a treasure she read alone.

"Chelsea . . .? What kind of name is that?" Barton asked.

"I don't know. It's unusual, isn't it?" she answered.

She did know, though. It was magical. A name to conjure with. She rolled the names around her tongue inside. *Chelsea Dingle Eaton.* Two towns in England and one in Ireland. What would it be like to have a son with that name instead of an ordinary one like John or Frank? The name was his mother's concoction. His parents had spent their honeymoon in the British Isles. Belle Eaton thought Chelsea Dingle a great name for their first son. What his father thought, Chel did not mention. He called his mother by her first name, Belle.

"Belle looks like a strong breeze would blow her away, but you better not believe it. She uses whatever wind comes up to fill her sails and get where she wants to go."

Shades of Lizzie. "Does she ever want what you don't want?" Molly had asked.

"We see alike most of the time, or I talk her round."

Molly raised her eyebrows.

Chel gave her a broad smile, "Oldest sons do have some leverage," he'd said, then added that he and his mother had a face-off when he decided to go West for his surgical training. Belle believed families should be able to see one another at least once a week, if not every day.

Belle's family was from Charleston, and that is where his parents had met, married, and still lived. Chel did not talk much about his father, or his brother who had just been appointed to Annapolis.

Molly wondered if she would like them. And if they would like her.

She moved swiftly into the heavy fog of California Street and did not see him at first. Her breath caught, then she saw his Chevy coupe rounding the corner. He reached to open the door for her. His voice warm and cheerful, he asked, "What kept you? I've been around this block four times!"

She smiled at him. Some questions didn't need answers.

"Let's see. We'll have dinner at Bernstein's on Powell, then how about we go to the fights at Winterland?" he asked. Her heart sank. She hated to sit and look at games and sports; particularly she hated looking at fights. Besides, she needed to talk to him tonight. Then she saw his naughty look and pursed mouth. He was teasing her.

"Okay, okay, you win!" he said. "I'll just have to accept Rusty's key to his cabin in Half Moon Bay for the weekend. A cabin stocked with food, drink, and oak logs, a cabin made to order for wild, passionate, love-making . . . Uh-oh, I feel your critical nose wrinkling . . . I should stop thinking in clichés, right?" He reached over and smothered her giggle with a kiss. Molly breathed her relief. The cabin — just what she wanted — and time, lots of time to talk.

The Ten Mile Road House on the coast highway was an unpretentious wooden frame structure known for its barbecued oysters on the half shell and jazz dancing 'til dawn. As Chel downshifted his car looking for a parking place, they heard the brassy sound of the band. The inviting garlicky smell of the grill reached them through the light drizzle of chill night air.

"Hop out and find us a table," Chel commanded. "Juanita's expecting us."

Juanita, an amiable peroxide blond, smiled when she saw Molly. "You take a place by the fire, hon," she said, motioning toward the corner of the room dominated by a fieldstone fireplace, "I'll have your table ready in two shakes." When Chel entered, she led them to a wooden table near the waxed dance floor. A waiter flicked a starched red tablecloth and two settings into place.

"I've saved you two steaks of abalone, fresh from Pescadero. You'll love it, though the Dungeness crab is good too, if you want something lighter."

The tender abalone, with steamed artichokes drenched in garlic butter, a wooden platter of crusty sourdough and a bottle of white Bardola, lived up to its billing, although the band did not. It was too loud to talk. Perfect for dancing though — and they did.

"The band's going until four. D'you want to stay?" Chel looked at her with sleepy eyes.

Molly wrinkled her nose. "We have another hour's drive, a half an hour for you to make the fire —"

"Aw, don't be like that. My fire-making skills are improving," Chel interrupted.

"— and then we can get to bed. And bed's where I want to be!" Molly continued.

Chel leaned his head back, gave her a smile, and drawled, "Well, that's better."

Molly woke while it was still dark. The room was chilly and damp. A roos-
ter crowed somewhere in the distance, but there was no sign that the sun would
shine today. Last night's drizzle had turned into a steady downpour. Chel still
slept the sleep of the exhausted. He was no longer on thirty-two hour shift rota-
tions, but ten to twelve-hour days were common on the surgical service. Molly
slipped into the green silk kimono he had given her for her birthday the month
before and felt her way to the floor furnace. As she struck a match and the gas
flame caught, she fervently wished it were warmer. Montana reached much
colder temperatures, sometimes 65 degrees below zero, but somehow it did
not get into your bones like the damp of Northern California. She moved back
under the covers, careful not to touch Chel with her now-cold body.

The four-bedroom cabin was the vacation home of a large family. She had
noted the upended rowboat at the side of the house when they entered last
night. The landscaping of simple ice plants and other succulents matched the
interior rooms — scruffy, but comfortable.

The room she and Chel had chosen ran the length of the second story. It
was beginning to grow light. She could see the wood beamed ceiling, the high
iron-framed windows with small panes of glass that opened to the dunes and
restless ocean. Wheat-colored cotton drapes hung from wooden rings on a
twisted iron rod across one side of the room. Two canvas covered armchairs
strewn with brightly colored pillows and an afghan of crocheted squares edged
in black faced the water.

The bookcases lining the far wall were filled with dominos, checkers, and
other board games, as well as an eclectic collection of books. She recognized
several volumes popular with her adolescent brothers, *The Hardy Boys*, *The
Rover Boys*, and *Tom Swift* with his innumerable inventions. She laughed to
herself. The books made her feel closer to Rusty, Chel's short, freckle-faced
roommate.

Rusty felt lucky to have survived medical school and was now starting
practice as a GP with no intention of cracking a book again. He obviously had
not taken his childhood Horatio Alger to heart. She wondered if his family knew
he lent their cabin to his friends. Molly could not imagine why he went into
medicine if he disliked it so much. She puzzled out terms in medical books and
journals and found the articles fascinating.

If she had time to read, she could do anything Rusty could do, better.

Show her anything once and she could do it. She imagined she could learn to do surgery the same way.

Chel did not like to talk about medicine though, with her or with anyone else. She didn't question him much. He had a way of going quiet, or changing the subject and telling her a story. She suspected that perhaps there were not many people in his life apart from his family. He had a moody streak in him. The stories he wrote had peculiar characters in painful, lonely circumstances.

"Why do you write about these people?" she asked.

"Guess it's my Southern Gothic sensibility," he said.

They seldom encountered friends from his world. "There are ten hundred more interesting things to do," he said, "than spend time with doctors."

She did not understand why he preferred her company. She could remember and imitate, but she did not make stories from scratch as he did. However, she knew she glowed when she was with him. Her feelings brightened, she laughed harder, and her mind felt alive and on fire.

A bizarre image of slipping, falling, and tumbling flashed through her mind. She shivered. It made no sense.

Enough! Molly shook her head and stretched free from unwanted thoughts and the weight of the blankets. A long stretch, beginning in her fingers, arms, shoulders, down her spine and into her legs and toes.

"You move like a cat," Chel murmured, stretching his own arm out from the blankets to pull her closer.

She melted around his body. And then, he into hers.

When she woke again, it was mid-morning. The rain had stopped and an unexpected patch of sunshine opened up. Chel still held her close.

"Do you know you snore?" he asked.

She shuddered.

"A tiny snore," he said, "but it shows great potential."

He laughed and pushed her to the edge of the bed.

His warmth, the comfort of the house, this was the time to tell him, she decided, and quickly blurted out the words that had been filling her mind all week.

"Chel, we're going to have a baby."

"Oh shit," he groaned. "Not if I have anything to say about it."

She looked at him quickly, unable to breathe. She had not known what his response would be, hadn't been able to get past her own undercurrent of fear. The silence lengthened.

Chel shook himself loose from the covers, turned the armchair to face the bed, and sat down. "Molly, you know I didn't want this to happen. I've taken every precaution to protect you."

She looked at him blankly. She supposed he meant the rubbers he insisted on wearing, the diaphragm he wanted her to use.

"All I can do now is to help you get rid of the fetus as painlessly as possible."

Molly's tongue was so dry; she couldn't quite form the words. "That's . . . not . . . possible," she managed to say.

"Look, I should have talked about some things," he said the words bluntly. "You know I'm Jewish. We've never talked about marriage because I've got to marry a Jewish girl. It would kill my parents, if I didn't. And it's what I want, too."

Chel's expression was strange. The tight skin around his eyes — he looked tired, but also like a stranger. "I wouldn't ask you to convert to my faith any more than you'd ask me," he said.

She heard the words. Should she have known? True, he hadn't talked about marriage, and she had not dared to bring it up. She had been living in a dream, an unanticipated, unbelievable illusion. She had managed not to see, not to question what she didn't want to see. Questions she had blocked from her mind flooded in haphazardly as well as all the things she had not told him about herself and her family. She had known it would not do to let Belle know her mother was a chambermaid, but she hadn't admitted that it wasn't safe to tell Chel. Somewhere inside she knew that about him . . . She had not met his family or his friends apart from Rusty.

He was ashamed of her. Deeply, painfully, in a way that could not be extinguished she knew this. She had never, never lost her pride; never felt shame in her life. Now, seeing herself through his eyes, she felt worthless.

She was in a box of time that had no meaning. Something had ended — a dream. Only ashes were left. She saw with a sudden clarity the plight of women through all time. This was what Sister Magdalene had tried to tell her.

She felt a pure flash of contempt for Chel.

✖   ✖   ✖

Molly sat on the cabin porch in complete stillness waiting for him to finish loading the car. Finally, he dragged a wooden bench to sit beside her.

"Molly, talk to me," he said in a choked voice.

She glanced at this man who did not want the baby she was carrying, but she said nothing.

He reached out and clasped both of her hands between his.

"Molly, I don't know that you believe me when I say I love you. What we have between us has been — is — precious to me." He cleared his throat, as if he, too, were having difficulty framing words. "I can't marry you, but I . . . I want you to understand."

He paused and rubbed her unresponsive hands. Then, with a sigh, he continued,

"It was my fault not to stop our affair before this happened. I have known that we had to talk. You didn't ask me any questions and I assumed you . . ." He stopped himself, and shook his head. "No, I didn't assume. For months, I've been putting it off because I knew you would end it if you knew marriage wasn't in the cards. I couldn't face the thought of losing you, and the thought of loneliness again."

Several seconds passed.

"I'm part of a family; it's more than a religion. Traditions have separated us from other people for centuries," he said. "We've often had to hide and do things that allowed us to survive. I don't talk about religion because it cuts me off from people and things I want."

How dare he speak of religion? This disaster had nothing to do with God. He knew nothing of God. She shuddered.

Chel glanced away, his voice so low that he seemed almost to be talking to himself.

"My father changed his name, Anglicized it when he came to this country, so he'd be better accepted in business. I didn't write down my religion when I applied to medical school, because the admission quota for Jews is from zero to ten percent, never more. But, we keep our faith. When I marry, it will be in Temple, to a woman who continues our tradition."

Chel looked at Molly directly now. "That's the way it is. I'll do what I have to do, and I hope I'll want the woman I marry as much as I want you."

Molly continued to look at him silently.

He swallowed. His words were now pleading. "I don't want you to have a child I can't claim, or take responsibility for. This fetus is just a bit of protoplasm at this point. Molly, let me help you."

Molly interrupted. "Take me back to the city, Chel. I'll manage."

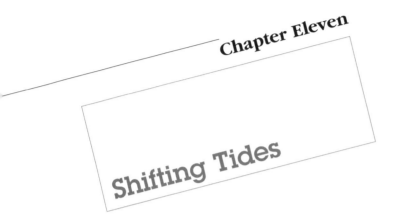

Chapter Eleven

Shifting Tides

M olly fumbled with her keys, trying to open the door before the flood-
gates inside broke. Thank God, Trudy wasn't home. She pushed
blindly past the living room to her bedroom, shut the door again and
flung herself on the bed. The wail could no longer be contained, an
animal sound high and thin, but on and on, inexhaustible. Ugly,
sobbing grief surged through her body. She pressed a pillow against
her mouth, but it could not smother the sounds of rage and despair.
She cried until she could cry no longer. One hour? Two hours? She
lost track of everything except the vortex of pain in every ragged
breath she drew.

Then it was over. Her mind began to wake again. The veil of
tears lifted. She realized that she needed to think what to do — but
she could not quite yet. She had to accept the numbness. Some
words pushed at the back of her mind. Sister Mary Magdalene said
a prayer. What was it? She said that everyone needs help at one
time or another. A cry, that was it, a cry, a silent howl of pain in the
dark night, reaching up to the heavens, demanding justice, but willing to settle for mercy.

Remember, O Most Blessed Virgin Mary, that never was it

known that anyone who fled to thy protection, implored thy help, or sought thy intercession, was left unaided . . . . Hear Me! Hear my prayer!

She could not remember how the words went from that point, or think what it was that she wanted. She had thought she wanted Chel — a chimera who didn't exist. The man she wanted wasn't the grim faced one who had brought her to the apartment house door and left without touching her. How had she let this happen to her? She couldn't think. She couldn't feel. What did she want? She wanted — no, she *needed* to mourn. Not the baby. God knows she did not want that; she didn't want to be caught . . . yet, she had known with absolute certainty that she would not let Chel take it from her. A fierce and primitive will was inside her — *I will not let this baby be killed.*

A noise in the hall. Trudy must be back from hiking Mt. Tamalpais with her crowd of hardy Germans. Someone was tuning a mandolin. Molly slid silently from her bed and locked her bedroom door and her side of the double-doored bathroom. She wanted neither distraction, nor intrusion in her grief. The last thing she wanted to face was a bunch of jolly hikers half sloshed after guzzling beer for two hours on the Ferry.

She consoled herself. They seldom stayed long after these forays; they soon reached the sentimental stage when hiking songs turned into love songs. Then they would ramble off to the William Tell to dance the Hambo and endless polkas.

No, this was only one person, she realized after twenty minutes. The lengthy patient tuning had been followed by an uncertain melody that the musician was either trying to compose or remember.

The lowest point of grief in her life, and she was distracted by rage that this dummy could not find the right chord! In spite of herself, she laughed. She needed to blow her nose, and then to put a cold wet washcloth on her eyes. Perhaps she would think more clearly tomorrow.

A half-hour and a hot bath later, Molly emerged from her bedroom in a fresh gown. She recognized the German who was still hunched over his mandolin, but had moved on to another tune. Hans Frings, a Rhinelander in his mid-twenties who had jumped ship after Germany's economy collapsed. He occasionally appeared with Trudy's hiker-friends, but he listened and seldom spoke.

"What are you doing here alone?" she asked.

"Maybe," he hesitated a moment, seeming to search for words. "I am here to comfort you," he smiled.

Molly's face flushed with embarrassment. "Were you . . .?" she asked.

"Ja, you don't see me as you rush by. I hear you, and finally I think you cry long enough, so I let you know I am here, so I pluck out my homesick song."

"But why are you in my apartment at all?" Molly raised her voice. "I didn't ask for your comfort and I don't ask for it now. I'd appreciate it if you leave immediately."

"Easy, easy," he said, throwing up his hands, the small smile still in place. "You are hurting. I know how it is to feel hurt and to feel alone. Better to be with someone to talk a little."

"I don't discuss my business with strangers," she said.

"Strangers . . . it is sometimes good to talk. They don't know; they see fresh."

Unwilling to admit his words pulled her, she made a feeble protest. "I can't talk about this to anyone. I don't want other people to know."

"Ja, ja, that's hard — but I will not say to anyone what you talk about."

"Where is everyone?" Molly asked.

"The Octoberfest at the Nature Friends Lodge. My back is too sore to dance, so I stay home to play my music. Trudy say I can stay here for weekend. Everyone is away."

In the year or so that she had casually encountered Hans, she had never heard so many words from him. Perhaps he was right. She might use him in this way to hear herself think. She could not write to her mother yet, nor her brothers. She had no one else. Trudy was, well she did not know what Trudy was, but in this, Molly knew Trudy would not be good to talk to. A part of Trudy would not be sad to know that Molly was in this kind of trouble. "You've got to get an abortion," she would say and, probably not think twice about it.

Molly glanced at Hans who sat with his arm across the back of the sofa. Physically attractive, but she had never heard him laugh. Dusty blond hair, gray eyes, a cleft chin, strong, lean body, he seemed utterly self-contained. But he was a foreigner, how could he understand? His English, if it could be called English, he had learned from Swedes in the lumber camps of Mendocino. His accent was atrocious. Nonetheless, he was right. She needed to talk.

✖   ✖   ✖

"That's how it was, right from the beginning, so many things between us we just understood," Molly said. "I thought when his residency was over . . . "

"He say you marry?"

"He said he loved me," Molly sobbed, then broke into heavy tears, "I thought . . . we didn't need to talk about it."

Hans put his arms around her and very gently kissed the side of her forehead. "Maybe he will think it over?"

Molly rubbed her eyes with her fingertips, and frowned. "No," she said. "When he offered to abort the baby, I knew . . ." She looked out the window for several moments, then shivered slightly, and continued, "This man wasn't . . . he's not for me." She finally turned her eyes back to Hans. "I'm a mess again. I'll go and wash my face."

"So," he said when she returned, "that wasn't bad to do. What do you want now?"

Molly felt confused and merely looked at him.

"Do you want supper?" he asked, rising to his feet. "I'll fix you the supper I make for myself. You like rabbit and spinach cooked with onion and little bits of bacon, and potatoes, ja?"

She had not eaten for almost twenty-four hours. She realized suddenly that she was hungry. "Yes, I'd like that," she said. "Yes."

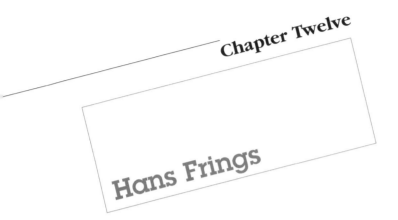

Chapter Twelve

Hans Frings

February 1929

It was 4 AM. Deep sounds of foghorns filled the night, identifying by their pitch and frequency each island, barrier, and obstacle in the bay. Heavy waves flung salt spray into the air and pushed against the piers. The creosote soaked pilings shifted and groaned. Red's Java Cafe by the pier was not yet open for breakfast, but its tin-roof canopy provided some shelter from the wet fog. Hans leaned against the side of the building, waiting.

Across the Embarcadero from the docks, a long row of ramshackle buildings held pool halls, seamen's outfitting companies, saloons, cheap hotels, tattooing parlors, and cigar stores. Behind these untidy shops, the narrow alleys of the wholesale and warehouse district, fruit, vegetable, and poultry centers, were already teaming with activity.

Hans poured a cup of coffee from his thermos. His hands were stiff with the cold, so he held the steaming cup more for the warmth than the brew. For two days, gusting winds of almost hurricane strength and the heaviest storms of the year had threatened to close the port. Hans looked over the men beginning to straggle toward the area where the shape-up would begin. A cattle auction, a slave market . . . what was the difference, except the men were white and thought they owned themselves. The early ones got near the front thinking they would be more likely to be picked for work. So they would, if they were also husky or had paid off the boss in advance.

Hans could not yet see faces, but the man he looked for had a distinctive bulk and gait. Henry Smyth and he resembled one another, but were not related. When Hans had first jumped ship, he had tried to get work on the waterfront as all seamen did. The shipping company boss hiring men from the pier that morning had taken him into a gang because he looked like Henry.

"You must be one of Smyth's cousins," he said.

Hans didn't like being compared to anyone. He had made his own way as a seaman, including two trips rounding the Horn in a three masted schooner. His skills, picked up on a German sailing ship known for its tough, tight discipline, outclassed those of ordinary seamen. His rigging lore matched anyone's on the waterfront. But he could not escape comparisons and Henry's impact on other men. He had to listen to dozens of stories.

Longshore gangs tended to be chosen from the same nationals, Finns, Krauts, Swedes, or Brits. They stuck together not only in the gangs, but also in the bars they patronized. Hans gathered that Henry was a Bavarian with a zesty sense of the absurd who loved filthy stories and practical jokes. Hans recognized him on sight when they later met.

Henry was taller, heavier, and older than Hans by ten years. An affable, hard-working, hard-drinking giant, he knew the wharf as few others did. One night he invited Hans to the German Fraternal Order that met on Albion Street, where an Australian with stiff curly hair and a long nose was talking.

"Every effort to unionize the wharf has been put down," Harry Bridges said. "Police and vigilantes smash whatever union picket lines get set up to protest wage cuts, speed-ups, or the staggering accident rates. The shipowners have used their power to destroy the legitimate union and force us to join the company union." Henry nodded to several men as he moved closer to the speaker and looked for a place to sit.

"And how does the company Blue Book Union work?" Bridges asked. "Remember Foghorn Charlie? A star winch-driver, he made the mistake of demanding American Hawaiian Steamship Line live up to the rules. They owed him two hours overtime. So he tried to get this so-called Union to represent him in a grievance. The Union got it for him all right, but from that day on the hiring boss looked right through him. In the shape-up, a guy to the right of him would be hired, a guy to the left, one in back, but never Foghorn Charlie. He was clear air to the boss and couldn't get work anywhere on the wharf."

Henry leaned over to Hans. "The ship owners set up that fink hall." Henry snorted. "It's no union."

"The Blue Book Union's function, even now," Harry continued, "is to maintain a spy system and a coast-wide blacklist of trouble makers, like Foghorn Charlie, who think they have rights."

"But, it's the only way to a job." Hans shrugged.

Henry and Hans continued to be thrown together in discharging and loading vessels. The piers were numerous and widely dispersed, so work locations varied. There was nothing routine about the work except that it was heavy, dirty, and required ingenuity. The character and size of each piece removed from a vessel had to be understood before it could be rigged with ropes and pallets. Then the equipment engineered to take it down and reload it into freight cars. The pace between dockside and shipboard work fluctuated however, so there was plenty of time for talk, and talk was what Henry excelled at. Besides, talk with Henry was easy. Hans could always lapse into German when he needed clearer thought. He mostly listened. Henry was always inviting sailors fresh off the boat to join them for a shot of booze with lunch in a local saloon.

"You had that Limey going," Hans laughed after one of their forays. "I thought you'd met your match. He was determined to drink you under the table."

"Before he listed portside, then slowly keeled over," Henry smirked. "But think what he said about the ports in Yokohama and Shanghai. Mark my words, there is going to be a shake-up in the Japanese military. Before long they're going to make their move into China."

"They may be preparing for something, but China, with the Brits there in force?" Hans scoffed.

Henry merely grunted. "Watch," he said.

"We forget already how it was in Germany."

"What happened to you?" Henry reached in his pocket and offered Hans a smoke.

"You ever eat nettle-soup? You're hungry to do that." Hans paused, thinking of the last weeks of the Great War — seeing the cripples, the dead and dying. All that talk, glory and honor, and the fatherland, and then the soldiers came home and nobody saw them because they had troubles of their own.

Memories of his mother stung his eyes. "I was fourteen. My mother hid my brother Karl and me. He was twelve. She hid us from the recruiting bands sending children to the front. She hid us even from our father, whose faith in the Fatherland would not let him see the truth — not even when the Brits occupied our home."

"And what was the truth?" Henry asked.

"I had been so naive, so patriotic as a child," Hans said with disgust. "The Fatherland above anything and everyone. We used to march to school singing:

Jeder Schuss ein Russ

Jeder Stoss ein Franzos

Jeder Truitt ein Brit

(every shot a Russian; every push a Frenchman; every kick a Britisher)."

Hans shook his head.

"The Kaiser and the rest of his family, his cousins — the Czar of Russia and the King of England, lived in a dream world. First cousins in a family fight, and they didn't know their ass from their toenails. They used men like scratch gravel for their peacock ambitions. No sacrifice of other people's lives, families, and land, the civilized world itself — nothing was more important to them than personal power. Not a scrap of difference between them.

"I learned the way to survive is keep my thoughts to myself — not make a move until I figure out what's going on." Like with Molly? The thought came unwilled to his mind.

Henry gave a short laugh. "Do you think it's any different with the ship owners in San Francisco? Put the Kaiser's head on Captain Dollar's body. Same show." Henry slapped Hans' shoulder. "There's one thing missing in your plan. You need to work with a partner so you can watch each other's back. That is what your mother did when she hid you and your brother. It is what you and your brother did for each other. It's what we need to do in the gangs."

Hans leaned against the pier and waited for Henry to join him; wife hunting was on his mind. Women, other than whores, were hard to find in San Francisco, but it was not a problem for Hans; finding one he wanted to *marry* was. Henry had a wife who catered to his every whim as far as Hans could tell. Had Henry trained her to be that way?

Molly would not be a Clara. She was too independent. Of course, he was too, and that part of Molly attracted him, but she needed to be taken down a peg. He threw out his cold coffee and put the cap on his thermos. It was lighter now, but no warmer. Still no sign of Henry. Hans' thoughts circled back to Molly.

The week after she had confided in him about the baby, he invited her to a picnic. "Have you thought what you're going to do?" he asked. They were on the dock, waiting for the Tamalpais ferry to join his friends.

She shook her head. "I haven't talked to anyone, even Trudy."

"Are you going to?"

"It'll be difficult for my brothers to hear I'm in trouble, but I can count on them to help me. Telling my mother is harder. My pride, I guess."

When they were on the bay, a breeze sprang up. Hans gave Molly his coat to shield her, but he could have squeezed a loaf of bread for all the response she gave when he tried to cuddle her.

"I wouldn't mind being married," he said. "I almost married in Valparaiso, a widow with two children, but I wanted to see the States first. Then time went on and she wrote she was marrying someone else. I still think of it, though," he said. "I wouldn't mind taking on a family." Molly just smiled, as if she didn't understand he was talking about her.

However, she did not discourage him. After the picnic, she had asked him to take her to some place — Coffee Dan's, with its silly slide instead of a door and stairs to enter, and its gangster patrons. It had not been the kind of place he enjoyed. He grimaced. Then she wanted to go dancing. His knowledge of dancing stopped with the polka. She made it clear that enthusiastic bouncing was not her idea of dance and declined to try any other steps with him. He was not used to feeling this way with women. She had refused his last invitation to dinner.

Back and forth, his thoughts circled. Should he pursue her?

A classy woman, but too many high-toned ideas, like why else did she fall for that phony doctor who knocked her up. He could not imagine her ever admitting that she was wrong about anything.

With Molly, it was like being in the Fun House of Mirrors at the beach. Push-pull and she was gone. The little glimpses he caught of her temper, fire, and humor sparked his fantasies. He wanted more, but when he tried to stroke her, she became the ice queen again. She was impossible. There must be another woman like Henry's Clara.

Hans remembered a dog, half wolf, half German shorthair, a little bitch who had tried to bite him when he was a small boy. It had taken a long time, but he had trained her until she was devoted to him — obeyed his smallest signal. He lost her, though. In the early days of the war, his father claimed she had gotten into the rabbit hutch and he killed her. Hans had never let himself want another dog. His father . . . Hans shook his head, willing the pictures to leave his mind. His father had not protected Hans' ten-year-old sister. He would have killed her too, if he had known the Brit soldier raped her. Hans pushed out his breath. Too many thoughts. Nothing connected. Maybe talk with Henry would help.

Henry arrived after the calling of gangs had begun. By the grim look on his face, Hans realized this would not be a day for personal talk. He became aware of the peculiar tension around him. The men were gathered in small knots, whispering. Joe Greeley, the company boss shaping up the gangs, was tight-lipped and hard-faced. The two thugs who acted as his goon squad stood beside him, running their eyes over the crowd. Hans caught Henry's eye and flashed an inquiry, as they moved toward one another.

"You haven't heard about Mickey?" Henry asked.

Hans shook his head. "Just that he joined the night shift loading scrap metal to Japan."

"He's at the County Hospital in a coma with a broken back," Henry said. "He fell three levels down into the hold. The fourth 'accident' this week. The poor guy worked fourteen hours. It was a full press speed-up." Henry shifted his eyes toward Greeley's shape-up trio, and then nodded toward the back of the crowd where Hans saw three other groups of unknown men. "They're expecting trouble — and letting us know, if we start something, we'll be squashed."

"What do we do?" Hans asked.

"Nothing, for now. The brew is not strong enough to be tapped. We'll talk tonight, but not a word on the dock. They'll have a company man in the gang."

Henry moved off, shouldering his way through the crowd.

Mickey Malone died that night. Money the men collected for the widow would barely cover a couple of months' rent for the hovel on McAllister Street, but the next day the funeral house was filled with men who knew and worked with Mickey. The goons stood outside the funeral parlor, ostentatiously marking lists of names. No violence occurred, nor would it.

Henry repeated his advice to men he trusted: "Don't risk your neck. Protect the guy you work with. Watch everything. See what's going on. Remember it and we'll talk about it later."

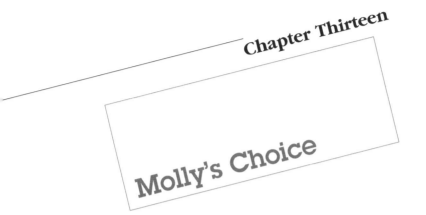

Chapter Thirteen

Molly's Choice

March 1929

M olly surveyed her body in the full-length mirror of the bathroom door. Her bath powder smelled of lilacs. Two months, at the most, before the pregnancy would show. She would have to leave Barton's before that — but where would she go? She wrapped herself in her green kimono, sat back in her bed, and picked up the two letters from Montana.

Ma's letter was emphatic. She should come home. The boys would take care of her. Her brothers had talked it over. Tom was getting married in the spring. He and Stella would take the baby.

No! This meant the neighbors would know, and it'd be a cold day in hell before Molly let them see her come trailing back to Butte like a beaten pup.

Frank's letter, postmarked from Missoula, was brief and matter of fact. A friend wanted him to join a family dry goods business. It was a good opportunity and, anyway, Frank figured it was time for him to get to work. He would take the job. Molly could count on his help in supporting the baby.

Molly's breath quickened, her hand clenched. This was

nonsense. Frank should not give up his football scholarship. She wanted him to get a university education. She wouldn't let him make the sacrifice. The boys still saw her as their big sister who had brought them home from the orphanage, and they wanted to take care of her in turn.

They loved her, but not one of them could imagine that she might want to be rid of this life growing inside, that her own life had been taken over and was now out of her control. She couldn't kill it and would not let Chel, but why wouldn't her body miscarry what her mind rejected?

Had Ma felt this way, trapped with her children, when Pa died?

What did God want of her? Why now — why couldn't she have had Chel — well, the man she thought Chel was — *and* the baby? She sighed, and then mentally shook herself free from that weakness. She needed her anger now. Whether he admitted the betrayal or not, Chel had treated her as if she and the baby were nothing to him. Like trash! Would her child feel that terrible feeling she had felt when Pa died . . . and when Chel left? That no one wanted him, or her?

Would the hurt and anger never stop?

She could put it behind her, and she would, she would keep the appointment this afternoon at St. Elizabeth's Home for Unwed Mothers. St. E's could provide her a place to stay anonymously for the months when her body would show the pregnancy. The baby could be placed for adoption immediately after its birth. Barton would think her family needed her in Montana for a few months and hold her job for her. Even if he wondered about Chel, he wouldn't presume to ask.

She did not know this baby. She did not need to keep it.

Molly's heart felt as gray as the fog that shrouded the squat, two-storied, red brick building. Each step up the broad, long staircase took enormous effort. The large, double-doored entrance was formidable. She heard the doorbell ring somewhere in the depths of the building and was dismayed at how swiftly it was answered.

"Come in," the tall nun smiled at her, "I'm Sister Agnella. Are you Molly? I was expecting you."

Molly nodded. Her mouth was dry as she said, "I'm not sure I want to do this, but I think I should talk to you."

"Of course." The nun pointed to a side room. "Let's talk in here. This first visit is not easy because you have difficult things to think about, and you want to make the best possible decision for your baby. Have you talked to a doctor yet?"

As she answered questions from Sister Agnella, Molly assessed her surroundings. All convents must be alike. This front parlor matched that at the Convent of the Good Shepherd. Same pictures on the wall — one of the Pope, but the other, a different founder for a different order of nuns. This nun had a brisk and competent air to her, getting right down to business.

What would Sister Magdalene say if she knew? That wrestling with the pregnancy and giving up the child would draw her closer to God? No, Magdalene was never simple-minded. She would say that painful problems were not always bad for us. She would say something about God, not just adoption arrangements.

Molly observed the nun at her desk, the notepad and what looked like contract papers close at hand.

Sister Magdalene would tell her to talk to God, and she'd remind her of St. Teresa of Avila's tart words to God about his gifts of suffering — "If this is the way You treat your friends, it's probably why You have so few of them."

Molly smothered her smile. She could almost hear Magdalene saying: 'You've got that same kind of spirit, Molly, and that's what God wants from you in prayer. Quarrel with Him. Tell Him what you need.'

"Have you thought of keeping the baby?" Sister Agnella asked. "Is there any possibility you might marry the father?"

Molly shook her head.

"Then, for the baby's sake, it should be placed in a good home where it will have both a mother and a father to love it. That makes sense to you, dear, doesn't it?"

Molly nodded.

"Can you pay something towards the cost, Molly?"

Molly wondered how many other girls sat in this chair, nodding, nodding their choices away. Did time feel as elastic to them, stretching into the vastness of an afternoon, then the months springing back, one small detour in a lifetime. The nun reached for the papers and a pen. Molly said, "Yes, I can. I have savings."

"I'll put you down for your board then. The rest can be paid from donated funds."

The sister was talking now about the adoption. How carefully those who applied were selected and matched to the baby in every way they could be. Molly looked through the half-open window at the squared off, clipped hedge. She nodded again, but how could anyone match this baby who was made of herself and Chel? They could care for her, but match her?

"During the last month of your pregnancy you'll stay here, but you can enter sooner if you wish. Beforehand, you can either live outside in a private home, in exchange for some light housework, or you can live at St. Elizabeth's."

Molly shifted her weight in the chair. Was the baby kicking her?

"You'll share a room with one other girl and can participate as much or as little as you wish in our community activities," Sister Agnella said. She opened a desk drawer and handed Molly a brochure with pictures of St. Elizabeth's and a description of the program.

"The obstetricians who provide medical care are always on call and will deliver the baby in our own hospital section," Sister smiled again. "You'll be as safe and well cared for as the baby is. You can see the baby after birth if you wish, but the adoptive parents will be ready to take it home when we notify them of the birth."

Molly could hear Sister Agnela's soft words flowing on and on, around her and over her.

NO. You can't have her. You can't make me give her up!

But no one was forcing her to do anything. The baby, a *her*? When and how had she become sure it was a girl — and equally clear that she would not give her up? This baby would not only be as smart as Molly herself, but would have all of Chel's talents — she would be able to do anything. If she were adopted, Molly would never know her! Another woman would mother her, but never know who she was, or what she came from. NO! No, Molly would *not* give her up.

She pressed her hands to her head. She felt like she was splitting into pieces. "Sister," she said, "this isn't what I expected to happen. I don't need . . . I think I can, no . . ." She could not return to Montana unmarried and hold her head up. She did not want a real marriage, not now at least, but perhaps there was a way. "I know I can marry another man. I can make a home and keep this baby, and that's what I want to do."

The nun sat up in her chair. "Molly, it's not unusual to feel torn when deciding to give a child to others, but you have to consider, for the child, whether you can give it such a secure home. Rushing into a marriage with someone other than the father may not provide what you want for the child."

Molly could barely listen. An image of Hans and herself married was growing in her mind.

"Let's talk about what marriage would require," Sister Agnella began.

Molly wanted only to be away and think of this by herself. She suspected her face had that provoking mulish look Lizzie accused her of holding. She caught the nun's words again.

"Marriage has many difficulties without adding the burden of caring for another man's child," Sister Agnella said.

"It's a wonder people who adopt can cope with it!" Molly said, then, seeing the nun's startled flinch, she could have bitten off her own tongue. Why was she so prickly and rude? This woman was only trying to help her. She quickly added, "You've helped me more than I could have imagined. I realize that I can manage this now, and I've got a family who will love the baby and help me."

Sister Agnella looked at her thoughtfully. "Molly, call me if things don't go as you expect. If there is any way I can help, I will."

Molly could hardly believe her sense of relief as the gate closed behind her. The decision was made. After so much protest, a Yes! She noticed the fog had lifted. A layer of light rimmed the horizon. She would leave a message for Hans at his waterfront rooming house.

✖   ✖   ✖

Hans returned to his boarding house and found a piece of paper under his door with Molly's message to call her at Barton's. He dropped a nickel into the cigar box his landlady kept beside the phone to pay for calls and dialed the work number Molly had given him. When he reached her, Molly asked him if they could meet on the weekend.

He said, "Do you want to go to the band concert in Golden Gate Park?"

"Fine. You can pick me up after the Ten, at St. Dominic's," she said.

"How about I join you at Mass?" he asked.

She agreed. Hans was perplexed as he hung up the phone. He continued to look at the telephone message scrap of paper without seeing it. He rubbed his chin slowly. On the phone, she did not seem her prickly self. He had a shrewd idea of what was troubling her. He had sensed from the beginning she wanted to keep that baby. He did not know whether to be excited or wary.

Excited, he admitted. He would make it clear to her that the baby was no obstacle. He could take care of both of them, but first he needed a wife. His father, a railroad stationmaster, would have been nothing without his solid, practical wife. Hans wanted to stay in San Francisco, and Molly was the best woman he had found — pretty and no dummy. She knew how to work hard and she was a Catholic, not that it mattered much, but it was good to have that in common. She was a challenge, but he had no doubt he could make her love him. He had always had the women he wanted. He knew how to plan and how to save. Then he laughed to himself. Wasn't he the guy who didn't make a move until he figured out exactly what was going on? The guy who wanted a docile hausfrau? He must be crazy.

✖   ✖   ✖

The Sunday band concert took place under the trees in the broad space between Steinhart Aquarium and the De Young Museum. People sat on the grassy banks surrounding the tall bandstand or on wooden park benches among the trees and fountains. The musicians in their uniforms of red jackets with brass buttons, black pants, and white, visored caps, lent a cheerful note to the foggy day. Molly wore a loose cream jacket over a lace-trimmed blouse and flared plaid skirt.

As they walked toward the benches, she gathered up a handful of field daisies that grew in the grass. While they listened to the first set of songs, she wove a daisy chain and placed it like an Indian band over her dark curly hair. She seemed distracted and not to be listening to the music.

"You wanted to talk to me," Hans prompted.

Molly gave him a side-glance and smiled. She said, "I want to show you a special place." She stood and after poking a daisy through his buttonhole, she led him through the under-road tunnel near the bandstand. She stamped her feet in the tunnel, which echoed with a large, ghostly sound. "We can pretend we're elephants," she said.

Hans did not understand playful fantasies. Seeing his puzzled look, Molly laughed and added, "Don't worry. We'll still hear the music."

Hans thought she was going to show him the rose garden, which he knew well, but he did not say so. He was touched that she wanted to surprise him. However, as they turned the corner, he saw an enormous structure of bones he had not come across before — a dinosaur? Maybe 75 feet long, about 10 feet at the widest. No, it was the skeleton of an enormous Blue Whale. Whales, he thought, the largest mammals still alive who feed on the smallest creatures alive — plankton. Why . . .?

Molly threw him an impish look. "Not very romantic, is it? Well, come on then." She ran up to the high hedge behind the shed structure, then disappeared through it. He followed her. She was sitting on the broad lower limb of a huge silver spruce in what seemed to be the alcove of another grove of trees. She laughed at his expression. "Magical, isn't it? This is Shakespeare's Garden. All the flowers mentioned in Shakespeare's writings are here and music playing in the background."

He attempted to take her in his arms, but she held him off, her face now quite sober. "I wanted to talk to you in a private place," she said. "It's about this baby I'm growing. She's mine, and I want to keep her." She twisted her body to face him. "I want to ask your help. You said you would not mind a ready-made family; you could see me as your wife. Did you mean that?"

Hans nodded slowly.

Molly looked away from him. "You and I don't know each other well enough, and I don't want to marry . . . but I want my baby to have a name, to be legitimate. I need some breathing time to plan."

Hans said nothing.

She gathered breath again and pushed the words out, "What I'd like us to do is to have a civil marriage, not a real one in the Church. You and I are both Catholics so we know a marriage by a justice of the peace would not be a real marriage for us. But I could go home to Montana with my family and the baby could be born with a valid birth certificate listing you as the father. I'd come back to San Francisco. We could get to know each other better, then decide whether we wanted to be really married, or we could divorce. What do you think?"

She looked at him expectantly. He thought she must have rehearsed that speech.

✖   ✖   ✖

Hans shifted his gaze to his hands, propped on the tree behind her head. Was this woman a trapped innocent or a schemer? An image of the whore in Valparaiso using her little daughter as a lure drifted into his mind. He pushed it away. Did Molly see him at all; have any idea what her proposal would do to his life? Was this some American idea, that a marriage could be thrown away depending whether it was convenient, or inconvenient? What was that word he'd learned on the wharf — cockamamie? This was a cockamamie idea. On the other hand, wasn't it close to what he hoped for? She needed him. He wanted her. Why shouldn't she love him? His parents had not known one another when they were married. Lost in his own thoughts, he didn't notice how long his silence had lasted.

Molly's irritated tone reclaimed his attention, "Well, I didn't expect the idea would knock you flat."

He looked at her then and smiled, for by now he knew Molly found it easier to feel angry with him than to feel hurt or sad. She was embarrassed. He pulled her close. "So how do we find this Justice of the Peace?" he asked.

Relief flooded her face and he felt the tension drain from her body. His instinct was right, she needed him now and all she felt was grateful, but she would come to love him. He hugged her then and lifted her mouth to his. He felt her response and pulled her closer.

Molly pulled him to his feet. She wanted to feed the seals in front of the Aquarium. She said, "Do you hear them barking?"

"Okay, okay," he said in his best American accent. "Then I'll row you around Stow Lake, and we can talk practical matters, like when do you come to my bed?"

She laughed, "Very practical."

During the next couple of weeks, Hans took charge of their planning. He was astonished to learn Molly bought stocks each payday following her boss Jay Barton's advice. They had soared in value over the past couple of years.

"Fifteen hundred dollars," Molly said. We can cash in everything except the gold stocks," She laughed. "Remember, I'm a hard rock miner's daughter and we hold on to our dreams."

They cashed in the stock and looked in the paper to find houses for sale. They had enough for a down payment on a house and the furniture to fill it. Hans swung her in his arms around the living room when they finally picked a home on 19th Avenue near Sigmund Stern Grove. "For the first time we share a big dream," he said.

They picked out furniture at Sloans; black velour living room set and a heavily carved dining room table and chairs that reminded Hans of his home, and a magnificent Wedgwood chef's stove that Molly fell madly in love with. "I'm not much of a cook," she said, "but with this I will be."

Hans drafted a change he would like to make to the kitchen, and brought her the drawings. She looked at them in surprise.

"I had no idea you knew how to do such things."

"Ja, you're getting to know me, now." They took the drawings into the kitchen to check the measurements.

"During the years I sailed, the ship docked at ports from Bremen to Calcutta to Liverpool, then round the horn to Valparaiso," Hans said. "In each port I look at the houses and their building materials. I read houses like books — the weather they face, the lives people live inside — how men protect what matters to them. Then back to the ship and my drawings."

"They're beautiful," Molly whispered.

Hans smiled. "One of my shipmates knew drafting and taught me so I see how architects think. Then I sent money each trip to my mother. I want to study to be an architect."

"What happened?" Molly asked.

"Germany went bankrupt in 1922. So, I lost that stake and I lost my last illusions about Germany." He paused, and then pulled Molly to sit with him on the kitchen step to the garden. The fog had lifted, but the day was growing dark. "We didn't have a dime when we jumped ship in California. Sailing ships were finished. I was lucky to find the lumber camps in Mendocino. A man who worked hard could make big money. Then Canada, this time, a legal immigrant." He held her close. "With a woman like you, Molly, the future holds everything I want."

Hans never did have the talk about women with Henry. For the most part, he was content. Molly had a good heart, although occasionally some things she believed just didn't make sense to him; her stories about her mother for instance. A monarchist chambermaid who put her children in an orphanage, a brave widow who had been a show girl? The stories did not jibe. Lizzie sounded like an ignorant Anglophile from his point of view, a feminine version of the Brits he had hated in Germany.

In June, a Justice of the Peace married Hans and Molly in Santa Rosa. The next day, Molly left by train for Montana.

✖ ✖ ✖

It was almost 9 AM on Caledonia Street in Butte, Montana. Nothing uptown was open. Molly quite urgently needed to find a rest room. The baby, now a week overdue, must have squeezed her bladder to the size of a teaspoon. She should not have tried to take a walk, but she was *so* bored sitting at home she could not contain herself. She spied a crack of light at the photographer's store window and hurried to bang at the door with her fist.

"I need to use your bathroom," she said, brushing past the young man who opened the door.

"It's through the door in back and to your right, Molly," he said.

She glanced back, but failed to recognize who he might be. Several minutes later, when she returned, she still felt puzzled. "Are you a friend of my brothers?"

"I'm Billy," he said, "Billy McPherson." His freckled face crinkled into a smile. "You don't remember me. I was only ten when you were our nanny."

Molly looked at him in amusement. Nanny? She had not thought of her stay at the McPhersons in that light. "And big as I am now, you recognized me," she said.

He flushed. "I shouldn't have called you Molly," he said. He looked at the cartons in his hands, as if just discovering them. He placed them under the counter before he looked at her again. "I thought about you forever, when you left," he said. "I knew you never took that ring. Mama 'found' it about six months later."

Molly winced. She had almost managed to forget that terrible day and that terrible woman. How funny that Billy MacPherson was so glad to see her — and apparently had his mother's number. He did not mention his father, equally despicable from Molly's point of view, but she now remembered Billy, a little runt of a fellow who loved her stories. No one else paid him any mind. She wondered again at the power of a little attention over someone who needs to be mothered.

Billy could not stop talking, now. He took his broom, held it without making a stroke, and then absent-mindedly put it back in the corner. "I'm entering Engineering at the Montana School of Mines this fall," he said. "Mr. Jacoby gave me a job when I was in high school, because I was the photographer on the yearbook staff. You remember Bobby? He's working for Hearst this summer, same alma mater and all, plus all that ACM money to slather in."

"How's Susan? Do you remember our play about Lady Ragnell and King Arthur?" Molly asked.

"Do I?" he shouted. "That's Susan to the life! A female Ambrose Bierce. She's got half the faculty at Montana State scared to death of her — can turn into a witch any time she pleases, or charm the birds out of the skies. Wait 'til I tell her you're here!"

Molly got carried away in their talk and found herself impressing Billy with the excitement of living in San Francisco and with her current status. She described her husband as an architect. Finally, she looked at the clock.

"I have to go, Billy, but it's been such fun."

"Please come back when the baby's born," Billy begged. "Mr. Jacoby loves to feature the portrait of a beautiful mother and child in one window. It's great for business."

Molly said, "At least, I promise to stop by to show you the baby."

She found herself grinning inside, as she walked out the door. What a great way to stick her finger in Mrs. McPherson's eye, after all these years. She felt a twinge of conscience, however, when she realized that she had again fallen into the exaggeration she had promised Sister Magdalene she would avoid.

Her marriage puzzled the family. They sat around the table drinking endless cups of tea. "Why do you want to marry a German?" Frank asked. "You're taking on trouble."

Tom added, "Stella and I are getting married in the spring. She has a big Italian family who love babies. We can take it until you find someone who isn't a foreigner."

"A couple of guys in Butte would still like to marry you," Frank said. He got up to look for Lizzie's cookie jar, then brought it to the table.

Molly squeezed Tom's hand and shook her head. "You want your own children. You'll like Hans when you get to know him." She sounded quite convincing, she thought, as she described this man who intended to take good care of her.

The birth went smoothly. On a warm August afternoon, Elizabeth came easily into the world. Molly's twelve-year-old brother, James, stayed at the hospital as long as the nurses would let him. He did everything he could think of for his sister, and then he carried the news to Lizzie and his brothers, who turned up en masse to welcome the baby. Everyone loved that she was a girl.

Lizzie was as proud as if she produced the baby herself. "Of course, I'm very young to be a grandmother," she said.

Molly was tired but happy the next morning. She burped her daughter and let her be taken to the nursery. The room was filled with sunshine and the scent of roses. Tom brought the flowers from his florist, future father-in-law.

Then the attending nurse remarked, while looking over her notes, "I see your husband hasn't come in to see the baby, yet."

Molly flushed with sudden anger. The woman sounded like Mrs. McPherson, condescending. How dare she! Molly found herself inventing a story of a business problem that kept her architect husband in California. She contained her temper and the story, but nonetheless the following day she signed the birth certificate, listing Hans Frings, Architect, as her husband and father of the baby. She worried though that she was losing control of herself. Mrs. McPherson, Trudy, Chel, and herself, each hiding something. Why did she lie?

Two weeks later, Elizabeth was baptized with Molly's mother Lizzie, and her brother Pat, as the godparents.

Having determined again that Montana held nothing for her, Molly took her 12-year old brother James and 6-week old daughter Elizabeth to San Francisco on the train. She left behind two charming sepia portraits in the photographer's store window. Billy McPherson forwarded them to her six months later.

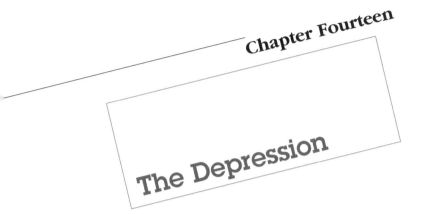

Chapter Fourteen

The Depression

September 1929

The train slowly chugged into Southern Pacific's terminal at the Oakland Mole. Molly, holding her freshly diapered and blanketed baby with one arm, gripped her handbag and a small valise with the other. James helped the porter move the heavy suitcases to the vestibule of their Pullman car. The car lurched back, then forward to its final stopping place before the porter swung the metal step out and allowed them to descend. Molly relished the small rituals of the trip. It was now a short walk to the ferry ramp. She could already smell the salt water and creosote from the wharf. The scent never failed to excite her. It locked into the first glimpse she had of San Francisco from the trip with Trudy years ago. James lifted the suitcases onto the wooden baggage cart, and Molly walked briskly ahead. She wanted a seat on the ferry that would allow her to watch the city grow closer.

When Molly reached the upper deck, she sat down on a curved wood-slatted bench, thick with layers of paint to protect against the weather. She settled the baby in her lap and opened her traveling blanket. With one hand, she reached into her hand baggage and put a bonnet on her daughter's head to shelter her from the sun, then sat back with a sigh of contentment.

Water sloshed against the pilings and gulls circled in the air as the ferry pulled away from the dock. It was still early morning. The Indian summer sun sparkled on the gentle waves of the bay, turning them into a sequined cloth. Molly raised her nose and sniffed. Not yet, but soon they'd catch the strong aroma of roasting coffee from the distant wharves in front of the Hills Brothers sheds.

"So this is Frisco." James was standing beside her, hands on his hips. The first sight of so much water and the ungainly, three-leveled ferry with the city in the distance had James goggle-eyed. Molly laughed.

"Yes, and where Butte has miners, San Francisco has tens of thousands of seamen, longshoremen, and all the other people involved with ships — and there are more musicians here than the doctors and lawyers put together."

James, with a Jimmy Durante grin, jumped into a sailor's horn-pipe stance and flung his hand out for applause. "I'll fit right in," he said in Durante's hoarse growl. He was Ma's son all right; Molly laughed to herself as he went off to explore the boat.

For her, sights, experiences, and feelings were the heart of San Francisco. The new house she and Hans had bought was far out in the western section of the city near Sigmund Stern Grove, with its eucalyptus trees and the sand dunes that stretched to the long beach. She had no idea what living in that district would be like, but she felt a bubbling happiness of anticipation as she watched the waves swirl around the boat.

They were approaching the harbor now. She could see the rows of pilings through which they would dock and the metal gate ready to be lowered as a passenger ramp. She thought she could see Hans in the crowd waiting for the ferry to dock.

She had thought about Hans in the long stretches of time on the train. She didn't love him with the wild surge of feelings she'd had for Chel, but he attracted her and she no longer wanted helpless fascination. She felt Hans was solid, practical, and steady; she could count on him. If he still wanted it, she was ready to be married in the church. The sacrament would strengthen their bond.

She snuggled her baby and murmured, "Oh Elizabeth, I am so glad we're home."

Hans smiled when he saw them and took the baggage from James acknowledging him, "Molly wrote she'd bring you down with her," then was pre-occupied getting them underway. He was not one for public display of affection any more than he was for conversation, but Molly did wish he had stopped long enough to look at the baby. Elizabeth was sound asleep despite the hubbub around her. So different from the boys Molly remembered taking care of as babies. Hans tucked James and her and the baby into his old Ford, and they were on their way to the Avenues.

The one-story stucco house with its red tiled roof was more beautiful than she remembered. Two small areas of clipped lawn flanked the entrance to the garage. The real surprise lay in the kitchen and stopped her on the sill of the doorway. Hans had enlarged the window that looked toward the back yard and the sea, and made an alcove bench around the kitchen table. Although there was only sand outside, a pot of Begonias sat on the table.

Hans pointed to the plant. "Our garden," he said. "Now see the rest of the kitchen."

She did, and gasped. It was a miracle of pale green counter space and cabinets and tidy as a ship's mess hall with everything out of sight. Hans grinned as she opened one door after another. A pull-down ironing board with a metal alcove for the iron; a cabinet for brooms and mops; cabinets for dishes, cups, and glassware; drawers for cutlery, silverware, and linens; below-counter cabinets for the cast iron pots and frying pans. There was even a new light over the sink. She could reach everything she needed for cooking from the magnificent Wedgwood stove which gleamed silver and black in pristine beauty.

Molly flung her free arm around him. "Oh Hans, it's wonderful! How did you ever do this in the few months I've been gone?"

He smiled as he held her in his arms. "It's good, yes." Then he glanced at the baby between them. "Let me take a look at this baby who kept you so busy in Montana." He cradled Elizabeth's head in his hand and looked at her, and then he took her in both hands and held her up to check her length. Elizabeth gurgled. "She's all right," he said.

"All right?" Molly said, holding her arms out to take the baby back. "You must be blind. Elizabeth's perfect. I can't ever remember seeing a more perfect baby."

Hans laughed and shook his head. "You see her with mother's eyes. Did I tell you I have a sister named Elizabeth? It's a good name."

Molly suddenly realized she had not consulted Hans at all. She could not remember if she had even mentioned that Elizabeth Patricia was named after her grandmother Lizzie, and her uncle Patrick. There were things she needed to talk to Hans about, but not with James around.

They took most of the afternoon to unpack. Earlier in the week, Lizzie had sent down a bassinet with baby clothes, blankets, and heaps of diapers. A baby carriage was due to arrive soon. The suitcases were crammed with Lizzie's sheets from the Finlan Hotel and other gifts. Then more unpacking. Molly's boxes of household goods and clothes from the apartment were brought up from the garage. James was ensconced in the extra bedroom, and the house settled.

Molly noted there was no food in the icebox, but Hans produced some cans of tuna fish, mayonnaise, and bread to toast from the pantry.

"I've something to cheer you up," he said. "My friends, the Burkarts, have been feeding me while you were away. We're going there tonight for supper, and tomorrow . . ." He paused and smiled. "Trudy is back and living in Mill Valley. You know that guy she went off with in his private rail car to New York?"

Molly nodded and her thoughts drifted to her last conversation with Trudy. Trudy had left shortly after Molly told her she planned to marry. What a day that had been! Trudy took Molly's break with Chel without surprise.

"I wish you had told me he was Jewish! I could have warned you. When Jewish boys want to play around and go too far, they do it with a shiksa, never with a Jewish girl," she had said.

"How come *you* know so much?" Molly had asked.

Trudy had just pursed her lips and nodded. "My mother told me things. I *know* what I'm talking about."

She was not enthused about the marriage plan, either.

"Oh Molly, are you sure you want . . ."

Molly had cut her off. "Hans is kind, practical . . . he wants a family and there's a strength in him I trust. He will do whatever it takes to protect me. I've never had that."

"But, you can do better . . ." Trudy had difficulty getting her words together. "He's different from us. He seems kind, but what do you know of him? You don't need . . ."

Trudy always thought she knew what Molly should do, and knew more than Molly did. Well, this was Molly's decision, not Trudy's. She told her so in no uncertain terms. "What do *you* know about making a family?" she had asked. "I bet you don't even know about Jews. You are making it up. They're no different than anyone else!" Molly's cheeks burned — all the insulting things she said — but she was sick to death of Trudy thinking she had all the answers.

Molly shook her head. Hans was still talking about Trudy and her ship owner boyfriend, Ted Cooke. "He must have fallen for her, because he's set her up with a bungalow on the side of Mt. Tamalpais. From its porch, you can see the entire bay. She wants us to spend Sunday with her. She says you can spend the week, if you want to, because the guy's away on family matters. She'd have gone with him, otherwise."

"Sounds like Trudy's following in her mother's footsteps. I don't know that I want to see her."

"Don't be that way, Molly. Trudy has a good heart. You know that."

"Maybe I'll get in touch with Trudy next week," Molly said, "but right now I just want to be here in this house. After the Burkarts, we can show James the city. Next week, I will have him take care of Elizabeth while I talk to Jay Barton about some work."

"I don't want my wife to work," Hans said flatly.

Molly decided to say nothing further. She did not doubt Hans was glad to see her, but he seemed subdued, almost strained.

The tasty dinner of pork roast and sweet and sour cabbage cheered Hans. He laughed and chatted with Mrs. Burkart and her teenage daughter, Alvina, as if they were his own family. Molly was glad to have James with her; she did not understand German. She would ask Hans to speak more English if they visited again.

It was late when they returned home. James had fallen asleep in the car, so he went to bed. Elizabeth, the world's perfect baby, had been fed before supper and slept through the talk. She now wanted more milk. Molly breast-fed her and settled her into the bassinet while Hans watched in sleepy-eyed contentment. He joined Molly by the bassinet and removed her night wrap. He kissed her eyes, the inside shell of her ears, then her mouth. "Now it is my turn to taste your breast," he said and pulled her to the bed.

Molly wanted to make love again in the early morning, and then she slept. She woke with a ravenous appetite and an urge to talk. She told Hans how much she had missed him. She did not mention that she had only realized this physically last night. She told him that she wanted to be married to him, and, if he still wanted this, they should get the marriage blessed without further waiting. She had not told her family it was a civil marriage, so she did not want James involved. Molly was full of words and plans. A half hour must have passed before she noticed that Hans had not commented on any of it.

"What's wrong?" she asked.

"Molly, I don't want to bring a cloud to your happiness. I've missed you. I want everything to be as you want it to be, but I am concerned how I will be a good provider for us if I do not get some good paying dock work soon."

"What do you mean?"

"You see how much work I've put into the kitchen. I wish I could say it was done at night and on the weekends." He pursed his lips together ruefully. "The fact is there's been almost no work. Everyday, first thing, I'm at the docks." His eyes hardened. "I've been lucky to get two days work a week. It was good to have this to do."

"You know so many things about wood, electricity, and plumbing. Could you find work like that?"

"I've tried," he admitted, "but carpenters are dime a dozen. They make less money than on the waterfront." Hans rubbed his forehead and grimaced. "Molly, the times are hard and getting worse. I thought of going back to the lumber camps, but no one is cutting."

Molly fought down a chill of fear. "It's been a long time, but I know what it was like when the mines shut down in Butte. There was no work anywhere, but people found ways to manage. We will too."

After a moment, Hans shrugged. "You're fresh home and now I make you feel bad. Don't worry. I'll take care of you. I will figure out how to do it, whatever comes. It's just that I saw the same thing in Germany. People stopped buying. Then the businessmen invested less money. Production went down, more workers were laid off. So, more people had less money to buy and more people were laid off. It's a devil's circle."

Molly decided to say nothing further. James would be better off with Lizzie in Montana, but for a few weeks more he could care for the baby while she looked to see what she might do.

✖   ✖   ✖

The stock market crashed on Thursday, October 24, 1929. The Depression, already begun, was finally acknowledged as a national reality. The small amount of gold stock Molly had kept was worthless. The following week yielded only one day's work for Hans. Molly visited Barton's to show off her baby.

"She's a beauty, Molly," Barton smiled.

"Mr. Barton, I might be interested in a short hours job, if you could fit me in." Molly said.

Barton bit his lip and looked away, momentarily. "Call me next month, Molly, but I don't know that I'll have work for you. I'm dealing with what you warned me about. Most of my accounts seem to be dead losses." He rubbed the back of his neck. "You were lucky to cash out your stock when you did and get it down on your house," he said.

She agreed with him, but did not mention that she was going to the bank to see if they would accept 'interest-only' payments for a while, until she and Hans could get more money. Six months ago, the payments on the house had seemed as easy as rent and the interest trivial. No longer. They had paid cash for most of the furniture, but had to make monthly payments on the beautiful Wedgwood stove.

"I don't see how we can keep it." Hans had said.

Molly argued passionately, "Let's not give it up until we have to. I'll find the money somehow."

Molly visited St. Dominic's parish rectory and talked to one of the monks about having their marriage blessed in the Church. She arranged to have this done on the following Saturday.

Macaroni and cheese with green peas wasn't much of a dinner, but she prepared it and set the table with a vase of white marguerites a neighbor, Mrs. Ortiz, had given her. "I talked to Father O'Dowd, today," she said. "He offered to marry us at two o'clock in the priest-house parlor."

Hans, looking at the paper, mumbled something that sounded like assent.

"That way we wouldn't have the expense of a wedding mass," she said. "But it seems too cold, don't you think? I told him, even without a Mass, we'd prefer to be married at the altar, maybe in a side chapel."

Hans glanced up. "Ja, that's fine. I have to be at a meeting in the morning, but two is okay."

"I'll have to buy some flowers, but the cost of candles is included in the stipend."

Hans was back reading his paper and waved off her information about the church arrangements "Whatever you want. Makes no difference to me."

They were married in St. Dominic's at a side altar, without guests. Two Dominican brothers acted as witnesses. The stained glass windows of the gothic church, brilliant gems of color in the sunlight seemed distant and cold on this foggy day. As she watched the flickering candles on the altar, Molly felt a shiver of terror invade her body. What a terrible time. Would they ever celebrate their anniversary?

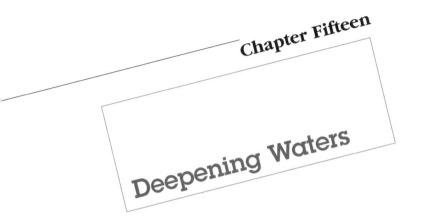

Chapter Fifteen

Deepening Waters

1932

H ans turned on the radio, waiting for the evening news. Molly sat at the table, darning his socks while he pulled out the percolator to make coffee. Elizabeth was already in bed.

"We went through bad times in Butte, but this is so much worse," Molly said.

Hans nodded. "Four million men without jobs last year, eleven million this year. Before Germany went bankrupt, this is what it was like."

"Why won't Hoover do something?"

"Huh? He doesn't believe in handouts."

"Good evening, Mr. and Mrs. America, and all the ships at sea. This is Walter Winchell with the news." Hans turned the radio knob to get rid of the radio's crackling sound. A clearer connection came in. *"Today the 'Bonus Army' Veterans' encampment in Washington, D.C. was attacked. Army Commander Douglas MacArthur and his aide, Dwight Eisenhower, with the men under their command, fired on the Veterans, drove them from the city, and burned their tents and possessions . . . ."*

"Do you wonder the homeless call their cardboard and packing case shacks, Hoovervilles?" Hans said.

✖   ✖   ✖

A group of dock workers sat over coffee at Red's Java Cafe after the morning shape-up. Red chalked the specials on a board near the window while Hans watched the whitecaps. The men had been on the wharf since 5 AM, with fifty men for each job available.

The door whipped open and banged the wall with the force of the wind as another seaman entered. Henry spoke in a low voice to Hans. "See the little squinty-eyed guy? That is Pete Ackerman, a union organizer. He was a news-paperman in New York. Then he came out to work for the *Examiner*. He lasted six months until he was fired for turning in stories opposite to the editor's point of view. He's got interesting things to say. You should stick around."

Pete nodded to Henry and carried his coffee and a plate of fried eggs and potatoes to the table. Henry said, "Hans here thinks a bigger crisis is coming, the same kind that's pushing Germany deeper into Fascism."

"Sounds like the roof's coming off," Pete glanced up at the rafters then out the window. He turned to Henry. "What do you say?"

"I think it's more likely we'll go socialist," Henry put his elbows on the table and leaned forward. "America's not bitter enough to go for the Nazis, but it's never been this bad. Half the country's going to be living in hobo jungles or Hooverville shacks before we know it. Every week I know someone else who's lost his home."

"It's been three months since I've been able to make a payment," Hans admitted. "We got a mortgage foreclosure notice last week, 'pay up or get out'."

"What're you going to do?" Pete asked.

Hans hunched his shoulders, his face blank. "One of my wife's friends has a two-room apartment over a saloon on Lincoln Way. We can use that for a while."

"People should realize what's going on," Pete said. "Almost everyone in this town, one way or another, makes his money from the cargo going in and out."

"I agree," Henry said. "But none of 'em speak out for us."

Pete signaled for more coffee. "Well, Sinclair Lewis does, and Diego Rivera did a great 'Up Yours!' with Lenin's picture in the Stock Exchange mural," Pete laughed.

"What grates me," Henry said, "is how Hearst with his anti-labor rag works hand in hand with the ship owners. All that law and order propaganda about anarchist Wobblies that Hearst put out was a smoke screen. D'you think the guys who live in the Sunset or Richmond Districts with their desk jobs downtown know diddily about what's really going on? The city newspapers don't write it and the Catholic *Monitor* won't touch it."

"Yeah." Pete pursed his mouth. "The Churches, someone like Archbishop Hanna, should say something about these mortgage foreclosures and guys out of work."

"And ruffle the feathers of big contributors to his Boys' School?" Hans raised his eyebrows.

The waiter limped over to the table with a metal coffee pot.

"How's the leg, Joe?" Henry asked.

"Days like this, I'm glad I got an inside job."

Pete said, "Ever seen the *Catholic Worker*, a newspaper Dorothy Day edits? It tells the truth and Church officials ignore it. But the point is, there is enough work to go around. Even with the Depression, we are handling millions of tons of freight."

Hans said, "There's work, but look at the dock. Most of the men who worked today are paying kickbacks to the crimp doing the hiring, or such kiss-asses that they're willing to take shifts of 24 hours overtime without extra pay."

"That's because we don't control the hiring hall," Pete said.

Henry took a small sack of Bull Durham from his shirt pocket and rolled a cigarette. "Right. Controlling the hiring hall is more important than money or the number of men looking for work. We could divide the jobs and see that each man got one."

"Fat chance," Hans grunted.

"The shape-up is a slave mart," Henry said.

"Yeah," Hans said, "but I'm nobody's slave."

Pete hunched his shoulders and put his hands palm up. "What else do you call it, hanging around the wharf all day in the hopes of getting two to three hours work in the afternoon — on the boss's terms?"

"Yet you think *this* is the time to organize, when men are so desperate?" Hans scoffed, "They'd leap at an opportunity to scab!" Better for them not to hope than be fools, Hans thought. To hope was to lose. He'd hoped to be an architect. What a dumkop*f.* He rose to his feet.

Pete leaned back to look at him. "I'm talking about organizing *us*," Pete said. "Getting us to figure it out. An injury to one is an injury to all of us. We've got to take over the hiring hall." Pete set his cup down and took out a cigarette. "There's a lot of organizing going on in most seaports now. We can link up the Atlantic and the Pacific with ports in Europe and major ports in Asia."

Hans shrugged. "I've never seen a union yet that stood up for the working stiff. Unions get sold out by their leaders," he said. "The officers sit on their fannies and play ball with the employers."

"We can make a different kind of union," Henry said.

"Strong workers do better to rely on themselves," Hans said. He put change for his coffee on the table and walked out the door.

The storm had thinned to steady drops of rain. Hans decided to pick up soup bones and vegetables from the Crystal Palace, but found himself veering toward City Hall. Men and a few women were milling around, some with signs demanding jobs. The streets had been blocked off to traffic. Motorcycle cops and police mounted on horses tried to keep the crowd of several hundred from reaching Mayor Rossi and the supervisors in their well guarded domed building. Hans had just walked past the demonstrators when all hell seemed to break loose. Police moved from their vans, clubs swinging. Mounted police pushed into the demonstrators. The people scattered, yelling, screaming and not knowing where to turn.

The cops spared no one and there were a lot of cops. Hans saw one hit a middle-aged woman hard on the face. She collapsed unconscious on the sidewalk. He reached out to stop her from being trampled, but he was clubbed aside. Others pulled her to safety.

Hans, his arm bruised and one eye swelling shut, continued to walk, disgusted that he hadn't been able to do more. He thought about the groups of police in front of City Hall watching their fellow officers pursue and club the fleeing demonstrators. Men fighting men was one thing, but to club a woman who hadn't lifted a hand? She should not have been on the street at a time like this, but something was wrong with men who would do that. This was what Nazis were like.

✖   ✖   ✖

Molly took her porcelain teapot to the stove. Her tears, seeping out, matched the rain. She turned the gas flame off beneath the steel kettle and poured the boiling water over a teaspoon of Lipton's black tea already in the pot. Lizzie's prescription for any time of trouble, "First, put the kettle on. We will have a cup of tea, then we'll talk about it."

Lizzie could not help her now. The trouble was too big. They were losing this house. When he got home, Hans would disconnect the stove and bring it to the Burkhart's basement for storage. She wished she could throw up. Hans was angry that she would not give the stove up and insisted on their trying to keep up the payments. The mortgage on their house had been foreclosed. They would be evicted soon. Their down payment, her savings, everything was lost.

"Molly," Hans had said. "We can't spend what we haven't got. God in heaven, don't you realize . . . when this house goes, my dream goes as well as yours? We have to live with the reality of these times."

"I earn enough to make payments on the stove."

"And you leave Elizabeth alone for three hours every afternoon while you work at the candy store to do it."

"It's her time to nap, she's all right."

"I don't want you to work. I have been finding enough work to pay for a small apartment and to feed us. We just have to live on what I make."

Molly closed her mouth then and hadn't said another word. He did not understand. She needed to work. She couldn't stand the silence. She could not stand her thoughts. It wasn't Elizabeth who caused this wild hatred of being shut in. Elizabeth was an easy baby, much easier to take care of than her uncles had been.

Hans was stubborn and impossible to talk with unless it was something he wanted to talk about. He would not talk to her about the waterfront. "It's men's business; better that you don't have to think about it." He was gone sixteen hours a day, sometimes more. There was no conversation between them; no shared dream. She felt nothing when she looked at him, only a panicky question: how did it happen she was married to a stranger? She felt so helpless. The city she loved had been taken from her. The house *wasn't* her dream. She didn't know that, until everything of her earlier life in San Francisco was gone. She felt her heart beating faster. She could feel the rage coming. She closed her hand around the cup and flung it against the kitchen wall.

We can survive, he said, just live on what he makes. She didn't want to *survive*. She wanted to have what she had . . . She had survived all her life . . . took care of Ma and the boys. When she stopped, she found she wanted something for herself — her life. Four years in which she could do, have, and be anything she wanted.

One stupid mistake, then another one . . . and another. Now everything was gone.

Molly grasped the saucer and hurled it after the cup. She pushed away from the table, stood and kicked the chair back. She wanted to yowl with rage and throw every piece of crockery in the kitchen, yes, and to break the windows of Hans' precious cupboards. Why should the bank get what he had slaved to create?

Like a splash of cold water on her face, her words woke her up. Hans had slaved to make this kitchen beautiful. It was beautiful. She flung herself down at the table and sobbed.

No, it was not Hans' fault, but she couldn't live with him. That much was clear. He acted like he owned her, that his decisions were best for them both. Well, he did not own her. Elizabeth was her mistake and she had to pay for it. She had used Hans; talked herself into thinking she cared for him enough. She couldn't forgive herself for that, but how would she survive in San Francisco without him? She went to the sink, ran a cloth under cold water, and held it against her eyes.

Lots of women would be glad for a few dollars a week to look after the baby. Maybe she couldn't find as good a job as she had at Barton's, but she was clever and she still could do anything she set her mind to. She would figure out how to manage. First, she'd line up a job, then she'd tell Hans she was leaving him.

Molly stood in the hall at the small ledge that held the phone. Six rings, did she have the right number? She dialed again. The phone was finally picked up, but she did not recognize the woman's voice who answered.

"May I speak to Mr. Barton, please?"

"I'm sorry. He's not available."

"This is Molly Dyer . . . Frings, I mean. Would you ask him to call me?"

"I'm sorry, Miss, it may be awhile before he gets the message. Mr. Barton filed for bankruptcy last month and we're finishing up the inventory now."

"I — I'm sorry to hear that." Molly bit her lip, close to tears. Jay Barton, but why? People always needed groceries. The accounts receivable? . . . his stock — probably everything was gone.

A week of looking for work, of calling everyone she could think of who might help her. Nothing. Two hours a day, five days a week at the Betsy Ross Candy Store was what she could count on, nothing more. Maybe she should call Gertrude. She might know somebody. Molly shook her head. No, Gertrude, the cynic who didn't believe anything, was the one who knew what was what. Molly no longer felt any certainty — about anything. She could not talk to Gertrude.

She was sick to death of everything. The nausea . . . when was her last menstrual period? NO. No, she couldn't be . . .

The door of the cage shut. Black, darkness closing in. NO! She shrieked. God, you *can't* do this to me.

Elizabeth woke and cried.

✖ ✖ ✖

Molly did not want this second pregnancy. She realized she was trapped. She could not face going; she couldn't face staying. She did not know what to do. It seemed bizarre that Hans took the news so easily.

"Aren't you worried about the expense?"

She wanted to fight with him, wanted him to protest, but he said only, "What expense is a baby? Cheer up, Molly, I'll find a way to manage." He lifted her chin. "Look, don't be so downcast. I've got some extra change. Ask the neighbors to keep an eye on Elizabeth, and I'll take you to see *Anna Christie* to celebrate."

Celebrate?

It worked. Molly was swept out of her problems for a while. Garbo was wonderful in her first talkie. The alcoholic father with his helpless daughter forced into prostitution oddly eased Molly's black mood. Her own life could be worse. She did not leave the theater with the sense of fury and despair she had felt while watching Marlene Dietrich's "Blue Angel."

✖   ✖   ✖

Pete Ackerman raised his eyebrows when he saw Hans at the Albion Hall entryway just outside the meeting room. Noise from talk and small disputes filled the air.

"Just the guy we need," he said. "Look here, the first step toward turning the tables." He handed Hans a mimeographed sheet titled THE WATERFRONT WORKER. The lead story was on the old frame-up of Tom Mooney in the 1916 strike and said he needed to get a new trial. Several spaces were blocked in with penciled titles for other articles.

"This is a mock-up of the paper we're going to put out next month. We're looking for stories about what's going on at the docks."

Hans said, "I'm not a writer."

Pete laughed. "What you are is such an independent cuss that none of the bosses would suspect you of distributing this gem. The stories are from the point of view of ordinary working stiffs," he said. "All you have to do is take a bundle whenever the printer sends them to us. Keep 'em under your jacket until you find a place where the men congregate, then drop them when nobody's looking. Others of us will do the same. Don't leave too many in any one place. People will pass them on. Are you willing?"

Hans looked at the clumsy format. Did these clowns think this was going to be a powerful public influence? "Ja, sure." Hans left then and pushed into the meeting that had already begun.

Harry Bridges said, "The ship owners have enormous incomes. We need to know how much and where it comes from." Harry believed in knowing who you were dealing with and having all the facts before you made a move. An attitude Hans approved of.

Harry Bridges and other members of the team sat at a small table beside a blackboard. Jim Liguori, a fact finder with a gravelly Brooklyn accent, walked to the front of the hall and pointed to a blackboard that had dates, names, and columns of figures chalked in.

"The ship owners worked a sweet deal to get tax subsidies for building ships during the war," he said. "Their Hearst flacks got Congress so worked up they ordered 3000 ships — more than the entire merchant marine of the world! The *first* ship they built came sliding down the ways exactly one month *after* the armistice was signed." A rumble of words started in the audience. "And they had 2999 boats still to build for a war that was over!"

"Wait," Liguori said, "there's more."

He moved to the next column of figures. "During the next three years, one million tons of wood and concrete ships were launched with no conceivable need for them. They were just lined up, more and more of them each year, one next to the other in the bone yard."

Liguori paused to let the absurdity of this sink in. Mumbling filled the room.

"Can you *believe* it!" he asked. He thumped the table with the flat of his hand. "If you want to understand something, you follow the money."

Liguori paused to light a cigarette. He drew in deeply as he glanced at the hall filled with men waiting on his words. "Get this," he said. "The majority of the ships were to be *scrapped* and the remainder turned over to the steamship companies to operate in foreign trade."

There was shuffling and murmurs in the audience, but the men were listening.

"In 1928, Congress passed the Jones-White bill that gave subsidies to owners in foreign trade," he said. "They gave them mail contracts. They *said* the bill was to get a high standard of living for American workingmen and develop a merchant marine. But what did this gem of legislation do?"

"For sure it didn't get us anything!" One of the men burst out.

A brief gap-toothed smile flickered over Liguori's face. "First thing, the government sold the ships to private companies for *two cents on the dollar.*"

He pointed to the black board again.

"An example of the miraculous good fortune that fell to these ingenious capitalists is the Export Steamship Company. They got 18 ships for two cents on the dollar. Then, in a single year, they transported *3 pounds* of mail, for which, the government paid them two hundred and thirty five thousand dollars."

Liguori squared his shoulders, then continued in a hard, rapid voice, "Last year they raised their capacity to *8 pounds* of mail and received one hundred twenty six thousand dollars *per pound*."

"Subsidy?" Pete yelled, "I call it a give-away of tax money, and Captain Dollar took another 10% for himself to *negotiate* the deal."

Harry Bridges opened the floor to questions and comments. Everyone seemed to have something to say, serious, funny, or obscene.

One man summed it up. "The S.O.B.'s are supposed to give us a living wage. We're averaging $10.45 a week, and they're raking in millions of tax dollars."

Henry spoke up from the audience. "Right," he said. "The Dollar Company, which had the lion's share of the earlier subsidy, didn't use *any* of it for American working men. They employed Chinese seamen and had the contract ships overhauled in Chinese shipyards by coolie labor, yet they got their entire fleet from our government."

Henry added an aside to Pete, "Someday we got to think about organizing labor in China. The capitalists don't get the connection between the civil war that's heating up there and their own skullduggery."

"I think they get it all right," Pete said. "They just won't stop as long as they can make a profit. In the past ten years, they've skimmed off almost $14,000 for every dollar they invested in that fleet."

"With the Hearst papers cheering 'em on, every step of the way." Liguori said.

"We need to get our side heard," someone said.

"We will." Pete Ackerman held the WATERFRONT WORKER mock-up in his hand. "We will."

Hans shook his head. A mimeographed sheet against Hearst?

✖ ✖ ✖

Molly sat ironing on the porch and thought about the snow. It was almost nightfall. The one-bedroom cottage they had moved into was not insulated. She had opened the oven door to help the gas floor furnace, but it wasn't doing much. San Francisco was not supposed to have snow.

Nothing was supposed to be the way it was in 1932.

Elizabeth had drawn a straight-backed chair to the window and stood on it, absorbed in watching the snowflakes turn to water and trickle down the pane of glass. She wore her one-piece dancing costume under the too-big sweater

Lizzie had sent.

Molly fingered the cloth of a lightly starched dress. Too dry. She flicked water to dampen it, then rolled it and put it in the icebox with Hans' one white shirt. "Your Gramma's coming next week," she said. "Pretty soon, we'll have a new baby sister or a brother come to stay with us in the house."

Elizabeth did not seem interested. She'd discovered the *inside* of the windowpane was covered with water you couldn't see, unless you made a line through it with your finger.

✖ ✖ ✖

It was an adventure, Elizabeth thought. Gram snuck her up a back elevator in St. Mary's Hospital. Gram held her close under her coat and they both giggled. They walked down a dark hallway with a high ceiling and turned to enter a room. A woman sat in a bed in the corner. She smiled at Elizabeth, opened her sheet and invited Elizabeth to come sit next to her. She held a small red baby in her arms. It made a sound like crying, but maybe not. Elizabeth pushed her face against Gram's stomach and clung to her. She would not go near the woman on the bed.

"Two weeks in the hospital is too long, Molly," Gram laughed. "She's pretending not to recognize you."

Chapter Sixteen

Confrontations

M olly bathed Frankie in the kitchen sink. She talked to him and he gurgled back as she toweled him dry, and then she powdered him with Johnson's Baby Powder. After she diapered him, she pushed her hands against his feet and blew a kiss into his belly button. He laughed, and she caught him up in her arms. "Such a handsome fellow you are!" She nuzzled his neck and put him into the wooden playpen on the living room floor.

Three-year-old Elizabeth had made herself a sloppy peanut butter and jelly sandwich. She now had a red crescent mustache, sticky fingers, and a brown streak on her pinafore. Molly carried the pail of diapers to the toilet for their first rinse. Absorbed in her task, she failed to hear the knocking at the front door. When she came back into the front room she heard the knob rattling and saw Gertrude behind the small window set into the door.

"Hi, I'm here. Come on, let me in."

Gertrude's mass of golden curls was newly styled, tucked in at the base of her neck. She wore an elegant mid-calf outfit that shouted City of Paris. Molly gritted her teeth and resolved not to let herself think about the cotton housedress she herself wore. A green

1932 Studebaker roadster stood in front of the house, no doubt a gift from her lover, Edward T. Cooke. Molly did not know how to drive. When last seen, Gertrude had not known either. The car and the lover, two other items not to mention. She would not let her see *any* touch of envy.

"Trudy, what a surprise!" she said.

They had talked a few times by phone during the past three years, but Molly avoided all invitations and didn't mention Hans' suggestions that she invite Trudy for Christmas or holidays. She didn't even want to think about why. Finally it seemed their break was complete. To find Gertrude on her doorstep, well — Molly pictured herself pushing Gertrude out the door, down the steps, then kicking the gate shut.

Trudy was her laughing, bubbly self. "What a darling cottage, Molly. I love the drapes you've made." She walked to the baby, bent over and touched his cheek. "So this is Frankie." He beamed at her. "What a devilish smile," she said. "You're going to be a mischief-maker."

Eventually it was clear her effervescence could not lighten the weight of Molly's reluctant responses.

She turned to Molly, took her by the hand, led her to the couch, and sat down. "I want to hug you, but you're giving me your silent, stiff-as-a-board look that says you don't want to be hugged. I feel totally disapproved of, so I've come to have it out with you. How come you're my best friend, and you won't talk to me?"

Molly stared at Trudy for several seconds, then suddenly the constriction that had closed her throat burst. Her jammed-up feelings pushed into an explosive sob, and fragments of incoherent thought tumbled out, "so mad, and scared, I don't know what I feel anymore. I love the babies, but I'm lonely . . . If I just hadn't gotten myself into such a tangle . . . This isn't what I want. I'm like a cow moving around, doing what has to be done. Hans, is so . . . stubborn and — no way out — I feel like I'm in a prison."

How long it went on, she didn't know. Her next conscious awareness was that her nose was both stuffed up and running, she was breathing through her open mouth, and her throat was dry. Trudy held her and was wiping Molly's eyes with an already soaked handkerchief. The baby and Elizabeth were both crying.

It was so absurd. Molly stopped sniffling and had to laugh.

"God, I don't know how to talk any more. Let me pull myself together and take care of the children," she said. "I haven't been able to talk to myself, much less anyone else." She rose and put Frankie in his crib. Trudy stood beside her as she rocked and patted the baby's back until he was calm. Molly gathered Elizabeth up and brought her to a cot on the porch to nap. She sat on the couch again, picked up the handkerchief and blew her nose. "I can't even cry gracefully," she said. "My nose is probably red as a lantern."

"It is, and your eyes are swollen, but you're beautiful just the same," Trudy assured her.

"Oh Trudy, I've missed you, and our life. I don't know what to do, but every time I think of what I really want, I go into a rage." She tightened her fists, and then stretched them into fingers again. She straightened her back and slowed her breathing.

Trudy massaged Molly's shoulder, but said nothing.

"Trudy, I've been so mad at you! You knew about Hans, didn't you? You tried to tell me, but I did not want to hear you. I thought you were being a know-it-all."

"I didn't know," Trudy said, "I just had some hunches."

Molly frowned, "He goes away inside, and there's no light in him, just his hard will." She paused, awkward in her silence. "Had you been with him? I didn't think so, but . . ."

"Didn't you ask him?"

"No, it's only lately I've wondered," Molly said. "You know I kept blinders on about a lot of things. Your affairs, for example."

"Yeah, well, it wasn't much of an affair," Trudy said. "I would have told you if you had asked what he was doing in our apartment the time you met."

Trudy pulled herself into a more comfortable position on the couch. "When I got back that weekend, it was clear that he wanted to pursue you. I knew you said something had happened between you and Chel, but I didn't put it together about the baby until about a month before you got married." Trudy cocked her head. "And after you blew up at me."

Molly glanced at her, her eyes bleak as stones.

"You don't have to —" Trudy said.

Molly brushed the comment aside and shook her head. "You were right about Chel. I never heard from him again after he offered the abortion." Molly pressed her lips together, her face expressionless, then she swallowed.

"I wanted to die with the shame of it. How could I have been so dumb?" Molly hesitated. "But I'd never met anyone like him, he knew so many things. I wanted to *be* him, I think. He filled my mind. I wanted to be what he wanted me to be. I felt I was, but . . . I couldn't tell him anything difficult."

Trudy motioned toward her purse. "D'you mind if I smoke?" she asked. Molly shook her head.

"I could tell him stories about Ma, a widow from an English family. Butte as a mining town was okay, but I couldn't let him see her as a chambermaid, or tell him about us at the Good Shepherd." She paused and frowned.

"Worse, when he left, without wanting to see me again, I adopted his eyes. I saw myself as nothing but — an easy woman who didn't matter."

"You've always been so religious. What happened to that?"

Molly rubbed her hands over her forehead, "God . . . disappeared. I still don't . . . It's as if a color that once filled my life didn't exist anymore. When the emptiness came, I only noticed this time it was different from when Pa died, or when I was sent to the convent. It was emptier."

"I know," said Trudy.

"I can't talk to Hans, or my brothers, and, of course, not Ma," Molly continued. "Every one of them has an idea of me that isn't — me as I know myself. Even I don't want this me that nobody sees."

"Oh, pooh, I don't believe that," Trudy said. "You've been through some bad stuff and forgotten what good times we used to have. That's all it is. You are fun. You love gossip and jazz and all kinds of dancing and underneath it all, whether you remember it right now or not, you're still Sister Mary Magdalene, Junior."

Trudy took a cigarette from the package she held, tapped one end on her thumbnail and stared at it. "Furthermore, Doctor Wonderful was *not* the end of the universe! In fact, that damn vampire almost killed you off with his exquisite Southern sensibility and wonderfully tragic sense of life." Trudy shook her head. "I used to listen when he'd deign to speak. He didn't have an ounce of humor. You were the one supplying all the life."

"But he . . . I didn't know you saw him that way!"

"Before he corralled you, you were having a fine time — apart from sulking at me, of course — but basically going around thrilled with everything — the museums, the theater, every movie that's ever been made, and all those crazy heavy books you read and . . ."

"Yeah — everything there's no room for in my life anymore."

"Doesn't matter," Trudy said. "That walking emotional sponge temporarily drained you and you weren't prepared for the economic pit the country has dropped into."

"Trudy, you never told me you thought Chel didn't have feeling."

"You didn't ask me, dear heart, and now you just got to remember who you are."

"But I'm not . . . I don't know, my anger is eating me alive." Molly paused and rubbed the handkerchief along the lower rim of her eye lashes. "I don't have all that many choices anymore."

"Well, our friendship's one thing to hang onto, because we know who we were and who we are."

"I didn't know you felt that."

Trudy groaned and grabbed Molly into her arms. "Oh girl, sometimes, you are pure blind wart!"

As Molly pulled out of the hug, she said, "Trudy, you're skin and bones!"

"Too many meals of booze and cigarettes — but you know what they say, 'A woman can't be too thin or too rich.'"

"It's not rich I'm worried about, just surviving."

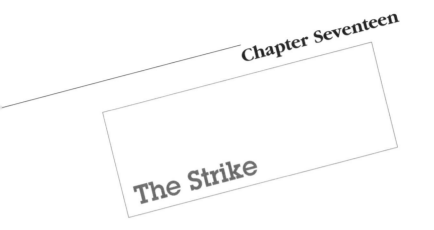

Chapter Seventeen

The Strike

February 1933

"What in hell were the ship owners thinking? A 10 cent cut to 75 cents an hour for dock workers — at Christmas, for Crissake?" Pete shook his head.

Henry picked up a copy of the *Waterfront Worker*. It was late Saturday afternoon and there was no other activity in the warehouse. A mote-filled slant of sun through the dirty window screened the far side of the room from view. The single cord bulb hanging from the ceiling provided barely enough light for him to read by. Printed sheets from three stencils Pete had cut the night before lay drying on the floor of the makeshift print shop until Henry could staple them. A printer friend of Pete's had lent them the room.

Pete snickered. "The rich guys' gift to themselves — ten cents an hour from each of us. Weird isn't it, just after the government dumped all that money in their laps!"

"Goes to show," Henry said, "there's no such thing as too much money for a capitalist, especially if he can take it from the wages of a poor working stiff." He braced his back against a barrel of lead slugs in the dusty warehouse office and settled down to read while Pete turned the mimeograph machine.

"Things are heating up," Pete said. "I'm tracking news stories and proclamations like that wage cut notice. Someday I'm going to make a book out of this stuff."

"Yeah?"

"That stack of yellow pages beside you on the filing cabinet."

Henry reached for the pages. He grunted. "They call us Communists, as if forming a union where *everyone* has his say would only make sense to a Communist. It used to be called democracy."

Pete nodded. "We don't need the CP to tell us about the class struggle. We spent fifty years in bloody union organizing before the CP existed."

J u n e   1 9 3 3

"We've got it!" Pete was jubilant. "Roosevelt's National Recovery Act says we have the right to join unions we choose and to bargain with the employers!"

Pete and Hans had joined Jim Liguori and Henry at Paddy Ryan's Bar, an enormous structure which ran from the entrance on the Embarcadero clear through to the next block. It was high noon, the place was crowded, and the air already stale with the smell of tobacco, sweat, and alcohol. Glasses lined the length of the bar, shot glasses for the most part, with water on the side. Henry hoisted his glass. "The sun's over the yardarm," he said.

"First one today, and God knows we need it," Hans answered.

Jim set his glass down. "D'you hear the Shipowners still claim 'the local doesn't represent the men.' This time they're going to up the wages a dime to see if they can knock some of us off."

"We weren't forced to join this union," one of the men standing next to Jim slammed his fist on the bar. "We've been knocking down the goddam doors to get in. If we start talking strike, they'll hear us!"

"It ain't easy to let everyone know what's going on," Jim said. "So we're going to fine anyone who doesn't come to the union meeting. That way we keep everyone informed and no little group of cronies can take over and run things."

May 1934 News releases

"Nothing complicated," Harry Bridges, chairman of the strike committee, said. "We want an hourly rate of one dollar, a thirty-hour week, a six hour day. Everyone gets a share of whatever work there is. And we regulate all hiring through the union hall. NO MORE SHAPE-UP."

(International Longshoremen Association San Francisco Union Local news conference)

The president of the Waterfront Employers told the newspapers, "Thousands of unemployed will be glad to get the jobs. I've already recruited 2,500 strikebreakers."

(Waterfront Employers Association news interview)

"On May 9 at 8 PM, we tied up the coast from Canada to Mexico when all West Coast dock workers walked out."

(Pete Ackerman's Journal notes)

✖   ✖   ✖

"The Embarcadero looks like a war zone," Hans said.

He and Henry were part of a thousand-man picket line parading two to four abreast. They walked the sidewalks in front of the docks where police guards were stationed. Two men at the head of the line carried an American flag and a Union banner. Heavy steel folding gates had been drawn shut at each of the piers and electrified barbed wire guarded the entrances. Additional police in radio cars, on motorcycles, and on horseback patrolled the wharf.

"D'you see the guy on the rooftop?" Henry asked. "He's a lookout with a radio phone. You can see the glint on his field-glasses when he looks this way."

Hans jeered, "Where's the hoard of scabs they promised would take our place — the colored folks and jobless who'd grab the chance to work?"

Henry turned to Pete, who had been double-timing his way up the line to join them. "You want to tell him, Pete?"

"Wait'll I catch my breath. I don't like the look of those black paddy wagons up ahead."

Three black police cars blocked the side street.

"They won't try anything today," Henry said. "They want to see how much strength we have."

"You want to know why no scabs?" Pete said to Hans, "I'll tell you. Bridges got to the ministers of every colored church in town and talked to the congregations. He told them the importance of this strike and said he knew they had been excluded from the wharf. He pledged, if they agreed to support the strike and refuse to scab, he'd see that everyone, regardless of race, would be included in full union membership. He got their pledge in return and they will be coming onto the picket lines tonight. I'm training three of them as recruiters."

Hans pushed his white longshoreman's cap to the back of his head. "I don't like the idea of mixed gangs with Negroes," he said.

"Well, you can stuff it," Pete said. "We aren't going to tolerate discrimination in union ranks."

Henry interrupted the tension growing between the two men. "Save it, you don't need to fight each other. Neither of you have dealt with professional strikebreakers. No sign of them yet, but they were all over the place in 1922."

"They're different from scabs?" Hans asked

"Yeah. Their specialty is slugging, not stevedoring."

Hans touched his belt. It held his cargo hook on the side. Pete nodded at him.

"Looks to me like the police are going to take the place of strikebreakers, but let 'em try," Pete said. "We're going to shut this town down if we have to."

Pete nudged Henry, "Look at the end of the line. They're here. Mike Casey, their president tried to block it, but Teamsters up and down the Coast are joining us on the picket line."

"The men are with us," Henry said. "So how come the union officers with salaries think like the ship owners?"

✖   ✖   ✖

Hans liked to have dinner on the table when he arrived home, but on Friday he was home early.

Molly asked, "How's the strike going?"

He yawned. "So-so." It was not worth talking about. He watched her prepare supper as he washed up at the kitchen sink.

She layered sliced potatoes into a black iron pot, alternating them with onions and bits of hamburger, salt, and pepper, then a small can of tomato sauce mixed with water. She covered the pot and put it into the oven. She put

Elizabeth on a chair next to her and, taking a bag of pea pods, showed her how to split the seam of the pod and push out the round peas.

Molly looked happier than she had been. Hans leaned against the door, thumbs in his pockets, watching her. "This morning we picked up some day old bread at Langendorf's," she said, "to feed the ducks when we walked home. Stow Lake was gorgeous. The azaleas are all out, and we found some sandboxes, swings, and a high round slide. But the real excitement was the merry-go-round. I had one nickel left and we spent it on rides. Frankie sat on my lap."

"And I had my own horsy," Elizabeth said.

Hans was too tired to talk, too tired to think. He couldn't imagine why Molly thought he'd be interested in the music of the carousel, how it made her feel, what it reminded her of. The Greens in Montana? Then she started with her questions, so many words. Hans admitted he was surprised at how rapidly support was mobilizing for the strike.

"What's happening with passenger boats?" Molly asked. She put the peas on to boil with salt and a dab of margarine.

"The Shipowners pretend everything is business as usual, but both Matson and the Pacific Hawaiian Lines have canceled sailings." Hans' eyes were half closed and he spoke slowly. "The Belt Line Railway's the only part of the wharf still working. Those guys with yellow dog civil service contracts can't strike without losing their pensions and seniority, so they go through the motions of work. Today, we parked our cars across the tracks and sat down on the rails. The crews were glad for an excuse to stop service."

Molly reached down plates from pantry shelves for Elizabeth to set the table. "I read the *News* and the *Call Bulletin* today. They say the ship owners are clamoring for the federal government to intervene. They also want Joe Ryan to come out from the International Longshoreman's Association in New York. What's that all about?"

"Joe Ryan may be the International President of the ILA, but he is *not* on our side. He has got his hands full trying to prevent the East Coast from going out. Listen though, Molly," Hans said, "don't bring a Hearst paper into this house. The union has heavy fines for that."

"I know. I read the Ortiz 's paper. I asked Mrs. Ortiz to give it to me instead of saving it for the ragman. I want to know what the ship owners are planning."

Hans tightened his eyes. "I don't want you putting your nose in this," he said. "I'll tell you what you need to know."

"Who do you think I am?" Molly sputtered. "I know as much about unions as you do. I want to know what's going on, but I don't need you to tell me what to think."

"You're my wife. This is far more dangerous than you have any ideas about."

"Hans, that's ridiculous. Pete's wife Nan volunteers two days a week doing office work for the union."

"That Commie, a crowing hen who acts and talks like a man," Hans' lips curled. "You shouldn't pay attention to anything *she* does. You've got me to make sure you and the children are protected, and I say you're not to get involved with this strike. You'll not go near the soup kitchen or the medical aid section. You'll do nothing, go no place at all. I absolutely forbid it!"

"Hans," Molly protested, "I don't know how you can talk this way. Is this some old country idea of what a hausfrau should be?"

"We should not speak any further of this now. We would both say things we'd regret later," Hans said.

Molly stared at him for a full minute. Then she finished preparing the supper and served it in silence.

He had not handled her right, he knew, but she needed to be curbed.

The strike was shutting everything down — lumber mills in the Northwest, grain shipments. Businesses everywhere felt the pinch as cargo rotted on the docks. McGrady, from the Department of Labor, sent telegrams to all employers and the ILA union asking that they appoint a committee to reach and sign an agreement that would bind both sides. On the evening of May 19 the longshoremen met at the Eagles' hall to consider McGrady's request. They didn't like it.

The close packed room was rumbling with talk when Henry and Hans arrived. Harry Bridges and the Local's team sat at the head table. Jim Liguori handed out ditto sheets so everyone could read the request and pro and con analysis.

"Where does the government get off asking us to sign a blank check?" Henry asked. "Accepting an agreement sight unseen!"

Pete added, "The seamen went out on a limb to support us. Signing a separate contract would leave them in the lurch."

Harry Bridges said, "We've already voted that any proposal negotiated must be sent to the Local members to vote on, *before* it's signed. And we'll stand by the seamen."

"McGrady's furious at involving dirt common workers in plannng," Pete snickered. "He says, 'Communists are throwing a monkey wrench into the situation,' and he isn't completely wrong." Pete held copies of Hearst newspapers with banner headlines, "STRIKE OUT OF HAND! Reds Lead Dock Strike, City Warned! Situation Hopeless, Says Mediator."

Pete and Hans let themselves into the print shop. The mimeograph machine stood ready to run the latest news handouts.

✖   ✖   ✖

Henry and Hans shrugged into their jackets. San Francisco weather had turned cold with summer's heavy morning fog. This morning the Strike Relief kitchen had received six truckloads of produce to be given out to the men from farmers in Salinas. It needed to be boxed.

"At least in San Francisco we're not going to starve," Hans said. "We've got vegetables from the Valley, and the Bay is teeming with crab, bass, sardines and salmon — all good eating for the effort of setting a trap or throwing out a line."

Henry flipped open another box to be filled. "You don't think of sardines as food, there are so many in the bay. And the stink they make when some fisherman hauls them in to rend them into oil right on board!"

"That's something I don't get about this country," Hans said. "Fresh sardines wasted as oil! Nobody thinks the bay can get fished out. Doesn't anybody know what it was like in Europe?"

What it's like today bothers me," Henry said. "You hear what that sailor said about the putsch in Munich?"

Hans nodded. "And they've damn near finished off the trade union movement." He found himself staring at a ship moving into the harbor, blowing its stacks, black smoke staining the sky. "Crud." He turned away. "What we're doing here is what will make a difference."

Pete joined them. "How about a doughnut and coffee?" He passed his copy of *The San Francisco News* to Henry, who glanced at it.

"What's this crap about Communism again? Last year we finally got rid of Prohibition. Are they going to prohibit thinking? I don't know if Trotsky and the rest of them will sort it out, but they are right about one thing. Workers have to stick together."

✖   ✖   ✖

That night, Hans got a surprise. Pat, Molly's 18-year-old brother arrived from Montana. Thin, covered with soot and a three-day growth of beard, he looked and smelled like a hobo.

"What're you doing here?" Hans asked.

"There's a fight going on — on the waterfront — that right?" Pat asked.

"Yeah."

"Well, you know us Irish. Is this a private fight, or can anyone get in?"

Hans laughed. "You look like you could use some grub. Come on back to the kitchen, and then I'll find some blankets and bring you down tomorrow. How'd you get here — ride the rails?"

Pat looked down at his overalls. "Freight train down to Ogden, then passenger trains. A hobo showed me how to ride the blinds. In the back of the tender, there is a space like the step on a passenger rail car. If you wait just past the rail station and jump on while it's in motion, you can stand up in there. It's faster than going by freight."

"I've heard it's tough. You have to stay awake, because you can't let go."

"I could use some shut-eye." Pat admitted.

Next day on the Embarcadero, the thousand-man picket line came under attack. Hans and Pat joined Henry on the line at 8 AM. Moments later, the police pushed into the line with horses and clubs without warning. The pickets used their fists. Henry twisted the arm of one club wielding officer until he dropped his club, but another on horseback brought his club down with a crack that broke Henry's hold and almost tore his ear off.

Molly didn't learn of it until Hans and Pat arrived home supporting Henry. Hans had made a rough splint from a board and improvised a sling from his shirt for Henry, whose right arm had broken under the police club. The bone was a simple break, so Molly strengthened the splint and tended his ear with iodine, gauze, and adhesive tape while the men talked.

"Pete's right, the ship owners aren't using strike-breakers," Henry said. "The police are doing their dirty work."

"How could they use shotguns against unarmed men?" Molly asked.

"We had arms," Pat said. "Whatever bricks and cobblestones we could pull up from the street."

"Are you sure you want to stick around?" Hans asked Pat.

"Your friend Pete asked me if I wanted to meet with some younger guys on Memorial Day. They're expecting some action. Should be fun."

Hans shook his head. "Not my idea of fun."

"On Memorial Day weekend," Pete wrote another note for his book on the strike, "Youth groups held their annual anti-war rally on the Embarcadero. The police attacked, claiming: 'They're Communists!' as if this justified anything. Then the parents came out. On Sunday, five thousand men and women marched up Market Street to City Hall to protest police brutality."

June 1934

"McGrady's gone back to Washington." Pete joined Henry at Red's Java Cafe the following Friday and helped himself to a thick mug of coffee. The fog was almost as thick as rain. "The Coast's deadlocked. We've gotten word from dock workers in New Zealand, Canada, and the Netherlands that they'll refuse to unload any cargo loaded by scabs on the Pacific Coast."

Henry finished off his plate of scrambled eggs and thick fried potatoes, and then pointed to his newspaper. "Says here they're going to open the port by force."

"Yeah, the Employers' Association has organized a little charade for the public," Pete said, "and the Governor threw in his two bits. Want to read some purple prose? Look here." Pete pulled a *Chronicle* newspaper clipping from his pocket:

> Governor Merriam, with whom the employers conferred privately, issued a proclamation attacking the irresponsible professional agitators, mostly aliens, trafficking shamelessly in the agonies of these stressful times, seeking revolution, not reform. Their alien creed of violence and sabotage strikes venomously at the heart of constitutional democracy.

"Hokum. So what now?" Henry asked.

"We're trying to get an injunction against the police chief to prevent inter-ference with peaceful picketing," Pete said. "The Machinists Union has sent out a General Strike Call to all other unions. Meanwhile, of course, Hearst is hinting at military action if the longshoremen won't go back to work."

✖   ✖   ✖

Molly was making her own statement about the strike at the Betsy Ross Candy Store. She stood at the counter putting toothpicks into red, white, and blue gum drops to form candy people. She lined them up across the glass counter and arranged several figures to carry tiny paper umbrellas. The leader carried an American flag, a toothpick toy from Japan.

"It's a Fourth of July parade," she said.

Nan, Pete's wife and another part-time worker at the Betsy Ross Candy Store, laughed. "Could have fooled me," she said, "I thought it was a picket line."

Molly grinned.

"Have you heard about our pay cut next week?" Nan asked.

"No!"

"Eric Robertson, the little dick himself, has decided he can save the company money by having us work 'on-call' and cutting our wages to 15 cents an hour."

Molly groaned. She remembered her feeling the one time the general manager came into the shop. He looked right at her and talked, but he still was not seeing her. His father had bought the Western Foods Company, then swal-lowed up the Betsy Ross Candy Stores to give his son something to manage.

"You know the books," Nan said. "This store makes a huge profit. If people can't do anything else, they can buy a bit of candy. People like Eric *Schmuck* Robertson know how bad times are, and they use it."

"Yeah, we need a union, but sometimes they can't be trusted either. This Joe Ryan fellow from New York is cozying up to the ship owners without a word to the local. What's a 'Judas-goat'?" Molly asked.

"The animal that leads the sheep up the ramp to the slaughter house," Nan said.

Molly nodded. "They call Ryan that."

Nan said, "Ryan and men like him think being elected makes them a cut above the rest of us — they can do anything they damn well please. Well, that's men for you, always strutting their peckers to see who's got the biggest."

Molly giggled.

"What's funny?" Nan asked.

"Nothing much, I just thought of something Hans said about your foul 'fowl' language, as in 'chicken-shit'!"

"Does it offend you?"

"No, I've heard it all."

Nan finished cutting the tray of walnut fudge and shoved it into the glass case. She picked up a pecan roll and started slicing. "I picked up words from my dad and his poker buddies. He thought it was funny when I was little, but then he told me to clean up my language with other people. It's good to have a few cuss words when you're mad."

"Yeah?"

"You have a good vocabulary, so you don't need them, but I can tell a lot about people from the way they cuss. What is the worst thing a man can say to another man? That he's a woman, or the son of a woman, or should be used like a woman — *you cunt, son-of-a-bitch, bastard, fuck you*. And men've got dozens of words to describe women they don't like — *hag, witch, ball-cutter* — and do we have even one word for men who lie to women, who beat their wives and children, and treat women so badly they have no self-respect left? Any words for men who do any of the other slimy things they do?"

"Pete been getting you down?"

"Naw, Pete's a love, always has been, but you know what some of his so-called friends say to him? They say he's pussy-whipped, because I've got a mouth and say what I think."

"Yeah, most men have got to feel in charge all right, even in Church."

"Hey, watch it," Nan laughed. "Are you turning into some kind of Commie radical?"

Molly was not laughing. "I'm right; you're wrong. If I can fire you or beat you in a fistfight, I'm stronger than you — and if I'm stronger, it means I'm right. I don't have to give it another thought."

"The way it's always been and always will be," Nan agreed. "Everywhere."

✖   ✖   ✖

Joe Ryan, the International President of the ILA, signed his agreement with the ship owners and the newspapers announced the strike was settled. It was the same document earlier refused by the local. Hans and Pat joined Henry at the back of Eagles Hall on Golden Gate Avenue. Henry had his arm in a sling and a bandage on his ear. Three thousand longshoremen packed the auditorium when Ryan arrived. A beefy, black-haired man in a dark suit, white shirt and tie, he walked up to the dais with the agreement he had negotiated with the Shipowners.

Jim Liguori was terse with his introduction. "Joe Ryan," he said.

Joe Ryan read the agreement, while the murmur in the audience grew to a loud rumble. The agreement continued the shape-up and excluded the seamen from Longshore negotiations.

A storm of boos and profanity shook the building. "Throw him out! *You fink, faker, Judas-goat.*" Obscene suggestions and every insulting name in several languages were thrown at him when he finished and sat on a wooden fold-up chair on the platform with the strike committee.

"Do we want this agreement?" Jim Liguori asked.

"NO!" The men turned it down with a unanimous roar.

Harry Bridges, his slight build half the girth of Ryan's, asked him, "Why didn't you report these negotiations to the membership?"

Ryan stumbled around, "I didn't — I thought I understood your best interests. I didn't know the seamen . . ."

"In our local, members decide what we want. Why didn't you confer with the men at any time?"

One man shouted, "Put a motion. We don't need these bums making our decisions."

Ryan pushed his hands against the table, got up and raised his voice against the roar. "Give me three minutes to explain. I didn't *know!* I wouldn't have signed the agreement had I known." His words were greeted with derisive catcalls. "Go back where you came from." "We didn't come here to listen to you."

A motion was made and passed to cut out salaried officers from the negotiations. Five men from each union on strike would negotiate any settlement, and then bring it to the members for a vote before it would be signed.

Henry grunted to Hans, "For sure tomorrow, Ryan will hightail it over to the employers and Mayor Rossi and tell them the union's been captured by Communists and is completely out of control."

Jim Liguori stood up and said to everyone, "A general strike is likely. All unions are going to vote this week whether to go out."

On July 3, Chief of Police Quinn warned the public, "Stay away from the waterfront. New supplies of tear gas and riot guns are being handed out to 700 police officers."

Hans adamantly insisted that Molly stay away. "But Mrs. Ortiz told me she'd watch the children so I could go." Molly protested.

Thousands of San Franciscans lined rooftops and filled windows overlooking the Embarcadero. Vendors pushed among the spectators selling candy bars, gum, and cigarettes. Pete stood with Pat on the rim of the crowd. "Look at those bastards," he said. "Out to see the show. Stick close to me, Pat. I'll show you how to get around when they start tossing grenades."

Pickets had been on hand since daybreak. At 11 AM the police on foot, horseback, and in patrol cars, concentrated on Pier 38. They forced the pickets back. A row of empty boxcars strung across the Belt Line railway blocked the south end of the street. The north end was barricaded by a string of police cars and cops, thick with guns and riot gear.

The steel doors of Pier 38 rolled open. Eight patrol cars guarded five dilapidated old trucks that moved out loaded with goods.

Angry shouts and obscenities came from the pickets the instant the wheels hit the cobblestones. A man shouted his contempt to the scabs. "The police are going to have to protect you the rest of your lives."

Police Captain Hoertkorn mounted the running board of a police car, revolver in hand, and hollered, "The Port is open!" He fired several shots in the air. "Let 'em have it!"

Police and pickets both surged forward. The Embarcadero was a tangle of fighting men. The police opened fire with gas-filled hand grenades. Hans picked up one and lobbed it back to explode behind the police line. Bright pools of blood appeared on the cobblestones. Chief Quinn arrived in time to get a brick through his windshield.

The wind carried tear gas all over the Embarcadero choking pickets, police, and bystanders. Fighting continued for four hours while news reporters circled overhead in a couple of planes. Sirens from ambulances could be heard up and down Market Street. Hans loosened a brick with his load hook and hurled it at a cop clubbing the head of a fallen man. He was still unscathed. That he could feel so frightened and keep on fighting surprised him. Corrupt police thugs — slime! He heaved another cobblestone.

Twenty-five men, including nine police, were hospitalized. Strikers took most of their casualties to private homes to avoid being arrested.

There was no fighting on the Fourth of July. That night Molly lay awake for a long time wondering what would happen the next day. She hated being side-lined, but what could she do? Or what should she do — what were the rules? Hans was sure he knew what was right, but who decided? Did it have to be this way? Why? She had been certain she knew the rules once. She'd been so self-righteous with Lizzie. Then she had broken the rules, and her life had fallen apart. Why? Was that the reason?

July 1934

At midnight on July 4th scabs attempted to run the railway. Stacked boxes from the Alaskan canneries swayed on a pallet. Two workers scrambled to steady the load, but they were as new to the ways of the wharf as the load, so the boxes came crashing down. They managed to shunt fourteen cars onto the Matson dock before Pete and Jim Liguori located and threw a switch that derailed several cars. The pickets advanced. Even with police protection, the scabs were no match for them. The clash played out in the pre-dawn hours on streets that resembled an Edward Hopper painting of the cold harsh lights of night. Half the scabs melted away before a single rock was thrown.

Governor Merriam ordered the National Guard to prepare for action. Adjutant General Howard told the press, "The National Guard won't monkey with tear gas. We'll use vomiting gas, the worst non-fatal gas in existence. It causes violent nausea, a splitting headache, and will knock the Commie thugs out for at least two days."

At 8 AM Thursday morning, police vans rolled onto the Embarcadero loaded with riot gear, sawed-off shotguns, and gas grenades. The police attacked with tear gas and clubs. Hans and Henry were in a sizable group driven back into the alleys off the Embarcadero and up Rincon Hill. Two boxcars standing on a siding burst into flames. Shots sounded. A dozen battles were going on. The police cleared a couple of hundred strikers from Bryant and Main by using tear gas. Pickets reassembled at Rincon Hill. Noise and confusion was everywhere. One police officer stood behind a telephone pole to shelter himself and started firing with his revolver. Henry was hit. He winced. It was his broken arm.

"God," Hans yelled. "They're trying to kill us!" He ran to Henry's side pulling out a strip of cloth Molly had stuffed in his shirt. There was plenty of blood, but it was a flesh wound. The bullet had glanced off.

The police swarmed up the steep grassy slope firing their revolvers. Bullets smashed the windows of private homes on the hilltop. Dry grass, ignited by tear gas shells, burst into a roaring fire. A fire truck arrived with sirens and aimed high-pressure streams of water at both the grass and the pickets. The police took command of the hill to the sound of shattering glass. Captain Hoertkorn ordered a squad of armed guards to surround the Hill.

"Don't let them take it again," he said.

Pete helped a wounded man get shelter in the print shop so he wouldn't be arrested. Maintaining a picket line in the face of gunfire and gas was hopeless. Most fighting was in an industrial section on the southern end of the Embarcadero. Men from all sections of the Wharf made their way to union headquarters a block from the Ferry Building. Strikers thought it was a neutral zone. A first-aid worker re-bandaged Henry's arm. Hans sat down. He could rest for a minute, catch his breath. Suddenly gas shells crashed through the front windows.

"Jeez, long-range guns!" Pete yelled.

The men were running. The telephone rang. Hans, a handkerchief to his nose, tears flooding his cheeks from inflamed eyes, picked up the receiver.

"Had enough?" asked the voice on the other end.

"Go to hell!" Hans hollered. He slammed down the receiver and stumbled down the stairs. A loud crackling of pistol shots. More men fell to the bloody pavement where they lay silent.

Two of them were dead.

Chapter Eighteen

Victory

P ete hunched over a battered oak desk in the print shop. He tore off
a sheet from the pad of yellow pages and crumpled it. Henry
glanced at him, "Tough job!"

"Yeah." Pete bit the end of his pencil, then started again to
write the news release.

July 6, 1934

> This morning we chalked an inscription on the sidewalk
> where Howard Sperry and Nick Bordoise were killed — two
> unarmed union men, shot in the back — murdered by the
> police. Their bodies lie in state in union headquarters. The
> waterfront is silent under armed guard.
>
> Howard Sperry was a World War Veteran. One of the
> sentries standing guard by the coffins wears a uniform of the
> Veterans of Foreign Wars. Nick Bordoise's wife of six years
> stands weeping by the other coffin. Nick, a native of Crete,
> a member of the Cooks' Union and of the Communist Party,
> was a volunteer who prepared meals during the long strike.
>
> Delegates from nearly every union in the city have
> voted unanimous approval of a General Strike.

On Sunday Hans gave up. Molly stood by the front door in her coat and hat. She pulled on gloves and picked up her purse. "I'm going, Hans. Nan wouldn't understand if I didn't come with her."

Hans slowly nodded. "There won't be trouble today."

Molly took a breath — she hadn't realized she was holding it — and touched him tentatively. "It must have been terrifying."

"Yeah."

From his closed expression, tight lips and blank face, she knew he still didn't want to talk to her about it. He told her the facts, but didn't want her probing. She knew better than to aim questions at him, but was he still training her to know her place, to stay out of his affairs?

"Why do you make it so hard for me?" she asked.

His face flushed. "Don't you know what you mean to me? I *need* to take care of you."

She dropped her purse to the floor, put both hands on his cheeks and kissed his mouth. "Try to trust me," she said. His face softened and he held her tightly.

Molly met Nan at the Ferry Building flower stand. She was dressed in black and carried flowers. "Have you ever seen so many people?" Nan asked. "There must be fifty thousand."

They joined thousands of others and waited, hour after hour to file slowly past the two coffins. Molly felt the sadness but pride, too. So many people were outraged and they were all showing it together.

"This strike is fierce," Nan said. "Working in the First Aid station was horrible. The Union Hall had a station, but most of the time, I was in the back of a truck with only one other nurse. We ran out of bandages, we ran out of iodine, finally we ran out of water."

Molly grimaced. "I wanted to be with you, but Hans wouldn't hear of it."

"Well, he was right about the bloodshed on Thursday. Pete told me Hans saved Henry's life in the Rincon Hill fight."

Molly wanted to be proud of Hans. She was proud of him, but why didn't he tell her these things? "Were you in the truck when the Police attacked?"

"No, in the office — and when the gas shells hit — I tell you, I thought we were goners," Nan said. "I've never been so scared in my life."

They reached the Union Hall and entered to view the bodies. Molly knelt, made the sign of the cross, and said a prayer. Why hadn't she thought that Hans might be killed? She loved Hans. She needed him, didn't she? This morning his tenderness startled her and she felt her relief. After losing Pa, she knew what misery death could bring, particularly without union benefits of any kind. Strange. Nan laid her flowers with others at the side of the coffins and raised her hand in a clenched-fist worker's salute — the closed fingers representing union, raised above the head, for the welfare of the group over the individual. The air was heavy with the scent of hundreds of wreaths.

Jim Liguori asked permission from Police Chief Quinn for a funeral parade on Monday. He asked that all police withdraw from around the ILA hall where the services were to be held and from the entire length of Market Street, the line of march.

"You keep away," he said, "and we'll be responsible for maintaining order and directing traffic." The request was granted.

The longshoremen in their hickory work shirts, black pants and white caps marched as a visible unit; Henry with his bandaged arm, Hans, Pat, and Pete among them. Pat had hit it off with Pete who gave him some pants, a shirt, and a white longshoreman's cap for the march. Other men carried the caskets down the narrow stairway from the union hall and placed them on a truck. Three more trucks followed heaped with flowers. A union band struck up the slow beat of Beethoven's Funeral March and the trucks moved onto Market Street. The giant procession followed in silence.

Molly and Nan joined the mourners moving onto Market Street eight, sometimes ten, abreast. From the Ferry Building to Valencia, the street filled with men, women and children. Streetcar men stopped their cars along the line of march and stood with caps over their chests.

Most people in the crowds on the sidewalk removed their hats. Others watched silently, some fearfully. Three hours went by. Longshoremen wearing blue armbands directed traffic. The parade ended at Duggan's Funeral Parlor on 17th Street and Valencia.

When the crowd of mourners broke rank, Molly knew the General Strike was certain.

Nan called Molly the next morning. "You haven't seen the papers, have you?"

"No, Ortiz's wasn't delivered." Molly said.

"Well, hold your hat," Nan laughed. "Hearst is saying that Moscow is trying to take San Francisco as a colonial possession. And get this one, *The Chronicle* reports a hoard of Reds are marching from the north."

"Sounds crazy," Molly said.

"It is! Those stuffed shirts are scared silly. Dad says his Berkeley neighbors have armed themselves with garden pitchforks and hunting rifles to defend their families. The highways are crowded with cars — people with money running from the bombs and rioters promised by Hearst."

✖   ✖   ✖

On July 16, 1934, the unions of San Francisco walked out in a General Strike. Molly walked next door with Elizabeth. Frankie was in her arms. "Mrs. Ortiz," she began.

Mrs. Ortiz had answered the door with her baking apron already smudged with flour. She laughed and reached out to take the baby. "You don't have to ask. I take these babies any time."

Molly felt like herself again. Hans didn't know she was out, but she felt completely safe. She decided to walk San Francisco. She liked the silence. Streets usually filled with activity were utterly quiet. No streetcars ran. Gasoline stations, saloons, small shops, and restaurants had signs in their windows: "Closed til the longshoremen get their hiring hall," or "Closed. ILA sympathizer." She saw most of the bigger stores had stripped their windows and pulled down the shades, preparing for the worst.

There was no violence — no bombs. The strikers weren't the ones with guns.

Kids and adults on roller-skates and bikes were everywhere. Here and there, a truck was turned over where a businessman had used scab labor to move his goods, but the streets were orderly under the direction of the strike committee.

She talked to her grocer, Eddy, an independent French-Canadian who worked for himself. "What do you think is happening?"

"I watched the big parade," he said. "Those men have courage. The

unions impress me, but a lot of people are terrified. They think brains and ability go with money, and the bosses not the strikers. They see their worn clothing
and think they're thugs and bullies."

Molly knew what he was talking about. She had met some of the skep-
tics. Mrs. Ortiz's son-in-law told her, "Strikers make me sick to my stomach. I'm
glad the country has a strong army and police force to keep these dim bulbs in
order." He was working 10 hours a day for $15 a week, and depended on
money from the Ortizes to keep his pants pressed. Yet, strikers were trash people to him. He could not see himself in their shoes!

On the second day of the General Strike, Trudy rang Molly's front doorbell.
"Enough of this living in a war zone! I've brought a hamper of food from Henri et
Marcel's. We're going to take the car and picnic in the park."

Elizabeth clapped her hands.

"It sounds great, but you don't know about naptime and meals for a food-
fussy one-year-old, and a four-year-old dreamer," Molly said.

"No," Trudy said. "We're bringing Mrs. Ortiz to deal with that."

They found their favorite place by the Azalea Garden pond, and Mrs. Ortiz
settled the children in sand boxes and swings.

"I've got something to tell you," Trudy said, "but you can't tell anyone, not
even Hans."

Molly nodded.

"You know Ted lives in Woodside," Trudy said. "Well, his close neighbor
and best friend is John Neylan, Hearst's right-hand man. Something big is happening this weekend. Ted's in town and they're planning a meeting with the
major ship owners and businessmen at John Neylan's house."

Trudy took out a pack of Chesterfields and fitted a cigarette into her pearl
holder. She lit the cigarette and slowly drew the smoke in.

"The folks downtown are getting uneasy about the strike. Some of them
think they went too far and brought it on themselves," Trudy said. "Ted called
me to come in last night and join him for dinner at the Flytrap. After dinner, we
went to Coffee Dans then spent the night at his place on Macondrey Lane." She
laughed. "What I want to tell you about is a tiny Mata Hari plot I launched."

Trudy poured them each a cup of iced tea from the frosted thermos and looked directly at Molly. "I haven't told you much about Ted. His idea of a joke is that his marriage was made in Boston, not heaven — a solid merger of financial dynasties. His wife went to school with Eleanor Roosevelt and she is a Republican, but with most of Eleanor's handicaps. She's a broom stick almost 6 feet tall and painfully shy at the dinner parties he insists on. If he lets fly even a tenth of the cracks he makes about her to her face, I think she's a saint to put up with him."

"Oh, Trudy, how can you stand him?" Molly asked.

Trudy widened her eyes, fingered the large diamond set into a band at her throat, and waved her hand lightly toward the roadster. "Teddy-baby has a *lot* of charm," she murmured.

"Seriously, Molly," she said, "Imagine this guy as a poor little rich kid — no one ever thought of rumpling his hair or kissing him on the nose, much less told him he couldn't go around kicking over everyone's sand castle, or he'd get booted out of the sand box."

"So you've been giving him the bad news?" Molly laughed.

"Don't be such a doubter! I learned a trick from you. I give him my total attention; say nothing, except your two thousand ways of saying, 'oh' and an occasional 'then what did you do?' He tells me *everything*, things he would not tell his brother, much less his best friend, John Neylan. When I Mata Hari-ed in my idea, I dressed it with plenty of sauce: 'Teddy bear, that's brilliant as a diamond. You've seen what the businessmen want and haven't been able to say.' He perked right up to see what he'd been thinking." Trudy drew on her cigarette, her eyes gleaming. "I sashayed on, 'They want the strike settled and out of the headlines. It's only served to get new unions started and all kinds of people are interested in labor conditions now. Businessmen don't *want* all that attention. It's got to be stopped, even if you have to *appear* to include the seamen in the negotiation.'"

"Bright, yeah and sharp as a diamond," Molly laughed.

Trudy shrugged modestly. "A lot of people see it, but someone has to say it out loud. Ted's still pawing the seamen idea around, but by Saturday, I promise you, it'll be his idea."

Molly hugged her friend. "Oh Trudy, the thing is that, for once, *ordinary people* stood up and we've won!"

October 1934

Henry slammed his paper on the counter of Paddy Ryan's bar. "Make it a double," he ordered and shook with laughter. "Look at this," he roared. "We got it all."

Pete grabbed the paper. "My God, it's over! The mediation board has handed down its decision! We got our six-hour day, a thirty-hour week and time and a half for overtime. The wage is set at 95 cents per hour. Higher wages for difficult or dangerous cargo."

"WE GOT IT!" he hollered, banging his fist against the bar. His eyes were wet. "After all this time . . ." He leaned forward and continued reading: "All hiring will be done by a dispatch hall controlled jointly by employers and the union."

Henry threw his good arm around Pete's shoulder. "It's true," he said, "and the God damn bastards have given away more than they know."

"What d'you mean?"

"Don't you see — we 'have the right to choose our work.' They give us any guff, increase the loads, or try to pass "hot cargo" from a strike area handled by scabs, we walk off the job."

"So?"

"The boss calls the hiring hall. Another gang is sent. If the grievance has not been fixed, *they* walk off the job. No matter how many gangs are sent, the men will stick together."

"We've won!"

May 1937

Bright sunlight flickered through the leaves onto the three-piece band dominated by the accordion player. The dancing platform was shaded by bay and redwood trees, except for the portion that seemed to float in the sky. Slapping shoes with hands and stamping their feet, Henry and his brother, a farmer from Wisconsin, spun around with elbows and knees gyrating. It was Henry and Clara's 20th wedding anniversary and the celebration was raucous. A roar of laughter and cheers accompanied the men when they finally finished, their faces and shirts wet with sweat. They wobbled off the floor, their arms around each other. Hans, with Frankie held tight to his shirt, brought them steins of beer, two of them in his right fist.

The music started again. A dozen couples took their places and whirled in the patterns of an old-country waltz. Guests stood and drank, or sat and drank, on the wooden porches of the Nature Friends Mt. Tamalpais Clubhouse and on steps up and down the hillside. The cliff-hanging chalet with its cutout wooden shutters and fenced walkways was brightly painted with flower patterns. Pots of geraniums hung from the porch rafters. Nan and Gertrude had found the club's outdoor sauna and shower, and now lay on the deck fenced off for nude sun-bathing. Molly was with other mothers and Elizabeth in the mountain meadow, pitching horseshoes and playing games.

Henry chucked Frankie under his chin and punched Hans' arm. "Meet my brother, Claus," he said. "I didn't think he'd make it."

His brother grinned. "I read in the papers you guys were so busy thumbing your nose at the Nazis, you didn't have time to dance any more." The cruiser *Karlsruhe* had arrived in port flying the Nazi flag, and the longshoremen refused to unload her. The Nazis destroyed trade unionism in Germany.

Henry chortled, "They could damn well fasten their own lines!"

Hans pointed up the hill. "Clara rings the bell — time to eat!"

In the upper hall, Clara presided like a golden gray-haired goddess over the food. One plank table was heavy with platters loaded with roast beef, fried chicken, pan roasted potatoes, sweet and sour red cabbage, cold-slaw, green beans cooked with onion and bacon, slabs of pumpernickel and rye bread, with pots of mustard, horseradish, and butter. Another table held pitchers of beer, with lemonade for the children. The harder liquor was down in the bar.

Henry pushed Claus ahead of him to the food. "Did ya hear about those smart asses, the University of California football team, who thought they'd take a little trip on the steamer *Yale*?" He gave his brother an evil grin. "Not only long-shoremen, but the seamen, refused to service the ship. The UC football team had scabbed on the docks during the strike. Hah! Now they carried their own luggage and found their own staterooms. No steward responded to the bells they rang for service."

Hans laughed. "I liked when we walked off the job to honor the picket line Chinese children set up to protest loading scrap metal to Japan, after they invaded China."

Molly stood with her hands loosely resting on the deck fence outside the hall. This party was the best she could remember. Even Pat had managed to get a three-day pass. He'd joined the Civilian Conservation Corps when the strike ended. He was balancing a mug of beer on his plate when he joined her.

"D'you like the CCC?" she asked

"Working on the road to Yosemite's not bad. The corps sends twenty five dollars a month to Ma," Pat said, "and I get five for spending money. It is kind of a toss-up, though. I'd like to study at the Worker's School."

"Why do you want to hang out with Communists?" Molly asked

"They're fun, and I like the girls."

"This is Pete's idea, isn't it?"

"You're trying to stop me from becoming a Red," Pat said. "But you and I are the ones who think alike! Don't blame Pete."

"Hm-mm."

"And speaking of the devil —" They could see Pete making his way over to them. When he arrived, Pat said, "I'm the new bantam weight boxing champ. The CO in Monterey says I can write my own ticket if I transfer into his outfit and sign up for another hitch."

"Do you want to?"

"I'm eligible for another six months, but I don't know what I'm going to do when I get out," Pat said. "Nothing is happening in Butte."

"Do you want to spend a couple of weeks learning something about organizing?" Pete asked.

"Why not?" Pat grinned at his sister. Molly shook her head. So much for "big sister" influence.

She had enjoyed the car ferry from San Francisco and the hike down through the redwoods from Mt. Tamalpias. How comfortable the men were with one another. She could overhear snatches of their talk. They mostly joked and teased about work matters, particularly Henry whenever he came near. Gertrude and Nan, now in dresses, were arguing something about Harry Bridges.

Nan shook her head, "I don't believe it. Harry Bridges? Rumba King of North Beach?"

Trudy's lips twitched. "I tell you it's true. I was right there at the Sinaloa. He and his partner had heavy competition, Ted and me included, but they gave him the crown. He is a dancer in addition to being the most important man in union-ism."

Nan made a face. "What I can't understand is why the ladies all fall for him. A good sport with a sense of humor, yes, and he's no fool — a genius in union organizing — but as a man? Homely as mud, without an ounce of feeling. A woman is a 'skirt,' end of his thought."

The music started again. Molly looked around for Hans. Maybe it was finally time for a polka.

Part III

Lizby

Prologue
Winter Sight

DAY 1931
In a blue room, under a gray skylight,
A tangerine orange bed.
Silence
There is no one else in the house.

NIGHT 1935
Fat rain drops streak down the window pane.
Lightening flickers, mumbles behind the Mountain, then
Crashes, hurling a roar of light.
My brother curls his hand in mine.

NIGHT 1936, OR 7, OR 9
Points of light in the sky
Stars in endless space, endless time.
Does God look through my eyes into my life?
Are we stories that He lives to pass eternity?

DAY 2007
A pencil and spiral notebook.
I reach back through body knowing
To find Before . . . and After.
My thought curls into You,
Cherishing.

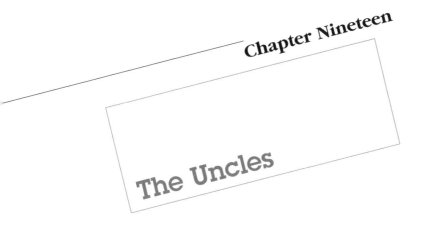

Chapter Nineteen

The Uncles

S e p t e m b e r   1 9 3 7

The Sunset District in San Francisco

"Flabbergasted . . . Molly, you can't — you *won't* get away with it . . ."

Elizabeth could hear her grandmother's voice in the living room, but at seven years old, she was quite sure the shut double doors meant 'Stay Out.' She fingered the crack to widen it where the sliding doors did not quite close, and then pressed her eye against it to peek.

The cardboard box Mother had hidden in the hall closet yesterday sat open on the floor and an inside-out blue lace dress lay over her knees. She was pinning white arm shields into the sleeves.

"Want to bet?" Her mother stood up, wiggled the dress over her head, and then twirled in front of the fireplace mirror. Her dark razor-cut hair rumpled into waves.

Elizabeth couldn't see her grandmother's face, but her posture was stiff with disapproval. Her mother, looking at herself in the mirror, laughed at Gram, picked up the red Maybelline box from the mantel and brushed her lashes darker. "I'll tell Hans I borrowed the dress from Trudy. On Monday I'll tell the sales lady at the returns desk my husband didn't like it, and they'll take it back," she said   "I already checked."

"Bold as brass," Gram laughed. "You *always* get your way."

Her mother took Gram's eyelash curler from the mantel, fitted its rims together to curl her eyelashes, closing one green eye, then the other. She used her lipstick to make a perfect cupid's bow, rubbed a bit more on her cheekbones and smudged it with her fingers.

Mother told a fib — it made Elizabeth's cheeks hot. She pushed away from the door; she knew she had better get dressed for the wedding. Frankie was still snuggled in his flannel Dr. Denton pajamas, eyes tight shut. She had to wake him. First she put on the pink dress with the satin sash that she hated, and the patent leather Mary Jane shoes Gram had brought down from Montana on the Greyhound bus. She would not think about her mother. She started shaking Frankie to rouse him.

The wedding did not take up much room in St. Anne's huge church. It was just like Mass on Sunday, except no incense, and with Uncle John and Kathleen standing in front of the priest at the foot of the altar. Most of the church was dark in the gray daylight, but candles lit up the sanctuary. Mother, in her blue lace dress, was right there in the Sanctuary, like she was being married too. *Bold as brass,* like Gram said. Kathleen held a bouquet of pink roses, and a lady sang, "Ave Maria" from the choir stall in back.

After the ceremony, their Montana relatives filled the flat — the men all with proper ties and jackets and polished shoes. Uncle Pat walked to the kitchen sink with Elizabeth at his elbow. He added gin to a glass with Party-Pak Lime Ricky.

"Cheers," he said to Uncle John who was holding a tray of ice cubes under the hot water faucet to loosen them.

"I didn't think you'd get here, riding the rails," John said. Then he sniffed the air. Elizabeth noticed it did smell funny. "Jaysus, don't light a match!"

Uncle Pat laughed. "The suit," he said. "If you don't stand downwind, it's okay. Maw brought it with her on the Greyhound — must have used a bucket of white gasoline to get the spots out."

"Sure, I thought I recognized that suit. Isn't it what I wore for Confirmation?"

Pat nodded, "Didn't we all? Hey, how 'bout that hobo jungle outside Salt

Lake? I got lucky — an old geezer showed me how to dodge the bulls."

Elizabeth drew in a sharp breath. Uncle Pat looked down and snuggled her between his arm and hip. He widened his blue eyes, as he did when he told an adventure. "Before the sun came up, the train started to slow. The old guy hollered in my ear, Git-uup, git-up, Kid." Uncle Pat scrunched his face and rumbled his voice from the back of his throat and made Elizabeth laugh. "He pulled me in front of the boxcar door. 'When I jump, follow me' he said, then he slid the door open, hunched his shoulders and landed with his knees loose, and rolled head over heels. I pushed off before I let myself think about it."

Uncle Pat was brave! Elizabeth thought maybe he would let her ride the rails with him someday. She would wear overalls and have a cap like his to hide her curls.

They walked back into the dining room. Pat pulled out his harmonica, leaned against the built-in sideboard and started to play, *The Lonesome Cowboy*.

She loved her Uncle Pat. He talked to her as if she was grown up and he had taught her how to draw — but the best thing he taught was how to be invisible. "Close your eyes, rub your left knee and watch your cloak of invisibility wrap around you," he said. "Then you open your eyes and do whatever you want. But don't say a word and don't look anyone in the eye, or you'll become visible again."

Mother stood at the table cutting sandwiches in half and then half again. She gave Elizabeth her 'Get yourself over here to help me' look. Uncle Pat winked. Elizabeth did a little shuffle-off-to-Buffalo step for him and he did it back while she picked up the tray with mayonnaise sandwiches of chopped egg and chopped olives and brought them to Gram.

Uncle Frank, her second uncle, was helping Dad lift a Victrola over the doorsill into the living room. She saw him through the open sliding doors. His rusty hair, thick eyebrows, and squinty eyes made him look like a lion; not the Cowardly Lion of Oz though, more like one you better watch out for at the zoo. After they put the Victrola in place, he took a swallow from his glass of whiskey and said something she could not hear. He and Dad laughed. Frank looked over at Pat and his eyebrows wrinkled together. He started to cross the room, and Elizabeth rubbed her left knee. Uncle Frank had not ever said anything scary to her, but it felt better to be invisible when he was around.

"I see you made it, Runt," he said to Pat. "Any of your Red buddies with you?"

Pat didn't say anything. He stopped *The Lonesome Cowboy* and held his hands closer to his mouth to start a tune Elizabeth didn't know.

"The *Internationale*." Frank made a disgusted sound with his mouth. "Gimme a break. When are you going to wise up? Bunch of anarchists."

"Pa didn't see them that way," Pat said.

"And look where it got him," Frank shot back. "A mile deep — dead at the end of a mine shaft. Huh, I suppose you're going to Spain, too — another dumb-ass idea."

She thought Uncle Frank would hit Uncle Pat, but Pat put his mouth organ into his pocket. "I won't fight you," he said, and slid his hands behind him onto the cupboard counter. Uncle Pat was a bantamweight champion boxer in Butte, but Elizabeth had never seen him fight. Gram came fussing across from the front room and put herself between them. What was she going to do? Dad said Gram had a nose for trouble twenty feet long.

"Give us a song, Frank," Gram said. "Your new sister's waiting."

"Don't push, Ma," he said staring at Pat. But then he turned and smiled and followed her to the living room.

Everyone knew Tom was Gram's favorite of the uncles because he was her first-born son and had a voice, but he had married an Italian girl and couldn't come down from Montana. Uncle Frank was her next best. He was also a Butte Bulldog in High School and Montana All-State football player in college. But Mother said he was an atheist and they argued a lot. Elizabeth was glad when Gram took him away to sing.

All kinds of things were going on at that party. And being invisible was fun. The sofa had been pushed out, and there weren't any chairs in the front room. One man played the fiddle and another had an accordion, but most of the music came from the Victrola.

Uncle John had one blind eye and pockmarked skin from a disease when he was little, but when he looked at Kathleen, all you could see was his great wide smile. He took her hand and they started to dance. Of all the uncles, Uncle John was the best dancer. In the morning, he had slicked his straight black hair back with Vaseline and he could not stop smiling. Uncle Frank leaned against the wall looking at them.

Kathleen, her new aunt, looked prettier than a movie star with her curly black hair and green eyes. She was her second aunt; Elizabeth had never met Tom's wife. No one talked about her. "It's better not to let the neighbors know this and that; we keep our business to ourselves." She knew better than to ask. "Little pitchers have big ears," they'd say, and they would not tell her anything anyway.

Mother danced the Charleston with Uncle Pat, but when she danced with Uncle Frank, she looked like a lion too, moving slow and keeping her eyes on him. Gram bragged to a friend that she, herself, could still do the splits, but she allowed that her daughter was a better dancer. "Molly danced on the stage before she injured her knee, got married and had the children. It's too bad Hans won't learn to dance."

It was already dark by the time Mother bumped into Elizabeth and she became visible again. Mother hustled Frankie and her off to their bedroom and tucked them into bed, but she didn't wait while they said prayers, just kissed them good night and went back to the party.

Their bedroom was beside the front room, so they still heard the music. Elizabeth felt it in her feet and arms, but she had lots of other things to think about. In some ways, Mother was more like a movie star than Kathleen even. Elizabeth didn't know if she liked that.

"I'm not sleepy," Frankie sat up in his bed. His bed had bars on it, so he would not fall out when he had nightmares. They had put a piece of clothesline through the bars and used a basket to play elevator games.

"Send me a surprise," he said. So, she hauled the basket to her bed and loaded it with a tiny white box that held a sliver of Gram's fruitcake.

"Put it under your pillow," Gram had said. "You'll dream of the man you're going to marry." She'd rather have a dream of roller skates — their metal wheels rumbling over the cement sidewalk, and then jumping over onto the tar street to slide like butter.

Frankie pulled the basket to his bed, opened the box, and made a face. She giggled. They both hated Gram's fruitcake. Frankie hiccupped, then lay on his side and soon fell asleep.

Elizabeth stared at the wallpaper they had helped Mother hang on the

bedroom walls — red roses in green trellis boxes. Their room smelled like the
lemon verbena leaves that Mother stored with the bed sheets.

Mother's voice floated up — singing a song from Elizabeth's tap-dance
class — "I'll be down to get you in a taxi, honey . . . Better be ready by half-past
eight. I want to be there when the band starts playing . . . I want to dance out
both my shoes, when they play those Jelly-Roll blues . . . tomorrow night at the
Darktown Strutters Ball!"

Their parents' bedroom was at the other end of the dark shellacked hall
that ran the length of the flat. Mother was not acting like herself. How could she
tell a lie about that dress? Elizabeth's eyes were getting sleepy. Maybe she'd
dream about running away with Uncle Pat to Spain.

She didn't. Instead, she had a nightmare — the same old one. They were
at a Fair and it was nighttime. Mother stood in front of a huge devil's head. She
had makeup on her face with red rouge like she wore when she worked sometimes at the Betsy Ross Candy Store. The devil's open mouth was the entrance
to a cave tunnel lit by flames. It stretched deep into the earth. Mother kept
motioning with her arm for Elizabeth to come with her, but Elizabeth couldn't
move. She was that scared.

Uncle Pat did not return to Montana with Gram after the wedding. Instead,
he stayed and worked on the waterfront with Dad for a few months, and then
he disappeared. Next thing they knew he was in Spain with the Lincoln Brigade.

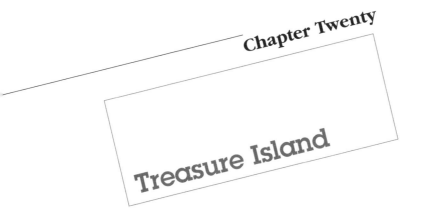

Chapter Twenty

Treasure Island

August, Summer 1939

Elizabeth watched the salt water lapping underneath them while they waited for the ferry to dock. The wooden planks soaked with creosote smelled like the sea. Squeaking timbers started to groan; the ferry pushed closer. THUNK, it settled in place. A heavy metal floor with chains clanking at both ends lowered to the deck. She and Frankie scrambled over it to board and ran up the narrow steps to the benches in front of the wheelhouse. She wanted to stand at the rail but knew they had to stay in their seats until Gram climbed up behind them. She and Frankie had gone to the World's Fair on Treasure Island three times already, but this was Gram's first visit.

Gram had taken off from her job as a chambermaid at the Finlan Hotel in Butte and arrived as a surprise the night before last on the Greyhound Bus. She'd be here a whole month and brought presents for Elizabeth's 10th birthday. She finally appeared at the head of the ship stairs, holding her hat in place with one hand and the map Mother had given her in the other.

"Can we go watch the ferry back out?" Elizabeth asked.

"Why not?" Gram lowered herself onto the bench. Why not? Mother would have given twenty reasons. Maybe the look on her face made Gram add, "No running though."

They were off like gulls skimming the water. The air was drenched with the smell of roasting coffee from the Hills Brothers plant that lined the waterfront. Funny that coffee didn't taste like it smelled . . . except when Uncle Pat would put just a spoonful in her cup of milk. She and Frankie hung over the rails for awhile, then went down to the main cabin to practice their sea-legs walking bow to stern and back. By the time she noticed the ferry was docking again, they had to race up the stairs to get to Gram. Gram didn't make a fuss about their not having come back sooner; she was talking and laughing with the man next to her.

"I've got most of it figured out," she tapped the map. "First we find the Court of Pacifica with the huge statue, then we'll see the panoramic open-air auditorium."

"I can find that," Elizabeth said.

"Will you go to the Cavalcade of the Golden West?" the man asked. "It's supposed to be the biggest stage in the world."

✖ ✖ ✖

They sat in the open air panoramic auditorium watching the Cavalcade. Indians, Gold Miners, Missionaries, and Soldiers crowded the stage along with two horses, a buffalo, and a cannon. They all made speeches except the horses and buffalo.

"We don't have to stay. D'you want to leave?" Gram asked.

Elizabeth nodded. Frankie, his hair falling into his face, was already pushing his way to the end of the aisle, smiling at everyone. "Boring," he said with Gram's tone of voice. Everybody smiled back, but no one else got up. The Cavalcade had an hour to go.

"The only entertaining thing was when the horse peed," Gram said.

"The horse pee-ed, the horse peed!" Frankie echoed. Elizabeth stifled her laugh with her hand and didn't say anything. Mother didn't let them say words like "peed!"

"Your mother would like it," Gram said, "but we have better things to do." They walked outside by the fountain in front of the statue of Pacifica. "What do you say to a cup of tea and a scone at the Scottish Village?"

Elizabeth would rather have had a glazed doughnut and cup of hot chocolate topped with whipped cream. But anything Gram suggested captured Frankie's attention, and besides, you weren't supposed to say what you wanted, even if you knew.

They followed Gram through the gate into the fenced village of thatched roof cottages. You could buy glasses with thistles on them, or packets of scones, or linen tea towels in the cottages. Gram led them to a table where she ordered a pot of tea and a plate of scones from the waiter. "Mind you bring the pot to the kettle, not the other way round," she called out to him as he turned to leave. The man laughed. The two of them had already decided that the tea would be black Lipton's — loose tea leaves, not in silly little bags.

"You sound like you're a Scot," the woman at the next table said.

"I was born in Newcastle-upon-Tyne, in England," Gram said, "but my mother was from Dundee." She turned to Elizabeth. "D'you know you're Celtic?"

"We're Irish and German," Elizabeth said.

"Your parents were born in those countries, but before there were countries, there were Celts in a lot of different places and what mattered was what your mother was. In fact, you're the oldest daughter of my oldest daughter and I was the oldest daughter of my mother who was the oldest daughter and so on, ever so far back. We're Celts."

"Sounds like the Druid priestesses," the woman at the next table said.

Elizabeth didn't know what to make of that, but it was interesting. St. Anne's parish had six priests, but no priestesses, just nuns. "What do priestesses do?" she asked.

"Oh, they had all kinds of powers. They knew how to heal, and where animals could be found to hunt. They also could look into the future and knew beforehand when troubles were coming. They knew where to hide," the woman said.

The waiter brought the scones and a pot of tea to the table. "All properly brewed and steeped," he said. Gram poured a few drops into her saucer and held it to her nose. "Tis fragrant," she nodded to him. She poured them each a cup of tea and added a generous amount of cream before getting back into her conversation with the woman at the next table. They agreed the scones were light as a feather and the secret was to use lard, just as you did with pie crust or pasties.

Elizabeth wished they'd talk more about the priestesses.

When they finished, Gram left enough money on the table to have bought another pot of tea. "You must always leave a good tip for waiters and chambermaids," she said. "They depend on it. That reminds me, I have a friend to see. D'you know where the Hall of Science is?"

Elizabeth did. "That's where a bowl's suspended in the air, like magic in OZ — but the attendant says it's a magnet in reverse that pushes the bowl up into the air. And a box, maybe a foot high that shows a little picture of some man who's talking on a platform at the other end of the room, and you can hear him. It's like Tom Swift's picture telephone invention in the books Uncle Pat left — except I don't know why anyone wants to look at a man just talking."

"We're not going in," Gram interrupted her. "I just need to know where it is to find our way to the back of it."

They were in a part of the Fair grounds Elizabeth hadn't seen before. It looked like a western cowboy town, with wooden fences and people walking around dressed like cowboys. A tall woman — Gram didn't even come up to her chin when the woman wrapped her arms around her — shouted, "Lizzie, you changed your mind! You're here. Are you coming with me, after all?" Gram, her face all rosy and laughing, shook her head.

"These are my grandchildren, Elizabeth and Frankie," she said. "With all you told me, how grand the Fair would be, I decided I had to see it myself."

"I'm Sally," the tall woman said to the children. "I wanted your Grandmother to travel with me, but she said she had enough adventures in the Finlan Hotel, without going on the road." She looked at a tiny watch on her arm. "I've an hour before the next show," she said. "We can sit down and have a cup of tea. I want to talk to you and have you read the leaves."

She turned to the children. "What do you want to do while we talk? Would you like to go visit the Hall of Food? They give out delicious little cups of rennet custard and cherry Danish pudding."

Elizabeth hesitated, and then remembered she was the eldest daughter of an eldest daughter — like a priestess. "I'd like to ride the Elephant Train," she said. "Does it come by here?"

"You've never ridden on the Elephant train?" Sally asked. "Would you both like to?" A bashful nod from Frankie. "Your grandmother and I will put you on the very next Elephant." Sally held up her hand to signal the man just coming around the bend in the road. She thrust a bill into his hand and told him he had two special guests. Her mouth widened in a laugh showing white teeth. Neither Frankie nor Elizabeth needed help to climb up to the bench seats, which were open on both sides. "It takes almost an hour to travel around the Island and we'll be right here to meet you, when you get back."

The train with its large elephant head, trunk, and tusks curled in front of the little motorcars it pulled, moved off. Gram, waving goodbye, was dwarfed by Sally, who in turn was dwarfed by the huge poster of a woman dressed in cowboy boots and a cowboy hat. She held balloons in front of her, so you couldn't see if she had anything else on. "Sally Rand's Nude Ranch," the sign over the gate read.

The lights inside the fountains were turned on, even though it wasn't dark yet. The drops of water sparkled blue and green and a pink that was like the sky at sunset. Elizabeth remembered Gram reading tea leaves for her friends in Butte when they went up to visit her last summer. After supper in the evening, they walked with her on the rail tracks used for carrying ore from the mines. They stopped in small houses to visit one or another of Gram's friends, then sat in the kitchen eating fresh baked cake, or saffron bread, and drinking tea.

"You've had a letter, have you?" Gram might start, eyeing the tea cup this way and that, to see how the leaves clumped. She'd show them to Elizabeth and then to her friend. "Mind, you see this bit here, and how it slopes?" The friend's head would nod. "Well, the fat's in the fire."

Gram's friends all marveled that she had the *gift*. She also could tell their fortunes from playing cards. She knows when the troubles are coming, Elizabeth thought.

Gram didn't tell fortunes in San Francisco. Mother disapproved of super-stitious nonsense so Gram gave it up for Lent, and whenever she was in San Francisco. But Treasure Island wasn't really San Francisco.

✖   ✖   ✖

"Why do people from Butte call you Lizzie?" She asked Gram when they were on the Ferry coming home.

"My christening name is Elizabeth, just like yours — except it's Elizabeth Lawson Dyer — and Lizzie is a more friendly name," Gram said.

It was dark, by the time they got home. The fog was already thick again in the Sunset District, and cold, but the kitchen was warm and filled with the smell of lamb stew.

"How did you like the Cavalcade of the Golden West?" Mother asked.

"Oh, it was grand," Gram said, "all those people on the stage. You couldn't do that in Butte. Just imagine pushing a buffalo up by his behind onto the stage of the Rialto!"

"I don't want to be called Elizabeth any more." The words burst out of Elizabeth. "My name is Lizzie," she said. Her cheeks were hot. She must have been blushing.

Her mother was speechless for a couple of seconds. "Now listen here, young lady . . ."

Gram laughed. "I like the sound of that," she said. "Perhaps we'll call you Lizzie, the Second." She pressed her finger to the side of her nose and looked at her granddaughter. "No, that's too long," she said. "You should have your own name. How about Lizby?"

So that's how she got a friendly name. Mother let her have it, but she wouldn't use it. To her mother she was always Elizabeth.

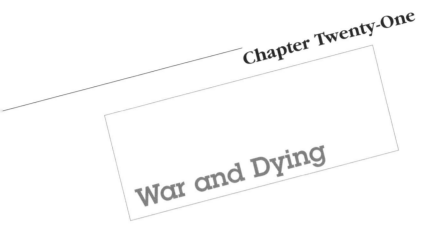

Chapter Twenty-One

War and Dying

D inner had to be on the table at 6 PM.

Their father, Hans Frings, belonged to the International Longshoreman's Union and he worked on the waterfront. Every day except Sunday he left early in the morning with his stevedore's white cap pulled down to his eyebrows and his wood handled cargo hook in his belt. The children did not see him again until dinner, unless he had a union meeting. Then, they didn't see him at all before they went to bed.

Dad had a cleft in his chin, like Errol Flynn in the Wednesday night movies, but he didn't grab ropes and jump around. He could have though. He had sailed all over the world on three and five-masted ships before he met Mother. He knew how to do everything, even make chairs.

After he got home at 5:30, he washed up and read the *Examiner* and *Call Bulletin* while Lizby set the table and Mother finished cooking.

This night was different. Mother was reading something. She hadn't even peeled the potatoes.

She looked as if she'd been crying when Lizby and Frankie got home from school, but she didn't say anything. Lizby put away her books, unbuttoned the stiff white starched collar and took off her navy blue uniform. She hung it in the closet. Mother still didn't say a word as Lizby picked up a potato and started peeling.

Frankie had one of his earaches and needed his mother to put some hot oil into it so he would feel better. He climbed on her lap and told her. She took care of his ear, but without hugging or teasing him. She again picked up the letter she had left by the medicine cabinet. "From your Uncle Pat."

They hadn't had a letter from Uncle Pat since he and his friend Pete went off to Spain to fight the fascists.

Frankie and Lizby missed him. Even though he had left all sorts of books — Tom Swift, and The Rover Boys — they didn't have him picking them up to give them a whisker burn, or sleep on the couch in the living room. They couldn't tumble on the cushions and bounce to make him laugh and wake up.

"Hans, I've had a letter from Spain," Mother called out to Dad when they heard him come in the door.

"Pat's not dead, is he?"

"No, this is from him, but he's in a hospital. He doesn't say how badly he's hurt, just that he's planning to go back to the front."

"What I hear on the dock, it's not going well. Brunete was a disaster." Dad tried to pull her into his arms, but she would not get up. He sat down beside her.

"He talks about Brunete. You didn't tell me," Mother said.

"There was no point."

Lizby felt a cold silence inside. Something had happened to Uncle Pat. She hadn't thought he might get hurt, just how much she missed him. No breath.

Mother told Dad what the letter said, then read parts out loud. Lizby pulled her chair out from the table to sit. Frankie did, too. Pat had been wounded in the leg at Brunete. His friend Pete wasn't so lucky. He had lost his right arm.

I didn't know what it'd be like in battle. I had a rifle, a can of ammo, and some odds and ends in my pockets, but my mouth was dry — scared spitless. The noise of shelling everywhere was worse than in the Frisco strike, because I didn't know where the enemy was. My legs did not want to move, but I had to.

Nine hundred of us fought at Brunete. The guy next to me got it in his neck. I still didn't know what was happening. There was a popping sound like pulling out a cork, before he fell against me. Then his blood was on my chest, pouring down my shirt. Six hundred of us were wounded or killed—but we won if you can call it that—we held the line...

Mother stopped. She couldn't finish reading that part, she was crying with tears running down her cheeks. Lizby and Frankie were crying, too.

Lizby sometimes had to sing a song at Mass on Sunday — "Blood of my Savior, gushing from His side . . . wash me in your tide." Ugh! She looked at the scar at the base of her little finger. She got it in a fight just before her First Communion. Joan Ackermann, the girl across the street, had picked up a broken bottle from the corner lot and gashed her hand. Lizby must have done something to make her mad, but seeing her own blood put it out of her mind. It made her stomach feel sticky like it felt when she looked at runny eggs, or spit.

Dad reached over to take the letter from Mother's hand, but she held onto it, just as she had all afternoon. "The next page is from Albacete, the headquarters for the International Brigades. He's been reassigned to the ambulance corps. There is not much equipment and too much to do. A young boy he picked up on the side of the road told him he lost his foot when the planes dropped bombs on his village."

Dad made a sound like a growl. "Women and children — target practice for Franco's Nazi buddies."

Mother skimmed Pat's description of his work: *". . . artillery and ammunition to the front, pick up the dead . . . bring the wounded back . . . try and get a bath, but you never get rid of the lice. The . . ."*

Mother stopped reading for a minute. "His language! He never used to use words like that . . ." She started again.

The last page described a Nazi Condor plane strafing Uncle Pat's truck. The truck crashed, and he woke up in a hospital bed. He had been there a week. He talked about Communist big shots, who came to visit — *"Jaysus, there's no time off, even in the hospital!"*

Mother looked up. "He ends with a laugh — he's just like Pa."

"The next batch who came in — we didn't give them a chance to make

speeches at us — we gave them some songs we made up to the tunes of the
'Bulldogs Fight Song' and 'Take Me Out to the Ball Game.'"

'Oh my, I'm too young to die . . .

Take me over the sea — where Franco, he can't get at me!

Oh how I wanna go home!'

The BS brass didn't get it — why were we laughing.

We'll stick to the end, but the few pieces of artillery we've got look like
they date back to Napoleon, so it'll be soon. We've been outnumbered and out-
gunned from the beginning."

"I don't know what to think," Mother said. "Monsignor Moriarity . . . all the
newspapers say Franco's protecting families and the Church against godless
Communists."

"They don't mention Franco's pals, the godless Nazis, killing children,"
Dad said.

"I just don't want Pat killed!" She started to cry again. "I've taken care of
him since he was in diapers. I protected him. Now, there's nothing I can do."
She let Dad put his arm around her.

✖   ✖   ✖

Lizby tried to think what it would be like if Uncle Pat died. She couldn't.
People died — most of them old and in Butte. She went with her mother to see
them in their coffins with all the wreaths. Bernadette, with her round head,
sleepy eyes and a wide smile was the only girl Lizby knew who had died. She
was a Mongoloid with them in the third grade.

Lizby was awake, but she woke up even more when Sister told them that
Bernadette had died suddenly. Everything was bright — the afternoon sunlight,
the dust in the air, the colors of everyone's hair and skin, the smell of chalk, the
sound of paper, and the way the room felt. Sister Alma stood fingering the
wooden rosary beads that hung from her leather belt. A starched wimple framed
her rosy-cheeked face and she smelled like Ivory soap. The white bandeau part
under her black veil cut into her forehead. Lizby could see just a peek of her
shaved hair in front of where her ears should be.

Sister said, "Bernadette died on Sunday. That means her soul has left her
body and gone to live with God." Sister looked around to see how the class

was taking this. "The body is like an automobile. The soul uses the body to move around in."

Lizby stretched her automobile hands on her desk. This was not what the Baltimore Catechism said, but it was much more interesting.

Sr. Alma went on. "Bernadette couldn't talk very well and she couldn't run like you do because her body was damaged, but she had a beautiful soul exactly like yours — and God loved her, the same as He loves you."

Lizby hadn't paid much attention to Bernadette, but now that she knew Bernadette had a body that wouldn't talk or drive the way she wanted it to, it made Lizby sad. But she still hated the smell of gardenias, when they went to see her that night. They all said the rosary and went to the funeral Mass the next day.

This could not happen to Uncle Pat. She would not let the pictures into her mind. He'd come home. She knew it. She didn't want his soul to be hurt.

✖   ✖   ✖

Molly sat in the living room surrounded by pages of the Chronicle. She had finished the wash and hung it on the line to dry. Fresh sheets on all the beds; at last, time for a cup of coffee. They had moved into the new house, a block away from the flat, two months ago. It surprised her that Hans had saved enough for the down payment, but she should have known he'd keep something like that to himself.

The house was quiet with Frankie and Elizabeth both at school. She looked through the glass doors into the dining room that overlooked the garden — a contented spot. She had to admit it would be pretty. Hans was looking forward to the birth of their baby in a short while — their family and their home pleased them both.

She took a sip of coffee and picked up Sunday's paper. Finally, a chance to catch up with the news. First the funnies. Maggie and Jiggs, Prince Valiant — she was as bad as Elizabeth in her reading priorities — then the front pages.

A half-hour later, she had worked her way to the Sunday society section. Her breath stopped, and she stared at the page. Under the picture of a pleasant looking woman, the article was about a well-known cellist. "On the other side of the footlights," it began and went on to describe the woman's forthcoming marriage to an equally talented physician, Chelsea D. Eton, whose paintings were currently on display at the Feingarten Galleries. The article noted Dr. Eton's memberships in the Olympic Club and the California Writers' Club.

Molly felt as if she'd fallen; her breath knocked out of her. The rest of the story . . . the cellist's accomplishments . . . parties her family and friends were planning. Nothing more about Chel.

Mind blank, then painful, prickling feelings, like blood entering a cramped leg. He had found the kind of woman he wanted to marry, someone who matched him. He had not given Molly a thought . . . Chel did not know or care whether he had a daughter or a son. That she still carried such bitterness stunned her.

She folded the paper slowly and sat in silence.

At last, she stood up and walked to the kitchen, twisting the news sheets into a tight ball. She lifted the iron lid to the wood-burning section of the stove, shoved the paper in, and struck a match. She watched the flames curl around the pages.

✖   ✖   ✖

James Thomas was born and like his brother John Francis, baptized with the names of two of his uncles. Elizabeth Patricia, of course, had been given her Grandmother and Uncle Patrick's name. Jimmy fascinated his brother and sister. If he was awake he smiled, and seemed totally awake noticing everything. As he learned to talk, his charm increased. Frankie began to spend more time with his father working at the workbench in the basement and going to Golden Gate Park to look at plants. Elizabeth discovered the library and reading.

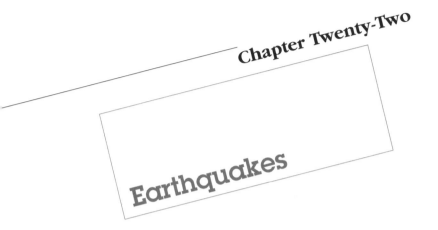

Chapter Twenty-Two

Earthquakes

Spring 1940 – Summer 1941

The ceiling lamps swayed a little and the house jarred as if you were in a car when it ran over a bump in the road. Sometimes there were two or three bumps, then nothing, and then another couple of bumps. What was scary — you did not know when it would happen. Things fell off the shelf, and the ground sounded like something deep under the earth wanted to get out and was pushing things out of its way.

Sometimes a long time would go by without an earthquake. At first there didn't seem to be any more quakes after they moved into the new house. But later they pushed through, one after another, and everything seemed shakier.

Lizby watched her father paint the pantry shelves.

"Can I do that?" she asked.

He grunted and handed her the brush. When she raised her arm, the paint ran back into the brush and onto her hand. Dad took the brush from her, and cleaned it.

"Watch," he said. She saw how he dipped only part of the brush into the paint, held the brush level, and then stroked. He always painted over the edge of his last stroke when he started a new one.

He didn't offer to let her paint again. "You're not a boy," he said.

Frankie's small workbench with his own tools stood next to Dad's in the new basement. A two and a half foot sailboat was braced on the bigger workbench. Its sails still had to be rigged.

"When will we sail it?" Frankie demanded.

"When it's finished." Dad looked at him with raised eyebrows. "Now, no more questions."

They followed Dad everywhere. He showed them the slips he had taken from the Rose Garden in Golden Gate Park and put into tin cans the year before. They had roots on them now, like little threads. The back yard, most of it sand when they moved in, changed after Dad put down mulch with gunnysacks of leaf moss he got from a forest down the Peninsula. It took weeks. He planted the rose slips and dahlias around a small lawn at the back of the yard.

Frankie asked if they could have a dog like Gram's, but Dad said, "No." Instead, he gave each of them a plant to water and take care of — Canterbury Bells for Lizby, and a Hen and Chicks ice plant for Frankie. He marked off the rest of the yard for beds of different kinds of flowers and a peach tree. Pots of begonias and a seed tray filled the sunroom back of the kitchen. When Lizby's plant had seeds, they put them into the tray.

A seed that looked like a grain of sand became a green thread with two tiny leaves, then a whole plant with stems of red bell flowers. She *liked* watching her plant change itself, even though it wasn't a dog.

✖   ✖   ✖

Mother called from the kitchen, "Library time. If you're going to come with me, get a move on."

Lizby hollered, "I'm coming," and raced upstairs to collect books from her bedroom. Frankie mumbled something about 'boat' and 'Daddy' and disappeared into the basement. While Lizby gathered her books, Mother folded freshly ironed clothes, now too small for the children. She placed them in a large paper sack near the front door.

They walked along Irving Street to the library. Her mother noted the prices of sidewalk fruit and vegetables and decided which stores they would return to on the way back. She deposited Lizby in the basement children's library and made her way to the upper floor. "I'm on the waiting list for the new Somerset Maugham novel," she said. "It must be my turn by now."

A half hour later, fresh books tucked under their arms, they strolled across the street to Mrs. Olsen's Swedish massage.

"Are you going to get into the hot-box with all the lights?"

"We'll see." When mother had a massage, Lizby sat in the outer room and read her books, but when she had a steam bath or sauna, Mrs. Olsen would massage Lizby if she did not have another customer waiting. Her lucky day! She felt like a small cat. She loved having her ears and toes rubbed. It made her tummy tickle at the same time.

An hour later, they shopped for groceries. Mother always bought more than they needed. They dropped the books and their groceries at home and picked up the clothes. Then they went by streetcar to Langendorf's on McAllister Street for day old bread, and to the Crystal Palace on Market Street to buy fish. Sometimes they brought the food to old ladies in the Fillmore district, but today with the clothes Lizby knew they'd be stopping by the Harrigans' house instead.

The Crystal Palace, a huge market with crowded aisles, was filled with noises that had a hollow sound. Shopkeepers shouted to one another and haggled with customers. Some of the fish markets smelled stinky, but Mother bought fillet of sole from a man who always had "fresh this morning!" fish for her.

"I thought you might be able to use some clothes the children have outgrown," Mother said when they reached the Harrigan family house. "Ma sends so many clothes at Easter, you'd think she owned Weinstein's Department Store."

"Ah, what a grand lot of dresses," Mrs. Harrigan, a thin little bird of a woman, said. "D'you have time to stop for a cup of tea?"

"Yes, and one of your oatmeal cookies."

This was what happened, Lizby thought. Soon Mrs. Harrigan would say that she was very, very grateful for the clothes, and wasn't it a shame that growing boys wore their shoes out so fast. Sometimes Mother had money to give to her, but mostly, she didn't. Lizby never heard her parents argue, but she knew Dad did not like Mother giving money away all the time. She also had a funny feeling that Mrs. Harrigan didn't like Mother.

Mr. Harrigan had something wrong with him, and milk delivery men only made $6 a week. There was never enough money for things the family need-ed.

"The milkmen need to join a union," Mother said.

"Isn't that the truth," Mrs Harrigan said. "The longshoremen are lords of the docks now with their short hours and good pay."

Afterwards, when they walked the two blocks home, Mother said, "No matter how much I bring, it's never enough for her." She was talking to herself, but Lizby would not have said anything anyway.

✖   ✖   ✖

One morning, Lizby sat, propped against her bed pillow, reading *The Seven League Boots*. She loved Richard Halliburton. When she grew up she'd dig up old cities like he did and figure out what happened — then she'd write books about her adventures.

Her small vanity with a white skirt stood next to the door. It was covered with library books, just like the desk next to the window — but that pile had Nancy Drew mysteries she wasn't finished reading. Books she wouldn't read again went on the floor. *Tom Playfair, Plebe at West Point, Percy Wynn* — Uncle Pat's books that he didn't want now he was back in the mines. Frankie might like them.

The half-open window brought in the sound of insects and the smell of flowers from Dad's garden. Sunlight slid across the floor and touched her toes. She stretched her feet to bring them closer into the sun. She was still in her pajamas. It wasn't time for breakfast yet.

The door banged open.

Mother moved into the bedroom holding Lizby's coat in her hands. Her eyebrows were tight together and her eyes narrow. She had red blotches on her neck.

"You're impossible!" She spat the words out. "Look at this room! Your clothes, books — nothing put away — your good coat tossed onto the tele-phone stand!"

She opened the window and hurled the coat out. Then she opened Lizby's closet and added all the clothes hanging on hooks instead of hangers and, for good measure, threw out the books on the desk as well. It was three floors down to the garden.

"You think I'm your servant, do you? Well, you've got another think coming. I've had just about enough of your not paying attention, eyes always drifting off as if you don't hear a word I'm saying." She drew herself up, hands on her hips, and glared at Lizby. "You are going to boarding school if you don't shape up."

Her red face and words were scary. Everyone left sweaters and jackets on the telephone post that stood between the clothes hooks and the desk in the front hall, even Mother, but she didn't allow talking back. Lizby bit her lips. She didn't know what to do.

"I . . . "

"Not another word from you," her mother warned. "I'm not going to talk to you again until you've straightened this pigsty of a room."

Uncle Pat used to say Lizby must not mind when Mother got angry. Sometimes she got up on the wrong side of the bed, and she didn't mean half of what she said. Lizby had asked him once what *exasperating* meant when her mother told her she was exasperating. Pat laughed a bit, and said it sounded like something the Green Hornet did. He figured her mother must want her to have a good vocabulary.

"But what do you do, when you're exasperating?" she asked.

"Well, you know how Mrs. Ackermann is with Goofus? She pulls one way, and he either won't move at all, or pulls the other way when he wants to smell something?" Goofus was Mrs. Ackermann's big dog, Gerhart the Fourth.

"You mean he has a mind of his own?"

"You said it, and it exasperates Mrs. Ackermann."

This time, Mother sounded a whole lot madder than that to Lizby. She didn't know whether she should run down to the yard and pick everything up, or wait. What could she carry the books in? She scurried down and up twice, before she thought of using her pillowcase, like they did for the laundry.

The next day, Mother took her on the streetcar to the Immaculate Heart Academy, a school in the Mission district that accepted boarders. A nun led them into a windowless office. When the nun in charge of admissions entered,

Lizby felt numb. This was a prison. Mother was throwing her away, like the clothes. Lizby heard their words, but couldn't understand them through her own thoughts.

The tuition must have been more than Mother could afford. She said, "I'll have to think about this for the fall, but for summer, I'd like to send Elizabeth to Camp Imelda, your camp on the Russian River." Mother used her church voice and smiled. The nun seemed to think she was wonderful.

Neither of them looked at Lizby. Mother filled out the papers and left a cash deposit. She said to the nun, "Would it be possible for you to show us the dormitories where the girls sleep, and the dining room and chapel?"

"This will teach you a lesson," she whispered in Lizby's ear as they followed the nun through the undecorated walls of the school. The dormitories, with neatly made beds in rows and chests of drawers between every two beds, looked tightly crowded. "This is where you'll go if you don't mind what I say."

Going home on the streetcar, Mother hinted she might send Lizby to an even worse place, the Convent of the Good Shepherd for Wayward Girls. "You're going to Camp Imelda this summer for your own good. You're becoming incorrigible."

For not hanging up her clothes? No, there must have been more. Lizby remembered her mother saying other times when she was mad, "Mind your tongue," and "Wipe that look off your face." Her angry spells were hard to understand though. She seemed to hate Lizby. Mother gave Dad the silent treatment sometimes when he got angry about the amount of money she gave away, but she'd never heard either of them shout at the other. She was the one Mother hollered at. Uncle Pat used to say not to cry, she just had to wait it out. Lizby decided to think of more interesting things when it got bad — but when she did that, her mother seemed to know what she was up to. It made her madder.

A month passed before her mother took her to the bus for Camp Imelda; her mother's mood had changed. She cried and said she'd miss Lizby, and gave her a dollar for spending money — the first money Lizby had ever had.

Lizby couldn't figure her mother out.

Camp Imelda, two weeks of swimming lessons, sleeping in a tent with other girls, singing at campfire and going for hikes was fun. She told the girls her name was Lizby, and that's what they called her. She did not know why her mother thought camping was punishment, and she wished she could stay longer.

Maybe it would be better to keep her eyes on her mother's face like she wanted. But sometimes she could not help it. Her mind popped her into a story someplace else. It happened other times, too. Like Saturday. Mother wasn't around, but she'd been told to have her tasks finished by the time Mother got home. Lizby almost didn't because of all the things there were to think about. Like Mrs. O'Connell and swimming pools, and neighbors in their houses.

She cleaned out her parent's walk-in closet, then took the dust mop and shook it out the front window. She looked at the houses on their block. A few had scraggly palm trees in front, because the sun didn't shine much in the Sunset District. Maybe half the houses had children, but all of them had a husband and wife. How could anyone fall in love with any of those husbands, any of those wives? Maybe 'falling in love' was just in movies.

No, Lizby decided. She would not fall in love and she would not get married.

She finished mopping the dust curls from under the two cedar chests in the closet, and then the laundry had to be put away. She opened the blue paper packages of ironed sheets and carried them to the linen closet in the hall between the bedrooms. She could imagine someone loving Mrs. O'Connell who lived around the corner on Lincoln Way, though.

She did.

Mr. O'Connell, a policeman who never in living memory said one word, was like her dad, who didn't look up from his paper or say anything when she and Frankie kissed him goodnight before saying their prayers and going to bed. Mr. O'Connell, when he was ready to marry, had gone back to Ireland and found Mrs. O'Connell. They had three sons and then a daughter, Frances, who was Lizby's age, but smarter. She had skipped a grade.

Mrs. O'Connell put sheets through the mangle in the Toulouse Laundry, where Mother sometimes did bookkeeping. She had a broad freckled face and curly hair bound with a thick shoelace tied around her head. She tucked her hair so it looked like a roll, except for one strand that usually slipped out near her ear.

People always laughed when Mrs. O'Connell was around. She told great stories about crazy things that happened to her. Like when she made ginger beer and it exploded in her basement. Every time Lizby thought of it, she giggled, "There the dim-witted bottles stood on the shelves, their caps firing off like rifle shots from the IRA." Sometimes Lizby laughed so hard at her stories she wet her pants a little.

After Lizby put the sheets on the shelf, she opened the white paper packages of rough-dry things that were not ironed — underwear, and towels. They had to be folded properly and put into the right drawers.

Mrs. O'Connell took Frances and Lizby swimming almost every week during summer. Lizby's nose prickled just thinking about the chlorine smell, the cold, wet, rubber mats, and the damp steam of the pools — and herself in them.

Each pool was different — the great jungle of ropes she and Frances swung on like Tarzan was at the Young Ladies Institute. The Art Deco Crystal Plunge in North Beach had walls with horizontal lines that looked like women. Then they had six salt-water pools of every temperature to choose from at Sutro's, plus its long slide down into its biggest pool. Fleischacker's pool, outdoors by the Zoo, was where the Elephant train went after the World's Fair. It went on for blocks and could have held all the other pools put together. Mrs. O'Connell took the girls to them all.

Mrs. O'Connell didn't swim or bike, but she taught the children how to do both. She stood at the side of the pool and moved her face and arms like the pictures in her book on swimming showed. Sometimes, they rented bikes on Stanyan Street for twenty-five cents an hour, and rode around the parking lot at Kezar Stadium. Mrs. O'Connell ran along with them holding the seat, until they got their balance.

She bought packages of square Walnetto caramels wrapped in wax paper or salt-water taffy when she took them to visit the zoo. When she took them home, she told stories about their prowess on the bikes and herself, 'losing her hairpins flying after the rapscallions to keep up.' Her stories pictured it all over again and made it funnier. Lizby's mother laughed too, so hard that she had to wipe her eyes.

Lizby crunched the laundry paper and the string and carried it down to the kitchen. Maybe it was worth being married if you liked children as much as Mrs. O'Connell did.

A week later, Mother and Mrs. O'Connell took the girls shopping downtown at the Emporium under the big glass dome. Frances and Lizby had on hats, and their white cotton gloves. Mrs. O'Connell held up a teal-green, terry-cloth, two piece swim suit. "This is just right," she said. "Lizby needs a proper suit."

"Two-piece? I don't think so," Mother said.

"Sure, it's perfect. All the girls at the CYO have them this year."

Lizby was ecstatic. Mother bought it!

✖ ✖ ✖

They must be going to Montana, Lizby thought, even though it was already the middle of summer. When her mother started losing her temper more often, and had a lot of headaches, it usually meant they were going to visit Gram. It'd be okay though. Her mother always calmed down again once they'd been on the train awhile.

Before they left, Mother had to work at the laundry to help with the mid-year accounting. Dad sat in the kitchen. No one else was home.

"This swim suit you brag about. Let me see it. Put it on."

Something felt wrong. Her father almost never talked to her, except to tell her to get the dishes done, or to sweep the floor. His eyes looked flat. She did-n't dare disobey, but she did not want to find the suit. She dragged her feet up the stairs. She found the suit in her drawer, the suit that had made her feel so special. She felt stupid. She did not know what she was afraid of, but she was bawling when she went down the stairs. Her father just looked at her with flat eyes and did not say anything else, so she ran back up the stairs, snuffling and wiping her nose with the back of her hand.

He did not ask her to do anything like that again. She told Mother she had not wanted to show Daddy her suit, and put the memory out of mind.

Two days later, they were on their way to Montana.

She and Frankie liked going to Butte. Waking up in the Pullman berth as the train crossed the Great Salt Lake was wonderful. First thing, they squeezed the little metal levers in the middle of the window shade and pushed it up. Water everywhere. They seemed to be moving right through the middle of the lake. *"Breakfast in the diner: nothing could be finer . . ."* than oatmeal with cream served in a bowl under a silver cover. Especially on a white linen tablecloth with a flower in a crystal vase, and the sound of rail wheels clacking under them. In the night, the sound of the wheels, the jerk and coupling of added rail cars, and the cry of the conductor, PO-CA-TELL-O, IDA-HO rocked them to sleep again.

The night sky was magic in Butte — San Francisco didn't have a night sky, only fog, but Montana had stars, and sometimes thunder clouds and lightning with sounds and smells. She and Frankie thought of their attic bedroom window up in Butte as a wizard's screen through which they could look at lightning, then a few moments later listen to thunder rumbling. The raindrops came streaking down flat against the glass. After the lightning, a funny warm smell would come in the air from the crack where they left the window open.

Gram didn't meet them at the station this time, but Lizby knew Spot, the tough mongrel who'd been with Gram as long as she could remember, would be waiting at the top of the alley.

She held Frankie's hand when they walked through the station. "Don't worry. We're going to see Uncle Pat and Spot," she said. "Butte's greatest dog."

Sure enough, when the cab let them off, Spot streaked over and hurled himself into their arms.

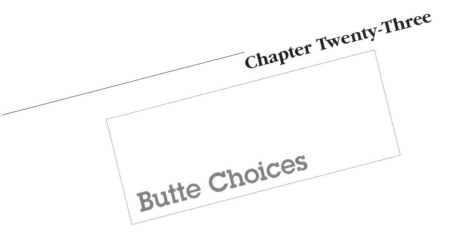

Chapter Twenty-Three

Butte Choices

Summer 1941

M olly was furious. If only she could throw something, or scream, or do anything to get rid of the volcano inside her. The train ride hadn't helped, and the lava inside her was turning to rock. Her face already felt like stone.

When they arrived in Butte, it was late afternoon on Elizabeth's twelfth birthday. Molly knew she should do something to celebrate it, but she did not want to. She would like to have left the children with Lizzie and gone on, but where could she go? Trudy, her only friend from the old days, was touring Europe with her current man. Sister Magdalene had been retired to the Mother House in Helena. Molly pictured the last time she had seen Magdalene, waving from the Convent of the Good Shepherd. She had hugged her close before they parted. 'You have a fierce sense of justice, Molly. But you need to learn how to use your anger — and when.'

The old nun was probably dead by now. There was no place Molly felt she could be herself. Alone. How she longed to be alone, away from the mess she had made of her life.

A bakery near the train station was open. She stopped the cab to buy a chocolate cake layered with lemon curd before they went home to Lizzie.

When Lizzie served the cake with tea after supper, it was old and stale. Molly wanted to put her head in her arms and cry, but she sent the children to bed instead.

"But Uncle Pat's not home yet. Don't you want us to do dishes?" Lizby asked.

"No," Molly said. "Just say your prayers and go to bed."

"Your uncle's working the night shift. He didn't expect you 'til next week, or he'd have been here," Gram said.

"We haven't had our bath —" Frankie started.

"GO," Molly shouted. "I don't want to hear another peep out of you!"

After the children scrambled up the stairs, Lizzie asked, "What's wrong? I haven't seen you this upset in years."

"Ma, you know my hair-trigger temper when I think I'm in the right."

"Just like your father's," Lizzie agreed.

"Well, I can't let it out with Hans. Never. He's right so much of the time, it gets strangled," Molly said. "But sometimes I know he's wrong — very, very wrong — and I can't tell him how he's wrong to stop it. I'm still upset so I take it out on the children. Gawd, today I couldn't even bring myself to say 'Happy Birthday' to Elizabeth."

Molly went to the stove and reached for the kettle to put more water in the pot. "Sometimes I act like a madwoman, then I'm so ashamed and I go to confession." She shook her head. "I do penance, but it doesn't seem to help. My temper flares up just the same the next time."

"You know I've never held with taking your problem to priests — or nuns," Lizzie said. "What do they know about married people? Besides why should you do penance for having a temper? Tell Hans what you're mad about, not some priest."

"But it's hard to think, much less say what the trouble is, and I don't know if I'm right."

"Well, that doesn't sound like you," Lizzie said.

"I know. I don't recognize myself." Seeing in her mind the unsayable, Molly took a quick gulp of tea and blurted out the latest reason for her upset. "When I was out of the house last week, Hans made Elizabeth put on her swimsuit for him to look at her."

"Well what was wrong with that?" Lizzie asked. "If I know that young lady, she'd been bragging about swimming and all the places she had been going with Mrs. O'Connell. Didn't I hear her myself, not a half hour ago? Has Hans seen her swim?"

"No, but Ma, I was out of the house. Why didn't he ask to see it while I was there? And why make her put it on? She was frightened."

"Well I wouldn't make too much of it. Fathers don't always know how kids take things."

Molly felt a mixture of feelings, mostly relief at Lizzie's explanation. But something similar must have happened before. Hans probably walked into the bathroom while Elizabeth was taking a bath and he did not back out, but stood looking at her. Now, Elizabeth would not take a bath when he was in the house. Molly knew this must have happened. There was no other explanation. Elizabeth had asked her, 'If maybe we could put a hook and latch on the bathroom door — so if someone's inside, you'd know and wouldn't try to open the door.' Molly hadn't thought about it at the time, but what else could have put that into her daughter's head?

A memory flash from years ago flooded her — Han's heavy lidded eyes watching her silently when she was in the kitchen, while she laughed and chatted and did her work. How it felt and how she ignored the melting emptiness swelling in the pit of her bowels until it reached her nipples and stopped her words. And he and she were drawn into one hard, pulsing fullness, rushing and gentling one another. What had happened to the passion between them? What had made her feel so trapped and angry?

A headache was starting . . . blinding little points of light that pressed the back of her eyes. She pushed her eyebrows together in a tight frown to hold the pain back.

✖ ✖ ✖

Molly typed a set of speed drills. She liked hearing the bell of the big Remington typewriter, snapping back the carriage to begin a new line, and keeping the even tapping rhythm of the keys. She was once again at Butte Business School, determined to improve her office skills. She looked over the next pages in the typing manual and decided against rote finger exercises. She'd write a letter to Hans.

She put a fresh sheet of paper into the typewriter and reset the tabs. She had packed up and left San Francisco without saying good-bye. Hans didn't understand children and didn't want to. She typed she was staying in Montana for a few months; he should send money to her. Then her fingers stopped. There was nothing else to say.

Hans would send money for their expenses without question. He probably missed having Frankie follow him around, but she and he didn't think alike — about the Church, about his crude friends, about the long hours he spent at work, or about anything. She did not recognize herself anymore; she was angry so much of the time. Hans hated that she worked and had any shred of independence.

She felt she was in prison in San Francisco.

She could not write this. She looked at the page blankly for a moment, then pulled it from the typewriter and jammed it into an envelope. He would have to convince her that he wanted her and would take care of the children properly before she'd return. She decided not to think about any of this any further. She would simply send it. Let him figure it out.

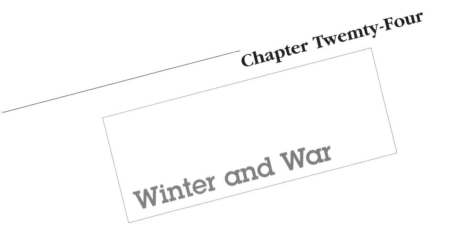

Chapter Twemty-Four

Winter and War

Sunday, December 7th, 1941

It was almost Christmas, and they were still in Montana. Uncle Pat shouted from Gram's front parlor, "You should get in here and listen to the radio." He fiddled with the radio knobs, trying to get a clearer voice. The news stunned them. The Japanese had attacked Pearl Harbor.

"What'll happen to Daddy?" Frankie asked. "Are they going to bomb San Francisco?" Mother and he were both crying. Lizby did not know what she felt — something terrible was happening. The little parlor, so crowded with stuffed armchairs you could hardly turn around, had barely enough room to breathe.

Mother turned to Pat, "Remember when the longshoremen refused to load scrap iron on boats going to Japan? The newspapers accused them of being Reds, but Hans said the iron would come back as bombs."

"He saw this war coming," Pat agreed, "but Germany . . ."

"Are the Japanese going to invade California?" Gram asked.

"Too far away. Hans says they have subs and airplanes though. Seattle and San Francisco may be bombed."

"Is Daddy a Red?" Frankie asked.

"Your father isn't a Red, and he isn't a Nazi. He's too practical," Pat blinked his eyes. They were shiny. "I need to find Pete," he said. He pulled his jacket and cap from the clothes hooks in the hall and fastened his gloves as he went out. Lizby kept looking at Gram's bronze statue of a cowboy tying up a calf, with his horse standing behind him. No thoughts came. She wanted to swallow, but her mouth was too dry.

They didn't see their uncle for a couple of days, but on Sunday night, after they were in bed, Lizby heard him come in. Something crashed in the kitchen and then Gram's voice. Her words were sharp. Pat mumbled. He must have been drunk. Gram was mad at him. "They need electricians in the mines," she shouted. "Getting yourself killed isn't going to solve anything."

When she saw Uncle Pat again it was Tuesday morning. She and Frankie sat at the table eating their cornflakes and grapefruit. Her uncle came to the table for breakfast. He hadn't shaved and his face was dark and thin. Mother asked him, "What will you do?"

He shrugged, "The army doesn't want me — that spot of black lung. Pete and I'll check out the Seabees. They're not so particular about seamen on the ship convoys. I can't fight with a gun, but there are other ways."

When Lizby thought of Uncle Pat dying, first blackness came, then her tears started so she stuffed the thought out of her mind, but she couldn't get interested in reading or anything else. No snow fell but it was bitter cold. The week before, the temperature had gotten down to 55 below zero. She pulled Spot from his place by the stove into the chair with her and kept her arms around him. He licked her fingers.

"Sit up straight, Elizabeth. Do I have to get you a brace?" Mother's words sliced into her mind. Gram shot Mother a look. Mother softened her tone, "She always slumps over," she said to Gram, "like she's carrying the weight of the world on her back."

"Balance a couple of books on your head, Lizby," Gram took the books she had put on a chair and placed them on her head. "Look, perfect carriage." She walked to the door and back. "Your mother needs to know there's nothing wrong with you." It was one of those times when they were not talking about what they were talking about — but Lizby didn't want to think about it.

During the days that followed until Christmas, Gram baked the fruitcakes she would send as gifts. Mother said to Gram that she didn't know what to do. She felt she should be back in California with Dad, but she still was not sure she could make things change with him. It was so much easier in Montana, where she was herself.

Lizby didn't know what she meant. How did she know when she wasn't herself? Lizby only knew when she was happy — like with Mrs. O'Connell, or afraid — like when she had a nightmare, or when she felt nothing—like now.

"The Mac," the grammar school of the Immaculate Conception, where they had been going for three months, did not feel like home to her. For one thing, they had boys and girls all in the same classroom, not separate like at St. Anne's. Nobody lived anywhere near them behind the San Anselmo mine, except the MacTavishes. And they were not much help.

They lived across the alley and went to public schools. Margy MacTavish, a little younger than Lizby, was very fat and blond and smiled a lot. Her older brother, Luke, had bad skin and stuttered when he talked at all, which was not much. He was in high school and spent most of his time tinkering with his short-wave radio.

Her classmates had crazy ideas about California — and her. They expected her to know all about Hollywood — as if it was Oakland, the next town over from San Francisco. All of them acted older, like they were in high school or something. She felt like a turtle, in her Sears-Roebuck catalogue snow suit, and all the other girls knew dance steps and words to songs — the 'Chatanooga Choo-choo,' 'Elmer's Tune,' and 'Down in the Meadow.' That one was about some "fishies" that "swam and swam right over the dam."

Dumb.

They invited her to be in their social club and in the weekly dance class. She knew they meant to be nice, but they seemed to want something from her, or think she was someone she wasn't.

Frankie, after a couple of fights with boys in his class, fitted in and liked "the Mac," fine. It was different for Lizby. She knew that she did not want to be there, but she didn't really want to be . . . anywhere.

✖   ✖   ✖

Lizby wound the metronome and started her scales again for the final go-through. The tall redheaded boy sat outside the music room, waiting. She could see him through the cloudy glass. He was the same boy who stared at her from his seat three rows over in class trying to get her attention.

Sister Mary James pursed her lips in disapproval of the sounds Lizby was making. "You must practice at home each day or there is no point to these lessons," she said.

Exactly right. There was no point to these lessons. Lizby slid Piano Basics 3 into her book bag and closed the piano. She hated scales. She hated piano. She hated the redheaded boy who could hear how awful she played.

"I see your boyfriend is waiting, but I want you here to practice for half an hour before your next lesson, Tuesday."

"He's not my boyfriend," Lizby muttered as she buttoned herself into her snowsuit.

When she opened the hallway door, the boy was looking at his high top basketball Keds, a broken shoelace in his hand. He immediately refocused on her and grinned. "Hi, I'm Red Mahoney," he said. "I'll walk you home."

"I don't need to be walked home."

"Aw, don't be that way," he wheedled. "Let me carry your books."

She kept her book-bag, but she could not think what to say to make him go away. He kept talking as if they were in a regular conversation. She didn't say a word. He told her about the open-air field near Gram's that would be flooded with water this week to make an ice-skating rink. "Do you know how to ice skate?"

"No," she said. "San Francisco doesn't have ice and snow."

"Would you like me to show you how?"

She knew Mother wouldn't buy her ice skates. Pink toe shoes, with lamb's wool to wrap around her toes, yes. She had let Lizby take toe dancing on condition that she practice the piano. But ice skates, no. Lizby knew without asking she wouldn't like the idea of a boy showing her anything.

"I don't think so," she said.

"At the end of January, we have a big holiday here, *Bohunkas Day*. Everyone dresses in crazy costumes and we have a dance. Would you go with me?"

She felt panicky. This boy was so pushy, and she didn't even know him.

"I think maybe I'm going with Luke MacTavish," she said. Suddenly, something happened in her, like when her mind popped her into a story. This time, it was as if she had popped into his mind. She *knew* what the redheaded boy was feeling. Confused and a little angry, but she also knew there was nothing for her to be afraid of in him.

"Looney Luke, the guy who can't talk straight?" he asked.

Whoosh, she was back in herself. "Uh," she said. "Do you know him?" Her fingers were crossed; she hadn't really said she was going, just maybe.

"My brother knows him."

Red Mahoney's conversation petered off after that, and he left her at the foot of the alley. She felt empty. She liked that he had asked her to Bohunkas Day and was sorry she had — sort of — fibbed.

✖   ✖   ✖

Mother finally bought their rail tickets back to San Francisco. Lizby tried to ignore the war. The one person she worried about was Uncle Pat. The newspapers did not report what happened to the convoys. It was like they didn't exist. But Lizby didn't like the reports of battles and deaths anyway, so she wouldn't have read them.

She felt terrible when President Roosevelt put Japanese families into the prison camps at Tanforan Race Track down the peninsula. Dad drove them down to see the camps. The prison was in the same place where they used to go for picnics and Uncle Tom used to bet on the horses. Now temporary army barracks filled the field. Dad had been born in Germany. What did this mean that Japanese were jailed and Germans were not? Would her dad be next? Would all of them go to a prison for Germans?

Then there was their house. It changed, too, although not like the Tanforan Race Track. First thing, when they came home from Montana, Mother made the house into a chapel. Father Monaghan came into the large front hall dressed in black. He kissed his green stole, placed it around his neck and blessed them all with Holy Water. Then he walked around sprinkling Holy Water in the hall and the rest of the rooms, except the basement. The ceremony was called the Enthronement of the Sacred Heart, so he said some prayers over the picture of Jesus pointing to his heart with one hand and up to heaven with the other. Mother hung the picture next to the front door in their hallway at the foot of the stairs. The hallway was as big as a bedroom, but a different shape.

They used to kneel by their beds to say an *Our Father* and an *Act of Contrition* before they went to sleep. But now, they had to say a decade of the rosary every night in front of the picture as part of their family prayers. Lizby always prayed that nothing bad would happen to Uncle Pat. Another difference was that her mother stayed longer, too, and talked to them.

"Each of us is a part of the mystical body of Christ," Mother said. "He lives in us and we are the means Jesus uses to carry out His work in the world. It is our responsibility to choose the best way to do this every day, and we have to examine our conscience every night to check how we've done."

"You're a toe nail," Frankie whispered to Lizby, "and you need to be clipped."

At the curve going up the stairs, a shrine to the Blessed Virgin Mary stood in the corner. Mother kept a bowl filled with flowers in front of her. The house turned into a magical fortress of protection against all the evils that worried Mother.

Lizby could not always concentrate on prayers, so she thought about books instead. Reading was the best place to disappear. She loved that nothing else happened when she was in a book. In bed at night with the light out, she became Jo in *Little Women*, and imagined different endings with more adventures before she went to sleep.

Mother bought shelves of, *"The complete Works of . . ."* Dickens, Hawthorne, Edgar Allen Poe, Washington Irving, Guy de Maupassant, Erasmus, and the *World Encyclopedia*. They always had something to read, but Lizby couldn't imagine herself into most of those stories. It was the way they talked, she thought. At school when she read the lives of the martyrs, particularly the French Jesuits who had explored Canada, she felt what happened. The Indians tore out their fingernails — it hurt. After Mass, Mother picked up all sorts of religious pamphlets from the racks in back of the church. So, Lizby also read about the rhythm method of birth control, but she could not picture it. Her mother gave her a Christmas present in the 8th grade — a book called *How to Think* by John Feardon that was about logic, syllogisms, and fallacies. She liked it. "It's like a code book," she explained to Frankie, but instead of reading, he kept looking for a match-up page in it like the one that came with his secret de-coder ring.

The hospitals in San Francisco did not have enough nurses for ordinary people, so Mother studied First Aid and how to be a nurse's aide. Dad worked double shifts on the bay. He was a barge boss with a huge crane and a gang of twenty men that had to be sent down the coast sometimes for days at a time.

Life was going on, but not much of it was in the Sunset District — at least not for Lizby.

Chapter Twenty-Five

San Francisco

Spring 1943

Rain and wind go together, but San Francisco fog holds stillness in the wet air. It just slips over the hills and up from the Bay close to the ground. Sometimes it is hard to see twenty feet ahead on the street. Then days and weeks, sometimes months go by when people walk around under what the newspapers call "overhead morning fog that will burn off in the late afternoon with temperatures in the low to mid-sixties." Tourists who come out expecting California sun shiver and wish they had brought something warmer to wear. San Franciscans don't hope for more; it is familiar, but the colors they see, both dark and light, are cleaner and unexpected.

✖   ✖   ✖

Molly clasped the railing of the bed so tightly her knuckles were white. She stood silent in a private room at St. Mary's Hospital. Trudy lay sleeping. The nurse told her Trudy had listed her as next of kin, so she could visit. Trudy's eyelids, white petals with pale blue veins, her face without makeup, expressionless, gaunt against the pillowcase, frightened Molly. Oh God, you can't let this happen.

She had known Trudy was ill, and worried about her cough.

Trudy's friend Ted brought her with him to Italy. He hoped the sun and easy life there for a year would help, but the War cut their trip short. Trudy called when they returned. She was better, she said, and any day would be scooping up Molly and the children for an adventure. But weeks had passed. Now, this.

Molly shivered. She knew the futility of arguing with God, of bargaining. She could only pray. She loved this woman . . . She glanced around the room. A huge bouquet, two dozen red roses at least, sat on the deep window ledge. From Ted probably, but where was he? Dark blood red roses. Whatever scent the flowers had was smothered by a heavier disinfectant smell.

A white metal chair, a side table cabinet with a half moon stainless steel bowl stood within easy reach to catch the blood, should it come gushing out again. The single high window looked out past Stanyan Street to a thick copse of eucalyptus opening into Golden Gate Park. How beautiful the day was, every precious moment of it.

Molly glanced back to the bed, her eyes caught by Trudy's. Trudy blinked, her eyes gentian blue as ever, but the whites like pale yellow clotted cream. She slightly crinkled one eye in a wink; her lips twitched a meager smile. The death mask was gone.

"Were you praying for me?" she asked in a husky whisper.

"How did you know?"

Trudy cleared her throat. Her smile deepened and her voice was stronger. "The Sister Mary Magdalene, Jr. look."

They smiled at each other. Molly bent, cradled Trudy's head, and kissed her.

"I've been thinking of the old days in our apartment, and our arguments about God," Trudy said. "How you believe that God exists — and I don't."

Molly waited.

"Are you talking to Him again about what's bothering you?"

"Sometimes. About stupid things I do, and my temper."

"Does he answer?" Trudy asked.

"Maybe. I sort of hear what He wants from what other people say, like you —"

"Me?"

Trudy sounded so startled, Molly laughed. "Yeah, sometimes you're a regular ventriloquist's dummy, a Charlie McCarthy — God's thoughts falling all over themselves getting into your words."

Trudy closed her eyes. She was barely breathing.

"Trudy, are you all right?" Molly pleaded.

A small smile touched the side of Trudy's mouth again, but her silence continued. "It's been like that . . . for both of us," she whispered.

Three days later, she died. Molly couldn't cry — or speak of it.

Guilt and Punishment

The new class intercom crackled. It was the Principal's office making an announcement. "We have exciting news. Our eighth graders have made us proud of them. Rosemary Lunkas has won a scholarship to the Convent of the Sacred Heart and Gertrude Miller has won the scholarship to St. Rose Academy." Sister Marcella led the clapping, congratulating Rosemary especially because the Convent of the Sacred Heart was the boarding school in the Flood Mansion that overlooked the bay.

Lizby remembered how awed they felt taking their tests in the school's marble ballroom. They sat in movable chair desks. The nuns were all called by their last name with 'Mother' in front of it, instead of 'Sister' or 'Miss.' Mother Mejia supervised the tests and afterwards led them into a wood paneled dining room with another marble fireplace. The serving sisters, who were called 'Sister,' passed plates of cookies and brought them little napkins, while Mother Mejia poured tea from a silver pot that hung in a silver sling contraption. Someone said her father was the ambassador from a South American country.

St. Rose Academy was not nearly as fancy. But the Dominicans taught it and they charged a lot more tuition than Presentation High School where the rest of the students from St. Anne's grammar school were going. It was great fun trekking around the city to all the different Catholic Schools — an adventure that Mother didn't object to Lizby having and enjoying.

Mother didn't let Lizby go on streetcars alone, but she couldn't object to something everybody in the class was doing.

Heidi Krois, who sat next to Lizby in class, thought none of the schools served cookies as good as her own mother made. Lizby agreed, and felt lucky to know the Kroises. Frances O'Connell was already at Pres because of her skipping a grade, and her family had moved out near the beach, so Lizby didn't see them any more. She missed them, and would have been lonesome, if it were not for Heidi.

It was funny how they got to be friends. When school started in the fall, Sister Marcella was new to the school and sort of frightened by so many students. She tried hard to keep them from making noise and talking. Lizby always knew when anyone was upset, but with Sister it was obvious. She got little beads of sweat above her upper lip.

At last, Sister Marcella thought of rearranging their seats, not alphabetically or according to height. She did not tell them what she was doing but it was easy to figure out. She put the smart kids who did their homework, like Janet Brown, on her right side near the windows. Kids who were dumb or caused trouble, she put on her left near the blackboards. In the middle were average kids who got average grades, like Lizby. Lizby understood Sister's view of her. She didn't do homework, didn't like to memorize poems like Longfellow's *Hiawatha*, and her grades said she was average. When Sister looked at her, Lizby knew she thought "a girl who isn't quite all there." And Heidi was, "a girl who has fits." Heidi sat in the blackboard side row next to her. She breathed through her mouth a lot, and Sister probably thought she might have a seizure any moment. But she had not had one that Lizby could remember since the fifth grade.

Heidi had a good memory for times tables and division. Lizby figured the fits were like Bernadette whose body had a few things that did not work right. Neither of them did well in anything except arithmetic — but that was fun. They passed notes to one another in arithmetic and always got everything right. Particularly, now that they had started algebra. Lizby read the problems and figured out the steps they needed, and then Heidi did the multiplication and divisions lickety-split. They also had fun going with Heidi's family up the coast on weekends when her father painted boats. The whole family sang songs with rounds in the car, some of them in German.

The crackling started again from the Principal's voice box. "This is extraordinary news. The school has never had *three* scholarship winners. You are to be congratulated, Sister Marcella! We've just learned that Elizabeth Frings has won a scholarship to Notre Dame des Victoires."

Sister Marcella looked strange, as if she had something in her throat.

Maybe Lizby did, too. Sister held up her hand to stop the clapping. "There may have been a mistake," she said. "Let me make sure, uh, before we . . . celebrate."

Lizby was scared. She couldn't breathe. Sr. Marcella was right. She couldn't have won anything, and she did not want it! She wanted to go to Pres with Heidi and where Frances O'Connell was.

Sister said she would check on the scholarship business and tell them after lunch. Lizby went home for lunch, as usual, but she didn't tell her mother. She was trying to think what had happened. She might never see the O'Connells again. Pictures whirled through her head. She had only wanted the fun of going around the city. Then she calmed down. The scholarship was a mistake, but she did not have to take it.

When they were back in the classroom, Sister said she's called Notre Dame des Victoires and they confirmed that it was Lizby who had the scholarship. Lizby couldn't smile, "I don't want to go to NDV," she said.

"Talk it over with your parents," Sister told her.

She couldn't.

After washing the dinner dishes, she went up to her room and lay on her bed. She could not read. She kept thinking about the French school. It was downtown on Nob Hill between Pine and Bush Streets on the top floor over the French Grammar School. During their class trip, Sister Emaline, who had a gap-toothed smile, had given them the tests and usual cookies. NDV had a gym and a basketball court, she said, but it didn't have a swimming pool. Students had to use the Fairmont Hotel's pool, a couple of blocks away. Tennis lessons were given in Golden Gate Park, as were the horseback riding classes once a week. They used the Stanyan Street Stables.

That was more interesting than the marble ballroom at Sacred Heart, but it didn't matter. She and Heidi were not going there.

The NDV tests had been different. They had been made up in Montreal, for kids who spoke English and French. They did not have to do the French part. The second section had a lot of questions about stories she'd read in Mother's "Complete Works of …" shelves, but also some questions about books she hadn't read that were interesting. Then there were two pages of math problems . . . *math problems*! She and Heidi had sat next to each other and shared the math problems as usual. Lizby held her head in her hands, tears springing from her eyes. That was it!

She had cheated — and she was so used to it that she didn't even think of it as cheating! But how could she explain to Sister Marcella? And Heidi — she would be telling on her. Sister Marcella didn't like Heidi to begin with — what would happen to her now? Maybe they wouldn't let them into Pres. What would happen to them both? Lizby put on her flannel nightgown, and got under the covers. Her hands and feet were cold. It was so dark. Neither warmth nor sleep would come.

It was beginning to get light. She was confused. Maybe she had slept, though, because she remembered having the same old dream that she used to have a lot when she was little; a Fair at night, with lots of sideshows. It was always the same — a big Devil's head with his mouth as the door; the path behind — inside the mouth — with flames on both sides; Mother standing at the entrance, with rosy make-up on her face motioning Lizby to come in. As usual, Lizby could not move, but the heat drew her. This time, she heard a sound like Sal, the Laughing Lady, above the entrance to the maze of mirrors in Playland at the beach.

The dream frightened Lizby, but when she turned away, she could see her window and knew she was awake.

Suddenly she knew what she'd do. She thought there was no one she could talk to, but there was.. She would go to Confession! The priest couldn't tell anyone and he would give her a penance, then she'd know God had forgiven her.

✖   ✖   ✖

Billings Dime Store, where Lizby worked for 20 cents an hour on Saturdays, was a block away up on Irving Street. She told Mrs. Billings she had to go to Confession, so she had to leave early about 3 in the afternoon. Mrs. Billings probably thought Lizby would confess she took pieces of candy from the fill-up boxes in the storeroom, so it was OK with her, particularly if Lizby'd stick with the 'firm purpose of amendment' part. When Lizby got to St. Anne's Church, the lines were still long around Fr. Monaghan's box, but nobody was waiting at Monsignor Moriarity's. Father Monaghan always gave three Hail Marys as a penance, no matter what you said to him, and he said things back that made you laugh, but Monsignor Moriarity didn't ask any questions, so it was quick. Quick was what she needed.

Quick it was not. He did ask questions. Then he said that she had provided an occasion of sin for another girl, a girl quite simple, and that she couldn't *not* tell her mother about the Scholarship. "That would be a sin of omission against the 4th commandment to honor your father and your mother."

"Do I have to tell her about my cheating?" Lizby whispered.

"It is sufficient that you've confessed this to God," he said. "But if your mother says you must take the tuition scholarship, you must accept that without any argument." Then he gave her a whole rosary to say and told her to meditate on the mystery of suffering as her penance.

She felt terrible. She prayed the rosary, and when she finished, she promised herself she wouldn't do anything like that again. She had to stay awake instead of just going off in her mind without thinking about how things always connected to everything else.

She thought she'd never forget about all the connections again — but she did.

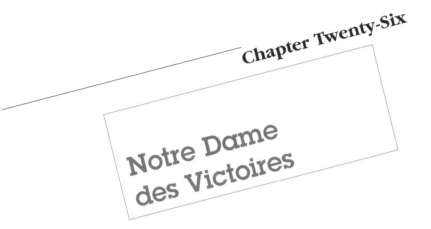

Chapter Twenty-Six

Notre Dame des Victoires

Fall 1944

Most of the sophomores sat together for lunch on the west corner of the school roof deck. It was Indian summer and their soft pleated navy wool uniforms were too hot, but that did not bother them. They had their legs stretched out for suntans, with their backs braced against the four-foot high concrete walls.

Clarise, with her dark eyes, perm-frizzed hair, and pock-marked skin, had a rubber face with a voice to create any character she wanted.

"Big Momma let out a holler and fell down." Clarise's body sagged against the wall as she said the words, her eyes barely open. "I could see her peeping under her eyelids to see what the motorman would do. He was hopping around, trying to get the gizmo connected to the overhead electric line again. We were all going crazy, he was so inept. Next thing we knew, she had rolled over on her elbow and was up on her feet. 'Give me that thing, you don't know how to do nothin' right. You probably let me stay on the street all day before you call an ambulance.'"

They giggled at Clarise mimicking life on the Municipal Railway. Her update on the shipyard workers, who took the Hunter's

Point streetcar with her in the morning, was their noontime soap opera.

Notre Dame des Victoires' multi-leveled school yards and buildings covered the central part of a block on Nob Hill. From the roof, they could see Chinatown's Grant Avenue half a block away on one side, and on the other, the downtown department stores with the Bay Bridge in the distance. Lizby avoided looking into the street, though. The height made her knees go weak.

"Ignorant Arabs!" Clarise hissed in a guttural voice. Sister Jerome, the heavy-browed nun from Paris who taught French, detested the horrid accents of the non-French speakers. Now Clarise was speaking French in a high-pitched monotone and the French girls howled. The way American girls spoke was a constant joke to them. Not funny to Lizby, one of the Arabs. She refused to read aloud in class. She could not get the sounds into her ears. It was weeks before she realized the 'Solly Molly' prayer they raced through in the morning was 'Salue Marie' — 'Hail Mary' in English.

"Don't worry, Liz," Pauline whispered to her. "Helen and I are just as bad."

Pauline was the one who had started everyone calling her *Liz*. She and Helen were her best friends, but Clarise was the one who made things so idiotic everybody had to laugh. Soon, she was laughing too.

After classes were out, they met again in the washroom on the first floor. They tried out different ways of combing their hair in front of the huge mirror that almost covered one wall, and complained about their mothers. They also examined their faces and decided which Hollywood actress they each resembled. "I've got freckles all over, more like Judy Garland," Pauline said, "but you could easily stand in for Elizabeth Taylor in *National Velvet*."

Helen disagreed. "Liz's eyes are more like Dana Andrews', even though he's a guy," she said. Helen was the only one who smoked. Tall and blond, she had a square chin and walked like she always had on riding boots.

"I took a pack of Lucky Strikes from Dad's dresser last weekend," Lizby said. "I squinted in the mirror and tried to hold the cigarette different ways to look interesting." She held her invisible cigarette between her thumb and her first two fingers, with her pinky up. She took little sips, as if it was a straw. "Then I placed it low between my third and fourth fingers, covering my mouth with my hand as I smoked, and stared into the mirror hard, like a French resistance fighter."

"I can see how *that* didn't work," Helen said.

"Well, I also tried dangling it from the side of my mouth like Rita Hayword in *The Lady From Shanghai*." Pauline was splitting her sides laughing. "By this time the inside of my mouth was feeling numb, my tongue tasted like cement, and I still couldn't figure out how to inhale without coughing. SO, I decided no, I'm not going to smoke."

"You need more practice," Clarice said. She was putting on pancake makeup to make her skin look smoother.

Pauline had a new tube of Revlon *Pink Lightning*. She blotted her lips and offered the lipstick to the rest of them. "Try it. It's a good color."

Lizby shook her head. Even as a sophomore, she would not dare go home with lipstick. She had told them some things about her mother, but not how mad she got, and the words she used — or that once, her mother had spat at her.

After primping, they walked down the hill to Chinatown and bought small bags of glazed melon, candied ginger, or coconut before catching their street-cars home.

Her friends made her laugh. She was awake. She had found a place where she was herself.

✖   ✖   ✖

They giggled when sailors whistled at them and shouted "hubba, hubba." San Francisco was filled with sailors. Of course, they didn't talk to them. A few classmates went to the USO to dance, but Lizby and Pauline just wished they could. All the songs were sentimental, *I'll Be Loving You, Always* and *Long Ago and Far Away,* and all the movies were romantic. Edith Piaf with an accordion sang "The falling leaves drift by my window." It made Lizby cry. She loved the way everything made her feel tender and romantic and doomed and invincible. *Casablanca* epitomized the spirit. Hitler and Hirohito were the enemy and the World had to be Saved for Democracy.

By 1944, all the cruise boats had been converted into war transport ships. Pauline's dad joked that his mother was in drydock for the duration — at the Fairmont Hotel. Mrs. Martin muttered, "Praise God, not with us."

The Fairmont was a couple of blocks up from Notre Dame des Victoires High School, so Pauline visited Grand-mère on Fridays, then they took the cable car down to meet Mr. Martin at Tadich's for a fish dinner.

"A ritual," Pauline said, "just like going to Mass on Sunday."

"Doesn't your mother come?"

"She says she doesn't like fish."

Pauline's dad, Lyman Martin, was the business manager for the Examiner newspaper, his office a short walk to Tadich's and to the Mechanic's Library on Post, where Lizby hung out.

Uncle Pat, Gram, Mrs. O'Connell, Pauline, Sister Emaline, and Pauline's father — they saw her. They all liked to laugh. They were her tribe.

✖   ✖   ✖

Sometime in 1944, Gram left Butte. Postcards came from various parts of Canada, also from eastern and southern states. None said what she was doing, or why she had left. One evening the phone rang.

"Yes," Dad said. "Ja, ja, I'll be there." He looked at Mother as he hung up. "Your mother's at the Greyhound station. Did you know about this?"

Mother shook her head. "That's Lizzie." She nodded to Lizby and Frankie. "You can go with your Dad. I'll try and reach Frank and John to let them know."

Lizby and her brother piled into Dad's company station wagon. He parked in the loading zone at the Seventh Street Depot. Ship chandlers could park where they wanted in San Francisco and Dad was now boss of one of Haviside's sea-going barges, the kind with the big cranes. The station was filled with sailors arriving, sailors sleeping on the benches, and sailors waiting for their girl friends. She and Frankie looked for Gram in the crowd. Families bustled around the ticket windows and listened to the announcements of arrivals and departures. Gram, an island of calm, sat waiting with a stack of presents and luggage taking up the three seats beside her. A cabbage rose was tucked into her pompadour.

"You found me," she said and hugged the children.

The bleary eyed sailor sitting next to her yawned and stretched. Gram said to them, "This young man has to wait another two hours before his bus leaves for Oregon." She smiled at him and said, "Would you be so kind again to help with the packages?"

He grinned. "For you, ma'am, anything."

Uncle Frank did not get down from Davis until the weekend. He was teaching agriculture at the University of California so he hadn't been drafted. When they gathered with Kathleen and John in the living room, Gram was all dimples and smiles as she sat on the couch. She cuddled Lizby on one side of her, Frankie on the other, not paying any attention that they were too big for that sort of thing.

"Sally Rand's ranch is south of LA, close to the Anza-Borrega desert," Gram said. "I stayed with her three weeks, resting up after our tour ended."

"We didn't know what you were up to." Mother said.

Gram made no excuses.

Everything about Sally Rand captivated Gram. "She's full of wise-cracks and laughs, but she knows what she wants and God help anyone who doesn't do what they agreed to."

"Like what?" John asked.

"She gets cash on the barrel head, in advance, for all our travel expenses, and full payment after the first performance, with a separate dressing room for her and me. She has nothing against the girls dating, but if there is a performance the next night, they have a strict curfew. The first time one misses it, there is a warning, the next time, a fine. The third time, the girl loses her job."

"She sounds like a tough broad," John said.

"Tough and soft," Gram said. "Sally's fun to be with and she protects her girls. They know it. One of the girls was in big trouble in Dallas with a boyfriend who beat her. Sally had a friend of hers on the police force arrange that the 'boyfriend' be held in custody and persuaded not to stay around."

"She has a good heart," Gram said, "and I enjoyed every minute as her dresser. But I'm ready to return to Butte. I miss my friends."

"Your gambling buddies and dance partners at the Old Timers Club!" John said.

"It must have been hard work, blowing up all those balloons," Aunt Kathleen joked.

Gram just laughed. "It was nothing at all compared to dusting off the feather fans."

✻   ✻   ✻

Sister Emaline used the biology lab to teach math because there was not any other space. It was a narrow room with three lab tables. There were sinks on one side of the room and glass specimen cases above them.

Six of them worked together. Cecile Gaillac said she would have dragged herself to this class, even if she had pneumonia. So would Lizby, but none of them ever missed a session. They seemed able to read each other's minds — to have one mind. One day, the six of them were piled around the end table where Sister had heaped books and magazines. She was doing things with numbers on the portable blackboard to show how magical the Fibonacci curves were. She had to use a stool she was so short, barely five feet high, but she took them out into the universe.

"Everything connects to everything else," she said, while her fingers marked down and added the proportions. "The Fibonacci numbers link the spirals of garden snail shells to the spirals of the galaxy and back again in the vibrations of sound and color. Let's look."

She spread the pictures out so they could check the proportions, then passed around a box so they each held a snail shell.

Cecile sniffed at her shell. "Now we need some chopped garlic and parsley, melted butter and a little crunchy black snail to put in under the broiler." She smacked her lips. Pauline made a gagging sound. They laughed.

Sister did too and continued to show them how the patterns flowed into one another, changing, growing. Lizby took a deep breath. She could hardly hold the beauty of it.

That night, in bed, she thought about the day. Sister Emaline once said what they were doing was like contemplation, a kind of prayer that cloistered nuns did all day, instead of teaching or nursing.

Her favorite scary thing to think about at night was time — when did it begin, and what was God. But she did not connect that to the life size figure of Jesus hanging on the cross in the corridor just outside their lab. Contemplation was different according to Emaline. She just had to see what she saw, and pay attention.

Lizby won Firsts in Biology, Algebra, Geometry, Trig, two years of History, and a blue ribbon in horseback riding.

Her father said, "You should take typing and office work instead of this nonsense." They sat at the kitchen table having supper. It was Friday, so they were having filet of sole dipped in batter and fried, with creamed canned peas over mashed potatoes. Frankie was separating green peas, which he refused to eat, onto the side of his plate. "If your husband gets sick," Dad said, "you can go to work and support the family until he gets better."

"I want to be a doctor," Lizby mumbled. Actually, she still thought she might be an archeologist like Halliburton, but it was better not to mention this.

Dad snorted, then looked at her with pursed lips. "Just who do you think you are? Take my word for it," he said, "You aim too high and you're going to fall flat on your behind."

"I don't know," Mother said. "When I was her age, if I saw something done once, I knew I could do it, too — even something difficult like surgery."

Dad said nothing.

Lizby took a sip of milk and said, "I read an article in the *Union Dispatcher* last week that helped me win an argument with Marion Nichols. It was about the government bribing witnesses to falsify the case against Harry Bridges as a Red."

"You don't know what you're talking about — and besides, it's none of your business," her father said and went back to reading his newspaper.

"But the court judge said the same thing, and threw the case out!" She was embarrassed that her voice squeaked. Showing any feeling at all in an argument meant she was wrong. The trouble was, Dad knew things and she wanted to hear him talk. He did not believe what he read in the newspapers. He compared what he read with what he observed and formed his own ideas. She liked that, but she thought it was fun to feel strongly. It did not make her wrong.

Marion Nichols, the only openly Republican student in their class, was her rival for Firsts in history. She did not concede Lizby had won about Harry Bridges. "Roosevelt has to be stopped," Marion had shouted. "No President should have a third term, much less a fourth. We need Wendell Wilke or we've got a dictator."

"How can you say that, after all Roosevelt's done?"

"He's bankrupting the country!"

"You're just saying that because your father owns a hardware store!" Lizby shouted back. "You're a capitalist!"

That was fun. Trying to talk at dinner wasn't.

Gossip was also fun. Mother had sent her to Dr. Bine to learn about menstruation, but some of her classmates seemed to understand more about sex than he did. Solange Labbe, for example. She had a tall Parisian model style of beauty with pouty lips. In gym class, Helen whispered to Lizby, "Do you know she shaves her pubic hair?"

"Why would she do that?" Lizby made a face, but looking at Solange, she could see she looked different from the rest of them standing on the basketball court in their blue one-piece bloomer suits.

Helen raised her arms, the Gallic open hands gesture. They both laughed. They were not sure why, but speculating about Solange's mysterious sophistication fascinated them. Maybe she was a courtesan.

Lizby was interested in her own face and body. Her breasts were beginning to round out and had pink nipples that she hadn't noticed before. In some places like her wrists, she could see blue veins deep inside milky transparent skin, but other places like her nose had freckles. Hair was beginning to grow under her arms and between her legs. She was surprised to see her eyes had yellow flecks in them and were gray or green at different times. Her wavy brown hair was quite ordinary, but at least she didn't have to have permanents.

She spent hours looking into the mirror.

When her father opened her bedroom door one day when she was dressing, her pleasure in her new body changed. She was not little anymore. She was embarrassed to have been so pleased. She wanted to hide. Another time he came up behind her in the basement when she was doing the wash, and tried to hug her with his hands on her chest. She dropped the hose she was using to siphon water from the washing machine into the sink. The hose sprayed out, and the clothes, soaking wet, dropped to the floor as she hollered and slipped from his grasp.

He did nothing further. It was like he was waiting for something. She was frightened and upset. She had to figure how not to be in the house when he was there. He knew so much — why didn't he act right? She remembered her fear as a little girl with the swimsuit.

It was OK when she got a job after school and had to spend all day Saturday at the Toulouse Laundry giving out packages. She did not ever have to be in the house alone again. This was a period when Mother was angry with everyone and everything, not just Lizby. Frankie spent most of his time with his fish tanks. He and Dad had built a room extending the garage basement to under the glassed-in back porch. It had two walls of glass windows, and two walls lined with fish tanks. Frankie didn't have a job, but bought and sold guppies and raised angel fish. Anytime he needed to escape, he slipped away to the Aquarium in Golden Gate Park, a half block away. He'd made friends with the director who let him in through the back door.

Their parents did not have friends that they spent time with. Lizby thought Mother had friends at work and at St. Anthony's Kitchen and in the hospital where she did volunteer nursing, but she didn't bring anyone home. Dad went to work early in the morning, except for Sundays, and always came home late at night. One time she heard them talking in the kitchen, when she was putting away dishes in the pantry.

"How is it that you suddenly have to be at work at six instead of seven every morning these days?" Lizby heard the irritation in her mother's voice.

"That's the way it is," Dad said gruffly.

"I suppose it has nothing to do with a WAAC who needs to be at her base by six-thirty." Dad didn't answer. Gas was rationed during the war and people shared rides whenever possible. On his way to work, Dad gave lifts to the two women soldiers who lived down the street.

"And your Friday late night shifts also conveniently coincide?"

"And you don't have anything better to think about." Dad ended the conversation.

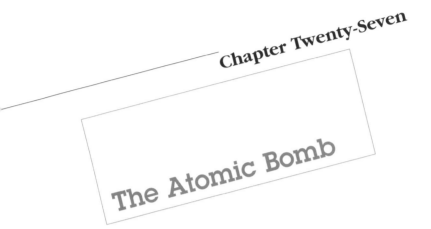

Chapter Twenty-Seven

The Atomic Bomb

S u m m e r   1 9 4 5

L izby was fifteen, it was a Sunday afternoon, and school was out. The summer program she had signed up for didn't start until the next week. She wanted to take physics, a course Notre Dame des Victoires didn't offer, so she'd decided to get it at the public school.

She sat on the cedar chest in her bedroom filing her nails. A month ago, Mother had called the St. Vincent de Paul truck to haul away her bed and the fluffy white curtained vanity. The same day Butterfield's Auction House delivered a dark mahogany highboy chest of drawers, a four-poster bed, and a dresser. This was supposed to be for her birthday in a couple of months.

She hated the dark furniture from Butterfield's, but she could not say anything because it was an expensive gift. She could not even see into the upper drawers of the highboy. And the dresser mirror needed to be re-silvered, or something done, to get rid of the rusty streaks. Mother loved auctions, but the things she gave Lizby were so peculiar, like a collection of porcelain dogs and the sad-looking clown lying with his hands around his knees to form a bowl.

She rounded her fingers, back filing so the nails wouldn't crack.

Mother threw the door open without knocking. Her neck and face were spotted with red splotches of anger. Lips pressed together and back stiff as a broom. Her eyes narrowed and sped around the room. Lizby felt her stomach muscles tighten. It was something she never got used to.

"What are you doing, all slouched over? Sit up straight." Her mother moved to the closet, looking for trouble. She picked up Lizby's waste bag from inside the closet. "A paper bag with your napkins that should have been burned!" The bed was made, but her mother swept the book lying on the bedspread onto the floor. "This place is filthy."

Instead of looking down and listening silently, Lizby continued to file her nails. This added to her mother's fury. "Take that look off your face," she shouted. "And you look at me when I talk to you." Suddenly, she screamed, "Do you know what you are? You are a bastard! You don't know who your father is. He could be anyone!" She flung open the window and called Dad to come in from the garden, then she started to tremble. When he came into the room, she said, "Tell her, Hans. Tell her you are *not* her father. She's a bastard." She ran out of the room, her face flushed red, crying.

He glanced at Lizby briefly, without any expression on his face, then followed Mother and closed the door.

Lizby continued to file her nails. She didn't know what she was feeling, just numb emptiness. Nothing came into her mind, except the stillness of the room, like the empty rooms of earlier childhood — long ago, before Frankie was born. A skylight that never showed the sun, a cold marble church where she had to wait, but no one came. No one could hear her or see her. She felt a glass wall building up around her. She could look out, but nothing would touch her.

Neither of her parents mentioned anything of this to her again — ever.

Afterward, she looked up the word *bastard* in the dictionary. It meant illegitimate. She . . . shouldn't exist. She didn't know how to think about that. There were other words and phrases, "child of the left hand," the Latin word, "sinister." Long ago she'd learned to put things out of her mind. She decided this was what she had to do.

Somehow, she pushed thinking about it out — except, for sometimes, when she had to file her finger nails.

✖ ✖ ✖

July 15, 1945

"Absolute zero is the point at which atomic energy, all activity of any kind, can be imagined to cease — an absurdity, of course." The teacher removed his chalk from the board.

Lizby sat in a classroom in Mission High making notes during the class in physics. The class was huge with more than thirty students, but a few students, most of them the Jewish kids from Germany, asked so many questions that it was hard for the teacher to link his points together. She looked at her notes wondering if they made any sense. They heard shouting in the corridor, and then a boy pushed open the door. "The United States has dropped an atomic bomb on Hiroshima!"

There was every sort of reaction from the students. Several boys ran into the hall cheering that 'we'd bombed the Japs', but another boy was crying. Girls followed the boys into the hall, but Lizby sat in her seat. She was frightened. What about the chain reactions that the teacher warned might happen if the atom was split — that enormous power released. Was this starting the end of the world?

Another bomb was dropped over Nagasaki a few weeks later, a couple of days before she turned sixteen. Shortly after that, the war ended.

On that day, she sat alone in the living room, listening to the bells ringing from Saint Anne's. They didn't stop for hours. The radio reported people were dancing in the streets, wild celebrations were going on in the city, and windows were being broken on Market Street. Lizby moved to the kitchen and sat at the table. The house was so empty without Frankie. He was working in the tomato fields for Uncle Frank. She wondered if he knew the war was over.

A story seeped into her mind. The man she was meant to marry had died in the war. She could see him — big, with freckles across his nose like hers — and his arms around her. She was filled with sadness. No one had ever hugged her. Some part of her had been killed and she had never known it, or him. The story tangled itself up with her bastard self who wasn't supposed to live. She shivered, and then wept. Once she started, she could not stop. She cried and cried as she had never ever cried, maybe for a couple of hours, maybe longer.

Finally, she blew her nose, and sat up straight. She felt dazed, puzzled —

this wasn't like her — then a niggling thought coming clear. She looked around — and remembered. The 'dead lover' was a story she'd read — not her, at all — it was from a magazine, *Redbook*!   Just a sappy story — but she felt better. She had barrels of tears inside waiting to be pushed over, to wash away all kinds of pain. To cry with all the stops out was so . . . wonderful!

She was glad the war was over. So many different kinds of feelings were crashing around in her, that she did not know what was coming out, or what to do with them. They were like a head cold. She didn't even know if they belonged to her, like with the Redbook story.

When school started in September, Lizby felt relieved. Frankie did too. He did not tell her much about what had happened with Uncle Frank, but he said he'd never work for him again. He mentioned a bracero who worked ten hours without water. Uncle Frank had beaten him up for complaining.

It was great to be back with her friends. She almost felt like herself, but not quite — as if there was something inside her that wanted to explode, or something she needed to do.

They were upperclassmen now and had responsibilities to carry. Right off, the faculty appointed Pauline as the editor of the school paper, the *Parlette*. She promptly designated Helen and Lizby as her staff. They met in the sewing room.

"We'll meet here after school every Friday until ski season," Pauline said, "Then we'll meet in the car while Dad drives us up to Norden."

Since Pauline's father worked in the newspaper business, she had a lot of ideas how a paper should work. He also was the one who sponsored them into the Sierra Club, which meant they skied at least once a month during winter at the club lodge in Norden.

"Liz, you'll write the movie reviews," Pauline said. "*Spellbound*, with Ingrid Bergman, is playing at the Orpheum. We'll start with that."

The staff, all three of them, went to the Sunday matinee after Mass. Lizby was entranced. All those dream images that meant something else! She found herself thinking about the Devil's head dream with the flames inside — and the memories of scary empty rooms when there was no one around. Had she really been left alone in the house when she was little? She and Frankie were left alone — but it wasn't scary like the early memories. In the movie, Bergman figured everything out, even the ski track memory that didn't make sense. She was smart. She watched Gregory Peck's face and the audience followed what she was thinking. The music made it clear what she was feeling. An iron picket fence scene looked like the front garden and the concrete banister on the side of the stairs to Lizby's family's old flat on 12th Avenue. The one doctor who thought Ingrid Bergman's thinking was too emotional was the head of the clinic — the bad guy.

Lizby knew now what she wanted to do with her life.

They sat at the Piggly Wiggly ice cream fountain after the movie. The three of them ordered cake doughnuts topped with vanilla ice cream and covered with hot fudge sauce.

"I'm going to be a psychiatrist," Lizby said.

Pauline laughed, "OK, so instead of doing the movie reviews, you get the 'lovelorn' column."

They all giggled. Lizby hadn't even had a date yet!

That did not matter. She had other things to think about — lots of other things. People really did see, feel, and explain the world to themselves — differently!

The next morning, Monday, she and Helen were in the room off the study hall planning the layout of the paper. They had to have it ready that week. Pauline banged into the room, late.

"The Battaan heroes are almost here," she said. "They sail under the Golden Gate this afternoon! All the public schools have off. They're going down to see the boats come in." They talked about it at lunch. Everyone was excited. They were only a few blocks up from the Embarcadero.

"We should take off, too," Lizby said.

"Sister Marie Jeanne already said it's not a holiday for us," Helen objected.

"Then we should have a sit-down strike," Lizby said.

One of the seniors, who had a sailor boyfriend, agreed. So did Clarise, but Pauline shrugged, "Heck, let's just go."

That settled it.

The others were milling around. Everyone seemed ready, so Rosemarie the senior, Clarise, Pauline, and Lizby declared it a school holiday and took off from the schoolyard and down Pine Street. Everyone was laughing and cheering.

Eventually, they noticed no one from school caught up with them, but it was easy to get separated in the crowd so they stuck together. It was fun to play hooky with the whole city in the streets. Of course, they could not get near the wharves where the ships would dock, but they got as close as they could and watched the boats come under the Gate.

It just seemed a prank that didn't mean too much, but Pauline called Lizby that night. "We're the only ones who left — and we've been squashed," she said, "suspended for a week."

Mother also got a call from the principal.

"This is the last straw," Mother said. She was on the phone that night, arranging with Gram for Lizby to go to Montana to live. "Elizabeth is unmanageable," she said. "Maybe you can do something with her, but I've given up."

"Unmanageable?" Pauline could not understand it when they met outside the principal's office the next day, and neither could Lizby. Pauline and Clarise sat beside her on the wooden bench in the hall waiting for Sister Jeanne-Marie to finish talking to Rosemarie. Their parents didn't feel the way her mother did. Clarise's mom thought it was funny.

Lizby couldn't put her hurt and bafflement into words. She must have been sleepwalking when they took off to see the ships come under the Gate. She had not let herself remember what trouble she was in — and how awful Mother felt about her. How had she done this without thinking about that — when she knew it? She was desolate at the idea of leaving NDV and all of her friends, her life.

"My Dad can talk to her," Pauline volunteered. "He can talk anybody into anything — and Sister Emaline would back him up."

Lizby hesitated. She felt confused. "He did talk her into letting me go skiing." But as she said the words, her mouth felt like acid at the base of her tongue. A feeling that she wanted to vomit . . . . "I don't know," she said, "maybe . . . I don't want him to do that."

Pauline was incredulous. "You want to leave us?"

"No, I want to stay here and to be with you, but . . . remember last year — when we were riding in the side of the park where we weren't supposed to go?"

"You mean when your horse bolted?"

"Yeah, the police shooting range scared him. I barely hung on when he tore off."

"But you got him under control, so what's that got to do with going to Montana?"

"I don't know . . . but I feel like I'm hanging on to something that's going to throw me. I keep getting into stuff that makes it worse. Maybe your father could talk Mother round, but Pauline, I don't think I can hang on with what's happening. I . . . don't think I can stay in my parents' house."

Pauline was crying. "So you're checking out?"

Lizby nodded. Pauline flung her arms around her best friend. They were both crying. Lizby wished she felt more certain. Pauline pulled back and looked at her. "Your mother — what a fishmouth, mouse-paw thing to do!"

Lizby had been in tears feeling sorry for herself, but Pauline's absurd words pulled her together. She laughed.

The principal called them in. She wanted them to understand why they had to be suspended. The girls understood. When the principal heard what Lizby's mother planned, however, she thought this more than was called for. She telephoned to tell her this, but Mother had made up her mind.

Sunday night before Lizby left, Frankie came to her room holding a big pickle jar he had cleaned and filled half up with water. "You'll have to hold this on you lap on the train," he said. His prize angelfish drifted in the make-shift tank, their inch high tails like purple-pink flowers. "Gabe died last month," he said. "Rafael and Mike need to be together or they'd get lonesome and die, too." He reached into the paper sack and pulled out a packet of food. "They need a pinch sprinkled over the top of the water every morning."

Lizby could see he did not want to cry, so she tried not to hug him, but she couldn't stop herself. She pulled him tight to her.

They both needed to blow their noses.

✖ ✖ ✖

Molly knelt at Mass. It was 6:30 Tuesday morning. She had put Elizabeth on the train for Butte the previous day. Molly's body trembled. She felt as if she had a fever. She tried to hold the disaster images at the altar in her mind as Sister Magdalene had told her to do. Why had she exploded? What was happening to her? She was almost forty one years old, middle-aged, and she felt helpless. These feelings of rage sweeping through her . . . . Everything was collapsing. This was the darkness. Her thoughts were not clear anymore. She had always controlled everything for everybody, now she wasn't able to control anything.

She must not judge herself, Magdalene said, nor God for sending her this darkness, nor anyone else. But Molly had judged Elizabeth — or had she? Was she trying to protect her? That day when she had exploded and called her a bastard — Elizabeth had looked so insolent, sitting filing her nails, with a face of ice like Chel's, not even looking at her. Molly wanted to shake her, to spit and scream, 'LOOK AT ME — all I've done for you — all I've given up.' Had she spit on her, or was that another time? And all the foul words she had called her, words she had forgotten she knew. Waves of shame swept through her. How could she not judge herself?

The nun had called her from NDV to tell her about the expulsion. "These four girls have to be taught a lesson; they're the leaders . . . ." the nun said. It was enough for the nun that the girls be kept home for a few days, but in Molly's mind she could see her daughter picking up with sailors and doing worse. Even Hans had his eye on her.

No . . . NO! What was she thinking? That was . . . unthinkable. No, this was her own madness. Her mind went blank again. This was impossible. She could not sustain it, could not stay with her anger, her fear, and hear it out. Why had Magdalene demanded that she do this? Sister Mary Magdalene, friend of God, senile old woman rotting in the Mother House, what did she know? Molly felt the sneer in her words and it terrified her. She shook with fear. NO, this was the evil spirit in herself! 'Our Father . . . deliver us from evil. Lead us not into temptation.' "Why are you doing this?" she whispered. "God, don't abandon me."

Swirling forces raged inside her. She was exhausted. She didn't know how long this wrestling with evil images went on. Then she felt the silence. Nothing but emptiness.

At least that voice was gone. But she had no one to help her. Trudy, her strong shelter, her friend, and the one person who knew her heart . . . was dead.

Molly put her head down over her arms on the pew and wept. She was alone.

✖ ✖ ✖

The train trip by herself to Montana was blurry in Lizby's memory. A confusion about Mother and her headaches, and what was really her — but she knew she had to be someplace else. She knew who she loved — Gram, Uncle Pat, Frankie, Pauline and her other friends, but . . . everything else was frozen. She did not know how to be angry, or to say out loud what she wanted. She had always known how to run away inside, but this was massive. She was . . . invisible.

Butte was in the second year of a strike against the Anaconda Copper Mining Company when she arrived. Gram met her at the station with a copy of *LIFE* magazine in her hand. Pictures of houses with the word 'SCAB' painted in huge black letters; pictures of picket lines and fights showed the violence and anger that filled the streets. Lizby read it and talked to the MacTavishes when they got to Gram's house; it was the first time she felt so pulled out of herself by injustice.

That is when she knew that in Montana everything would change. She was part of a world, not just a family. What the news stories didn't show was the warmth and strength of people like Gram and her neighbors. It is hard to see who people are. If you don't love them, you don't notice what matters. She began to feel herself again, just like with her friends. It was a great time to be alive.

The Angelfish, Rafael and Michael, did fine for the space of time they had there — and so did Lizby.

Chapter Twenty-Eight

The Waking

I learn by going where I have to go ...
— Theodore Roethke

San Francisco 1947

fter the war, the UN was established in San Francisco and Lizby returned to Notre Dame des Victoires for her last year in high school. She found her friends all considered themselves to be internationalists. None planned to do anything about it however, except perhaps to attend cultural events sponsored by the French consulate and, of course, to continue to see every French film ever made.

From her experience of the long copper-mine strike in Butte, with its violence to and from the miners, Lizby empathized with the socialist Wobbly movement, but she did not have a clue how to be useful yet. Eleanor Roosevelt had drafted a great document on Human Rights, and Lizby was confident the whole world was going to change. So, she followed other interests and studied Sculpture and Life Drawing at the School of Fine Arts in North Beach.

During the school year, Lizby worked ten hours each week as a lab assistant, and fourteen more on Saturdays and Monday nights at Macy's on the sales "flying-squad," selling everything from corsets to cutlery. Then in a summer of smothered, infectious laughter, she worked in Yosemite as a Camp Curry housekeeping maid — and experienced her first crush. A Cal Berkeley graduate in physics and philosophy, Ned was an amiable charmer who dropped into Yosemite with his younger brother to visit his sister, another Curry maid. The younger brother went home, but Ned stayed to work in the Grill and dated Lizby.

Sketching Mirror Lake in the sunshine, watching the nightly Fire-fall, hiking, soft-kiss necking, she felt an overwhelming pull toward him — like the tide sweeping sand from under her feet. It was only a few weeks until the end of summer, but when he called her in San Francisco to join a Beach party he and his brother were planning, she refused his invitation. She recognized this was a bit insane, but in her parent's home, her awakening body — was nothing to talk to her mother about, or even to her best friend. She simply could not deal with it.

This slipping from girlhood into a woman's body was going to be more than labor issues, working for pocket money, and family concerns. She did not feel ready. First Lone Mountain College to begin pre-med studies — then what would be, would be. Her own story had begun.

Part IV

The Unfolding

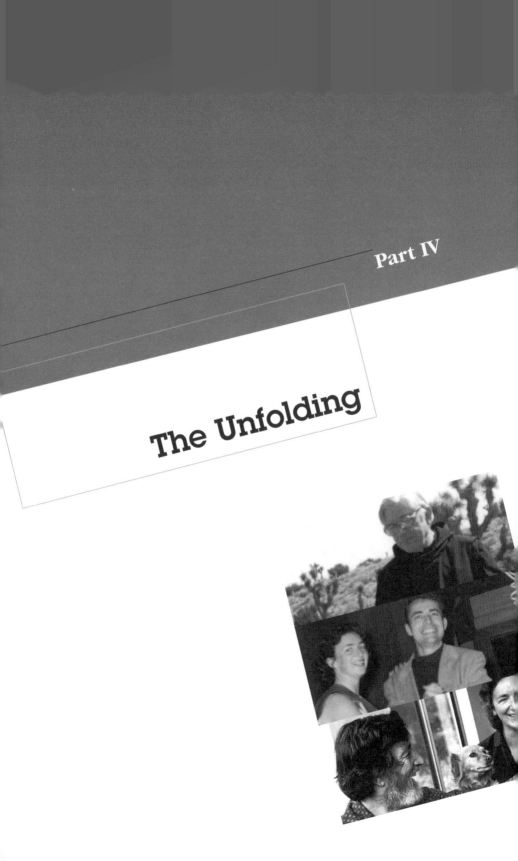

Prelude

There is a story:

Memory and Reality were fighting. "This is what happened," said Reality. "It couldn't have been that way," said Memory. Memory won.

All story is selection. I ought to know, I've spent seventy some years listening to people tell their stories. Stories change as they are told; so do the storytellers.

Stories belong to time regions in our lives. Time and experience strip them of illusion and fantasy. Reality then can claim its truth and reveal the pattern and meaning of a life.

There are some stories in what follows but, mostly, it is the tale of a search, a quest; sometimes perhaps, only a glimpse of the road.

The segment on Mentors and Maps is really about Acquiring Power. The stories of Men as Partners and as Puzzles tell of an Inward Journey into personal shadows and unexpected archetypal wisdom to find What Women Really Want.

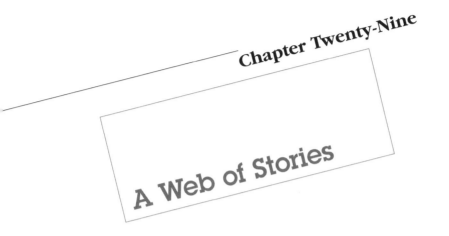

Chapter Twenty-Nine

A Web of Stories

fter her third year at Lone Mountain College, Lizby spent the summer of 1950 in Europe. Seemingly freed from her fears and suspicions, Molly gave Lizby eleven hundred dollars she had saved from her work at the Toulouse Laundry to fund the trip. It was exactly enough for everything.

Vienna, July 1950

Lizby paused on the corner of the Ringstrausse, the broad street that surrounded the central city. The air was softly past the chill of early morning and filled with small rustling sounds of a breeze through the trees and insects in the dappled sunlight. There was still massive evidence of bomb damage from the War — two-thirds of the city had been destroyed — but the sidewalk was wide with coffee and pastry shops and a sprinkling of people sitting in the sun.

The streets were largely silent. Only one patrol jeep passed. It had the usual quartet of military police — a single French soldier plus one American, one Russian and one British. Vienna was a city still under occupation. A film, *The Third Man*, had just been made in Vienna. Lizby heard it dealt with current black market corruption, but there was no hint of that in the city she experienced.

More important to her, were the heavily shaded trees with birdsong and glimpses of doves and other birds she could not identify. She laughed to herself. 'A ten minute walk' the portress had said. That was an absolutely standard European description for everything — no matter the country. The post office, the rail station, whatever you were looking for, you were given very good directions followed by this tiny measure of time and space. A small pursing of the mouth, shrug of the head in the appropriate direction, waving of the hand and the phrase to start you off, 'It's just a ten minute walk!'

Yes, now she could see it — a couple more blocks, next to the rail station.

The tightly scheduled European trains strongly contrasted with the small funny hotels, uncertain travel arrangements and personal adventures she and her friends had enjoyed in the south of France, even in Rome and Barcelona. Pauline and Lizby simply wanted to be there, any which way, and it often was just that. Heat, monuments, and a sense of centuries in Paris, Florence, Assisi, and Venice impressed them, but what mattered most was the fun of the trip. Their group of twelve girls altogether had blocked out student contacts and the places they would stay — but things fell apart regularly and had to be knitted together again. The young men they met — students at Oxford including one journalist, American Coast Guard cadets in Paris who were sailing the Academy's three-masted Eagle to gain seamanship skills — all of them showed off their skills, made the girls laugh and took them to beer gardens, dancing and sports competitions. Lizby had never had such attention, nor imagined such fun. Even the journalist had already posted a letter to her from Kenya.

Standing on the corner, she had one of those moments from childhood where her mind simply swooped her into another story. Austria, the Hapsburg Empire, and before that, the invasion of the Mongols — with people like her who weren't any part of the power structure simply surviving, keeping their heads down, hiding their animals, taking care of their seeds and fire, growing plants and harvesting them where they could. They probably saw the Mongols, like the American Indians saw the 'white man,' as invaders, conquistadors. She thought of how she loved Gram's dog Spot; her Celtic ancestors probably felt the same way about sheep and goats and pigs. She wondered whether there were chickens; you never saw them in museum paintings. But she knew her forebears must have looked into the same skies of sun and clouds, and night stars — and wondered about them, as she did — and about what god was. How close it all felt — them and her — in space and time . . .

Now, startled, she woke up. A compact, blond young man was signaling as he approached that he would like to talk to her. "I'm Rudolph," he said. "A law student here in Vienna. Would you allow me to accompany you wherever you are walking. I would like to practice my English." Lizby explained she was going to the post office to see if mail from home had arrived, and would be pleased to talk for a bit. "How did you know I'm an American?"

"Your shoes," he said. "No one else wears such shoes here."

She laughed. White, with strips of brown leather in the middle to hold the laces, she said, "We call them saddle shoes as if our feet were horses."

"I have a couple of friends. Perhaps you will join us for coffee?" He motioned toward the sidewalk café where several other students watched with interest. Joining them was a perfect way to see the city, the Rhine River and the Vienna Woods — what a thought! "I have friends back at the hotel," she said. "Let's gather them up after I collect our mail, *then* coffee."

The Austrians impressed them with their deep voices and accents. "Older brothers have a duty to teach younger ones how to deepen their voices, so we sound like men, not the high-pitched English," Rudolph explained.

The girls felt quite cosmopolitan when the law students invited them for a formal dinner dance at the Schoenbrun Palace for the next evening. However, two of the other girls had met several American Army sergeants, who sincerely informed them that the entire United States European Operation was run by sergeants. The girls explained that they could not date them; they were firmly scheduled to leave for Bavaria the next morning. The sergeants said that then, the least the girls could do was join them for a brief visit to a small cellar café after their palace dinner-dance.

At 2 AM after they said good night to the lawyers, Lizby and Pauline joined their friends for hamburgers and milkshakes. The sergeants explained nothing, but somehow the girls were not surprised to find them with their jeeps in Bavaria two days later. They had written themselves 4-day passes and followed. They took Lizby and three of her friends to Garmish, Hitler's resort in Germany, where they paid for Champagne, a nightclub ice show, and an evening of dancing, with a single carton of cigarettes. The soldiers were homesick for peculiar things like singing commercials, which the army radio screened out — but mostly they missed girls who understood their jokes — and who laughed.

When Lizby returned to San Francisco, she felt she had made her debut and become an adult. She had roots, not only in the Catholic underpinning of European culture, but also in family ties — particularly a warm-hearted, great aunt in the north of England and an Irish cousin who edited the *London Daily Express*. She thought, "I'm a citizen of the world." Braving Molly's disapproval, even though it was her senior year, she transferred alone to the University of California. Berkeley.

Hubris — and naiveté.

During that senior year at UC Berkeley, Lizby didn't have the money for room and board so she lived at home and felt almost invisible as a commuter on the eleven thousand-student campus. Her attempt to get on the *Daily Cal* news staff was rebuffed. That she had edited 400-student Lone Mountain's college newspaper during the year before mattered not at all.

In addition, she was humbled to receive her first D — in Symbolic Logic, of all things! Scholastic Logic had been an easy A at Lone Mountain. The source of difficulty was the meaning of truth.

One sunny fall day, Lizby sat in a smallish class of forty-some students. She could see the campanile clock tower through the window as the professor explained that an "arbitrary cosmos of coherent, consistent meaning can be developed, even when the symbolic content of the premise is something stupid like 'Snow is Green.'" A mundane statement — nothing really — but suddenly her unshakable universe cracked. No one else seemed bothered and Lizby had no one to talk to. She had glimpsed a void, but was unable to understand her terror, unable to make it clear to anyone else. The first strong choice of her life, to go to Berkeley, had resulted not in freedom but self-doubt, a shattering of how she thought, loneliness, and an unchosen invisibility. She had no context for this numbing experience of blankness that followed. She wondered if her state of mind had been related in any way to the emptiness that Tibetan monks worked to cultivate — she thought not. There was no under sense of calm. Many years would pass before she heard the term *fertile void* and connected it to the first step of a shift in knowing. Something, no-thing was beginning to move in her mind. It was terrifying — yes, but . . .

She gradually suppressed the fright of blankness by plunging into stories. Lizby had always been an avid reader like Molly, her mother. Now plots and the patterns of stories drew her. They were doors to other worlds, as important as food, almost an addiction — but they felt necessary to something she could not yet see.

For graduate school Lizby took an-easy-to-get scholarship to the Catholic University of America in Washington, DC — primarily because it was three thousand miles away from home. She always felt a deeper sense of being herself in Montana, in Yosemite, in Europe, anyplace far away enough from home — and from Molly.

Train travel across the south, life in a dorm, weekends in New York, Christmas with her roommate's sociable family in Florida, tennis and twice a week folk-dancing with Jake — a New York-born Jewish physicist from the Bureau of Standards, dates listening to opera with Dick Connell — a cab driver graduate student in philosophy. All this, and not having to work, only study — restored her well-being with only rare flashes of self doubt in her first year.

However, in Psychiatric Social Work, her chosen field of study, she found Freudian theory bizarre. The 'Oedipal-complex' did not make sense to her, and she certainly was not aware of 'penis-envy.' She disliked the term 'object relations' for people, but she knew the jargon. Her 'resistance' supposedly showed she was 'threatened.' Huh!

Lizby did volunteer work at Fides Settlement House; met 'colored people' and began to find out what segregation meant. Emily Milburn, a middle-aged, brassy, pushy, competent, black woman was the boss volunteer. A birth scar covered half her face. She took Lizby under her wing to educate her in street life. She wanted Lizby to understand what it was to live in the courtyard alleys behind the once elegant street-front mansions. Rats ran in the night; children slept in shifts sometimes four to a double bed. Oil was used for heat, and a single outside toilet for several families.

The alphabetized blocks of Washington, DC, designed by L'Enfant, radiated out from the capitol center. The single letter alphabet streets, originally fronted by homes of the wealthy, had inner courtyards that once held stables and carriage houses. Now they were the slums of the poor. Mothers living in poverty did day work for white folks; the fathers, unable to find work, drank and shot craps in the alleys. Emily and Lizby could not eat together except at Penn Station, nor could they attend the same movie theater. Washington, DC was the South. Segregation ruled, even to the extent of having separate drinking fountains for white and for colored.

Lizby's vote for Adlai Stevenson the next year, 1952, was the first of many she would cast for losing candidates. In addition to her psychology studies, she read the Papal Encyclicals on social justice, the novels of Bernanos, Leon Bloy, and Francois Mauriac, Charles Peguy's poetry, and Jacques Maritain's new scholasticism and art criticism. Instead of studying for finals, she read Graham Greene's novels of faith and doubt. She worked that summer at Gallinger Hospital as a social worker in the Emergency Admitting Room. Young men bleeding from knife wounds and 13-year old pregnant girls were new and troubling to her. She needed a two-hour session with her supervisor to learn street language. She had not heard the word "fuck" before, much less "cunt" and similar terms. All of which were missing from the books she was devouring.

It was while working with unmarried mothers to place their children for adoption that she came home one night and started a marathon two-day crying jag. Finally, she went to the room of a kind, somewhat older student, Ursula, who was working on her doctorate. She helped Lizby to tell her bastard story. At the onset of puberty, Lizby's mother in her anger had labeled her, but had not told her anything about her biological father. Lizby could not question her mother and had not spoken to anyone about the shock she felt. It was a relief to finally talk about it.

Lizby needed the 3,000 mile distance between them, but her mother did not take her chosen absence lightly. During Lizby's second year away, Molly traveled cross-country by bus with Lizby's 14-year old brother, Jim, to spend Christmas in DC. Nineteen year-old Frank, came up from Ft. Benning, Georgia where he was in OCS preparing to leave for Korea. Lizby arranged for her family to use a friend's apartment, but still could not talk about things that mattered with her mother. The family habits of silence were too strong.

Lizby had begun to realize that the way her family talked was peculiar. Things that happened were reported, especially things that happened to family members, but never chewed over, analyzed, or discussed. Somehow, questions made everyone uncomfortable and were seldom asked, except as accusations or from a judgment perspective. There were anecdotes and stories, but the past was seldom mentioned and the future rarely anticipated. Questions might imply disloyalty, incorrigibility. Ask the wrong one and you might get thrown away.

Lizby did not want to go back to San Francisco when she finished her degree, so she sent for information on joining the Baroness de Hueck's commune in Combermere, Canada. She also checked out Dorothy Day's Catholic Worker settlement house on the Bowery in New York, but dealing with derelicts was not her interest.

Ultimately, a telephone call from Molly on the night before her comprehensive exams changed her plans. "I'm going to be operated on, possibly for cancer. I'd like you to come home." Lizby completed her exams the next day and flew home. Her mother was still asleep in the recovery room when she arrived. The surgeon told Lizby, "We opened her up, but it's too far advanced. We doubt she'll live another three months."

Molly lived three years.

Lizby felt compelled to stay close, but bought a cabin on Mt. Tamalpais to keep a sense of herself. Her father helped by backing the bank loan she needed. The cabin became a meditation poustinia. She covered two of its walls with burlap, and remodeled the kitchen. Lizby even painted a Steinberg cartoon naked lady in the shower. She sewed loosely woven drapes, hung them on wooden rods and filled the kitchen shelves with her hand thrown pottery.

Drinking a cup of espresso, in the quiet, heavy sunlit morning above the fog, blocked out the horror of Molly's illness with moments of perfect contentment. Lizby gradually re-entered San Francisco life with friends.

During the year after surgery, Molly went to Europe to visit Lourdes, Rome, and the Rhineland. Meanwhile, Lizby took a burro trip into the High Sierra for a few weeks, and climbed Mt. Brewer, the third highest mountain in the Sierras. She climbed the difficult 10 to 14 foot talus stones of the last portion, but stopped about 70 feet from the top. A tedious stretch of gravel-like scree remained. She asked her companions, "Can you imagine the view is any more spectacular from the top than it is here? The rest of the climb isn't important." The two young men continued on to the top of the mountain to sign the register. As she waited for them to return, it struck her that this not signing the register symbolized her attitudes. The name on her birth certificate wasn't right. She had not bothered to pick up her diplomas from either the University of California or from Catholic University's School of Social Service. Papers were not what mattered.

When Molly returned from Europe, Frank graduated from Officer's Training and married the girl he had dated throughout high school. Joan, a second child like himself, was anxious for independence from both their families.

Lizby's youngest brother, Jim, did not marry until after Molly died. He was then a nineteen-year-old Marine, stationed in Hawaii. When he did marry, the family of his San Francisco Italian bride swept Hans and Lizby into their family life. Noni, the grandmother who ran the household, taught Lizby to cook Florentine style. Family feasts were formidable and unforgettable. Each year they seemed to enter an identical time capsule with the traditional food, even the same conversations. There was no outside world. The warmth and cheerful family caring was deeply comforting to Lizby. For years, she felt at home there for every holiday. Even Hans, so stolid in his home role, unbent and laughed with Pete, the small, rotund, truck-driver pater familius.

Nothing like the Fides Settlement House of Washington DC existed in San Francisco. Instead, Lizby found the Junipero Serra Book and Art Shop on Maiden Lane, a center for Catholic intellectuals in the Bay Area. The winds of change that would lead to Vatican II were already blowing. The shop had spidery ties to the Sheed and Ward publishing house in England, to priest workers in Paris, to theologians in Germany, Holland, and Yugoslavia, and to artists throughout the Catholic world. She met the founder, Ethel Souza, a woman with a great gift for gathering people with interesting life stories around her and was swept up in the flow.

At the Serra shop, Lizby's craving for stories kicked into high gear. Listening to talk was better than reading novels, especially in combination with dinner parties and marvelous food and wine.

Ethel lived in the Piedmont home of Kai, an artist, and Kai's two small daughters. Their home had been built for Kai's father, Xavier Martinez, in exchange for one of his paintings. Ralph DuCasse, Kai's homosexual husband, lived in San Francisco and taught at Mills College. Although the connection was quite unclear, the CIA, according to Ralph, sponsored exhibits of his large abstract paintings throughout Brazil and other South American countries.

The background stories that captivated Lizby had to do with turn-of-the-century early California writers. Kai's mother Pellie was much younger than Xavier and the daughter of Herman Whitaker, a *Harper's* magazine writer. He was also Pancho Villa's one-man air force in the Mexican Revolution. In his early days, he had founded the Bohemian Club together with Jack London, the poet George Sterling, and journalist Ambrose Bierce, whose *Devil's Dictionary* made Lizby laugh. These men, with very different values from the billionaire power brokers of the Bohemian Club today, also belonged to the first socialist party in California — with its own set of highly entertaining tales.

Pellie, who knew them all, currently lived in Carmel with her friend Pal. Pal was Harriet Dean, a musician, and graduate of Radcliff who had sponsored *The Little Review*, which first published James Joyce and Ezra Pound in this country.

These stories with dinners and weekend parties in Piedmont and Carmel became a central part of Lizby's life. She learned to bake bread and to construct easy, elegant meals from Pellie, and enjoyed conversation at their table with a constant stream of guests. For more than a decade, it was as if she had fallen down a rabbit hole like Alice, into a timeless wonderland filled with stories, people, and ideas that enchanted her.

The resulting friendships informed her heart and woke her mind.

One such lifelong friendship was with Dom. Vincent Martin, a Benedictine monk who had been in China, a prisoner of war of the Japanese. When all European males were imprisoned, he was with Teilhard de Chardin, the Jesuit paleontologist who discovered the Peking Man cave tombs. Lizby had a regular review spot on the weekly KGO radio show, "Talking about Books," run by Joe Golden. Teilhard de Chardin's books were a major interest to her, so Vincent, who knew him in such difficult times was a great resource.

Vincent had graduated from the London School of Economics and was now getting his Ph.D. in sociology at Harvard — with his dissertation on the Collective Mind. He was also looking for land to build a priory to resettle his fellow monks expelled from China. He finally found it in the upper Mojave Desert.

Lizby's friendship with Vincent was to become a cornerstone in her life for forty-five years. He talked of God in a way that connected deeply with her for the first time. The trinity notion of 'three persons in one God,' he explained was simply about the mystery of existence itself. The 'holy spirit' meant *relationship* energy, so essential to our being, something she could feel and know directly. His work on the 'collective mind' provided seeds for one of her books to come.

Her other close friend, Del Lederle — tall, dark, handsome, and with a wild sense of humor, had studied liturgical art in Paris under the GI Bill of Rights. He painted flat tempera gouache icons, and used colors as if they were chords of music. He also cut out paper sculpts, and drew cartoons on paper napkins of most of the things that happened to them. Ethel wrote the captions. Liturgical art was flourishing at the time of Vatican II. Lizby met him when she was 23, and they went everywhere together, making pottery, listening to Beat poetry, and visiting friends. Everyone wrote, painted, operated small print presses, or crafted wooden furniture. They traveled the road south between Piedmont, San Francisco, Carmel, and Big Sur to Partington Ridge; or north up the coast to Mendocino and Bill Zacka's Art Center.

With endless conversations, beaches and beauty — great meals and wines, Lizby began to see bits of herself that Del — then others — saw. Her eyes, newly skilled hands, and the fun of her mind surprised her.

Lizby worked as a family service social worker, participated in peace groups, and learned to throw pottery with skill. She also studied with Ruth Cravath, a sculptor second only to Benny Bufano among San Franciscans, and took part in Charlie Farr's life drawing sessions. After two years, she changed jobs to become a medical social worker at UC Medical Center, where she worked in the Hypertension and Psychosomatic Clinics and the Internal Medicine Unit of the hospital.

As Lizby began to come alive, Molly's condition continued to worsen.

She died at 51, alone at home with everything still unsaid between herself and her daughter. It was February 14, 1956, when Lizby found her body — Valentine's Day and Mardi Gras that year. Books that had absorbed Molly's attention in the last months — Thomas Merton's *Seven Story Mountain* and a book of poetry, *The Woman Wrapped in Silence* — lay on the bedside table, silent witnesses of her isolated journey.

It was a difficult time for both Lizby and Lizzie, her grandmother. They could not cope with whatever Molly was wrestling with. When she died, Lizby knew she was willing that she die. She felt that she had failed Molly and had failed her training. She should have been more compassionate. It was impossible to acknowledge the legacy of love, anger, wary hope and edgy despair her complex mother had left.

She sensed the legacy would need to be dealt with. She had only one gift her mother did not — her capacity for friendship, a gift much like her grand-mother's.

Several years before, Lizzie had moved to San Francisco and lived two doors down the street from her daughter's family in a warm, high-ceilinged flat with a back garden filled with trees. After Molly's death, they sat together in her grandmother's kitchen. Lizzie rose to fill the kettle for another pot of tea. The night was black outside the kitchen windows.

"I didn't know how Molly felt about leaving Butte," she said. "Good riddance, maybe. Her penny postcard said: 'We've arrived & are staying at the Y. Love, Molly.'"

Gram's stories had been skimpy with lots of gaps. But Lizby had hunch-es to think about and fill in later. At the time she only said, "She didn't tell me stories of her childhood, but I imagine she was sad to leave you and a little scared."

"Not a bit of it. Molly always knew exactly what she wanted. I did question her friendship with Gertrude, though. They seemed exactly opposite to one another, but now, I wonder. . . ."

Lizby asked, "Did you ever meet, or did Mother ever tell you about my blood father?"

"She didn't talk to you?" Lizzie asked.

"Only to tell me when I was around 13 or 14, that I was a bastard — and I could never — I didn't know how to ask her about . . . anything."

"You have a proper birth certificate," Lizzie protested. "But, . . . well, I should have said something, but I didn't know you knew even that. It wasn't my place to ask." Lizzie looked at her miserably. "I couldn't bring it up to her either."

They sat in silence. Finally, Lizzie sighed. "I didn't know him — just that he was a doctor — a surgeon — in Oakland. I think she got to know him when my sister Betty was visiting from England. He was English and had a peculiar name, I can't remember. He wouldn't marry Molly when she became pregnant. She didn't tell me, until she had to. I know he committed suicide in a downtown hotel in San Francisco sometime around 1950. She did call me about that. I guess she had to talk to someone when she read it in the newspaper — but she hadn't been in touch with him and didn't know why."

1950 was the summer Molly gave Lizby her trip to Europe and seemed to relax her fears — but Lizby had no awareness of pain or trouble in her mother's life.

Her grandmother didn't know much about the strikes of the thirties — or about Molly's relationships. But before their night talk was over and she had nodded into sleep, Gram had given Lizby facts to frame her questions about the complexly independent woman who eventually became her mother.

Later, Lizby told Ethel the suicide story. Ethel went to the newspaper morgue and searched the news stories and obituary columns until she found it. Lizby's father's name was Chelsea Dingle Eaton. He was a surgeon, a member of the California Writer's Club, and a past president of the Medical Arts Society. His hobby was painting portraits. His wife, a musician, survived him, as did his brother an Annapolis Navy career officer, and his parents. His mother's name was Belle. No children were mentioned.

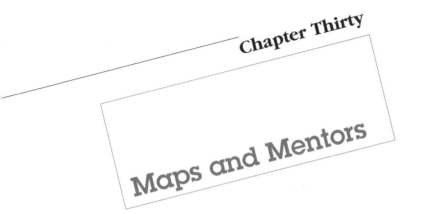

Chapter Thirty

Maps and Mentors

August 1956

A|bout six months after her mother's death, Lizby entered psychotherapy. It was difficult for her to understand what kept her in therapy except a pent-up hunger to talk. She did not yet understand she was beginning a journey with different roads, different languages — every one of which she would need to know.

First, she chose Dr. Carl Jonas, the head of Langley Porter and father of nine children. He saw her for three months then said she should consider analysis for a couple of years of two to three times a week therapy. He referred her to Don Brown, whose rates he thought she could afford better than his.

Not a good choice.

Don Brown, then a closet homosexual and orthodox silent Freudian, was a cerebral psychiatrist, the last thing in the world Lizby thought she needed. Abandoned by a father who did not know her, she felt disliked by Hans, the substitute father who did, and cast off by the 'father of nine' psychiatrist she had chosen. Lizby could not let her grown-up self know how painfully she wanted a daddy. Yet, UC Medical Center was the right place to be. She had six well-paid years of postgraduate education. She attended every

lecture and every seminar that interested her in both UC and LPNI (Langley
Porter Neuropsychiatry Institute). She also went to the weekly psychiatric
rounds at Mt. Zion Hospital.

She needed its laughter, yes, but there was still so much more that she did
not yet know, or feel . . .

Common Sense and Laughter

Eric Berne, tall and skinny with tufted hair, resembled the comedian Danny
Kaye, as he presented his theory of Transactional Analysis at a Mt. Zion noon
lecture. After his talk Lizby came to the podium and told him it was the first time
she had laughed at any psychoanalytic thought.

"I like you, too," he said. "Come over to my place on Sacramento Street
— the back side of Grace Cathedral — next Tuesday night. A bunch of us get
together each week to talk about this stuff."

So began Lizby's three-year association with a small group of psychiatrists, psychologists and social workers in Eric's apartment on Nob Hill. After the
discussions, the group usually drank beer; sometimes they went out to play in
North Beach, but they each always left a dollar in the basket for their adopted
Greek orphan, Can-You-Turn-This-Page-George. Can-You-Turn-This-Page got
his name from the phrase under a pitiful child photo, part of an ad campaign to
sponsor foreign children in need. Even their own heartfelt gestures were
couched in flip language by these therapist-iconoclasts who took on the psychoanalytic establishment.

Eric acknowledged each member of the group in his published books. He
had been kicked out of the SF Psychoanalytic Institute and was determined to
prove to that enclave the usefulness of his ideas, which avoided sickness labels.

He developed an easy to understand 'pop' form of Freudian therapy that
identified recurrent behaviors as *games* with hidden *payoffs*. The games were
all versions of parent\child interactions with catchy names. They could be quickly understood in contrast to the insights of four times a week psychoanalytic
sessions. For example in the game, "Why Don't You . . . Yes, But . . .," one person in the child ego state can drive any number of other players giving *helpful*
advice from their parent ego states, up the wall. "<u>Why don't you</u> try X?" parent
player says. "<u>Yes, but</u> that won't work because Z," child player answers. The

exchange is repeated until numbness sets in. Parent is defeated; child wins, proving he has this interesting problem no one can solve. It keeps everyone's attention. The only counter that cuts through the game is NOT to provide an answer to the problem, but simply to ask, "What have you tried?" The point of the game, oddly enough, is not only the small gain of substitute power, but to avoid the painful problems of true intimacy.

Lizby thought her own childhood game must have been the Invisible Watcher, strengthened by the pleasures of reading, and then a variant became the Invisible Listener, reinforced by gathering real life stories through friendships, and by her profession as a psychotherapist. The payoff was to avoid danger — but what kind of story has an invisible protagonist?

What do people in stories want — power, sex, fame, recognition, revenge — what? Her hunger was for stories, and more than that wasn't clear. Except maybe knowledge, and how to know what was worth living for. She felt like she was looking for a map without knowing her direction.

The Berne version of her game had to be GWPYW/YUP. Here the name of the game uses the first letter of each word, Gee Whiz, Professor, You're Wonderful, to which the reply is YUP, You're Unusually Perceptive.

Benign, but not enough.

Eric built a profitable training empire by cultivating the para-psychology agencies with training budgets — for probation officers, ministers, school counselors, any group that could ante up. He mocked Carl Rogers style groups, which produced "*feelings*, as if for a National Feeling Show." Lizby considered his least known book, *The Structure and Dynamics of Organizations and Groups,* the most interesting. It was like anatomy and physiology, the skeleton and the muscular processes of *life* in real time.

Something Berne did not write, but talked about one night, was the creation of institutions. There is a saying attributed to Carl Jung, that "an institution is the lengthening shadow of one man." Lizby considered Eric's account the tightest possible description of the pattern behind ALL institutions.

He understood the role of the Euhemeri (e.g. Jesus, Freud, Karl Marx) who start a movement; the Apostles (Peter et al, Otto Rank, Stalin), who collect the sayings and start organizing training institutes; the Heretics (Judas, Carl Jung, Trotsky) who develop alternative points of view; the Canon of Approved

Scripture and Commentary (The New Testament, the Psychoanalytic Journals, The Daily Worker) largely done by students of the Apostles; and the continuing interpretations which provide a livelihood for graduate students and instructors down the years.

The lineup of euhemeri amused Lizby. The only disagreement she had was that she thought the apostle Paul, rather than Jesus, was the man whose lengthening Shadow stood behind the corporate institutional Church. A man who hadn't even met Jesus in person!

Eric Berne charted the formal and informal lines of power influence and taught his trainees how and when to use them. Lizby learned about the principles of neighborhood community organizing that Saul Alinsky was developing in Chicago. Eric used them for his own purposes. For example, any hospital has a natural conflict of power interests between lay administrators and the medical staff. Skilled bureaucrats exploit this intuitively. Lizby got Berne into UC by requesting him as her consultant to do group therapy in the Psychosomatic Clinic. It was an administrative ruse. Psychiatric residents, hearing of his unorthodox methods could, and did, attend their sessions. Berne's empire eventually extended to thousands of people, and finally went worldwide.

It was an entertaining period and several years passed before Lizby realized how much her truth and personal knowledge differed from Eric's. Healing was impossible for anyone without the feeling of being cared for in a relationship — particularly in therapy. Rational Information alone, no matter how attention grabbing, was simply not enough. Eric saw the patterns of relationship, the games, and knew that they were always used to avoid intimacy. He was fun to be with, both loyal and devoted as a friend, but he seldom showed any hint of intellectually disarmed feelings. And for a long time, neither did Lizby.

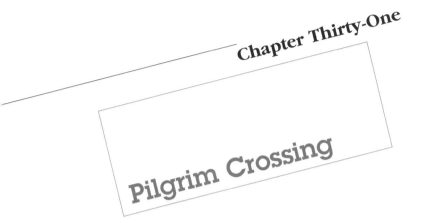

Chapter Thirty-One

Pilgrim Crossing

UCSF Medical Center 1958

There was a knock on the door of the Department of Internal Medicine. Then it opened.

"Is this w-where the Psychosomatic Clinic meets?"

Lizby glanced up from the charts of patients scheduled for the day's discussion. A gray-haired man in an ill-fitting business suit stood in the doorway, hands hanging helplessly at his sides. A new patient? Surely . . . this couldn't be the psychiatrist from Chicago scheduled to take over the Tuesday afternoon clinic. He had not been at the orientation for new resident physicians starting their training.

"Uh, yes," she said, "the others will be here in a few minutes. I'm Lizby Frings, the clinic social worker."

"I'm Mike Agron, the psychiatric c-consultant." His voice was husky, the accent probably Russian-Jewish. "We'll be teaching together this semester."

He took one of the oak chairs in the circle and placed his back against the light.

"Oh, hello," Lizby said. "Let me fill you in on how we run the clinic. The residents rotate in three-month shifts, so most treatment is short term, but a certain number of legacy patients continue from doctor to doctor throughout the year. The residents choose teaching rounds with either a psychiatric consultant — that's you — on Tuesday afternoons, or a psychoanalyst on Friday mornings. During rounds, they present medical data from their cases to the group. I add information about the patients' living circumstances, family support, and emotional or financial troubles that seem relevant, and they link this to the treatment plan. You can work in any way you prefer."

Agron listened with one leg crossed over his other knee, his hands relaxed on the arms of the chair. His face, which seemed to have a paralyzed muscle on the left side, was expressionless. The drooping lower lid of a pale blue eye created the slightly gargoyle profile associated with Bell's Palsy.

When the six residents trooped in with noisy good humor, he watched them silently. Then with the bare hint of a one-sided smile, he suggested they introduce themselves. During the next two hours, he listened in the same quiet stillness. Occasionally he asked a question. He did not stammer when he worked.

"When your patient described his pain, how did it make you feel toward him?

"Any idea why this old lady's flirting made you uncomfortable?

"As you remember him walking out of the room, does any image come to your mind?"

The silence would lengthen as the young doctors undertook the unfamiliar task of looking at how they had felt or what they'd seen and their fleeting mental images to learn what was going on in the patient.

The one uncomfortable with his patient's flirting, flushed when he said, "Her rash didn't need treatment. She was wasting time and, besides, she looked like a freak with her frizzy hair and cheap perfume."

"The hair and perfume bothered you?"

"No. She was just so . . . intrusive."

"She wanted to get to you, or get some feeling from you?"

"I felt disgusted and didn't want to show it."

"Strong feelings, good. Your feelings can be an emotional stethoscope to locate what the patient is struggling with. Old women often feel invisible, even repellant. How do you connect this with her physical symptoms?"

Lizby noticed how difficult it was to see Agron clearly in front of the light.

When the session ended, she felt like someone coming out of a hypnotic trance. She commented, "I like the way you didn't let that fellow get away with denigrating his patient."

"Four s-syllable words" — a brief flash of his crooked smile — "Do you want to say you like me?"

She laughed, "Maybe." His question made her uncomfortable. He was doing the same thing to her he had done with the students. He made her aware of her feelings, and she became unsure of herself. She wanted to be a watcher, not a player. Mike was the wrong name for him — too open. This was a devious man.

The weeks went on. Lizby continued to administer the clinic and, to her surprise, found she trusted Agron's style of teaching. There was kindness in his clinic. Gradually, the residents became less inclined to talk about a patient as "an interesting colitis problem," and more likely to say things like, "Billy Joe had an asthma attack after dinner with his mother-in-law last weekend."

In contrast, the psychoanalyst with the Friday clinic taught the *flight to health* method of healing. He chewed an unlit cigar throughout his morning clinic.

"Nothing short of four days a week analysis for several years would accomplish any *real* change in this guy's life," he said of one patient. "Psychosomatic symptoms come from the unconscious and the patient is afraid but can't tolerate knowing what he is afraid of." He picked up a piece of chalk. "Your task is to make the patient *more anxious*, not more comfortable. Only in this way, will the natural defenses of repression grow stronger — the flight to health." He sketched a little diagram on the black board. "The pathology remains securely buried under the strengthened defenses and the patient returns to normal functioning," he said.

A vaccine model, Lizby thought. Sure enough, the patients rarely returned, but what was normal about the inducement not to return?

During the following spring, Lizby learned that Agron was experimenting with some new drugs said to offer the equivalent of a round trip ticket into schizophrenia. A current theory of schizophrenia blamed parents for sending double messages to the child who became schizophrenic. Parents' words said one thing, but their actions showed another, so the child used garbled talk and actions to answer both levels. This was an outside view of an illness. Agron was looking for an inside experience of how the mind worked — but the research funds were in schizophrenia.

One afternoon, Mike Agron showed up at Lizby's office, a small cubical behind the hypertension clinic. Betsy Adams, a curvy botanist working on her doctorate, was with him.

"I'd like to talk to you about what I'm doing. You might be interested in taking part in the research," he said. "It will begin next weekend and take about three months, one weekend each month."

Betsy and he carried chairs in from the waiting room. Lizby's uncluttered desk, a sumi ink drawing on one wall, and ceramic pots on the windowsill gave the room an air of quiet simplicity. A tall window filled the room with light and space, but it now felt crowded to her.

"Have you come across Aldous Huxley's book, *The Doors of Perception*?" Mike asked.

"I haven't read the book. Some friends in Big Sur were talking about it last month. I figured he was another English poet like what's-his-name who wrote the stuff about the stately pleasure dome of Kubla Khan, and Alph, the sacred river that ran down to the sunless sea."

"'Through caverns measureless to man . . . ' Coleridge." Mike smiled slightly. "No, this has nothing to do with opium."

"Aldous Huxley is an important writer," Betsy said, "and his brother Julian is a research biologist. They've both done these experiments."

"What are the experiments?" Lizby asked.

Mike sat down and placed his notebook on the desk. "Sandoz Pharmaceutical Laboratories in Basel, Switzerland has produced a new experimental compound called LSD-25," he said. He settled back in his chair. "They claim it has extraordinary psychoactive properties. They've made it available to researchers throughout the world. We're interested in its use for training mental health professionals."

Betsy said, "That's the round trip into schizophrenia part."

"It's more like a visit to a different part of our mind," Mike said, "a part that's more aware of nature, and what life is. That's why I asked if you had read Huxley. He's described what he saw and felt." Mike stopped a moment and stretched his neck, then turned back to Lizby. "I'm interested in how our minds know what the world really is."

Lizby was fascinated. This sounded in line with an idea that absorbed her — that the whole vast world of creation was moving toward a point of unified consciousness. She and Betsy had shared books by Teilhard de Chardin, the French paleontologist who documented the evidence for such a vision.

Betsy, who had hung on Mike's words, pouted. "I don't see why I can't be included in the next experimental group."

Mike said, "I need you on the observation team." She gradually let herself be persuaded as he took her hand and held it.

Lizby saw Mike, and the experiments, in a new light as the target of Betsy's flirtation. He was moving up in the medical power hierarchy if he had attracted *her* attention.

Mike then stood and asked Lizby, "Do you want to do this series? We're comparing the effects of two additional substances derived from plants used in religious ceremonies by Native American Indians that seem to have similar effects — mescaline and psilocybin." Lizby hesitated only briefly. She simply suppressed a fleeting thought that she had been manipulated to bypass any objection or normal question of risk.

"I think so. What are the arrangements?"

Sterling Bunnell, a third year medical student interested in becoming a pathologist, and Rex MacAlpin, an internist, whom Lizby regarded as a rather stuffy first year resident, were to be her companions in the experiments. Sterling, the son of a well-known San Francisco surgeon, was a loner who raised falcons and kept snakes in the attic of his family's Pacific Heights mansion. From childhood, he had studied whatever and however he chose. This included field trips to gather peyote buttons in the desert. He was the one who suggested comparing the effects of drugs used by the Indians. An unlikely trio, they arranged to spend the weekend in Mike's home in Palo Alto and to take the first drug, LSD, in pure Sandoz quality.

Sterling had his own agenda before they left for Palo Alto. He was in the dissection room at UCSF and late in finishing. He had Rex MacAlpin and Lizby meet him there and stop to look at the corpse of a young redheaded woman, whose lungs he had removed. Years later, Lizby still would not have to close her eyes to remember flashes from the green operating room, the stainless steel table and containers, the stillness of the corpse with her orange hair and gaping, red, empty chest.

Driving down, Sterling took some pills from his pocket and directed the others to take them. He said he had collaborated on a number of similar experiments with Mike. It would be a couple of hours before the effects took hold. He would drive, so the others could start. When they arrived Mike said nothing, but Lizby sensed his irritation. Sterling had insured there was no turning back from a dosage he selected.

The living room in Mike's peninsula home was comfortably carpeted. A wide fireplace, a few wooden chairs, a large aquarium, a glass cage in which a boa constrictor lay curled, and a table were the only furnishings. A blood pressure cuff and various medical measuring devices lay on the table. The kitchen on one side of the living room overlooked trees and a road in the distance. A bathroom opened to the other side and on either side of the fireplace, glass doors led to the patio of a rear garden enclosed by shrubbery.

Sterling gave Mike a sunny smile and took his pill. Mike looked at him without expression and directed Betsy to begin the baseline tests. Lizby learned later she had a panic pulse in these measurements although she was unaware of her fear. It still did not occur to her that Sterling had constructed the possibility of a "bad trip" for one or more of them. The objective curiosity of the research pathologist was unfamiliar to her.

However, as the drug began to take effect Sterling's pre-set variable dropped away. It was as if lights had been turned on in a dim room. Everything had a hard-edged brilliant clarity. Soon her senses washed clean, and sensory data flooded her body. Utterly absorbed, she watched an ant walk across a cement patio, his perfect little body and the movement of his legs like a small machine, a tiny packet of life. The three experimental participants, Rex, Sterling and Lizby were taken to a hillside and she stood by a tree feeling the movement of the wind sweeping up, waves rippling through the grass, as she had never felt wind before, completely, with all of her senses. She touched the bark of the oak tree, and then clung to it. She wasn't the tree, but felt at one with it. They shared the same life. Everything she knew about cells, the movement of water and nutrients from the earth, the chemical interplay of leaves with the sun, was in her mind at once with an amazing sense of finally understanding — as if dry facts had turned to poetry.

Like a baby, however, she had no sense of her separate self and no power to *decide* to move. She simply received how utterly beyond all previous imagining, how wonderful, was life. During the course of the weekend, she watched without judgment or protest while a boa constrictor swallowed a live mouse. She ate a roasted chicken, exploring the slimy underside of its skin, the muscle meat, and its bones with her fingers. The smell, touch, taste, and visceral aftersense of satisfied hunger were part of the meal. Even as the drug began to wear off a day later, she still could be captured by the movement of wood grain in a chair or light refracted through a water-drop on the rim of a glass.

The next month they worked with mescaline, a derivative of peyote. Lizby was astonished when she fell into a waterfall being pulled deep into a mountain stream — in a Hokusai woodcut print. When the print was taken from her, the break in closeness felt like a boot being pulled out of mud. She looked deep into the heart of a flower—pistil, stamens, corolla, and calyx — with equal surprise. The incredible bi-polar nature of sexuality that ran through all life and into her own body saturated her mind. The florid colors and textures, the roaring tumescent fullness amazed her senses.

During the third month, with psilocybin from hallucinogenic mushrooms, Lizby experienced one sense translated into another inside her. She lay on her back on the living room rug; her eyes closed while she listened to Raga music, and saw a tree design that resembled a Persian rug. Small bits of light flowed in intricate circuits, periodically pulsing with color beats of bright intensity. The sound-sight and her fascination with it seemed to go on forever.

When Mike Agron presented his observations at Langley Porter Neuropsychiatry Institute, they were not well received. His imagination and care in constructing the experience was not seen, only that he had not established the connection to schizophrenia in a way that was conventionally obvious to the medical audience. It is not easy to explain the relevance of an answer if the question has not been felt, or carefully framed.

Seeds can be tossed anywhere there are cracks, however, even in the hard ground of orthodoxy. Then all that is needed is water.

What Lizby got from the three month series — she never took such drugs again — was her own understanding of how her brain worked. Sensory data was constantly flooding into all her receptors, not merely the five senses. The drugs apparently removed all the structural filters, like a box with its cardboard dividers taken out. Everything was present at once. It crossed the sense barriers and she experienced the chaotic but marvelous flood again that she must have known before she knew her child self as separate from her mother and the world. Now, as then, unless she filtered out most of the information, she couldn't move or think. Her language and European Catholic culture had taught her how to shield herself from the immensity of knowledge, and how to find and use fragments to survive. Emotions were the genius shortcuts mammals used to call up survival connection data quickly. She appreciated them with newly informed respect.

She knew, too, that although filters were absolutely necessary to have enough of a sense of herself to walk around and to make decisions, she was asleep to the degree she did not know the screens were there, and did not know *a deeper Self connected to everything* was also inside her, every moment of her life.

Lizby found how to concentrate her passion with her mind to re-enter this other level of reality eventually. She needed to keep her ego, the sense of being herself, *in* the experience rather than to let it be overwhelmed by sensory data. The major obstacle was that her sense-of-self was sustained by daily life situations where her ego as the actor claimed almost constant attention. She tried a variety of meditation exercises — mind disciplines.

Self-forgetting occurred while paying attention to others. In her work, she could reach stillness and look as deeply into a person as into a flower. It didn't last, and didn't always happen, but it was possible. The world opened and she was there, able to know and to act on what she knew, if only to say 'yes.' Choices and changes appeared. Creation was a *constant* process and she learned to recognize it.

She then realized she had become a pilgrim, and that a time stretched before her of seeing and serving the quiet choices of life. There would be other parts to this journey.

Mike and Sterling, both as physicians and subjects, carried on their research for several years. As far as she could tell, neither man had any interest in working with the societal implications of their work. Each had a slightly megalomaniac quality.

A few years later, Timothy Leary and Richard Alpert seized the imagination of the country and drugs went to the street. Lizby would see and recognize the intricately detailed flower paintings with their harsh colors that the drug users made. She knew what they were trying to show, but like beauty in the valley of Shangri-La, it could not be carried back.

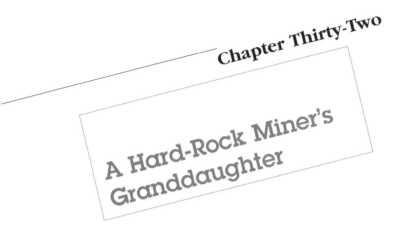

Chapter Thirty-Two

A Hard-Rock Miner's Granddaughter

Esalen and Four Springs

Henry Miller cast a long shadow but no longer lived on Partington Ridge in Big Sur. The handful of artists and writers who lived on the ridge worked in hermit-like isolation. They gathered each day at the mailboxes on the highway and socialized occasionally in the sulfur hot springs at Esalen with its rusty looking tubs. Men went to the right and women to the left into separate quarters, but both overlooked the vast peaceful ocean.

Toward the end of the decade, Mike Murphy inherited the land nearby and, with Dick Price, started inviting people for poetry readings and weekend seminars.

Lizby stayed with Louisa Jenkins, an architectural mosaic-maker who lived on the ridge, and she loved the stories of Louisa's friends who visited — particularly, the playwright Clare Booth Luce, and inventor Bucky Fuller. In turn, Louisa used Lizby's Mt. Tam cabin when she came to the Bay Area. On one such visit, she took Lizby to meet the Jungian analysts who had started the Guild for Psychological Studies.

The Guild was the somewhat disreputable cousin to the official Jungian Institute associated with UCSF. Disreputable because these women analysts, who had studied with Carl Jung in Zurich, openly used some of Jung's more occult metaphors — astrological and alchemical ideas — ideas that tend to make establishment academics nervous. They used them in common, everyday psychology.

Elizabeth Howes and Sheila Moon were at Four Springs, their 400-acre study center retreat near Middletown in Lake County. They had just concluded a ten-day seminar on Dionysus and Apollo and were obviously pleased to see Louisa. Lunch was served outdoors on a stone table under a forty-foot tree near the grape arbor—fruit, cheese, and wine with fresh baked bread. Sheila read some of her poetry, and afterward the four of them swam without suits in the rock-sided pool.

"Alchemy is a symbolic system of classification. You have to be able to use metaphor. And most people don't use or understand metaphor well," Elizabeth explained to Lizby. "That's the problem with fundamentalists."

"Well, another aspect of your work that makes people nervous," Louisa said, "is your point of view that Jesus was a fully individuated man — the epitome of what the Jungian process is about."

Sheila just laughed. "We don't accept the 'Christ' archetype the early Church projected onto him. Nonetheless, if you focus just on what we know he said in the stories, the parables alone — they are brilliant. In the Records seminar we analyze them in the same way we analyze dreams."

She said they focused their principal study on the Records of his life and teachings, as they called the synoptic gospels. They analyzed them as if they were dreams and a product of the Collective Unconscious. They worked in a similar way with the myths of other cultures.

Dreams and archetypes? Lizby took their thoughts home with her and thought about universal characters like the Wise Old Man, and the Fool, situations like the Night Sea Journey, and Choices, and Three Magical Wishes — the elements of fairy-tales and myths. Who was the Hard-Rock Miner archetype — one who went into the caves of the earth, and made them deeper, more dangerous for others to follow, while searching for hard metal that would be worked with fire — always fire — and hammered into other forms? The uses of metal by Vulcan: in coins for exchange, tools, armor, weapons, strength, transport, and bridges — each of them holding the power of hardness and endurance. Who would the daughter, or the granddaughter of a hard rock miner be in such a story? Persephone — or some connection to life to contrast with the deadness and weight of stone?

The strange dream she had as a child returned to Lizby's memory. Again she stood frozen in front of a mouth-cave, its sides filled with flames, and leading deep down into the earth, the land of Dwarfs, Hades, and the Inferno. The place where Dante had found not heat, but cold avarice. Which somehow must be avoided at all costs by giving away everything. Were these matters somehow connected to a story—the story she was *not* living? A cul-de-sac she decided, but something she would think more about.

In fact, Lizby was questioning what she was doing with her life. She had expected marriage to just happen to her somehow, but it didn't. Del was tall, handsome, knowledgeable, and witty, but the song, *I don't know why I love you like I do... The only time you hold me is when we're dancing,* said it all. There was no fire between them. She dated a few men she met on Sierra Club high-country trips and a couple of physicians at UCMC, but there was nothing other than smallish sparks.

Alan Balsam, a Quaker whose father taught sociology at Harvard, took her to his family's home in Monterey one Thanksgiving weekend. His agnostic family quickly established her Catholicism, formal education, family background, and intuited that Alan and she had not slept together. The combination apparently was sufficient for them to hate her. His father attacked in ways Lizby had never experienced and, at first, she could not imagine what he was doing. The father, a polar opposite to Alan, arrogantly lumped her with know-nothing fundamentalists and baited her to defend positions she had not taken. Alan seemed paralyzed. When they returned to SF, he said it did not matter. That was just his father's way.

She went with Alan on one other trip. They visited Indian reservations, where he might take a medical position after he finished his residency, but she looked at him with different eyes. He read widely and had a quick sense of humor based in puns. She liked his Quaker integrity, but he could not stand up to his family.

Something felt terribly wrong with her own life. Analysis with Brown had been useless, she thought. There was no sense of direction, much less a journey completed. She decided to take a pilgrimage to the Holy Lands. Rome, Delphi, Istanbul — which she thought of as Constantinople — and Jerusalem, and began a six-month study of Hebrew. Ethel and Del joined her. Del by this time had returned to Paris to live, and they wrote long letters to each other filled with plans and cartoons.

Her trip lasted almost four months, the first two with Del and Ethel. They stayed briefly with friends in Paris and Zurich, then onto Yugoslavia, where the family of a San Francisco colleague took them in hand. Lizby had read Rebecca West's *Gray Lamb and Black Falcon* and found the region fascinating. It had four languages, two alphabets, and three ethnic groups who hated one another, yet lived as communists under their common hero Tito.

The Voduseks, siblings of the brother they knew in San Francisco, were a mixture of communist academics, the last physician in private practice, and anti-Communist fighters. The two communists were the head of the Chemistry Department at the University of Lubjiana and in charge of collecting and publishing folklore and art books to help Serbs, Croatians, and Slovaks find some common ground. One of the family's anti-Communist resistance fighters had edited a national newspaper and then fled to Trieste when Tito took over. He presently beamed radio programs back to his homeland. His wife, who had stayed behind to care for their invalid son, worked as a charwoman.

Del and Ethel then traveled with German friends by car down Italy's boot. Lizby flew to Greece where they joined her, visiting Mt. Olympus, Delphi, Epidarius, Corinth, and the Greek Islands. Lizby went on alone to Istanbul, down to Jerusalem in Jordan, and through the Mandelbaum Gate to Israel. She visited several kibbutzim and talked to Arabs and Jews from Tiberius to the Negev. She wrote an article on the life of Palestinians she met in Israel who had a problem with water rights. Her Swiss publisher friends helped her to sell it to a US monthly magazine, *Jubilee.*

Lizby liked Israel and considered taking a job as a mental health consultant. In the end, although she fantasized that her blood father was probably Jewish, she knew that she was not. She also came back with the knowledge that Del lived a homosexual life in Paris. He no longer focused her vague yearning.

Lizby's sense of self shifted. Again, the blankness she had first felt in Berkeley surfaced. After hearing Jo Wheelwright talk at Langley Porter, she wrote to him and asked that he accept her into a Jungian analysis. He was one of the two principal training analysts and founder of the SF Jungian Institute. She felt incredibly bold to ask for one of the few training hours he had each week, but he accepted her and she worked with him for over a year to gain a clearer understanding of dreams and how to work with shadow issues.

She learned that inner shadow drives are first seen as belonging to other people and outer matters. The work required owning them as one's own — seeing what she was contributing. For example, she selected friends who rarely demanded strong feelings or physical closeness. As soon as a man wanted a serious relationship, she lost interest. This was *her* process of leaving, not his. With consciousness, comes choice, and she began to recognize that being loved did not necessarily come with the baggage of ambivalent feelings she had experienced with her mother. Del had been an ideal friend to experiment with closeness. He had not engulfed her, but they genuinely enjoyed each other's considerable gifts. That was the demand she was making in all of her friend-ships. But following her own path was her *choice* and it could include *mutually chosen* intimacy.

That fall she applied for an NIMH (National Institute of Mental Health) doc-toral fellowship at the University of Chicago. Wheelwright urged her to go to Zurich for training as an individual analyst, but her interests were turning to the communal again and her grandparent roots.

Eric Berne recommended her for a NIMH Fellowship grant to cover room, board, tuition, and $20,000 pocket money for two years of more study. Her friends gave a surprise crab-curry dinner party for thirty people to celebrate and send her on her way. Her personal revolution and return to roots was about to begin, but again it would not take the shape she expected.

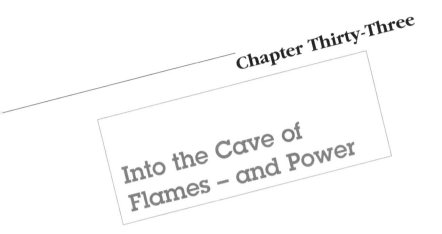

Chapter Thirty-Three

Into the Cave of Flames – and Power

P ower is an interesting word, associated with taking charge, decision-making, money, action, energy, life — and fuel. It is not usually used to describe nurturing and love. There is something paradoxical about training to heal the wounds of society. This was particularly evident in the Sixties, a time of revolution in civil rights and sexual rights — the anti-authority, anti-institution, and anti-war revolutions — were flourishing. Everyone who lived through the beginning period was swept into them, one way or another — and changed. It was necessary to find how to get, and use, power.

Chicago 1960-61

In the fall of 1960, with her NIMH Fellowship grant at the University of Chicago and living in International House, Lizby anticipated the freedom of student life. She did not expect to study intensively ten to twelve hours a day, every day. A quick revision to thoughts of freedom, but ideas continued to seduce her — and new seeds were everywhere. She sat in on the Committee for Cultural Thought and audited a class by Mircea Eliade. The class felt completely over her head. The first three pages of Eliade's reading list were in German, the next three in French, and one in English. She had read and enjoyed his books, particularly *The Myth of Eternal Return*, but clearly here, she was an amateur in a pick-up street game.

The University of Chicago was *the* school for training administrators for national programs. The training required a broad understanding of economic forces and political thought. Lizby spent hours reading legal arguments and dissenting opinions in Supreme Court decisions. The students studied evidence of declining jobs and a shift away from manufacturing in this country so that doors were closing even for skilled workers. They knew that trouble was brewing in the cities, that income distribution had to be solved, and it would not be through jobs. Corporations attracted by cheap labor and tax avoidance were already building their plants in third world countries. As little as a 1 percent increase in unemployment meant increased rates of admission to mental hospitals, and prisons, and correlated with increasing family violence, alcoholism, and suicide. They did detailed analysis of administrative problems in the Harvard Business School Case Books. As they studied research methods and statistics, she felt her anger growing, along with contempt for fuzzy thinkers.

One night, however, she woke up with a frightful dream. She was skiing down an icy mountain path. The track was very straight, carved into the snow by previous skiers, so her speed was picking up. On either side, she could see burning animals. She had spent the night with Ramesh, a sweet East Indian man with whom she liked to dance. As she sat up in bed, the stars were winking out, one by one in the stillness before dawn. A Hindu god figurine with an elephant head sat on the windowsill beside a guttered candle. It was a week before Prelims, the examinations before final acceptance as a doctoral candidate. She remembered the Snow Queen story from childhood, with little Hans "learning to play the games of icy reason." She thought, 'I am doing something wrong. My instincts are being destroyed,' but she could not face the implications of her dream and fell into magical thinking. 'If I'm not meant to go on this path, I'll fail a key segment of Prelims,' is the thought she later remembered.

Nine students took Prelims that year, including two repeaters. Five passed. She did not. Unbelievably, she had failed her strongest subject, administrative theory.

D'accord! She did not look back. She would not take the prelims over, for she knew she did *not* want to administer a government program.

Phyllis Dunne, a great old social worker from days of the Depression, asked her to take a job in Marin County, as her director of professional services, when she returned home. In the next few years, Lizby worked four days a week for the agency and each month took time off from the 25th to the last day of the month to write. Her articles began to be published.

She redesigned the agency program; started group, couples, and family therapy; peer group supervision; and added the use of a sociologist consultant. Psychiatric theory was not enough to create the public mental health model she sought.

She also did consulting-evaluation work for the Office of Economic Opportunity, and learned some difficult things about politics. The Headstart program was a simple notion. Preschool children, given attention and opportunity to learn, learned more when they got to grade school and had higher IQ test scores than comparable children who did not have preschool attention. Unfortunately, only a small amount of the OEO money actually got to the direct child contact.

There were layers of bureaucracy involved, staffed by people with "don't look closely" busy-ness similar to her own. She was well paid for her time, board, room, and all transportation as a consultant. She was required to write a site report with copies going to the Lear consulting corporation in Texas, the Western Division of the OEO, and another to the DC office. None of these reports were used for anything. She sent an extra copy to the site officials; at least, they would know how she thought about the site and what she recommended.

Her DC line officer requested her picture, and then invited her to an event with Schriver in Washington, DC. There was no reason for the expense. She began to understand how difficult it is to legislate 'good works,' and how necessary a spiritual vision is.

Her grandmother Lizzie died of a heart attack when she was 76 and Lizby was 34. Lizzie's eldest son, Tom had taken Lizzie to live with his family down the Peninsula toward the end of her life. He had always been her favorite, the 'one with a voice,' and a sense of humor close to Gram's own. An unsuccessful bank robber and ex-convict in the thirties, Lizby's Uncle Tom had become a successful building contractor. He bought his mother a highly dignified cockatiel bird, they called Sir Wilfred Lawson, in honor and parody of Gram's grandfather for whom she was named. When Lizzie died, Tom brought her body back to Montana to be buried. He rounded up her remaining friends and they had a grand wake, he said. Gram, known for her 'racy' tales, was sadly missed by her friends, her sons, and by Lizby.

✖   ✖   ✖

Another crisis: Lizby almost died when she lost two-thirds of her blood in undetected internal bleeding. A silent tumor had burst in the inner lining of her stomach. After multiple blood transfusions and a quick surgery, the tumor was found to be benign, but she knew death had brushed her. She also knew she still had not rethought the mystery of her 'unknowing hunger' touched earlier.

✖   ✖   ✖

Mike Murphy invited Abe Kaplan, a philosopher featured on a *TIME* magazine cover as one of five top teachers in the country, and Bill Schutz, a psychologist interested in Encounter Groups, to help Esalen define its direction.

Lizby attended a weekend with them. She was intrigued enough to stay for 5 days more in Kaplan's 7-person group. With a combination of Zen and Hassidic tales, encounter group techniques, gin, and Abe's sexual charisma, she learned about the permeability of ego boundaries, for the first time connecting it to the 'Group-Mind' studies of Dom. Vincent Martin. She had learned to pay close attention to the underground noise of her own feelings, which often started, but sometimes contradicted, her thought. But now, she could see body and speech shifts in other people as their feelings moved into conflict or harmony. Utterly new and fascinating to her.

One night after a late session, the group went to the baths. Although separate in the daytime, the baths were used for mixed nude bathing at night. The night was bright with moonlight, waves crashing on the rocks, and the sound of crickets and frogs. They went down and she joined the others, but she felt anger at this Esalen norm, an illusion of 'instant intimacy.' What was she doing here?

She was preparing to leave when Abe came and asked if she would take a walk with him after she dressed. They then had what to Lizby was a perplexing conversation. This man knew her and she knew him after four days of this intense group encounter they had been through, but he was asking her where she lived, what kind of work she did? These facts had not entered their talk before.

Identity was not in identifications — nor in norms. They had been interacting from immediate thought and feeling, rather than screened through role layers that usually limit what we say and see.

She learned more than she knew that night. It was a first step to questioning the cultural bedrock of assumptions she had taken on in earliest childhood. For example, her Esalen Hot Tub flash of anger touched her cultural upbringing's resistance to sexual curiosity about her changing body, but eventually widened to many other areas of belief and doubt.

Lizby changed her agency's way of staff training to include what she had learned about groups. She orchestrated weekends using video taped sessions with groups of families and a mixed staff of professional caseworkers and graduate students from Cal. They moved into a new building that she designed to include a children's play therapy room with a mirror-window observation room for research and supervision. One additional program, Jacob Moreno's psychodrama, was, to her mind, the most powerful tool in psychotherapy. More journal articles came from her study of gestalt therapy with Fritz Perls, and she worked to understand her resistance and cultural defenses — the shadow issues work begun with Wheelwright.

Fritz Perls was an outrageous but powerful mentor. In Enneagram terms, he was an EIGHT, cruel, sadistic, occasionally kind, but always a flamboyant, fascinating and comic teacher. The Enneagram, a Personality Classification system with Sufi roots, uses 9 types of personality each with 7 variables to establish an individual classification. It was developed as a psychiatric instrument during the 70s by Claudio Naranjo and is largely used to describe normal range tendencies rather than pathology, i.e. Fritz was *not* a sociopath.

Lizby found his attacks usually served the truth efficiently. He would go to sleep if he was bored, but he was more often mischievous and infuriating. Once in a week's training group putting in hours to be certified as a Gestalt therapist, she beat him at his own game. The setting was Janie Rhyne's studio attic in the Victorian house on Ashbury. Fritz announced that he was going to the opera the next night. This was such a small group; he had given them more than enough attention.

"Not with my money," Lizby said. "If you require the hours for certification, I require you or my $20 for the evening."

He smiled benignly, took a $20 bill from his wallet and handed it to her. "The first direct talk from you. You graduate."

He looked around the room challenging. "Does anyone else dispute me?" No one did. The next morning, Lizby was on his list of teaching associates.

One further experience with group added unexpected muscle. She wanted to know more about character disorders and how to *use* anger. Judith Goleman suggested she learn to play the Synanon Game.

Chuck Deterick had bought a mansion on Cherry Street in Pacific Heights to use as his drug treatment facility. There were games every night in the high-ceiling rooms, with sideboards of bagels, soup and endless amounts of coffee. The Game was NOT about short transactional exchanges; it was a no-holds-barred verbal encounter between peers, i.e. *everyone* who came — psychologists, real estate agents, ex-prostitutes and ex prison inmates.

In an effective game, one person at a time becomes the target of the group's probing attention. Small deviant behaviors and minor incidents are engrossed, magnified into major story-building character flaws; evidence of why one has become such a 'thoroughly discredible public figure.' A good game is wild and funny in the same way a cartoon can be. Fear and fury change through hooking into the powerful energy of humor. Defenses fall when they are seen as absurd. Not the slightest touch of physical violence is allowed. A target of the group can become the leader, if he or she is fast with words and funny enough to turn the game — the skills are learned. Not before blood is drawn, however. One's ego has to be punched into a more truthful self-knowledge.

Like war buddies who have survived the trenches together, friendships from this period were deep and permanent — including that between Lizby and her book collaborator, the photographer Michelle Vignes. Lizby probably would not have married, had it not been for the Game's harassment. "How much of a broken-down, middle-aged, bleeding-heart social worker did she plan to become?"

One other group of people mattered to her during this period — an archetypal story in themselves. Mother Humiliata rated a *TIME* magazine cover when she led her nuns in defying the Cardinal of Los Angeles, a former Wall Street stockbroker, who wanted these religious women to confine their activities to teaching. The 800 nuns, included Sister Corita (little heart), an internationally recognized artist and innovator of a new style of commercial art, Sister Fleurette (little flower) Ph.D. in drama from Stanford and producer of avant gard plays, Sister Lucita (little light), et cetera. They were a group of highly educated, beautiful, and charming women who laughed. Half of them had been or were 'in therapy,' and all had experienced encounter groups. The modestly educated priests of the Los Angeles dioceses did not know what to do with them. Some of them had met during Co-operation Church, a series of weekends the Junipero Serra Shop sponsored for priests, nuns, and lay Catholics to share their insights and concerns about the Church. Their lives entwined for several years while the Church was sifting ways to think about itself as 'the people of God' rather than the institutional corporate body of the Church.

Eventually Liz (Sister Fleurette who looked like Marilyn Monroe in a habit) left the order to marry her first analyst, Jim Bugental. They moved to the Bay Area and later many other nuns left; but some remained to form a lay institute outside the Cardinal's line of command.

Joan Lark, from the Grail, a Catholic lay group in Ohio, usually stayed with Lizby when she was in San Francisco. Lizby rented a large Victorian flat facing the reservoir park at the foot of Russian Hill, for $110/month. Its kitchen table overlooked the Bay, Aquatic Park, and the Wharf of historical sailing ships. Her Italian neighbors mostly owned small Fishermen's Wharf restaurants nearby. Friends stayed with her when they came to San Francisco and she enjoyed their long weekends of talk. Joan, however, always attracted her own entourage, most of them ex-New Yorkers.

One who came to visit was Ettore, an attorney working for the Franchise Tax Board in Sacramento.

Chapter Thirty-Four

Marriage and Partnership Puzzles – Night Vision

izby met Ettore exactly two months after the break-up of her relationship with Art Rogers, a psychologist video-film maker and a post-grad Fellow at Esalen. She was ready for a return to her family roots. Ettore, like her—a cradle Catholic, had graduated from the Coast Guard Academy, USF Law School, and two years of tax law study at NYU. He had not been married before and was going on 39, her age. He came from a comparable socio-economic, and cultural background — an Italian-Irish family in Brooklyn. Dark and attractive, he was down to earth, smoked cigars, liked country western music — especially Johnny Cash, knew local politicians, and seemed tough and street smart. Perfect, Lizby thought, she could not have written a better description of a man she might want to marry.

The Seventies

A difficult time — signs of world-threatening dangers and personal peril were everywhere. Carl Sagan warned of the incomprehensible nuclear arms threat this country was building. Michael Harrington wrote of the consequences of poverty in *The Other America*. Caesar Chavez was fighting for his Farm Workers Union with Grape Boycotts. One homophobic reaction to the *Gay* movement strengthening in San Francisco was the murder of Mayor Moscone, and Supervisor Harvey Milk by Supervisor Dan White. Jonestown mass suicides in Guyana and other Bay Area cult excesses indicated dangerous extremes in the hunger for new structures.

As old institutions experimented with change for survival, Catholics began to hear about Liberation Theology in Central and South America. The poor and their priests were re-reading the gospel in new politically activist ways. But some in Rome did not like it.

Lizby's personal sense of economic reality was also darkening. The country was in recession. Ettore worked for the Franchise Tax Board in Sacramento and they dated on weekends in San Francisco, but he was also looking for work in the Los Angeles area as a specialist in tax law.

When Lizby and Ettore decided to marry, she gave notice to the family service agency that she was leaving her job. She planned to join Ettore in Orange County, where he had found work with a small firm of trial lawyers. The agency conducted a well-publicized search and brought a man from the east to take Lizby's position. Then a week before the wedding, Ettore was fired. He sent up his books and belongings C.O.D. to Lizby's San Francisco flat and moved in.

Lizby's feelings were confused. The prospect of two of them without a job gave her pause, but she decided to go ahead. She could not let herself feel her Depression-child terror. This was a good man. She could help him through this period. She had no investments, but substantial savings. She spent little and banked her salary without thought. Bill Lamers, a psychiatrist friend, invited her to join his office. Ettore set up her books for private practice, tax returns, and a Keogh retirement account. She found it hard to understand why half her Keogh money went for life insurance, but she changed her bank accounts to joint savings and checking when they were married.

Sixty thousand dollars gradually went to set up Ettore's office in Marin, and to pay the MasterCard charges for his seminars, tapes, books, and other business expenses. He thought it would be at least three years before he could take any money out of the business. She had never really thought about money before, much less that she was responsible for planning its use.

Her father Hans had watched a small apartment building being built across the street from their family home in the Sunset district, and recommended she buy it. Ettore viewed debt — working with other people's money — as business common sense. He drew up the necessary papers for her to make a down payment. And again, he urged her to borrow money to buy the house of a friend on Potrero Hill. The sculptor, Suzy Coons, was going home to Virginia to retire. Then one of Ettore's clients came to him with a Muir Beach property problem. As a Coast Guard officer before law school, he had liked this beach, relatively unknown to most Californians. His client had a buyer who wanted to back out. Ettore, knowing that Lizby and Bill Lamers were looking for a place to do weekend couple groups, had her buy the property. The only money she had to put up was the thousand dollar closing cost.

Lizby, although she recognized the value of what Ettore was doing, had never owed money to anyone and was taken aback by the high monthly payments and the idea of being a landlord.

Born at the beginning of the Great Depression, she had absorbed its lessons from her family. Phobic about being in debt, she increased her workload. She took a job teaching in Lone Mountain's Graduate Psychology program, then added weekend courses at UC Santa Cruz Extension and UCSF Extension; summer courses at the Graduate Theological Union in Starr King and the Pacific School of Religion; then Sonoma State and Antioch West in the next few years. She was on the Board of Directors of the Legal Aid Society, the Berkeley Center for Human Interaction; later, the Strong Center for Environmental Action, and a couple of think-tanks that decided they needed a woman's input. Everything was interesting. It just did not leave much time for critical thought.

One of her students at Lone Mountain, Ruth Kramer, owned a publishing house with her husband. She urged Lizby to write a book about her use of art methods in psychotherapy.

The Inward Journey became a best seller in the new field of Art Therapy that was starting to develop. It was written in a week spent at St. Andrew's Priory in the Mojave Desert while Lizby visited Vincent Martin. The publisher asked for another book, *Staying Married* on the couple group therapy she and Bill Lamers were doing.

Lizby recognized this was work-a-holism, but thought it temporary and due to her lack of experience. She did not have family knowledge of business or private practice. That it might be partly a response to Ettore's unease did not occur to her. At first, she was too busy to realize how over his head he felt in practicing tax law, especially in light of her easy transition to private practice.

As the 70's began, she wrote occasional newsletters — soft sell publicity for classes, therapy groups and a monthly, no fee, drop-in group to discuss ideas. Work with Bill now included two more psychiatrists.

Jim, born in Iran, had been raised in this country by his divorced mother and played All American football. He later changed his first name to Jamshid, kidnapped his children and returned to Iran, where his father was physician to the Shah. Howard, who had just finished his analytic training at the Jungian Institute in Zurich, was attractive, intelligent and flirtatious. He generously gave guest lectures for Lizby's class at Lone Mountain. His wife Sally told her that he kept an ongoing fantasy about her in his journal. Peculiar, but without any basis in reality. It was an odd period in her life, every corner crammed with some form of work — and puzzles. Not without laughter, but with little time for dinner parties and talk that had formerly filled her life.

UC Medical Center had finally recognized the importance of training physicians in sexual information and started the Human Sexuality program. (Informally it was called the Fuck-a-Rama.) Rev. Cecil Williams of Glide Memorial Church co-sponsored and opened it to other therapists. The initial training consisted of two days' saturation viewing of films and slides simultaneously projected onto four walls and the ceiling. Films of gay and straight, male and female, young and old, handicapped and healthy couples were sometimes lyrical, often funny. One film, called *The Quickie,* was shown in Chaplin style fast motion. Another cartoon of two frogs demonstrated sexual positions. Lizby brought some of these SAR (Sexual Attitude Restructuring) films to the couples groups Bill Lamers and she taught. Most of the middle-aged couples they worked with had never before talked about their preferences, fears, and distorted understandings.

Part of the training took place in the Santa Cruz Mountains at a facility called Getting-In-Touch. Rita and Lorne Bay taught various kinds of mind control and body knowledge, including several systems of massage. Rita, a comfortable, grandmotherly, woman announced, "The easiest way to deepen and prolong sexual response is to place your awareness inside the body area under your partner's hand. It can be your backside, your tongue, your ear rims or your toes."

Ettore's work prevented him from attending although he went down to Esalen for a week, but this was a long way from Brooklyn.

Lizby's' spiritual life, although thin, was deeply rooted in Catholicism. Her prayer life fluctuated, but the Church's tradition of care for the needy continued to be a driving force in her life. That a celibate clergy defined rules for sexual behavior she found absurd, but she also saw that the temptation to legislate rather than educate for choice was not solely a defect of the church. She felt guidelines for developing healthy and caring sexual relationships should be knowledge of sexual responses, awareness of relationship issues, plus a strong commitment to staying with difficulties until they were understood. That would strengthen both partners.

The hetero- and homosexual problems of Catholic priests and nuns and the marital difficulties of Protestant clergy she had as clients led her to think not of sex education, but of the use and misuse of interpersonal power. Another way of saying, we don't see our own blind spots.

What troubled her the most during this period was not the anti-choice, anti-birth control and anti-sexual information stand of the church — that would have to shift or the church would not survive — but the lack of human warmth and kindness in many religious communities facing greater freedoms. Even Vincent Martin was expelled from his community and put into exile, apparently for his power to draw money to his causes. This in some way threatened the Cardinal of Los Angeles. Exile apparently was a price exacted from his community. He did not speak of it, but the mother Abbey in Belgium sent someone to investigate. Eventually, after several years, all was well and Vincent returned from Israel to his community, but that it could happen in this century, made Catholicism problematic for Lizby.

She was also troubled by her own marriage. She had married Ettore because he was very much like her family. What she failed to consider was that *she* was not very much like her family. Her values, her way of thinking, her interests, and her profession were difficult for them to approve of or understand. Although she loved her brothers, she did not really talk to them about the things that mattered most to her. They shared some traits. Frank's work-a-holism defense against knowing anger, for example, was exactly like hers. Neither of them knew how angry they could get until they found themselves in an outer situation that was intolerable — and then demanded change.

She talked to Ettore. He was a good listener, although he did not comment much. There seemed no time in his life for anything except survival. In their marriage, they had taken only one brief vacation. Ettore canceled scheduled trips to the Navajo Indian Reservation, cross country skiing, and river rafting citing 'business conflicts.' She was used to living in contact with friends. He did not seem to like many of them.

Eventually she realized that Ettore was taking money from rents to pay off a debt to his mother. She had no particular problem with this, although she *felt* he should wait until he was earning money. It was peculiar and difficult for her to put this in words. She said she wanted him to tell her before he used large amounts of money, e.g. for this debt, or to buy a car as he had the year before. He continued to take money without mentioning it. She felt petty to make a fuss, as if it were her problem; this was a hard period for him.

Ettore was not succeeding in the law partnership he had established with a friend. When his law partner finally sent Ettore a telegram notifying him that their partnership was over, Lizby helped him to deal with this, but she felt increasingly uneasy. Her marriage commitment was to stay with difficulties; strength and ability to cope would come. But that should not rule out anger. Why didn't she *feel* it? She had little experience with seeing her needs as valid rights. A need for straightness was a valid right. She did see that she was not treating her husband as a partner. Instead, tacitly, it was as if he was an incapacitated patient and should not be held accountable. That bothered her.

Some months later, she was listening to a series of tapes by Carl Faber, a Jungian Analyst who was absorbed by the phenomena of *Lying*. Lizby recognized the things Farber said matched her experience of living with Ettore. "You begin to doubt your own perceptions. You say to yourself, 'I think he said this, but maybe I am wrong. Maybe he really meant . . . Maybe I let him down . . . or he *thought* I let him down . . .' and you create scenarios to justify his doing terrible things, because *you* betrayed him by your doubt," Faber explained on tape.

Lizby heard and knew Faber's words as true.

Shortly after this, Ettore took her last savings, a treasury bill. Her book, *Staying Married,* had been published just the month before. She did not learn the money was gone until it was time to roll over the T-Bill.

"Why?" she asked, "and what has it been spent for?"

The usual expenses . . . he would not explain further, but if she really loved him, she would trust him . . . No, he would not leave the house.

A blinding, shocking moment of clarity exploding! Dante's Inferno around and inside her mind, her heart, her body, her spirit. Her Italian-descent husband could not, NOT have known he was punishing her hubris in thinking and writing about marriage while feeling none of the passion that should give it meaning. No matter that neither of them brought this force of love, nor even the blaze of anger to their particular relationship. No matter that she wrote only of what she knew, information and processes that were useful, practical, and healing. They were not what either one needed. It was not what they had.

Lizby's grief came with a monstrous storm of tears as she truly recognized that she had created this marriage out of smoke and mirrors.

Ettore knew her values stated in *Staying Married,* and gambled their marriage would continue. Her image in the community was important to her. However, she met what had to be met with open eyes. TV Channel 7 had taped and publicized a one-hour special program on her book to be shown the coming Sunday morning. KGO radio had scheduled her for a two-hour call-in radio program that would follow. On Saturday, she had another crying jag.

The pre-taped Sunday TV program would be televised. A friend came with her to help deal with the live radio calls that would follow the showing.

"When do you recognize you can't 'stay married,'" the first caller asked.

"When one or both persons are lying to the other," she answered.

Lizby filed papers for divorce before she went on a month's book publicity tour around the country. Inside, she knew her grief. When she came home, she refused to take any client for marriage counseling for a year. She needed to feel and understand what she had not known and how to know it.

Then, one day, she walked down the street and noticed a commercial jingle was echoing in the back of her mind, "Plop, Plop. Fizz, Fizz. Oh, what a relief it is." The ad from Alka Seltzer — it told her the headache was over. Clearly, her unconscious was *not* viewing all this as a tragic failure!

The comic unconscious — amazing that she'd not noticed before. Lizby also suddenly realized the number of times in her life she'd had crying jags in an important transition — the end of the war when the atom bomb was dropped, her exile to Montana, then dealing with the bastard issue in graduate school, and even earlier with the unwanted scholarship. What purpose did each of these serve? A clearing of the air, a clearing of the mind, seeing more clearly — almost literally a washing away of something noxious. Cleaning out a wound was better than not seeing it and it swept away the little pretensions of exaggerated self-importance it attracted. But deepening feelings were even more important, not her head knowing.

When she finally could laugh, her life was coming into balance again. Sadness stopped.

She would have to pay more attention to the Iron Lady sub-personality in herself, who thought she could deal with anything, and to the comment from her inner Stand-up Comic, "So, you want a medal for it?" Actually, she HAD paid attention in the past. Most humor involves a rapid shift seeing things in two frames at the same time — dignity and farce, tragedy and pretension — like at Synanon, or in Del's cartoons and Pellie's stories, or in studying with Eric and Fritz. La Professora and the banana peel! Laughter, a quick trip to the unconsciousness, brought truth. It was embarrassing that with all the psychology she knew, not to mention having written a book on staying married, she had to divorce. But when that time came, *she did know* and she knew it through her feelings.

This experience had its lesson, and it was not about blame.

Love is an on-going process of *two-way learning*. She *needed* to be cared for and to feel her own caring was seen. A baby teaches a mother how to love it and care for its needs without knowing it is teaching. In falling-in-love, partners see themselves shift, as much as they select and see their partners.

She sighed, but also knew she needed to laugh, hike, dance, and talk more with friends to feel loved.

A gift — her godchild Monica came to live with her when she moved to Muir Beach full time. Monica attended the College of Marin before she transferred to Cal Berkeley. That Easter, Lizby gave a great beach party with a whole lamb roasting on an iron spit a friend had constructed. About seventy people danced Greek line dances to music from amplified speakers — the beginning of spring.

Later that year Lizby went to Britain for a walking trip through Wales, Scotland, and the Lake country in England. She borrowed a pen from a man sitting next to her waiting in the Oakland Airport. She needed to write a check for the friend taking care of her pets. By the time of departure the man, a London broker, had arranged with the steward to sit next to her. When they got to London his Jaguar was at the airport and he drove her to Wales. As one who knew about trekking the Australian outback, he quickly outfitted himself with hiking boots and joined the Sierra Club trip. When it ended, he invited her to his home in the south of England to visit Avalon, King Arthur's traditional site, and took her to London where they saw several plays, 'third row Orchestra, two in from the aisle.' It did not matter that Ted was a 63-year-old man she would not think of marrying. He woke Lizby's sense of being herself again. She was very much Gram's granddaughter.

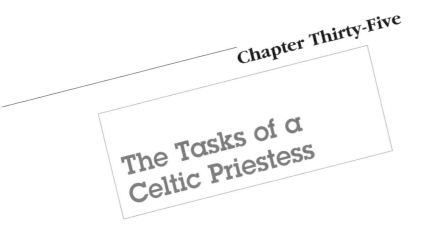

Chapter Thirty-Five

The Tasks of a Celtic Priestess

A typical August day at the beach with coastal fog condensing to a drizzle from the branches of Cypress trees, Lizby was writing a play with Liz Bugental tentatively called, *The Cardinal and the Mother General*. Liz, who taught drama, set up scene situations. They took opposing roles and improvised dialogue. Lizby, in the role of the Cardinal, found herself asking, "What in the name of heaven do these nuns want, anyway? — to be Priests?" It made her laugh, as she remembered her childhood fascination with Celtic Priestesses —'the eldest daughters of eldest daughters, ever so far back.'

"Gram explained to me that priestesses knew how to heal and where the animals hid," she told Liz. "They also could see the future, knew when Troubles were coming and how to prepare."

"That's exactly what our nuns needed to be and do when we were dealing with Cardinal McIntyre," said Liz.

The two of them had worked four hours non-stop, but now were bogged down. Lizby decided to look for inland sunshine. She would go to the Goldstein party in Berkeley. She never stayed at parties more than half an hour so she didn't think she'd be gone long. Liz stayed at the beach to nap.

There were two main attractions to any Goldstein party — conversation and Norman Goldstein's fresh baked bread. Lizby was enjoying a handful of herb-cheese and onion rolls when she went out to the deck. A tall-bearded man held the attention of a handful of people under the eucalyptus trees. Still talking, he reached out and claimed one of her rolls, while he continued his story of a radio station in Seattle.

When he was a mathematician for Boeing in Seattle, he found he had some surplus money and tithed — gave 10% of his earnings to this listener owned station — for a couple of years. The jocular owner finally called one day to tell him he owned half the station now, did he want any input on programming? "For sure," he said, and the story continued, with Lizby listening in. She became part of it as they went on to discuss the political battles of KPFA, Berkeley's own local alternative news station. This man was clearly a political radical — with an attractive sense of humor.

When the discussion was over, he introduced himself. Scott O'Keefe, who had just returned to Berkeley from a large family reunion in a coastal town near Boston that included more swimming and boating than he had had since childhood. Lizby said she regularly swam at Muir Beach. He had not realized it was a swim-able beach, so she invited him to come by when he was in the area. After several weeks, he did and their friendship picked up. He had dropped out from mathematics when Boeing started making Minute-man missiles and now did plumbing—but he also was writing a book on differential equations. She hired him to put copper pipes in the rental house on Potrero Hill.

The *Cardinal and the Mother General* play collaboration fizzled. The arc of the real life story was too depressing to capture. It was definitely a time of troubles in the corporate church.

During the next two years, Lizby lost her two dearest friends. Del returned from Israel and was living openly as a homosexual when he had a heart attack and died in a bar south of Market. He had listed her as his next of kin. Ethel suffered a stroke approximately a year later. Her outer personality was destroyed although she recovered enough memory to function. Friends helped her with several living arrangements, but finally she had to go into a nursing home. Experiencing Ethel's under-personality, where once there had been intelligence and charm, was difficult, and at times terrifying to Lizby.

Lizby and Scott began to live together in a loosely structured way. He kept a cottage in Berkeley, but they spent hours walking the beach, and talking. He read widely, quoted poetry and told her stories from Francois Villon, Henry Miller, the Arabian Nights, Ezra Pound, and *Archie and Mehitabel.* She found him fascinating, a bit careless as a worker, and shockingly indifferent to his clothes and money. He also overestimated his knowledge of French.

Nonetheless, he was always amusing, always had something relevant to say, and had a far broader range of knowledge to draw on than she did. The cottage in Berkeley where he spent about half his time was on property he owned with Barbara Lashley, the black jazz singer he had met in Washington, DC after he left Boeing. Babara and her four children had come to Berkeley with him while she completed her studies at UC. Two of her children were still in the home when she and Scott had separated as a couple, several years before. Her Jazz career and subsequent marriage was flourishing. She and her husband remained good friends with Scott and Lizby until her death, in 1992.

Scott attracted Lizby physically and in terms of his story, but he was difficult for her to understand. In her adolescence, Ned had captured the physical desire she did not yet have courage to follow. Del had catalyzed her creativity in her twenties. Ettore mirrored her middle-years over-focus on work. Scott, with his unconventional standards, seemed to her to be half Fool, half Wise Man. She knew she wanted him in her life, but puzzled why.

She had forgotten one of the tasks of a Celtic priestess — to read the changing patterns. A court jester has his own sources of wisdom and is a great companion.

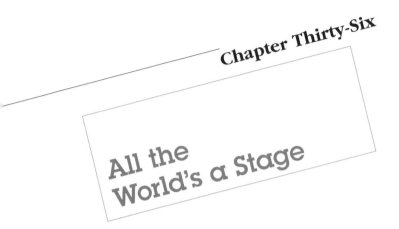

Chapter Thirty-Six

All the World's a Stage

An ancient description of a surgeon's training is: "Observe one. Do one. Teach one." If you multiply the sessions by several hundred and add the ethical imperative — do not do unto others what you would not have them do unto you — you have a skeletal description of apprenticeship training in psychodrama.

Lizby studied Psychodrama with Elaine Goldman in Phoenix, Arizona, with Dorothy and Mort Satten, in New Mexico, and then went to the Moreno Institute in Beacon, New York, to study with Zerka, Jacob Moreno's widow. Jacob, a Viennese contemporary of Freud, had invented Psychodrama — the powerful method for re-entering and changing early-in-life blocks to particular feelings.

Each of us seems to have a life-long issue to solve that touches intimacy and the use of power. Lizby's tendency to prefer feeling depressed rather than to feel angry is a common experience among women taught to regard showing anger as doing harm to a vulnerable other. Psychodrama allows practice to find other possibilities.

Other methods exist for studying the relation of individual and group consciousness. Hypnotic methods including their offshoot

NLP (neuro-linguistic programming) can be manipulative and easily misused. Lizby studied hypnotism with David Cheek, a physician in San Francisco, and with Milton Erikson, a psychologist in Arizona, both highly skilled and reputable. Lizby always worked with a contract understanding with her own clients. The goals of therapy were explicit and clear as well as knowing when the work was finished.

Werner Erhart impressed several of her graduate students at Lone Mountain, so she attended his EST seminar at a downtown hotel in San Francisco. Erhart, an Encyclopedia salesman who had changed his name (from Jack Rosenberg), put together a set of exercises to market for the public. The exercises were taken from contemporary psychology gurus; from L. Ron Hubbard's Mind Dynamics, to some Eastern philosophical concepts on the nature of Being, and wrapped up with sleep deprivation in marathon, encounter-class sessions.

Erhart courted local psychologists to validate him. He introduced them to the group at critical points in the fatigue cycle, emphasizing their credentials and accomplishments; and they, in turn, spoke of the great usefulness of his methods to their clients. He held graduate seminars and used the graduates to proselytize new members. They used his phrases, e.g., "being at cause instead of being at effect," to gain a sense of being in the IN-group. Everyone clapped and made everyone "who got with the program" feel great. It was fascinating to watch and, in fact, many participants learned enough to function better in their daily lives. Others took their learning into political life.

Lizby thought that, like Synanon, EST provided a parental shape-up structure for people who needed it. In terms of therapy, it was similar to the rewards reinforcement of B.F. Skinner's Behavior Modification.

Through her friendships with other therapists, Lizby brought her graduate students on field trips to experience different forms of therapy. For example, during the month long training groups at the Western Institute for Group and Family Therapy run by Bob and Mary Goulding, Lizby taught a day of art methods. The Gouldings were developing re-decision therapy, an offshoot of TA and Gestalt. Lizby's students assisted her with materials when she taught, and then sat in on the Goulding lectures. Bob, a bombastic psychiatrist but a good clinician, taught that close attention to the client's actual words, particularly verbs, could identify his or her operative ego state.

Lizby considered what had and what had *not* been useful about the help she received in understanding her own consciousness and blind spots. She then designed an intensive therapy program that became quite successful. Individual clients spent ten days or so with her in a residential treatment period at Muir Beach that was half a Jesuit-style life-review retreat and half an intensive psychodrama. She used art methods, journal exercises, and videotape and experimented in using these methods in small groups.

Helen Luke, the Jungian analyst and professor of medieval literature, provided another influence on Lizby, particularly her interpretation of Dante's cantos in the *Divine Comedy*. Lizby compared it with Claudio Naranjo's work on the Enneagram in a journal article on Dante and the tasks of Individuation. She wrote a chapter in Paul Olsen's book *Emotional Flooding* put out by the National Institute for the Psychotherapies, and another for John Staude's book, *Aging*.

To witness, to celebrate the patterns of life and death and to sense the future — the summary tasks had begun.

Chapter Thirty-Seven

Sifting Seeds

L izby and Scott were social activists, donating an increasing propor-
tion of their time and income each year, and joining other friends to
fight the growing threat of nuclear weapons. When Helen Caldicott
started the PSR (Physicians for Social Responsibility), UCMC and
Stanford created *The Last Epidemic,* a film to show the medical
effects of dropping a nuclear bomb. Lizby purchased tapes and two
videotape machines to show it to every group she was involved with
— neighborhood, professional, and religious. She donated one
machine to the Social Justice Commission to use in the schools.

In 1984, Lizby was appointed Distinguished Scholar for the
Julie Cunningham Chair at Notre Dame, Belmont. It entailed teaching one class and delivering one public lecture. She used two polar-
opposite images — the mushroom cloud of the nuclear bomb
(expressing utter destruction) and the image of the earth as seen
from space (showing the unitary nature of life). She talked about the
power of images and the importance of waking to these in our collective psyche.

Lizby's godchild, Monica Moore, who had studied ecology
issues in Scandinavia and in South America, started PAN, the

Pesticide Action Network, with an international campaign against the "Dirty Dozen" international corporate polluters with the worst environmental records. It became a significant force in the environmental movement. Monica introduced Lizby to groups working on Corporate Social Responsibility.

John Lind's group, the California-Nevada Interfaith Committee on Corporate Responsibility worked at the international level with banks on policies dealing with South Africa — and he was effective. He also worked with local area banks on such matters as "red-lining," proving statistically when loans were being restricted from qualified blacks. Lizby, attentive to systemic influences, was expanding her social work influence.

Scott worked with the Livermore Action Group and was frequently arrested in their protests. He spent weeks at the gates of the Livermore Campus reading aloud the arguments of the anti nuclear war thinkers. Both he and Lizby took part in interfaith social justice work and several San Francisco Organizing Project actions for unions and church neighborhood causes. The often-simple results, e.g., getting Safeway to hire a night guard for the parking lot after one shopper was badly wounded, meant that people could buy their food locally and neighborhood disintegration was held back. Small victories, but they provided hope for the larger actions that followed.

They also took a deeply caring interest in one of the families who lived in the public housing projects. It would last for the next twenty years. Lily Bruno, mentally ill but devoted to protecting and keeping her three children in school, lived in the projects with her 10 year old daughter Pearl, one brother 2 years older and one 2 years younger and her husband a much older black man. Scott and Lizby made sure the children grew up with good memories — travel to national parks, city and beach experiences, train travel and educational opportunities. For Pearl, this included college admission test coaching, then residential college, graduating from Mills with a university education.

Scott joined in the Sanctuary Movement, protecting Salvadoran refugees, and visiting that country to provide medical supplies. Both of them went to Nicaragua when one of Monica's sisters was translating for a radio station in Managua. They traveled everywhere and talked to everyone they could. When they came back, Lizby wrote newsletters and occasional op-ed pieces for the *Marin Independent Journal.*

The different points of view between the US Government and the RC

Church on what was happening in El Salvador and Nicaragua reached the crisis point. St. Teresa's parish church on Potrero Hill, was a leading Sanctuary Church in the country. St. Teresa's parish, with the pastoral team of Fr. Peter Sammon, Sr. Kathleen Healy, and Sr. Lucia Lodolo was almost unique in having thoroughly adopted Vatican II's view identifying the "people of God" as the Church rather than the Institution. The parishioners worked to shelter their refugees and to bring pressure on the government to stop the lies. Our USA government's projection of Shadow elements, ("We're OK, but the Evil Empire is godless and materialistic"), the selection and slanting of news according to "defense" strategies and policies closely parallels what people do in their individual lives. The systems aspect of individual and group behavior began to interest Lizby even more.

She rediscovered the writings and work of Don Brown, now dead from AIDS. Although not useful to her personal therapy, Brown's conceptual work on group process was superb. Astonishingly so. She became active in the professional associations of group therapists.

Lizby used the Enneagram as a system of personality classification. It included a wider range of attributes, and therefore, had greater explanatory power for the correspondences between the outer world and the inner world. She had been looking for a way to write about the things she knew worked in psychotherapy. It seemed that the Enneagram might provide that structure. She started making notes.

One summer, Lizby traveled around the world visiting socialist countries with a group of people gathered from the *Nation* magazine readers. They had been attracted by the low fare $3,400 for a month's inclusive travel. They flew to Belgium where they boarded a Soviet plane bound for Moscow. They traveled the Volga by boat to St. Petersburg-Leningrad, then went by train down to Tashkent, and up into Siberia. They took the Siberian Express down into Mongolia. Finally, they entered China, then Hong Kong, and home. Everywhere, they were treated with immense courtesy and care. If it was propaganda, so be it, she thought. Their experiences deepened the reading Lizby had done for months beforehand. The people she traveled with, most of whom had grown up in NYC or Philadelphia as "red-diaper babies," were unforgettable. As a not-too-opposite ideological "cradle Catholic," Lizby understood them well. They drank together and sang labor songs with their hosts.

Scott and Lizby took other trips for fun, river rafting on the Rogue in Oregon, traveling to various regions in Mexico — Hermasillo, Lake Patsquero, Oaxaca, and Copper Canyon — then a sailing trip to whale watch in Alaska. They visited old friends, Vincent in Jerusalem, then Monica Hannasch in her villa on the coast of Salerno.

After Lizby published her first two books on the Enneagram, they traveled on AMTRAK to do a publicity and workshop tour around the country, then to the British Isles, France and Germany. They especially loved train travel, talking with different people at each meal in the dining car, reading books to one another in their roomette, and falling asleep to the sound of clacking rail wheels.

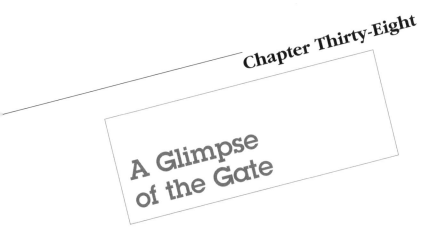

Chapter Thirty-Eight

A Glimpse of the Gate

"The crop of livers to transplant is slim," the doctor said. "Since the motorcycle law passed, the usual 'donors' have had to wear helmets. More of them save their own lives these days."

It was 1995. Dr. Joanne Imperial, the hepathologist, had just told Lizby her diagnosis — Hepatitis C. Thirty years in the past, Lizby had needed seven pints of blood in a transfusion. Hepatitis C was not yet known, and about one in three pints of the nation's blood supply was contaminated. Now the condition was known.

A year passed, then two — the time the physician had thought Lizby could live without a transplant. Yet nothing changed. There was no pain, or even discomfort, just gratitude. Each day, each meal, in her home or walking the beach and the streets of the city — everything and everyone was stunningly precious. Then Lizby realized she was as healthy as ever. The physician had been just plain wrong about her dying.

Gradually other concerns moved back into her life again, even disagreements and grouchiness. However, Lizby puzzled why her feelings of anger or sadness had not been stronger. She was much like Hans in this. Hans had died at the age of ninety-one. He lived in the Napa Valley vineyard home of Lizby's brother Frank. He had not remarried and all of his companions from the great strike years were dead. His major interest had become the beauty of his begonia flowers and of daily life in his son's home. Although he and Lizby saw each other a few times a year, they were not close. When he died, what she felt was her brother Frank's sadness.

Life took back its ordinary acceptability. Scott moved east to look after land he inherited, and worked on the Underground railway for refugees from El Salvador.

Then, a major shock for Lizby — the death of her brother Frank in 2002. All of her memories, all the things she cared about in childhood were entwined with Frank. He had been her extra eyes, her ears, her other self, before and during their early years of school and when they traveled back and forth to Montana. His teasing, funny stories and affection had continued throughout their adult years as her bedrock, even when they were not in close touch. There was no one else who mattered to her with such unconditional love — he had been the family structure of her life. She now crossed over the sill of knowing that, even if her own death was not immediately about to happen, she was in the last portion of life.

A different sense of death — and life — came in losing precious friends. A note from her journal on the long years of friendship with the Benedictine monk and sociologist, Dom.Vincent Martin, O.S.B, when he died at 84:

> *Time spent with V. was not linear. Past centuries crowded in as per-sonal yesterdays. Intuitions of the future flamed out as he casually gath-ered the passions and politics of today into patterns of vast movements and gropings of the human spirit.*
>
> *It is difficult to admit that in 40 years, I seldom had a back and forth ordinary conversation with him. Not that he didn't know my heart. Every major decision, every disgust with the Church, with the Academic world and with my professional career, I've detailed to him, as well as my love affairs, the decisions to marry, to divorce, and not to remarry — but I don't recall that he ever gave me a word of advice. Questions, yes — questions that stuck in my mind like foxtails in my sock. Questions sometimes so maddening that I sulked for as long as three years — but questions so*

objective that bit-by-bit, very gradually, they shaped and formed my world. Intimate conversation, however, that casual give and take between peers, we never had.

Initially, I simply did not know how to brush past the screen of his sophisticated European charm, his vast learning, and amusing sense of the absurd. I was entranced, instructed, astonished, sometimes amazed, never bored — but return his thought in kind? No way.

Scott died in 2003, after a heart operation in Holy Week — the same week Lizby lost her 15-year-old Siamese cat, Aida, and her 91 year old mentor, Sister Dorita Clifford with whom she was studying the patterns of eastern civilizations. A year after Frank's death, she grieved for them all. It was a difficult time. We share our identity in our shared webs of memory. Although without children, Lizby was fortunate with a loved god daughter and assorted "adopted" grandchildren — but the real tasks of age were beginning.

Grieving, followed by a time of return to ordinary life — perhaps a year, or more. Then an unexpected experience. The puzzle of the intense feelings that usually emerge in adolescence — surfaced at age 73 for Lizby. Paul, an agemate widower, and Lizby fell jointly in love. While studying at Ghost Ranch in New Mexico that summer, Lizby had created and pit-fired a sculpture — a political chess set. It depicted the natural resources of the world arrayed against the pre-emptive war politicians then in office. Paul admired it — as well as a light essay she had written using Marilyn Monroe as Dante and Eleanor Roosevelt as Virgil. Paul and she agreed politically, and both of them enjoyed writing and making art. Their hot e-mail fueled, adolescent passion was a snuggling delight. It seeped into everything, for days, weeks, months, before it slid into a durable friendship, softer than most. There was no question of partnership, nor sharing of living space, only life — and, again, gratitude.

Time reverses itself, glowing. Everything, everyone matters.
This gifted see-er and I do not think alike. He is an atheist, while I see
Myself as one of billions of peepholes into the universe
One-ness uses to cherish its unfolding
And tussle with its meanings.

A partner captures my feelings and mirrors my waking questions.
As doubt is essential to belief
Dealing with other possibilities — replanting "Reality."
D'accord. C'est bien

Life was not only astonishing, Lizby found, it was more creative than she had imagined possible. The tasks of Age had to be actively engaged.

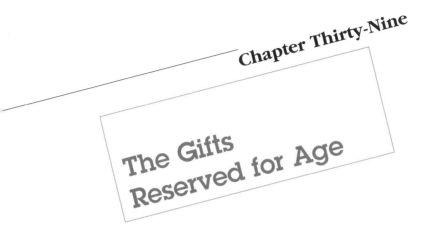

Chapter Thirty-Nine

The Gifts Reserved for Age

Age needs more than thinking about, Lizby realized. Helen Luke, a Jungian analyst with a poet's gift for the emotional issues of real life, examines William Shakespeare's plays, *The Tempest* and *King Lear,* in her book, *Old Age: Journey into Simplicity*. Both Prospero and Lear were men dealing with their age and legacy.

Prospero, a magician, lived on his island with only his daughter and Caliban, the half-human brutish son of a witch who originally owned the island. He had promised to free his slave Ariel, the spirit who powered his magic.

Ariel, a metaphor for our spirit of personal meaning and accomplishment, leaves each of us in the end whether or not we are willing to see it go. A particular problem for those of great accomplishment, or those with delusions of entitlement. Prospero manages it well in *The Tempest*, and his story is absorbing.

King Lear, by contrast, was a soldier used to living with his men in the field and in his Court. His tragedy is common to many who think somehow they can transfer power and still hold on to it. He announced he was dividing his kingdom among his three daughters. He expected each daughter receiving her portion to speak of her gratitude and her affection for him. Regan and Goneril, the hypocritical elder daughters already married, competed in describing the depth and breathe of their love for Lear. Cordelia, however, spoke proportionally of her care for her father and a devotion, which she would give to her future husband, the King of France. With this — from his once favorite daughter — Lear felt betrayed and furious at what he interpreted as humiliation before his Court. To the dismay of his Fool (the primary wisdom figure in the play) Lear banned Cordelia from his sight.

The transfer of lands and castles took place. Lear expected to divide his time visiting, and that he and his attendants would be welcomed and entertained by each of the elder daughters in turn. Not so, and the tragedy began to unfold.

In her analysis, Helen Luke uses T. S. Eliot's description of the "gifts reserved for age — the loss of energy and enchantment, the rage of projection of our hidden darkness onto others or onto circumstances, and the suffering hidden in our memories—all of these, once they are accepted, become the essentials of liberation . . . ." A love is born from struggling with these realities — a purging flame to integrate these strange *gifts* that can free us at last, from both future and past — and from identifying our small ego with Life itself.

Jungians really believe in looking at one's archetypal Shadow, Lizby thought, but how odd that Luke's examples were all about male hubris. There were some similarities. Certainly, she knew personally Prospero's pitfall of identifying oneself with one's work, and that Lear should have stated his expectations, rather than assuming he had an agreement with his daughters. However, were there no literary examples to model a *woman's* ending life tasks?

Lizby's "gift" came — and this one she recognized because it *was* a feminine version of the tasks/gifts given to both Prospero and King Lear. Yes, and common enough to be recognized by every parent puzzling through the reality of an offspring's separate, "other" point of view and values alien to the parent's own frame of knowing. It took several months for Lizby to realize what might be happening, and a deepening depression before she recognized Prospero's loss of Ariel's understanding and power — her own clinical diagnostic skill — might be an additional issue for her in this crisis. So, enough metaphor — on with the story.

✖   ✖   ✖

The daughter from the Bruno family that Lizby and Scott had shepherded in many different ways through school then college was now 30 years old, divorced and living with her pre-school age daughter. She asked Lizby for money to purchase a neighborhood business. Lizby suggested she look into a government program for minority women setting up new businesses, and learn about loan possibilities. A financial advisor friend of Lizby checked out the sales conditions and prices of similar businesses for Pearl's use.

Pearl was not a suitable candidate for a bank business loan, nor for financial help from community programs it turned out. She had neither business training, nor experience. When Pearl said she could get a partner — a male schoolteacher with business experience, Lizby gave her the name of a business specialist attorney and agreed to give her money for a 50% partnership if they worked out legal papers for the partnership and their purchase of the business.

Pearl said she had done so, and that the sale was arranged for the 1st of the next month. Lizby had her attorney draw up a promissory note that specified the partnership and purchase of the specific business for which the money was provided.

A couple of days after Pearl signed the note, Lizby asked when the deal was closing? Pearl said she was looking for another partner. Lizby asked Pearl to return the money until she had one. Lizby knew that when she had previously paid off Pearl's car loan, Pearl had not followed their verbal agreement — to continue putting the monthly payments she would have had to make into a savings account to build some capital. Pearl now refused to return the loan, saying the money had no time limit on it and that Lizby was unreasonable.

She did not respond to telephone, mail or e-mail.

Lizby, (like King Lear) saw herself as 'a good-hearted, generous woman who had been betrayed.' It seemed quite clear. EXCEPT that Lizby, had a levelheaded God-daughter, Monica, who like Lear's daughter Cordelia, could imagine a different way of looking at the situation — that Pearl felt betrayed. She was a self-reliant young woman with a great need for independence, who had an actual opportunity. She had asked for help and felt betrayed that Lizby was asking for that back when Pearl felt she could find another partner if she were given more time.

Learian indignation from Lizby. Lizby certainly had never betrayed anyone. This had been a clear agreement between them.

Roughly 24 hours of simmering — before Lizby woke with the memory of a long forgotten striking instance of her own betrayal of a confidence — one she had rationalized and buried long years ago.

Hmm — so this is what Helen Luke meant.

There was no question of Pearl's unjustified refusal to return what did not belong to her. Her indifference to 20 years of kindness and affection was also difficult to understand. What Lizby realized — one of the *gifts reserved for age* — was a vision of shared shadows, and that she, too, had once failed someone she loved.

No one is completely good and no one is completely bad. We all have to realize we do wrong to other people and we try to rationalize it. When we get this right, and it is never comfortable to admit, we can both give and receive a different kind of knowledge. If we do not "get it" we sink into delusions of entitlement — a type of mental disturbance with a self-willed element to entering it.

To own up to our act of harm, we simply end it clearly and quickly pay our debt of truth. Pearl had not yet realized this was both an objective reality and a developmentally crucial decision for her. Lizby had not assessed the situation critically, or accurately, for there was still something she did not want to see.

Three months passed. Pearl prepared to move out of state. Another important person in her life, however, would not accept Pearl's rationalization for keeping the money. Pearl came to Lizby's home with a check. Lizby welcomed her and had the good sense to ask only four questions: What had happened to the partnership? What had Pearl learned from the experience that she could use in the future? What was she planning to do now? And was there someone where she was going who shared this same understanding of what she wanted to do, who would support and perhaps mentor her?

✖   ✖   ✖

The experience was unnerving to Lizby. Pearl had no interest in Lizby's point of view — no curiosity — no apparent sense that she had misled her — or anyone else.

"What actually happened with your partner—that you didn't buy the business together?" Lizby asked.

Basically they had only two face to face meetings and nothing developed. "He refused to answer my calls."

"You didn't answer *my* calls, was it the same sort of thing?"

"No, if he didn't want to talk, that was it. I had someone else, who was interested in going in with me, but the owner started acting funny and would not answer our questions about the business tax records — probably he hadn't been giving that information to the IRS either. We realized it wouldn't work."

"What did you learn form this that you can carry with you and use in the future?"

"Nothing," she said. "Well . . . maybe I'd do things differently — not just assume that somehow things would work out."

"Why didn't you return the money?" Lizby asked.

"I was angry at you, because you were angry at me and I don't deal with anger."

"We've never had any anger between us that I can remember."

Pearl shrugged.

Lizby asked, "What are you planning to do now in moving out-of-state?"

"I'm leaving so my daughter can be closer to her father and his mother. I've got some job leads through the Internet, and I've always known how to survive."

She did not anticipate any difficulty in making new friends. Her mother-in-law wanted to help her and her former husband to work out some counseling to deal with the problems they have understanding one another.

"Do these people know and support your plan?"

"Well, I know that this is what I want to do and I'm going to give it a trial. I will know if it will or won't work out."

Lizby gave her some books she had for her daughter's birthday and said the questions she'd been asking were the sort of things she used when she was figuring out what to do — objective questions.

It was difficult for Lizby to realize that after 20 years, she did not know Pearl well enough to see how little emotional understanding existed between them. She had assumed a greater degree of trust and closeness, and failed to check it out. She had not thought about Pearl's characteristics she did not want to see — her self-defined sense of justice — that considered only her personal interests. She was bright and had a gift for writing poetry—but they didn't share feelings.

Lizby sighed.

✖   ✖   ✖

Gifts ARE gifts, however, as she, Helen Luke, Prospero, and Lear's Fool knew well.

The process goes on — taking responsibility for one's blindness without false guilt — the self-pity of ego drops away. Self remains — our individual consciousness from bits of choices. We glimpse finally the possibility of new life in even briefest meetings. We are part of a cosmic system itself with properties quite different from ours — an evolving consciousness different from any we can imagine — an amazing oneness with everything and everyone. We know the gift of our hunger to experience the creation reality of atoms, galaxies and everything in between, freshly. It is so much MORE than we can know.

This comforted Lizby. Yes.

Aftermath of a Two-Year Conversation: The Net of Consciousness

(concluding excerpt from 7/3/08 dialogue about social intelligence)

LIZBY: I can see how the future will be massively different — every decade is speeding up — changes beyond imagining.

DAVE: Yeah, the Mayan calendar ends in 2012, and it's a spiral. During the last twenty-five years – the most happens during that span.

LIZBY: The Mayan calendar . . . ?

DAVE: Yeah, I guess the Mayans thought that we would have a choice — whether we wanted to continue.

LIZBY: It's odd to think what parts of our stories belong to us—and what parts simply hold the spirit of the times. The Egyptians, the Mayans, the Romans had empires for centuries before they declined—but in my one lifetime the Ottoman Empire disappeared the decade I was born, then the Axis of the Nazis and the Imperial Japanese, the old Chinese Empire, the British Empire, the South African Apartheid Government, the Soviet Union as such, even Mao's form of Communism in China ended — to say nothing of all the changes in Africa at this moment!

DAVE: And now the United States has lost world leadership, at least in moral and economic terms. It's weird how easily militarism infects government.

LIZBY: It's like a disease of decay. The coinage, the money supply and the Economy get debased — in mysteriously uncounted ways. Supply lines to battlefields lengthen and weaken. People hardly notice the corruption of central government because they're being entertained and distracted. It's the same script for *every* Empire that's gone down.

DAVE: — and they all have.

LIZBY: What scares me are corporations with legal rights as if they were individuals who do not die. Nothing is required from them for their privileges. Only that they make a profit—which means treating people only as consumers, instead of conscious humans who care about one another. They should be licensed with an oath: DO NO HARM TO LIFE.

DAVE: Group minds are always vulnerable to infection.

LIZBY: Uh-hu, 'Memes' — the sticky ideas and ideologies that spread like viruses. I have been obsessed by patterns, so I know how obsession and decay work.

DAVE: The double-sidedness of Technology doesn't help. Have you heard about MMOGs? That's massively multiplayer virtual reality games, thousands of players can play at the same time. For the last three years they have been growing exponentially — and they're as addictive as drugs . . . The Chinese are beginning to see it as a public health problem.

LIZBY: Alternative realities — but without our wonderful *senses* — who wants that??

DAVE: Particularly now with what we're learning about our brains — the parallel processing right hemisphere with the totality of NOW sensory data pouring in and the tyranny of our left hemisphere sifting every-thing into past and future boxes labeled "little old ME (a separate human being)."

LIZBY: Yes — consciousness isn't just US, much less ME — it's incredibly multi-leveled!! We've got to figure out how to use our natural empathic intelligence better. Actually, *that's* one thing that pleases me most about growing old. So many of us are altruistically concerned about life . . . each other, our planet and how dependent we are on all forms of us-ness.

DAVE: Spiritual traditions are being re-packaged.

LIZBY: I woke this morning after a tussle thinking about betrayal. I realized this state of mind was similar to an upwelling of regret — an indigestion of obsession, something difficult to swallow. It connected to upwelling images of currents in the sea and air and wind layers.

Stuff and nutrients get moved around — and other things happen — in us as well as the universe. Like the saturation limit — the limitation of the sea to take up excess CO2—before it begins to acidify and destroy calcium in shells and fish bones.

Universal patterns aren't good or bad — they just have effects. Then my mind turned to Lear and his relation to Goneril, the insights of age; then to Theodore Roetke's "In a Dark Time, the eye begins to see." Yes — "I begin to see."

This is an incredibly rich period. The deepest questions (Quests) of my lifetime are being swept up, clarified, brightened in docent study at the California Academy of Science. All the religious, mystical issues are being reframed. I am happy — there is no other word for it — what a gift, this life.

DAVE: Sounds like a spiritual practice.

LIZBY: I do use a journal to write truth carefully. When I was a child, we were taught to offer up our thoughts and actions to find whatever 'God' wanted us to do each day, and then at night we had to examine our conscience, and say our night prayers — which included contrition, petition, saying thanks, and expressing awe. 'Awe' meant seeing how wonderful life was. I guess my journal still is a version of that — mostly thanks and awe, and hope for courage. Do you have a practice?

DAVE: The journal — yeah. I use it to find out what I'm thinking.

LIZBY: Getting thought past the *noise* of empty words is hard. We are parts of one reality like an immense animal – with a living nervous system meant to last for centuries that the messages navigate. We're designed to connect with one another — designed to link up. Physicists, as well as biologists like Rupert Shelldrake and economists Paul Krugman and Robert Reich, Clinton's Secretary of Labor, are thinking about our human connections through time and space. The metaphor of money is just one of the flows of energy being repositioned.

DAVE: Yeah. We don't have the words for what we're beginning to sense.

LIZBY: It's coming, though — and fast.

An Afterword:
Cast of Characters

Part I Butte Montana (1918-1923)

"Packy": Francis P. Dyer, 37 y.o. copper miner, b. in Sligo Ireland,
    killed in Montana Mine Accident, actor, musician, athelete
"Lizzie": Elizabeth Lawson Dyer, 32 y.o. with 6 children, widow,
    later hotel chambermaid, dancer, 'little-theater' actress
Dyer children: Molly 14, Frank 11, Tom 12, Johnney 6, Patrick 4,
    James 1
Flanagan: Lizzie's best friend, a gambling hall hostess
Mrs. Bonner: hotel housekeeper
Jocko: hotel bellboy
Bill Hendersen: Anaconda Copper Mining Corporation official,
    ranch owner
McPherson family: Molly's employers
Gertrude: Molly's best friend
Sr. Magdelena Convent of the Good Shepherd
Jeanette Rankin: Congresswoman who voted against WWI

Part II San Francisco (1924-1937)

Molly: 21 y.o. bookkeeper for a gourmet grocery
Trudy: her roommate and best friend, a receptionist at a shipping
    company
Chelsea Dingle Eaton: physician finishing his surgical residency,
    Molly's boyfriend

Hans Frings: sailor-longshoreman from Bonn, Germany, Molly's husband

Henry Schmidt: Hans' friend and 'gang boss'

Harry Bridges: Australian founder of the ILWU, the Waterfront Union

Lizzie Dyer: Molly's mother, a hotel chambermaid in Butte

Molly's brothers: Frank Dyer, football hero, at college in Montana;
    Pat Dyer, ALB vet; Tom, John, and James Dyer

"Lizby": Elizabeth Patricia Frings, Molly's daughter

Part III   Lisby (1937-1946)
San Francisco and Butte

Lizby: 7 y.o. observer

Frankie: 4 y.o. brother

Molly Frings: mother

Hans Frings: father, ILWU Longshoreman and Ship Chandler

Gram (Lizzie): grandmother

Trudy: mother's 'best friend'

Frank Dyer: teacher at agricultural college,

Pat Dyer: miner, artist, member of the Abraham Lincoln Brigade in the
    Spanish Civil War; alcoholic

Spot: Gram's large mongrel dog,

Sr. Alma: at St. Anne's Grammer School

Sr. Emaline: at Notre Dame des Victoires

Pauline Martin, Helen, Cecile and Henri Gaillac: Lizby's friends in high
    school

Part IV   The Unfolding (1947-2007)

San Francisco '47-53

Molly: mother, French-Laundry bookkeeper

Lizby: college, graduate school, professional career, marriage into old age

Hans: father, ship chandler

Frank: brother, army officer in Korea, later years: general manager of a
    candy factory, Napa Valley wine grape-grower.

Washington, DC '51-53

Emily Milburn: Fides Settlement House, black pragmatist

San Francisco-Big Sur-Mendocino '53

Ethel Souza of Junipero Serra Art and Book Store and Del Lederle,
  painter, sculptor: Lizby's best friends
Pellie and Pal, Ruth Cravath, Bill Zacha, Louisa Jenkins: friends
Vincent Martin OSB: lifelong friend
Elizabeth Howes and Sheila Moon: Jungian founders of the Guild for
  Psychological Studies

UCMC and Univ. of Chicago Legacies '55-'75

Eric Berne, Michael Agron, Jos. Wheelwright, Fritz Perls: physician-
  psychiatrist mentors

San Francisco, Synanon and Sufis '65-'95

Monica Moore: god-daughter
Judith Goleman: Synanon Game proponent
Michelle Vignes: book collaborator, photographer
Bill Lamers: psychiatrist partner
Ettore Keyes: Lizby's husband
Joan Lark: friend from New York Ciry
Corita and Fleurette: nuns from the Los Angeles dioceses
Zerka Moreno, Elaine Goldman, Mort & Dorothy Satten: psychodrama
  teachers, mentors
Claudio Naranjo: psychiatrist, Enneagram teacher.